THE
JOURNEY

THE
JOURNEY

Jiro Osaragi

Translated by Ivan Morris

TUTTLE PUBLISHING
Boston • Rutland, Vermont • Tokyo

This edition published in 2000 by Tuttle Publishing, an imprint of Periplus Editions (HK) Ltd., with editorial offices at 153 Milk Street, Boston, Massachusetts, 02109.

Cover photographs © Horace Bristol; background image: "Pedestrians walking along a street in Japan," November 1946; inset image: "Walking Under a Japanese Torii," ca. 1946-1956

Library of Congress Cataloging-in-Publication Data in Process
ISBN: 0-8048-3255-2

Distributed by

North America
Tuttle Publishing
Distribution Center
Airport Industrial Park
364 Innovation Drive
North Clarendon, VT 05759-9436
Tel: (802) 773-8930
Tel: (800) 526-2778
Fax: (802) 773-6993

Japan
Tuttle Publishing
RK Building, 2nd Floor
2-13-10 Shimo-Meguro, Meguro-Ku
Tokyo 153 0064
Tel: (03) 5437-0171
Tel: (03) 5437-0755

Asia Pacific
Berkeley Books Pte Ltd
5 Little Road #08-01
Singapore 536983
Tel: (65) 280-1330
Fax: (65) 280-6290

05 04 03 02 01 00   9 8 7 6 5 4 3 2 1

Printed in the United States of America

CONTENTS

1 · *Between the Trees* 3

2 · *The House* 14

3 · *Aged Youth* 21

4 · *Dislocation* 30

5 · *Among People* 41

6 · *Dim Light* 56

7 · *Island of Fire* 86

8 · *The Guest* 116

9 · *The Staircase* 140

10 · *Where the Clouds Went* 159

11 · *The Spider's Thread* 173

12 · *The Traveling Companion* 209

13 · *An Autumn Night* 226

14 · *The Wild Goose* 255

15 · *By the Wayside* 265

16 · *The Glacier* 272

17 · *The Warmth of a Winter* 310

18 · *American Village* 330

Consonants are pronounced approximately as in English, except that g is always hard, as in Gilbert. Vowels are pronounced as in Italian and always sounded separately, never as diphthongs. Thus Taeko is pronounced *Tah-eh-ko*. There is no heavy penultimate accent as in English; it is safest to accent each syllable equally. The final *e* is always sounded, as in Italian.

THE
JOURNEY

1 · BETWEEN THE TREES

THE TRAIN left North Kamakura station and after running through a cedar forest emerged into the open between a cluster of hills. From here one could see the roofs of the temples and the peaceful-looking houses. The next station was Kamakura, where Taeko Okamoto was to get off. She stood up and removed the bouquet of flowers from the rack above the seat. It was wrapped softly in cellophane paper. The flowers were white and dark purple clematis, and their color peered vaguely through the thin paper.

It was Sunday, and Kamakura station was crowded. Taeko managed to get away from the crowd and crossed the square in the direction of a teashop where she had been once before. She found the place after a short search and opened the wooden door.

"May I use your telephone?" she said. "You have one, don't you?"

The phone was on a small table just in front of the entrance. Still dazzled by the glittering daylight, however, she had not noticed it on first entering the dimly lit shop and could not help feeling slightly embarrassed.

She looked in the directory to make sure of the number of her uncle, Soroku Okamoto. Leaning on the table, she listened through the receiver to the distant ringing of the phone bell. She was conscious of the languor of noontime on a spring day. In the glass case in front of her was displayed a group of attractively decorated cakes and lemons. The lemons were fresh and looked beautifully glossy.

"There's no answer," said the operator.

"Really?" said Taeko frowning. "Please try again in a while."

She ordered some coffee and, as she sat waiting, examined the pictures on the wall.

Her Uncle Soroku was alone now. He had lost his wife nearly ten years before, and his only son, Akira, had been killed in the war in Southern China. He had a woman, however, to take care of the housework. Someone should certainly be there to answer the phone. It was a large house, to be sure, but the phone was in the corridor right next to the kitchen.

Taeko picked up the receiver again, and once more she heard the distant bell ringing repeatedly. In her mind's eye she could picture the loneliness of her uncle's house.

"There's still no answer," said the operator.

"There must be a mistake. Are you sure the phone isn't out of order?"

She had spoken without thinking, and at once the operator answered touchily: "The bell's ringing, all right, but no one answers."

Taeko had been planning to visit her uncle's house after first going to the cemetery where Akira was buried. Now she left the teashop, crossed the crowded street next to the station, and began to walk through the residential area of Kamakura with its many trees and bamboo fences. As usual when she came to the town, she was struck by the contrast between the dusty main street with its crowds of sightseers and these quiet back streets where one hardly ever met a single person. From every point one could see the wooded mountains that surround Kamakura, and a Tokyoite could hardly help feeling envious.

There was not a person in sight as she passed through the temple gate, and in the cemetery it was utterly quiet. The cemetery stood at a slight elevation behind the bamboo fences and the rows of private houses; the mountains seemed very close. The gravestones were clustered together on the side of the mountain slope, which the inhabitants called Yato. They provided a unique sight, each one of them situated in a small cave excavated from the side of the mountain. The trees threw their shadows over the graves. The stones were covered with moss, and the winter leaves still lay thick on the ground.

Taeko had not expected to see anyone here, but now she caught sight of a shadowy figure next to her cousin's grave.

"Oh, so Uncle has come to visit Akira's grave," she thought.

It was a calm afternoon in the late spring without even a trace of wind. The only sound was the chirping of a bird that sounded like a sparrow from among the trees. The person by her cousin's grave was busily sweeping with a bamboo broom and did not even look up as she approached.

Taeko saw that the profile was not that of her Uncle Soroku but of a young man. He had removed his hat and coat and from his crumpled shirt emerged a pair of sturdy arms. No doubt this was someone her uncle had sent to sweep the grave.

"Is Uncle at home?" said Taeko.

"Who?" said the young man, looking up surprised.

Taeko was puzzled and did not answer. The young man set himself again to the task of sweeping the fallen leaves.

"What a lot of leaves!" he said, as if addressing himself and Taeko simultaneously. "I've been at the Kamakura tennis courts and just stopped by here on my way back," he added.

Taeko noticed that a tennis racket lay in its press on the hedge underneath his coat and hat. The young man had a tense expression.

"Are you a friend of Akira's?" asked Taeko, getting ready to help him with his cleaning.

"Yes, I was a school friend of his. Terrible thing about his dying, isn't it?" answered the young man. "Well, that's what happens in war. I dare say it couldn't be helped. But, you know, Mé always took the most dangerous things on to his own shoulders. He was like that at school too. . . . A terrible shame, his dying like that!"

"Is there any water around here?" asked Taeko.

The young man had finished clearing away the leaves, and

he was now crouching down picking weeds. He turned around, still in his crouching position, and said: "I believe there's a well down that way."

"I'll go and have a look," said Taeko.

Behind the cemetery she found an old open well. The wooden pail for carrying the water was broken, and so she had to use the old well bucket. When she returned the young man was standing smoking a cigarette.

"How are you related to young Okamoto?" he asked.

"He was my cousin." Taeko realized that she had answered rather brusquely, and she added in a politer tone: "My name is Taeko Okamoto."

"I didn't think Mé had a sister," said the young man with a smile. "I don't know if he ever told you anything about me," he added. "My name's Tsugawa. Mé and I were together from when we entered the college preparatory course until we graduated. My home is in Wakayama, but I lived in Kamakura while I was at school, and Mé and I became good friends."

Through the drifting cloud of cigarette smoke he added emphatically in his youthful tone: "He shouldn't have died."

"Do you know my uncle?"

"Yes, I met him two or three times—oh yes, and I must have seen him a number of times on the street. I should say I've come across him about four times altogether. . . . The truth is," he added after a pause, "he was rather frightening. He really had nothing to say to young people, and I always had the impression he was about to scold me for something."

"He really isn't like that, you know," said Taeko.

She filled the flower vase with water, and what was left she poured quietly over the gravestone. She wasn't quite sure why she did so, but vaguely she remembered that it was customary when visiting a grave to sprinkle it with water. The stone had been made three years before and still looked new. Where the water had fallen it appeared slightly blue.

Taeko unwrapped the flowers she had brought and began putting them in the vase.

"What sort of flowers are they?" asked Tsugawa from behind her.

"They're clematis. Aren't they pretty?"

"I'm afraid I've never taken much interest in flowers. I certainly didn't think of bringing any myself."

There was a relaxed, unreserved manner about Tsugawa as he spoke.

"I've never had much to do with flowers," he went on. "I don't even know the names of most of them. Clematis? Never heard of them."

"We had them in our garden when we lived in Kyoto," said Taeko. "They used to bloom about this time of the year. There are some lighter ones also, but I think these dark purple and white clematis are the prettiest."

"Mé didn't know much about flowers either. He never reached the age of buying flowers and sending them to people. When I set out today to visit Mé's grave, flowers were the last thing I thought of bringing him. I brought him something proper!"

"Incense sticks?"

"No, nothing gloomy like that."

Tsugawa opened the Boston bag which lay beneath the hedge, fumbled with a perspiration-soaked shirt, and from below extracted a small, pocket-sized whisky bottle.

"The bottle's cheap," he said, "but inside is pure first-class saké. A friend of ours that we used to play tennis with at school returned home and went into his father's brewery business. He sent me this saké with a letter saying: 'This is saké which I brewed myself. Please pour it on Mé's grave.' "

Next Tsugawa took out a small saké cup.

"Now we're ready," he said.

After leaving the cemetery, they went to the Modern Art Museum in the precincts of the Tsurugaoka-Hachiman Shrine.

"Frankly, I don't know much about paintings," said Tsugawa.

They hurried through the galleries, only hastily glancing at the famous French paintings on the walls brightly illuminated by the fluorescent lighting, and entered the tearoom. It was a light, cheerful place, and Tsugawa introduced it to Taeko as being the most pleasant spot in all Kamakura. She agreed with him. The room was so designed as to protrude from the wall of the building, in the style of Le Corbusier, and from their table they could look over the whole pond of the Hachiman Shrine and see beyond it the mountains covered with their beautiful trees.

The pond was covered with thick duckweed, and at first sight one might have thought that it was just a green lawn without any water at all. Only here and there could one see little patches of water reflecting the blue sky.

"It's worth paying the entrance fee just to come here, isn't it?" said Tsugawa. "I don't care a rap about the pictures myself."

Taeko smiled at his words. Then she noticed that the man sitting at the next table with a catalog was glancing at them. He did not look like a native of Kamakura, but like someone who had come from Tokyo specially to see the exhibition. He had the air of an artist.

"The camellias are in bloom," said Taeko to change the subject.

Between the bushes on the small islands of the pond, camellias were blooming; next to the red flowers the leaves shone brightly where the light fell, but underneath they looked black in the shade.

"Camellias!" said Tsugawa. "Even I know the name of those flowers."

"I had no idea there was a place like this in Kamakura," said Taeko.

"A little bit of the modern world at last," said Tsugawa. "Until now there's been nothing here but old temples and ancient villas."

The streets of the town were hidden by the trees which towered round the pond, and only parts of the roofs were visible. The tearoom was on the second floor of the building, and from its windows the sky looked wide; there was a stagnant quality about the afternoon light. One could vaguely hear the sounds of the town, but compared with the noise of Tokyo, where Taeko lived, this was a different world. Tsugawa's teaspoon glittered in the spring light.

As she sat opposite Tsugawa, it struck Taeko that until an hour before she had not known anything about him. Since she worked in an office, the company of young men was not particularly new to her, and there was really no reason, she told herself, that she should think of Tsugawa as someone so special. Yet it seemed strange to her that she should be sitting here unexpectedly drinking tea with a friend of her dead cousin. It made her feel that she was very much alive. She thought of her cousin who now lay peacefully under the winter leaves.

"Akira was just my age when he died," she said.

With her words a cold shadow passed over the table.

Tsugawa's expression did not change.

"Hm," he said, nodding. "You know, Mé told me that his father used to charge him interest on the money he advanced him—right up till the minute he paid it back."

Taeko was lost for an answer.

"Yes, he used to complain about it a lot," continued Tsugawa with the same impassive look on his face. "I don't know if his father made him give an I.O.U. or not, but I remember how Mé hated to pay that interest."

"It seems impossible," said Taeko. "A father taking interest from his own son."

"Yes, he figured it out to the last sen."

"But surely the father's money was Akira's money also. At least his father gave him money for his school expenses."

"Yes, he gave him that in advance for each term. That was fine; except that getting the money in advance like that, anyone —not only Mé—would be bound to use it all up long before the term ended."

Tsugawa laughed suddenly, relaxing the tense expression on his sturdy face.

"It was our fault too," he said. "Since his secondary-school days Mé enjoyed drinking. He was a generous fellow, and as long as his money held out, he used to take us along with him when he went drinking."

"Really?"

"That's why his money never lasted till the end of the term. He used to have to figure out good excuses to get money from his father. He was pleased to be able to borrow the money, of course, but he hated having to pay interest on it from the moment he got it. At the beginning of each term, when it was time for him to get his expense money, his father used to tell him exactly how much had been advanced to him and how much he would have to repay. He never let him off with a single penny either from principal or interest. According to Mé, his father was much stricter about collecting the money he owed him than they were in the Ginza bar where Mé used to go."

The memories of the past made them feel cheerful. Under the direct spring sunlight Tsugawa laughed: it was a gay, manly laughter.

"It must all be true," he continued, "because Mé told me it himself. In the course of a single term Mé used to be flush for just about one month. During that time we all profited. But when the month was over Mé didn't even have enough money left to buy himself a cup of tea!"

Taeko laughed.

"Yes," said Tsugawa, "we certainly were more easygoing and lighthearted in those days than the present university students seem to be. Old Mé certainly had a tough time with his father, though! I remember how once he pinched a picture scroll belonging to his father. It didn't take that scroll long to turn into beer, cutlets, and what-not and to disappear down our gullets! Do you know a painter by the name of Yanagi Kyori?"

Taeko shook her head.

"Well, I don't know much about artists, either old ones or new ones, but the name of Yanagi Kyori has certainly stuck in my mind, because he was the man who painted the scroll that Mé went and sold. Before long his father missed it, and it looked as if he'd soon find out what Mé had done. So we all got together in a hurry and collected enough money to buy it back."

There was a look of happiness on Tsugawa's face as he talked about the past days.

"The person who'd bought the scroll from Mé had already sold it to someone else."

"Good heavens, how terrible!"

"So we went to see the present owner. He turned out to be the director of a large company. He had a large house with a garage. As soon as we explained what we wanted, he answered: 'I've bought what I wanted to buy with my own money, and I have no intention of selling it back to anyone!' Mé turned white with anger. He realized that the man was treating us like fools just because we were students. Worst of all, the painting didn't even belong to Mé's father. If Mé couldn't manage to get it back, there was going to be real trouble. I don't suppose what he'd done could actually be called a crime, but it was almost as bad. I wonder if these things disappear completely when one dies. . . .'"

The story made Taeko smile. That young and rather weak-looking cousin of hers, who had died at just about her present age, came to her mind as someone very dear.

"What on earth did Akira do then?"

"Well, we were all sitting there in the drawing-room discussing the picture—and there it was hanging right in front of our eyes. I haven't the faintest idea whether it was a good picture or not. I remember it was a painting of some fruit lying in a red basket. On the floor next to the painting there was the stone head of a Buddha, a folding screen, and lots of other things. I remember thinking at the time that he must be a *nouveau riche.*"

Taeko nodded.

" 'Anyhow, I can't let you have it back,' said the man. 'I've got some business now. I have to go out. Please excuse me while I go and get ready.' He stood up, with the very obvious implication that we should leave.

"Mé, who'd been silent till then, suddenly uttered the word 'Money!' and laid the money we'd got together for the picture scroll on the table. We had no idea what he had in mind. Next he walked over to the wall, seized Yanagi Kyori's scroll with all his might, and started tearing it to pieces."

"Good gracious!"

"I was thunderstruck. The owner shouted at Mé and rushed up to try to stop him. But he was too late. Mé had already torn it. Other members of the household came running in, and there was talk of calling the police. Mé told us we should all go home and he'd handle the matter himself. Then in a quiet tone he said to the owner of the house: 'I know it's no excuse, but the fact is I just wanted to tear that picture!' The man, needless to say, was red with rage, but seeing that Mé had calmed down now (though his face was still pale), he told him to sit down and asked him if he didn't think what he'd done was pretty bad. Mé, still very quietly, said he agreed it was bad.

" 'I'm going to let the police know about this,' said the man, 'and your school also.'

"Mé suddenly started crying and muttered: 'There's nothing I can do about it now.'"

"So then what happened?"

"'But look here,' said the owner of the house seriously, 'why did you want to tear the scroll? It's completely unforgivable.'

"'If I didn't tear that picture,' said Mé, 'there'd be no meaning to anything.'

"'But why?' said the man. 'That's what I don't understand. Try to explain in a little detail.'

"Mé kept silent. He didn't seem to be able to explain the matter clearly even to himself. Then after a while he said that he couldn't express his real feelings, but he simply couldn't leave the picture where it was. Since the man hadn't let him take it home with him, he had to tear it to pieces. It was the man's turn now to be silent. He put a cigarette in his mouth and was reaching for a box of matches when he noticed the money that Mé had laid on the table. Seeing this, his expression became even more serious."

Akira Okamoto, the university student, had been restored from death and was alive to Taeko and to Tsugawa at this very moment—alive only as a shadow, it was true, yet in the spring air that wafted over the mossy pond, it was a very light and cheerful existence. The near-by mountain and the willows by the edge of the pond were bathed quietly in the afternoon sun.

"That man hadn't become a company director for nothing. He struck me as a very mature person. Looking up he said: 'Let's all go somewhere and have a bite to eat.' Without waiting for our answer, he bent down and picked up the torn scroll from the floor. 'This can be repaired,' he said. 'As soon as it's been repaired, I'll let you know and you can come and fetch it.' We were all pleased, except Mé, who still looked dejected. He didn't seem to like the idea. He probably wished he could have torn the picture even more thoroughly. He was just like a child who gets angry when things don't turn out exactly the way he's planned. It annoyed him that the matter was being smoothed over. That was the willful side of Mé's character coming to the fore."

"Just like my uncle."

Tsugawa did not seem to hear what she said. It did not interest him whom Mé might or might not resemble; at the moment he was overcome once again by his familiar regret that on the particular front where so few people had been killed, his friend had been one of the casualties.

"Well, one way or another the case of Yanagi Kyori's picture scroll was settled," he said after a while. "But the interest he owed on the money his father gave him while he was at school accumulated to such an extent that in the end he never returned it."

"I'm glad to hear it," said Taeko, smiling lightheartedly. "After all, they were father and son, weren't they? It seems unbelievable that Uncle should have behaved as he did, but if it's true, it's a good thing Akira didn't pay him back. In fact, I wish he'd caused his father more mischief than he did! Well, now I'm off to visit my uncle. Do you suppose he knows the story about the picture scroll?"

"It doesn't make much difference now one way or another. But at the time, when we saw how completely Mé had lost his head, we really thought he was going to be cut off without a penny!"

"It can't have been as serious as all that."

For a moment Tsugawa seemed to be thinking of something else. Then he suddenly remembered something and said: "I'd better go home."

"I'm sorry to have kept you," said Taeko. "But I'm glad to have had a chance to talk about Mé."

They walked down the museum steps and crossed the garden with its bronze statue. "My old man's a usurer!"—Tsugawa remembered the words that Akira had once spoken to him in a violent tone of scorn. It was not the way a son would normally speak of his father. He had said this, Tsugawa realized, not because he begrudged paying interest on the money he had borrowed; there was something else—some intolerable aspect of his relation with his father.

Near the shoulder of the bronze statue, which stood there with its bent arm, a spring butterfly fluttered about in small circles.

2 · THE HOUSE

Between the dark cedar forest and green of the copse that covered the near-by hills the Tsurugaoka-Hachiman Shrine stood out distinctly in its vivid red. Taeko and Tsugawa walked together as far as the Shinto gateway in front of the arched stone bridge outside the shrine precincts. There they parted ways.

A few moments later it occurred to her that she might have asked him to accompany her to her uncle's house, but now she had missed the chance. Her uncle would certainly have been pleased if he had come along. Near the gateway was parked a row of cars belonging to Americans who had come to sightsee in Kamakura. When Taeko reached the road, she turned back and saw the tall figure of Tsugawa striding along with the tennis racket in his hand. A group of girls on a school excursion walked along in a crooked file toward the shrine. The air seemed weary.

"He doesn't have a very high opinion of Uncle," thought Taeko to herself as she set off in a new direction.

Uncle Soroku's attitude to Taeko was one of cold indifference. Perhaps, she thought, it was because he was so far removed emotionally from her own father; the two men had no connection with each other at all.

She remembered how once when she had returned home to Kyoto her father had said: "Akira has died. If you like, you can go to Kamakura and stay with Uncle Soroku. He's rich enough so that you can live there in comfort for the rest of your life!"

It had been meant half as a joke, but Taeko had turned red, as though she had been insulted, and had not said a word. Something in her father's tone had made her feel that he wasn't joking at all, and this had hurt her deeply.

No, there was no love lost between Uncle Soroku and her father, and that, no doubt, was why the former treated her so casually. At least when Akira had been alive he had treated her as his younger cousin, and she had been accepted as one of the family. But all this had changed when he had died. Just at this time Taeko, who was still at school, had been taken into a factory as a volunteer warworker. It had been a period of rapid development for her. After the war she had graduated from school and decided that she would work on her own. Taeko had resolved to cut herself loose from both her home in Kyoto and her uncle in Kamakura. Her parents supported her in this decision, and her uncle was still indifferent. Her knowledge of English had been useful: first she had worked at the Allied P.X., and from there she had joined her present trading firm.

She wasn't quite sure when she had got into her habit of being alone. Because of this habit, most of the people at her office thought her arrogant. Only when one came to know her did another side of her character appear.

She came to Kamakura only on brief visits, and now she felt completely estranged from her uncle. Just as Uncle Soroku didn't want to know anything about her, she wasn't particularly interested in knowing anything about her uncle. She was distinctly aware of the loneliness he had suffered since the death of his only son, Akira; but he made it quite clear that he did not want to be comforted by Taeko. When she discovered this she thought she might come to like him.

Uncle Soroku was in his fifties. He had lost his wife when he was about forty. From then on, despite everyone's expectations, he had remained single. Taeko and her family thought that it was because of Akira that he did not remarry. The story which Tsugawa had told about her uncle's lending money to his own son with interest had been new to her; yet from what she knew of her uncle it did not strike her now as too incongruous. Soroku had started as a banker and had made a name for having a very hard head when it came to money matters.

As she now approached the entrance of his house, she remembered that no one had answered when she had telephoned from the station.

The front gate was closed, and Taeko went into the garden by the wooden side entrance. The house stood there quietly between the budding trees: it gave a distinctly gloomy impression. Perhaps it was simply the result of dilapidation caused by long neglect. Just as elderly men and women so often became suddenly old during the war, old houses also seemed to age all of a sudden due to the privations of the long war years. The drainpipes of her uncle's house had been contributed to the war effort, and the roof-tiles were broken. Taeko had never noticed until today how antiquated it all was. It occurred to her that during the war the effects of malnutrition had shown most distinctly on the faces of old people.

Taeko remembered hearing that the house and its grounds had come into her uncle's hands through the foreclosure of a mortgage. The garden was spacious, and the house, being an old-fashioned wooden structure, was solid and had a secure and dignified look. The hills approached on the east side. The house was situated in a sort of hollow; in former days of prosperity this had given it a quiet, pleasant atmosphere, but now in its dilapidation, with fallen leaves and dead branches all around, the place seemed dim and one was immediately reminded that it really was very unfavorably located. The awful scars of war were visible everywhere. A wooden building, unlike those of brick or stone, is unsuited for the rigors of war; even if it happens to escape direct damage, it inevitably undergoes serious deterioration. In her uncle's home only the plants and trees retained any semblance of their former grandeur. The spring was drawing to a close.

"Oh dear, how dark and gloomy it all is!"—Taeko wondered whether it would be all right to say this to her uncle.

If there is such a thing as the "expression" of a house, she thought, it must surely be attuned to the person who lives in it. When the interior is left unswept, then one can expect that the outside will be in a state of disorder—and, by the same token, that the owner of the house will be disheveled. Should the house itself be a mess and only its master neat, one would hardly be mistaken in assuming that he must be a hypocrite.

Taeko knew that she could never live in a gloomy house. She would do anything to change it. In fact, she would probably tear the whole place down and build herself a small, light home —a Western-style house, she rather imagined, painted in white or cream.

Her Uncle Soroku was a man of means. For a person with money to live in such a somber place as this could only mean that he lacked all zest for life.

When she reached the main door of the house, she found it was locked. On the ground she noticed a pile of newspapers that had evidently been delivered over a period of days; her uncle must have been away for some time. Taeko walked along the bamboo hedge to the kitchen. Here again the sliding-door was firmly secured. In the silence she was suddenly startled by a noise. A cat on the roof had seen Taeko and leaped onto the fence. Taeko caught a glimpse of only the buttocks and the tail of the cat as it disappeared over the other side of the fence.

The southern side of the garden consisted of a spacious lawn with a small pond. She was struck by the springtime animation of the trees. The remains of the cherry blossoms lay on the ground, muddied by the rain and covered by thick leaves. There was a gaunt quality about the scene. The shrill small voice of a frog sounded rather endearingly from what must be the middle of the pond. . . . Was it the light that streamed in from the wide sky which made this spot seem so desolate?

"What on earth can have happened?" Taeko thought to herself. "Can the housekeeper have gone out shopping?"

On the left-hand side of the house there were Western-style glass windows, and for a moment Taeko thought of climbing up and looking in through them. The old large house gave her an uneasy feeling. The fact that she could see no one made her imagine that something mysterious was lurking inside. She turned her back to the house with a peculiar sense of oppression.

It would have been different had her cousin still been alive. Taeko felt so utterly removed from her uncle. Her own world was, she sensed, a more alive and stimulating place than her

uncle's. Yes, it would have been better to have gone to the
beach after leaving the museum rather than here. On a pleasant
spring day like this the beach was bound to be crowded with
people from the city.

A large dog came running up to her from the opposite direction. She recognized its red hair: it was her uncle's dog. At the
same moment someone appeared round the hedge.

"Friday!" Kaneko called out, and the dog stopped. He
looked doubtfully at Kaneko for a moment, then approached,
wagging his tail.

"You remembered me, did you, **Friday?**" said Taeko, patting
him on his head. Then she looked **up** at the old housekeeper
who now approached.

"What's happened?" she asked. "Is **Uncle** away?"

"Oh yes, he's been gone for three **days** already. It's a shame
you came all this way for nothing."

"Is he on a trip?"

"He said he'd be gone for some time."

Taeko was surprised: it was rare for her uncle to leave like
this.

"You mean he hasn't just gone to Tokyo?"

"He said he wasn't quite sure where he was going, but that
he'd wander around where he felt like."

"Strange," said Taeko. "Did he ever do anything like this
before?"

"I don't believe so, Miss," answered the old woman. "Three
days ago," she added, "he left all of a sudden."

"Aren't you lonesome looking after the house all by yourself?" asked Taeko.

The old woman did not seem fully to understand the question. Her wrinkled eyes started to smile. "It comes to about the
same thing," she answered after a while. "Even when the master
is at home, he hardly ever says anything to me. . . . All the
same, to be on the safe side I've asked my grandson to come
and sleep here at night. The young fellow started in middle
school this year, you know."

Taeko remembered that the old lady's son was a carpenter
who lived near one of the temples in Kamakura.

"Please come in, Miss, and have a cup of tea. After you've

gone to all the trouble of coming here, that's the least we can do for you."

"I'm afraid I'm in a bit of a hurry."

Taeko was in no mind to return to the house where even the sliding-doors were firmly locked.

"Actually I came to visit Akira's grave. . . . Friday was alive in Akira's time, wasn't he? He must be a pretty old dog now."

"Oh yes, he's getting on," said the old woman, and smiled at the dog, who now ran up to her. "I wonder just how old he is. He's on the timid side, you know, and he barks at the slightest sound. That's why he's such a good watchdog at night."

"All the same it must be lonesome for you in a big house like this."

"Not really, you know. It's only recently we got rid of those evacuees from Tokyo. They finally moved back to the city. It's a lot better now with only one family living here. Those people had been here ever since the war, and they really got on the master's nerves. Well, Miss, please come in and rest a while."

"No thanks, it's quite all right. I shall drop by again when Uncle gets back."

"Well then, I'll come with you part of the way."

The old woman and the dog joined Taeko as she left the house. Living in that lonely house made Kaneko friendly, thought Taeko.

"I was really shocked to see how dilapidated Uncle's house has become," said Taeko.

"Well, it's not as bad as all that, you know. Still, if it looked too good, the taxes would be even worse than they are. It's better this way in the end."

"Well, really!" Taeko was about to say, but instead she asked: "Is that what Uncle said?"

"No, the gardener mentioned it in passing the other day. 'The master must be having a hard time with his taxes,' he said. He told me that if you've got a house with a garden in Kamakura, they tax the garden also."

As the old woman spoke something else seemed to come into her mind. "Oh yes," she said, "I'd forgotten. After the master left, Madam came here also to see him. What a shame for her —coming all this way and not finding him here."

"Who came?" said Taeko, surprised.

"Mrs. Terada from Kobe."

"My elder sister, you mean!"

So Tazuko, who was even more estranged from Uncle Soroku than she was herself, had come here from Kobe just to see him. Obviously she had come on behalf of her husband to get some money out of Uncle. Perhaps it was an unfair conjecture; yet Taeko could think of no other possible reason.

3 · AGED YOUTH

As THE ship moved out of Ryozu Bay, leaving Sado Island behind, the vibrations from the engine seemed strangely enough to become more subdued than when they were in the harbor. Perhaps it was that their ears had become used to the sound of the ship. It was a calm spring sea.

"I should have liked it to be a bit rougher," said Professor Yoshitaka Segi suddenly. His corpulent body rested on the couch of the special first-class cabin; he had been gazing at the ceiling, but now he turned his bespectacled face to his companion.

"Don't you agree?" he continued. "After all, we had a quiet crossing coming over to the island, and now it's just as dull going back to the mainland. What will we have to tell our friends when we get home? Apart from everything else, this calm sea rather belies Bashō,* the god of the *haiku,* doesn't it? He described this stretch of water quite differently!"

His companion had been examining the map that lay on the cabin table which was covered with its neat nylon cloth and

* Matsuo Bashō (1644-94), famous *haiku* poet.

decorated with a vase of flowers. Now he looked up with a calm smile on his young face. It had been Professor Segi who had been afraid of being seasick and who had insisted on buying some special medicine in the pharmacy at Niigata before they had embarked on the boat for Sado.

"Look, Suté," said Professor Segi with a grin, "don't you agree?" His tough beard looked like pieces of wire evenly arranged over his face. "When the sea is as quiet as a pond, it's hard to get the real feeling of Bashō's poem: 'It is a rough sea —the Milky Way that lies athwart the isle of Sado.'" He paused for a while. "Besides," he continued, "it makes me wonder whether the Emperor and Chunagon-no-Suketomo and Nichiren, who were all exiled to this island at one time or another, really suffered as much as we always thought they did!"

Sutekichi Ata laughed with his eyes and replied: "It's because it's spring."

This down-to-earth reply failed to silence the professor. His bristling mustache seemed to move mischievously.

"That sounds rather cheap, you know—like something out of a popular song. You know the sort of thing: 'I can't help feeling the way I do. It's because it's spring!' Oh well, enough of that. I only mention the matter because of Chunagon-no-Suketomo and Nichiren. If exiled people are going to be as thoroughly melancholy as exiles are supposed to be, it's better that the island they're going to is far away. And the sea they have to cross had better not be too calm—otherwise how would the great priest Nichiren be able to calm it down by his special prayers? There'd be no chance for a miracle. And if a priest can't perform a miracle, he becomes just like some corrupt labor-leader or some undertaker who coins money by disposing of dead people's bodies! He certainly can't be a saint if he doesn't perform miracles. It worries me, you know, just as if I were personally involved."

"But have you forgotten, sir? It was you who were looking for that medicine against seasickness in Niigata."

"Ah yes, but I haven't been exiled for committing some crime. I came here as a tourist to enjoy myself!"

Before the ship had left Ryozu harbor they had each drunk a bottle of beer. The professor had declared that he was going to sleep during the two-and-a-half-hour crossing to Niigata. He had shut his mouth, closed his eyes behind his glasses, and turned toward the wall of the cabin. But he hadn't dozed off: evidently he hadn't yet chatted to his heart's content.

"Really, you know," he continued, "that *haiku:* 'The sea of Spring/ Rising and falling/ All the day long,' doesn't form the basis of any history or tragedy, does it? To have history you've got to have something dangerous—a Molotov cocktail, for instance. If I were the director of the Sado Steamship Company, I'd arrange for the captain to get the ship pitching and rolling somewhere in the middle of the quiet spring sea. That would give the tourists a taste of history—as well as a touch of seasickness! 'Ladies and gentlemen, that's the island of Sado over there. It's a peaceful spot, but the sea is rough. It's all just as Bashō said, isn't it?' After that the tourists wouldn't forget Bashō in a hurry, would they?"

"Well, perhaps they wouldn't forget him," said Sutekichi, "but I don't expect they'd come sightseeing to Sado again, would they?"

There was no answer from the professor. He was as quiet as a badger who has crept into his hole. Having had his say, he let the conversation drop.

"Suté," he called after a while.

"Yes."

"How about our budget? Can we afford to have them beat the barrel in grand style till the train leaves Niigata? Will we have enough left to get back to Tokyo?"

The young man burst into laughter. He had immediately understood the odd reference to "beating the barrel." On the evening that they had arrived in Niigata, they had gone to a high-class restaurant and seen a Niigata Jinku dance. An elderly geisha had appeared with an empty barrel on which she kept on beating cheerfully to keep the rhythm.

"No barrel-beating for us tonight," said Sutekichi.

"Really?" said the professor with an air of disappointment. "Well, what are we going to do until the train goes? You surely don't expect us to go and sit in a movie, like a couple of fools, after we've come all the way from Tokyo to Niigata."

"No, not that, I agree," answered Sutekichi.

"Well then, let's have them beat the barrel for us. Can't we, Suté?"

"I'm afraid it's no good, sir."

"All right then, we'll travel third class instead of second. After all, if we've had enough to drink, we won't know the difference! In fact, I'll wager we could even go back on a freight train."

The professor stopped talking, and after a while he fell asleep. His regular snoring was interrupted for a moment, as if he had woken himself up with the noise he himself was making. Sutekichi quietly opened the cabin door and went out on deck.

The deck had been crowded when they had left Sado, but now it was deserted. Evidently the cold evening wind had scared people away. It certainly was not a spring wind, thought Sutekichi.

The sea was completely still. The only waves were those that the ship itself made as it glided through the water. Gazing back at the distant island of Sado, he could see the mountain peaks, some of them still covered with snow. The city of Niigata was invisible. With the distant spaces all round him, Sutekichi thought with a certain nostalgia of his mother, whom he had left behind in their Tokyo apartment. While visiting the island his mind had been full of the new things he was seeing—the Ogi harbor, which had once been so prosperous, but now gave a feeling of desolation; the Renkaho Temple with its Ashikaga Period pagoda hidden in a ravine; the remains of some ancient goldmine, whose seams made the mountain look as if it had been sliced with a knife; the waves biting into the lonely rocks on the north coast, which, he had been told, lay directly opposite Siberia. Now that he was on the ship returning to the mainland, however, he felt for the first time that he was in the midst of a journey, and the thought of his mother flashed through his mind.

Since graduating from school, Sutekichi had been teaching history. It had already become clear to him that his real scholarly ambitions could not be realized and that he would have to struggle along on his meager salary; it was improbable that his mother would ever be able to enjoy those small comforts in the hope of which she had so eagerly looked forward to his graduation—all these thoughts came to him now with a feeling of coldness.

In the distance he could see a group of small fishing-boats.

"Well, there's another life," thought Sutekichi to himself. "No doubt that's how they all end their days—setting out to sea to work."

Was his own life all that much better than theirs? The same thought had occurred to the young man when he had walked through a bleak fishing-village in the northern part of the island. It lay amidst the roar of the waves on a narrow strip of land, hemmed in by the mountains on one side and the rough waters on the other. Along the coast the water had eaten into the rocks, which stood there gaunt and angular. On a narrow plain facing the sea cows were grazing desolately. The steep, naked mountain rose directly behind the village, and on the lower slopes the villagers had built their enormous gravestones. These were the graves of the people who had been born in the village and who had died there after spending their lives at sea. The graves appeared so numerous that Sutekichi had wondered whether there were not more of them than of living people. Compared to the poor state of the village, the graves looked elaborate. . . . Yes, it had been a lonely place, but one could not deny that there was something noble about it. Sutekichi could imagine the firm-rooted life that was lived there, a life unburdened with superfluous doubts.

When Sutekichi returned to the cabin, he found that the professor had put a newspaper over his face and was lying on his back in a deep sleep. The sinking sun was shining through the small porthole, illuminating the professor's outstretched legs from the knees down to the socks on his feet.

Sutekichi picked up a history book and began reading. After a while the professor's voice emerged from under the newspaper: "Haven't we turned back toward Sado?"

"I hardly think so," said Sutekichi, surprised at the question.

"Hm," said the professor. Then after a while he added: "I had a feeling we'd turned back."

"But surely the ship wouldn't turn back, sir."

"Perhaps they left something very important behind," said the professor banteringly. "Now, what could they have left behind? They couldn't possibly have forgotten to take the captain on board, could they?"

Sutekichi was moved to laughter. There was an expression on his face as if to say: "What can you do with a man like the professor?"

"Did you have a nice nap, sir?" asked Sutekichi.

"Very much so," answered Professor Segi, removing the newspaper from his face. "It's just like paradise, lying like this," he added. He lay on the couch with a dreamy expression in his eyes.

"Ships make one sleepy," muttered the professor. He stood up abruptly. "We've stopped moving," he announced.

The throbbing of the engines had gradually ceased. It was strangely quiet. Sutekichi stood up and looked out of the porthole. Under the evening sky there was nothing to be seen but the colorless sea. High above, the clouds were dyed with the colors of sunset.

"I wonder if we've had engine trouble," said Sutekichi.

"I wouldn't like us to run into a floating mine," said the professor, putting on his shoes. "It would hardly do to become a war victim now that it's all been over for so many years."

"Can you see anything, sir?" asked Sutekichi.

"Well, if the ship has broken down, we're really in the soup! It isn't like having a breakdown in a taxi in the middle of Tokyo when one can just get out and walk if one's patience gives out."

Sutekichi left the cabin and hurried onto the deck in order to ask a crew member what had happened. The first-class deck was still deserted, but when he looked over the rail he saw that people were running about agitatedly on the lower deck; something had obviously happened. A crowd of passengers and crew were gathering in one spot and gazing out to sea. On the surface of the water about ten yards from the ship Sutekichi saw a group of three or four swimmers. It did not take him long to realize that someone was drowning. Now some other members of the crew had stripped off their clothes, jumped into the water, and swum toward the drowning figure. With the help of a life buoy they began pulling the body back toward the ship.

The only person who was dressed was the drowning man: the coat of his suit was spread out on the surface of the water. He seemed to be unconscious; his head rested on the buoy, but when the latter slipped down, his head also began to sink into the water. One of the swimmers righted the buoy and adjusted it so that it would support the man's body. In the gray sea the swimmer's feet looked strikingly white.

From the lower deck other members of the crew were loudly shouting out instructions. Another buoy was tossed onto the surface of the water, describing a wide arc as it fell.

"Get the trunk of his body into the buoy," someone shouted. "Keep him up on the surface!"

The drowning man's head was still partly submerged. Sutekichi noticed that his hair was short and partly white. As he watched, the young man felt his heart pounding. He noticed that the professor had also left the cabin and was standing next to him.

"Man overboard, eh," said the professor. "Attempted suicide?"

"It looks like it," answered Sutekichi.

They gazed silently as the buoy was gradually pulled alongside and the ship's ladder was lowered. The drowning man's clothes stuck closely to his body. He managed to cling to the ladder with his own strength.

"He's alive," said the professor.

"Thank the Lord!"

The crowd which had gathered at the ship's rail broke up suddenly to form a circle around the man, who had now been helped onto the deck. There was a large number of middle school students, evidently on a school excursion.

When he reached the deck, the man got to his knees and knelt there with his head down. One of the crew members thumped him on the back with his fist. The men who had swum to the rescue returned now to the deck, one after another. They were all sturdy young fellows. They shook their shoulders, as if cold, and stamped their feet, laughing merrily in spite of it all and talking loudly to each other.

"I'm glad they managed to rescue him," Sutekichi heard the professor say. "But it's a really cold evening, you know—no time to be throwing oneself overboard!"

Sutekichi was suddenly amused.

"A man who is going to throw himself overboard hardly stops to think whether the water's going to be cold or not," he said.

The professor moved his thick eyebrows and looked laughingly at Sutekichi's face. "Well, once he was in the water I bet he noticed it was cold! He seems to be on the old side. He's at the age where he needs a hot-water bottle when he goes to bed. It's quite cold enough just standing here on deck, isn't it?"

"Indeed it is," answered the young man. "There's still some snow left on those mountains."

"That's right. The Shinano River is pouring that melted snow right into the sea. Our friend evidently didn't consider that point before he went for his swim!"

After he had spoken, there came onto the professor's face the look of an old man, a look, indeed, that befitted his age.

"Yes," he went on, "I'm glad he's been rescued. Very glad. It'd be awful to know that someone had thrown himself overboard and then not to be able to find the body. Awful even if it were a complete stranger. The captain or whoever it was really deserves a word of praise."

The crowd that had gathered round the man on the lower deck was gradually growing as people emerged in little groups after hearing what had happened. He lay there listlessly, without sufficient energy to stand up. One of the crew tried to make him disgorge the sea water which he had swallowed. The passengers stared curiously. It was usually an uneventful two-and-a-half hour crossing, and this provided a welcome distraction.

"Because it doesn't concern them, they don't feel the slightest sympathy," commented the professor.

When they returned to their cabin, the professor soon became cheerful.

"Well, I was right, wasn't I," he said, "about the ship turning back? You kept on saying it was impossible. Once they knew there was a man overboard, they turned back to search for him. I knew perfectly well that we'd changed course. I may not look so bright, but my senses are as keen as a carrier pigeon's! I haven't aged for nothing, you see."

There was a discreet knock at the door of the cabin.

"Come in."

The door opened, and a man stood there in ship's uniform.

"Excuse me, gentlemen," he said, removing his cap. "I'm the purser. Very sorry to disturb you, but we've had a man overboard. We managed to rescue him, but now we'd like to put him in here where he can be away from the other passengers.

Would it be troubling you very much if I asked you to join the other passengers in the first-class lounge?"

"Well, of course," said the professor lightheartedly. "You want us out of here, you mean?"

"I'm very sorry to trouble you, gentlemen, but I'm afraid that's it."

The professor was about to stand up, but then he sat down again and asked suddenly: "If it's all the same to you, it won't bother us in the slightest if he joins us in here. He isn't dead, is he?"

"Oh no, sir. We managed to rescue him all right."

"In that case we'll certainly have no objection to his coming here."

"Well, if it's all right for you, sir, that's splendid," said the steward, and left the cabin.

"You don't mind, do you?" said the professor to Sutekichi. The latter nodded his assent automatically.

After a while they heard someone outside the cabin. So he had come, they thought. It gave them a queer feeling despite their matter-of-fact approach to the whole matter.

It was the cabin boy in his white coat. He carried a hat, overcoat, and suitcase evidently belonging to the unfortunate man. Sutekichi noticed that there was a calling-card attached to the case. After the boy had left, he looked at it. It was an extremely old card. On it was printed the name SOROKU OKAMOTO.

4 · DISLOCATION

●

THE TWO men sat in the cabin, each absorbed in his own silence. Even the vivacious professor was now quietly smoking a cigarette.

The cabin door opened, and the purser appeared again.

"Please look after him," he said apologetically, and stepped aside to make way for the man he had brought with him. The professor and Sutekichi looked up at the same time. The cabin boy stood there supporting the body of the man, who had a blanket round his shoulders. The head with its closely cropped whitish hair was the one they had seen a short while before bobbing up in the water.

Sutekichi noticed the professor tapping the ash from his cigarette into the ashtray and looking out of the porthole.

"Why don't you have a nap, sir?" asked the cabin boy solicitously. "Wouldn't you be more comfortable lying down?"

But it seemed to be too much of an effort for the man to walk even as far as the couch. Instead he sat down on the chair in the corner of the cabin and leaned back against the wall. The collar of a bathrobe showed underneath the blanket; they must have got him to change his saturated clothes.

"You aren't cold now, are you, sir? If you are, we can put on the heater," said the cabin boy.

With a vacant look on his face, the man slowly shook his head to the side. Then his wide-open eyes turned, as if by chance, to the professor and Sutekichi. For the first time he appeared to notice that there were other people in the cabin.

The professor, who until now seemed to have been bereft of speech, turned suddenly to his companion. His prominent mustache appeared to move, but the words emerged slowly as he began to tell a story.

The professor himself seemed fairly unconcerned as he talked; yet because of his companion's youth, he could not help feeling uneasy about the proximity of the man who had so recently been on the verge of drowning. As for Sutekichi himself, the name that he had read on the card remained vividly in his mind.

The professor's characteristic technique of telling a story made most people who heard him for the first time look at him with some puzzlement; his commanding presence and his personality did not appear to be those of someone who speaks with his tongue in his cheek. After one became accustomed to the professor's manner, one automatically adopted a cautious attitude in listening to him, but at first people were usually bewildered and astonished by his nonchalant air. But on this occasion Sutekichi noticed that the professor's story was not having the slightest effect on the other man. He could not even tell whether or not he was listening. Soroku Okamoto slouched forward in the chair with the blanket wrapped around him and his eyes closed. Deep agonized wrinkles were drawn on his face. Now and then his shoulders heaved under the blanket. His breath seemed to come in painful gasps. Evidently he was not unconscious, for suddenly his eyes would open widely as if he had momentarily returned to himself. At such times he would glance around timidly, then close his eyes, and subside again into torpor. One could feel the agony of his bitter self-restraint; in both his posture and his expression one could sense his utter instability.

All this seemed fairly natural to Sutekichi. For whatever reason this man had tried to take his own life, some very exceptional circumstances must have led to the decision. Then after all that, at the very moment of consummation, he had un-expectedly been rescued—no wonder that he felt bereft of all security. . . .

The professor finished his story, abruptly crushed his ciga-rette in the ashtray, and a moment later his large back disap-peared through the cabin door. Passing Soroku Okamoto, who was sitting by the entrance, he said: "Excuse me" in such a matter-of-fact tone that Sutekichi was impressed by the profes-sor's good grace. Mr. Okamoto had straightened himself up in his chair, but now he slouched forward once more and returned to his original position, with his face buried in his hands, as though he were crying, and his elbows resting c the his knees. There was something so utterly debilitated in his whole at-titude that one felt he might fall to pieces at any moment. His hair was white. Sutekichi had never seen a person of his age and distinction in such a state of agony, and it was almost un-bearable for the young man to look at him.

Why had he tried to die? He must have had some strong reason. How terrible it must be, thought Sutekichi, to have failed in his attempt at suicide and before he knew it to find himself surrounded by the curious eyes of his former fellow passengers. Surely it would have been better for the old man to have died as he had intended.

There was something suffocating about being alone so long with this silent companion. Sutekichi gazed through the port-hole at the sea. By now they must be nearing the harbor of Niigata, yet the water spread out before his eyes as unruffled as before.

The professor had been away for some time now from the cabin. What business could he have had except to visit the lavatory? Yet still he did not return.

Eventually the door opened, and the professor strode in.

"One can see Niigata already," he informed Sutekichi. "There's a good view of the lighthouse at the mouth of Shinano River."

He sat down in his former place and then, much to the young man's surprise, suddenly addressed Soroku Okamoto.

"Excuse me," he said, "but from the look of things I'm the oldest man here, and so it's for me to start the conversation."

The professor smiled and continued: "I may have been taking a liberty, but the fact is I've just been to see the captain and asked him whether he really has to hand you over to the police when we dock at Niigata. What d'you think about it? You don't really need the police to look after you, do you?"

Soroku Okamoto raised his head. He seemed to understand what the professor was saying, yet he looked absently at him without a word, as though neither his feelings nor his will were capable of motion.

Sutekichi was impressed by the professor's kindness. So even while the professor had been telling his story about the goblin cat, his brain had been working on the problem of how to help their unfortunate companion. Behind the superficial humor, his heart had been filled with sorrow for another person.

"After all, you are all right, aren't you?" continued Professor Segi. "No, there's no need for you to go to the police station," he said, answering his own question.

He took out a cigarette, thrust it in his mouth, and then laid his hand on the one that was already resting on the table. Sutekichi could feel in the professor's quiet attitude the strong will of a man determined to carry out what is in his mind.

"Your home's in Tokyo, isn't it?" asked Segi. He spoke slowly, as if to adapt himself to the slow tempo of Mr. Okamoto. "I think the best thing would be to telephone someone in your family. But that doesn't have to be done through the police. And, anyway, that's all that the police could do in any case."

Okamoto remained silent.

"If you don't think we're butting into your personal affairs," continued the professor, "I don't see any reason that we can't phone for you. We should try to get someone to come and fetch you—your wife, your children . . . or someone. As soon as we reach Niigata, we can get in touch with them by telegram or by phone. They could get on the night train from Tokyo, and they'd be in Niigata by tomorrow morning. Quite simple, you see."

But even now Okamoto did not answer. An impatient shadow seemed to pass over his spiritless face, and a restless light appeared in his eyes; but he did not speak.

"Where do you live in Tokyo?" said the professor.

"Well," murmured Okamoto with an uneasy look, and then suddenly he closed his eyes tightly as though overcome by confusion.

"Is it your wife," pursued the professor, "or is it your son that you'd like me to call?"

"Yes, my son," answered Okamoto, as if the words had suddenly torn themselves out of his throat.

"A boy?" said the professor.

"Yes indeed."

Okamoto blurted out the words, then stopped abruptly and turned his gaze to the sea beyond the porthole. His cheek muscles twitched violently, and his eyes were wide open. He put his hand to his eyes, then tapped his forehead repeatedly with his fist, as if to force himself to recall something forgotten. What he said next came as a shock to both the professor and Sutekichi: "Isn't it a fact that my son has died?"

The professor controlled his surprise and curtly answered: "I don't know," staring at Okamoto. The latter appeared to have retired deeply into himself.

"Yes," he continued, "he died. Akira is not here any more. That's quite certain." His tone had changed, and now he was speaking entirely to himself. "No, he's not here. . . ." said Okamoto.

As they stepped off the boat, it was getting dark. There was no taxi to be found, and they decided to walk to the hotel. By the time they reached the center of the town it was completely dark and the lights were blinking brightly. The atmosphere of spring was more intense here than it had been on the somnolent sea.

In the daytime the old canal, which was the distinguishing mark of Niigata, was rather an eyesore with its turbid water; but now at night it softly reflected the city lights and the willows along its banks, providing, in fact, a lovely image of the ancient port town. And the wooden bridge, along which during the day people hung their bedclothes to air, became at night a bit of graceful scenery.

"Listen," said the professor, "how about this? I've just thought of a *haiku*: 'Among the spring lights/ Hiroko and

Kimeko/ sit side by side.' Not bad, eh? You remember those two geishas the other day at the restaurant—the two sisters."

"I'm afraid I don't know the first thing about *haiku* poems," answered Sutekichi.

"That's just why I'm telling you this—because you don't understand. What's the point in telling someone who knows all about it? But seriously, don't you think it's rather a charming little *haiku*? The two geishas neatly arranged side by side. Not just one, but two sisters—that's the central idea. And all this set among the lights of a spring evening. We might even put a golden screen behind them as a sort of backdrop. . . . Hm. What about beating the barrel again tonight?"

"I think you'd better ask a goblin cat to do it for us!" said Sutekichi.

"Damnation!" said the professor.

"You see," said Sutekichi, "we ought to be able to get a cat to dance for us free."

"Free, eh?" said the professor. "You know the old proverb: 'gold coins before a cat,' or, as the Westerners say, 'pearls before swine.' Supposing the cat wants some gold coins! But then, of course, it's true that cats have had the reputation since ancient times of being very disinterested."

The professor spoke with seeming cheerfulness; yet it was clear that some trouble lurked in his mind. The source lay, of course, in the person of Soroku Okamoto, who was walking beside them.

It was all right to have helped him on the boat, but the trouble was that now they couldn't very well abandon him. Sutekichi was wondering the whole time what the professor was planning to do about the situation. The easiest thing, of course, would be to hand him over to the protection of the police. Even now if the professor were to ask Sutekichi's opinion, that is what he would suggest. Actually, thought the young man, it really couldn't be called unkind if they were simply to take advantage of Okamoto's vague state of mind to slip off and leave him by himself in the dark. After all, they hadn't invited him to accompany them. He had simply left the ship with them and, without the slightest attempt at explanation or apology, had tagged along with them as they walked to the center of the town. He hadn't said a single word, but had just drifted along beside them, as though utterly winnowed of all will power.

Sutekichi noticed the professor smiling to himself. What on earth was in his mind? All he had said was: "We'll go along to the hotel." As to the object of their attentions, he had been completely vague when they had suggested telephoning or telegraphing his family to come and fetch him. Was this because he did not want his family to know what had happened? Whatever it was, reflected Sutekichi, glancing at Okamoto, there was definitely something wrong with his mind. As they walked, Okamoto kept looking at his suitcase with the card on it, which Sutekichi was carrying for him. He seemed greatly concerned with this case, but he hadn't once touched it since they had started walking. Suddenly he looked up at the professor and Sutekichi and said: "Is that my suitcase?" After that there was no doubt left in their minds that something was seriously wrong with the man.

Fortunately before leaving the ship they had found a change of clothes for him in his case. The young man remembered how Okamoto had fumbled with the dry suit, turning it inside out and examining it with a suspicious look in his eyes. He had handled the clothes as if they belonged to someone else. Later they had stuffed his water-sodden clothes in the bag. Now Sutekichi was carrying both the professor's suitcase and Okamoto's.

"Excuse me, sir," said Sutekichi.

"Yes," answered the professor.

"Why don't we make ourselves scarce?"

"Hm."

"Let's just give him the slip. There'll be no end to it if we go on like this."

The professor let out a deep sigh: he was obviously considering the young man's suggestion. Just then they had to stop at an intersection while a large bus passed in front of them. Neon lights flashed busily on the wall of a large building opposite, which looked like a department store. As soon as the bus had passed they hurried across the street. Okamoto fell behind. Sutekichi glanced back and saw him searching for them goggle-eyed.

"The police will do something for him, sir," said Sutekichi, taking advantage of this development to establish his position.

"It's a real case of bats in the belfry," he continued, tracing a counter-clockwise circle on his forehead to emphasize his point.

"Bats?" said the professor.

"I mean to say, he's plumb crazy."

The professor glanced back. "Look at him standing there," he said, "wondering where we can have possibly gone. Well, I suppose you're right. It doesn't matter too much if we leave him. But what about that bag of his? You'd better hand it over to him."

"All right, sir, I'll go and give it to him right away."

"Just wait a moment," said the professor, seemingly annoyed at the young man's impatience. "He seems to have spotted us. He's coming this way." The professor smiled grimly and raised his hand as a signal to Mr. Okamoto.

"You see, my young friend, he's relying on us entirely. In fact, you know, he's a rather pathetic figure."

"This is no time for such reflections," said Sutekichi.

" 'In our journeys, a companion; in life, sympathy.' I suppose that from your point of view that saying seems a bit old-fashioned."

Okamoto approached them now, but he did not seem particularly pleased to have caught up with his companions. There was the same vacant expression on his face; at the same time one felt that he was possessed of some implacable purpose far removed from his present circumstances.

"Aren't you hungry?" the professor asked him. And receiving no answer, he said to Sutekichi: "What about treating ourselves to some *sushi* rice-balls with raw fish? I imagine there's a *sushi* place round here."

"Anything will suit me," said Sutekichi curtly.

"No need for you to get into a huff," said the professor. "After one's been for a swim, one's likely to be hungry. After all, even the sea breeze on deck is enough to give one a good appetite. Well, Mr. Okamoto, how about some *sushi?*"

"*Sushi,*" said Mr. Okamoto. It was not an answer, but a simple parrotlike repetition of the other's word.

"Yes, let's settle for some *sushi,*" said the professor. "After all, we're all Tokyoites, so *sushi* is our speciality. Come on, let's have a bite, let's have a bite, as they say in Tokyo! Isn't there a *sushi* place somewhere round here, Sutekichi?"

"Yes, I expect there is."

"Well, please find one. And don't be so cross. After all, I haven't said anything about calling for geishas and getting them to beat the barrel! All I'm after is a little *sushi*."

"If that's the way you feel, sir, I certainly have no objection to a bit of barrel-beating!"

But the professor did not laugh. He had suddenly become uneasy as he realized that Soroku Okamoto really did not understand what *sushi* was. From the very beginning, of course, it had been clear that there was something peculiar about Mr. Okamoto; now the peculiarities were emerging one by one.

"You do like eating *sushi*, don't you, Mr. Okamoto?" asked the professor.

"Okamoto, you say," came the answer. "Do you mean me?"

There was an earnest, seeking look in the man's eyes. The professor was startled and for a while remained speechless.

Mr. Okamoto's face was rigid, but his eyes were intent. "Okamoto . . . you said Okamoto. You're talking about me, aren't you?"

Sutekichi suddenly became irritable. "Let's not carry this too far," he said.

"Wait a minute!" said the professor in an unusually severe tone, and stepped directly next to Mr. Okamoto. Through his glasses the professor's strong eyes peered directly at the man. "That's right," he said. "You are Mr. Okamoto. You are Soroku Okamoto."

When he heard this, the man smiled, and for the first time a look of relief appeared on his face. Yet even now there was something vague and unreal in his expression, which made it impossible for his companions to feel any true relief.

"Yes, yes, I am Soroku Okamoto," he repeated to himself.

Sutekichi was reminded of the "Who Am I?" program on the radio. At first it struck him as amusing, but then he felt annoyed when he realized that in this case the man was actually identifying himself and not some other character.

The professor's thoughts were evidently of a different nature. As they passed a shop window, Sutekichi noticed a slight, mischievous smile playing on his face.

"I'm amused," said the professor all of a sudden, catching up with the young man. "I've thought of another *haiku*, you see. Here it is: 'A hazy night/ Bewitched by a fox/ We walk along.'"

Sutekichi glanced intently at the professor.

"You mean to say he's trying to fool us, sir?"

"Oh, dear me no!" said the professor hastily, as if trying to intercede on behalf of their companion. "Not at all. Nothing like that. If my poem can be taken in that sense, it must be very poor indeed. No, our friend here is bona fide, absolutely bona fide. It isn't a case of his bewitching us. Let us say that it is we who are in a state of bewitchment. He is completely innocent, you see."

"What exactly do you mean by that, sir?"

"I don't know. Oh look!" said the professor, suddenly coming to a stop. "What on earth is that? It really gave me a shock. Cherry blossoms! I couldn't imagine at first what flower it was."

In the darkness of the canal one cherry tree remained in full bloom. Some petals also lay on the somber ground at their feet. And no doubt the pink petals were floating along the stagnant waters of the canal.

"Stubborn things, these cherry blossoms!" commented the professor. "Blooming this late in the season. I suppose it's because we're fairly far north here."

"There are still some cherry blossoms left in Tokyo," said Sutekichi.

"That's not good, you know," said the professor dogmatically. "These blossoms are like elderly women who remain amorous beyond their time. Heavily rouged, you know, to disguise the encroachments of age."

Along one side of the canal was a row of small restaurants and *cafés;* the lights from their windows fell onto the road along which the three men were walking. They soon managed to find a *sushi* shop.

They went in and sat down at the counter with Mr. Okamoto in the middle.

"I'll take some oily tuna," said Professor Segi to the man behind the counter.

"Some conger eel for me," said Sutekichi.

Mr. Okamoto alone remained quiet. He was a man whose

spirit has slipped away, leaving only an empty husk. He sat on his stool gazing vacantly at the various slabs of raw fish that lay behind the glass pane ready to be rolled into *sushi* rice-balls.

"Well, Mr. Okamoto," said the professor, "what would you like to eat? You can have anything you like."

No doubt he was hungry, yet for some reason he sat there looking absently in front of him without giving any order.

"Yes indeed," he murmured. "This is *sushi*, isn't it?"

The professor felt like jumping up from his seat and shouting to the man to shut up. But looking at his serious face, he knew that there was no deception in him.

5 · AMONG PEOPLE

As soon as Taeko had entered the Kabuki Theater and gone up
the main stairs, she caught sight of her elder sister, Tazuko
Terada, standing by one of the large pillars in the foyer. They
nodded to each other from a distance.

Taeko walked up to her sister. She noticed that she was
wearing a heavy kimono of bright green silk decorated with a
fine pattern; her *obi* was of a blackish shade. It was some time
since they had met, and Taeko was struck by how young her
elder sister looked. Her hair style, also, was different from when
she had last seen her in Kyoto. Tazuko's face was quiet and
slender; she reminded Taeko of the French film actress Vivienne
Romance. Since Tazuko was greatly interested in the latest fash-
ions, this resemblance was no doubt far from being accidental.
During their father's years of affluence he had brought her up
indulgently, and Taeko remembered that Tazuko had since her
childhood always enjoyed getting herself up as impressively as
possible.

Taeko noticed that her sister was watching her carefully as
she approached.

"So you didn't put on a formal dress," said Tazuko, with a slight nuance of reproach in her voice.

"No," said Taeko nonchalantly, "I've come straight from the office." She looked at her wristwatch. "At any rate I've come on time," she added.

As they stood side by side, the two tall well-built sisters attracted a good deal of attention.

"There are some other guests coming as well," said Tazuko.

This suddenly reminded Taeko that her sister had sent her the theater tickets by special delivery, and she now thanked her warmly.

"I knew that you'd come up to Tokyo," said Taeko, "but I thought that you'd probably already gone back to Kobe by now. Did you come with your husband this time?"

"No," answered Tazuko briefly and in a rather cold tone.

Taeko knew that her sister tended to be self-conscious when she was with people. That, no doubt, was why she made such an effort when she came to Tokyo to speak standard Japanese instead of her usual Western dialect.

"I visited Uncle Soroku the other day," said Taeko. "That's how I knew you were here. The old housekeeper told me."

Tazuko turned her dark eyes onto her sister. "When was that?" she asked.

"Well, I should say it was about four days ago. Last Sunday, it was."

"Was Uncle at home?"

For a moment the image of her uncle's dilapidated and deserted house with its bolted shutters flashed through Taeko's mind.

"No, I gathered that he was away on a journey."

Tazuko closed the fan which she held in front of her breast —a Kyoto fan made of sandalwood. Her eyes were fixed to the entrance of the theater, and she seemed to be waiting intently for someone to arrive. Taeko noticed the slender bridge of her sister's nose. It was a shapely nose inherited from her mother; Taeko, who had been born of a different mother, remembered how she had envied it when she had been younger.

"I came up to Tokyo because I had something to ask Uncle," said Tazuko. "He wasn't at home when I arrived, and since then I have been phoning him every day from my hotel, but they tell me that he still isn't back. Do you often go to Kamakura?"

"Not very often," said Taeko. Because she lived relatively near Kamakura she knew that her sister imagined Taeko was probably on close terms with her uncle. Her sister expected some more detailed reply, but she did not feel inclined to elaborate.

"I was hoping to get some funds from Uncle Soroku for my work," said Tazuko, being characteristically forthright. Then, in just the same tone of voice, she moved on to a completely different subject of conversation: "Taeko-san, you really ought to be getting married now, you know. And the fact is I've found someone very nice for you."

Taeko pouted, as if to make light of what her sister was saying. She had no intention of taking this subject seriously.

"I've invited him here tonight," said Tazuko.

Taeko's features tightened. The program tonight was a performance of Japanese dances to which she hadn't really wanted to come in the first place. It was particularly annoying that her sister should have forced her to come here without any proper notice when she had such a scheme in her mind.

"Is that why it would have been better for me to wear a formal dress?" asked Taeko.

"Well, as a matter of fact, you may make a better impression in your simple everyday clothes."

"What does he do—this gentleman you want to introduce me to?"

"He's a graduate of Tokyo University. He has a position in a bank now. He's a very bright fellow."

"It all makes me shudder!" said Taeko.

Tazuko looked at her younger sister with surprise.

"Why, Taeko-san, what on earth do you mean?"

Her sister's formal manner of calling her "Taeko-san" instantly brought back old memories to the girl, reminding her sharply of the fact that they were only half-sisters.

"I've been planning it all for you out of the kindness of my heart," said Tazuko. "I've been thinking it over from every point of view."

"But the trouble is," said Taeko, "that your way of thinking and mine are utterly different. My goodness, do people still go in for arranged marriages in this day and age?"

"I wanted you to get acquainted with this young man and to have a good talk with him."

There was a clarity about the elder sister's words which perfectly matched her features. "You know, Taeko-san, I was really expecting that you would thank me for this," she added.

"Has he spoken to you about it all?" asked Taeko.

"Oh, he's very popular, I can tell you. He's getting offers of marriage from all over the place."

"Well, that makes it even worse!" said Taeko, laughing now and recovering her good spirits. "I can assure you that I don't want to become one of the candidates of whom he says later: 'That one's no good at all,' or 'I'm afraid she isn't quite right'!"

"His family were very interested in you. I just thought this would be a good chance for you to meet him and see what he's like."

"Oh yes," said Taeko, "I'll see him with pleasure. But I don't specially care about his seeing me. And if he does see me, you can tell him it's no good. I just don't happen to like the idea of being 'seen' by men in this way!"

"What are you saying?" said Tazuko. "Is that how people talk in Tokyo these days?"

"I don't know about that," answered Taeko. "In any case, I can assure you that there's no one else involved."

"Just as you like," said Tazuko. "But we were only doing all this for your sake. We thought he'd be a very good candidate for you as a husband."

"Well, thank you," said Taeko.

They were very conscious now that the atmosphere had changed, although they were standing in exactly the same position as before. The crowds of people coming up the stairs increased, and then the curtain-bell rang.

"Don't you think I'd better wait here too till he comes?" said Taeko.

Tazuko looked at her sister with an expression of utter astonishment.

"It's all right," she said. "Come along. We'll go in now. And by the way," she added, "you're going to pay dearly for what you've said!"

Since it was a performance of Japanese dancing, the proportion of women to men in the audience was greater than usual. Particularly conspicuous was the large number of kimono-clad women, both young and old, professional entertainers from the demimonde. Taeko remembered that her sister had studied Kyoto-style dancing as a girl. She herself had never had this opportunity, although as a younger sister it would have been normal for her. Partly this was because things had been so utterly disrupted during the war, but more important, thought Taeko, was the fact that she had never been loved as much as her sister.

As the curtain was pulled aside for the first dance, Taeko glanced around and saw that a large part of the audience had not yet arrived; there were a number of vacant seats surrounding her and her sister. The people who had arrived in time for the first number were no doubt the real enthusiasts. She glanced at her program: the first dance was called "Plum Blossom" and was to be accompanied by a classical Tomei tune. This, as a matter of fact, was the first time that Taeko knew there was a school of music known as "Tomei-bushi."

When the curtain had been drawn aside, she saw that the enormous stage was occupied by just one man. He was standing at the front of the stage attired in a crested kimono and a formal divided *hakama* skirt.

"That's Eitaibashi," said Tazuko, but it was not clear whether she was addressing her sister or murmuring the words to herself. In any case, Taeko had no idea of what she meant, and it took her some time before she realized that Eitaibashi must be the place where this particular dancer lived. Her sister was indeed well versed in matters of the theater.

Taeko looked without interest at the stage. The white Japanese-style *tabi* socks and the bluish-tinted *hakama* gave it an atmosphere of particular purity which one would not normally notice. As the man started to dance, she found in his generous movements a peculiarly attractive grace and elegance, and it no longer struck her that the stage was too large for a single person.

The slight deliberate pauses in the middle of the movements of the dance were also of great beauty. For a fraction of a second one wondered whether the dance was coming to an end, but then the previous movement would blend softly into the next, and this in its turn would come to an end, giving rise to all manner of unforeseen variations. Taeko found it hard to follow the words of the song, but there were moments as she listened when she could clearly understand their connection with the forms that the dancer was displaying on the stage. At such times she was vividly aware of the plum blossoms and of the nightingale delicately alighting on the branch of the tree. She could even feel the cold bracing air that fitted the season in which the plum flowered. Taeko's eyes involuntarily followed the dancer's every movement. Compared with Western ballet, this seemed to be a far gentler type of expression. It occurred to her how difficult it must be when dancing to such a slow tempo to support the tension of each stylized movement without ever giving the slightest overt indication of tension.

Taeko suddenly came to herself when she heard the man in the seat next to her exclaiming: "Splendid!" For a moment she thought that he was talking to her. "Yes, that really was very fine," said the man again after a pause. Her attention had now been distracted from the stage, and she felt annoyed at the interruption. No doubt her neighbor was in the habit of expressing his artistic appreciation aloud to himself. This was the mark of an elderly person, but when she glanced at him she noticed that his face was that of a young man. He was dressed in a Japanese kimono, and the bold striped pattern was one that was not often worn these days. She could not see too well in the dim light, but her impression was that it was an old kimono with well-worn sleeves and collar. The man had been silent now for some moments, but just when Taeko thought that he had given up his vocal comments, he let out a loud sigh. Taeko stared directly at him, but this did not appear to affect him in the slightest. She decided that as soon as the lights went on, she would give him a really cross look.

A late-comer was ushered into the aisle and took a seat on the other side of Taeko.

"Ah, Hoshino-san," said Tazuko, and Taeko knew that this was the man of whom her sister had spoken. He had come with another man, and now as they sat down they both exchanged greetings with Tazuko. Taeko did not even bother to look up to see what he was like.

"Well, the first scene is over," said Tazuko to her belated guests with a slight tone of reproach in her voice. "It really was a lovely dance." It occurred to Taeko that there was something familiar and unceremonious about the way in which her sister addressed the men.

The second dance had begun now, but, although Taeko had her eyes fixed to the stage, she was not following it closely. The scene came to an end amidst a burst of applause. The dancer finished his movements by striking a delicate, doll-like pose. Though the audience was clapping, the singing and the music of the *samisen* that had accompanied the dance continued. After a short delay Taeko's kimono-clad neighbor joined in the applause. "Damn it all," he murmured, "people shouldn't start clapping until the music is over!" As soon as the curtain was drawn the man jumped to his feet and hurried into the aisle, leaving his program, his evening paper, and a deerstalker cap on the seat. Taeko noticed that he was wearing an old-fashioned stiff *obi* round his striped kimono and that he had on a pair of formal white *tabi*. What sort of person could he possibly be, she wondered, and what did he do in life? It would be possible to imagine that he was a clerk who had undergone his apprenticeship in some very old-fashioned shop in the old business section of Tokyo. But were there many people of that kind left these days? There was a weakness in the line of the man's mouth, and his face had a rather unmasculine pallor. Well, thought Taeko, at performances of old Japanese dances it was no doubt common to find rather out-of-date people among the audience. She had already noticed that so many of the women in the audience obviously belonged to the traditional demimonde.

"Let's go out for a while, Taeko-san," said Tazuko. As Taeko got up from her seat, she glanced at the two men who were now following her sister into the aisle. They were both wearing spring suits, and their hair was neatly brushed in the back. As she walked down the center aisle, Taeko felt annoyed that her heart was beating rather faster than usual. She would have liked to have been able to look at this gentleman when she was introduced to him with an expression of utter indifference and even a little haughtiness.

The foyer was packed with people, and despite the old-fashioned aspect of much of the audience, the atmosphere was quite lively. Only a few of the women were dressed in Western style, and most of these were young girls.

"I shall introduce you all later on," said Tazuko to her guests. "Let's go up to the bar on the second floor."

Taeko nodded slightly to the two men, then hesitated for a moment, wondering whether she should go up the stairs ahead of the men or whether she should follow them. Her face flushed at the thought of a desire to make a good impression on the young man her sister had chosen for her. They both looked like ordinary young men of good family—the type of young men one can see by the dozen walking through the Ginza. They looked so commonplace, in fact, that they might have been picked up at random off the street. Taeko was already bored with them: she no longer cared in the slightest about finding any individuality in either of them.

When they reached the bar, they sat down at a table and Tazuko ordered some cold drinks. It was a quiet and cozy place, and considering that it was inside a theater, it had a rather luxurious atmosphere.

"Hoshino-san, I'm sure you'd like some saké, wouldn't you?" asked Tazuko.

"Thank you so much," said the young man shyly, "but I think I shall decline at present."

"In our work," added his companion, "there are all too many occasions when we simply have to drink. And Yo-chan here isn't one to drink on his own. You never do any drinking by yourself at home in the evenings, do you?"

"Hm, no I don't," replied Mr. Hoshino sullenly.

Something in the manner of the two young men reminded Taeko of the smooth capsules in which is enclosed some dose of bitter medicine. On the surface their bearing was relaxed and youthful, but inside they seemed stiff and affected.

"Excuse me," said Mr. Hoshino's friend, standing up and leaving the table. "I've got to go and buy some cigarettes."

A moment later Tazuko also said: "Would you please excuse me for a while?" and left Taeko alone with Mr. Hoshino.

Taeko understood the game at once. It amused her that her sister thought she was manipulating everything so adroitly. In Tazuko's mind this was no doubt the tactical moment to leave 'the young couple'—that was probably what she called them to herself—to talk.

Taeko felt certain that her sister would be the subject of Mr. Hoshino's conversational opening.

"That's a very nice sister you have."

"She's not a bit like me," said Taeko. Then, as she thought of what she wanted to say, she gazed at the little translucent bubbles attached to her cold drink glass.

"You see," she said, "we're different, both to look at and in our characters."

"Yes, I'm sure," said Mr. Hoshino in a gentle tone. "It's quite right that you should have your own character and individuality."

"Yes, but my sister wants to make me exactly like her," said Taeko forlornly.

"Well anyhow she's a very clever woman. We all admire her."

So the subject of her sister was going to continue, thought Taeko. Yes, it was no doubt one aspect of Tazuko's nature that she should be the subject of men's conversation.

"Isn't that a bit dangerous?" asked Taeko. "Especially from the point of view of you men who work in a bank."

"What do you mean by that?"

"She always thinks she can make everything work out just as she plans, doesn't she?"

Hoshino appeared not to understand what Taeko was driving at, but he was very adept at evading the question. "I hear you're working at the Daiwa Trading Company," he said.

"Yes, I'm a typist there," said Taeko.

"It's nice that you work on your own like that, isn't it?"

"If I didn't," said Taeko, "I couldn't eat."

"What a thing to say!" exclaimed Hoshino, and it was clear that he was referring to her parents and her sister. It all seemed rather tiresome to Taeko.

"Anyhow," he continued, "a new beauty has sprung up among the Japanese women who've begun to work on their own—a beauty which one didn't find when they were all closeted permanently at home. Don't you agree? Perhaps one might say that it's a beauty which comes from contact with life."

Taeko shook her head slightly, as though to indicate doubt.

But she answered gently: "Well, I'm sure there are some very pretty girls in a place like your bank. But I know that where I work it isn't so much life that we're in contact with every day as our typewriters. I really don't believe that working makes people beautiful in the way that the women's magazines pretend. I just don't think they're telling the truth when they say that."

Her words sounded too harsh to her, but she was doing her best to speak honestly.

"It's true," she continued, "that there may be something a little more lively about those of us who work compared with women who spend all day at home. On the other hand, we often get miserably tired—much more than conventional housewives. Haven't you ever noticed that at your bank?"

"Yes, to be sure," said Hoshino. There was something vague and gentle about the way in which he reacted to her words.

"Perhaps I didn't express myself properly," said Taeko. "The very fact that we're obliged to work gives us a certain strength. In a sense we're pursued by life and that builds up something new in us. That's all true. But at the same time, when the evening comes we're usually dead tired. . . . I wonder if it's because we're physically weak," she added after a while.

"What do you really like?" asked Hoshino. "What are your tastes?"

"Surely that's what our go-between should have told you!" said Taeko. Once she had started like this, she knew there was nothing for it but to continue in the same vein: " 'Excellent marks at school; learned the Japanese harp; studied the tea ceremony and flower arrangement. . . .' That's what the go-between would say, isn't it? But the truth is I'm hopeless at that sort of thing. What I really like are the *pachinko** parlors!" Taeko did not hesitate to confess her tastes honestly. "Yes," she said, "when it comes to Lux soap, I'm a real millionaire!"

Just then her sister returned to the table. "What are you two talking about?" she asked.

"I'm telling Mr. Hoshino about my treasures!" said Taeko. "When it comes to Lux soap, I've got so much I could open a shop all on my own. And I've won the whole lot by playing *pachinko*."

* *Pachinko* is a pinball game, extremely popular in postwar Japan. The winners receive prizes of cigarettes, soap, chocolate, etc.

"You really are the limit!" exclaimed Tazuko. "Do you honestly mean to say you play that terrible game?"

"Yes, I play it every day on my way back from the office," answered Taeko.

"Well, really," said Tazuko. "It's all right to do these things in moderation so long as they don't cause any harm. But if it's become a craze with you, I'm really going to have to tell Father about it."

It did not stike Taeko, however, as a particularly appropriate occasion to introduce her father.

"It's got absolutely nothing to do with Father," she said.

At this moment the bell rang to announce the beginning of the next part of the program. Taeko decided to leave the bar and to let her sister and Mr. Hoshino argue it out between themselves as to who was going to pay the bill. The main doors to the auditorium were already closed, and the spectators were hurriedly emptying the foyer.

Well, thought Taeko, it was a good thing she had been a failure. Of course, it was something she had expected all along. Yet at the same time she was aware of a certain sense of dissatisfaction. What made her hate occasions like this, she reflected, was the fact that there was always an odor of hypocrisy in the background. Her sister's officious, self-satisfied behavior had amused her. About Mr. Hoshino she didn't have any strong feelings one way or the other. She would have liked to return home by herself ahead of the others, as she had seen quite enough of the dancing.

Tazuko joined her, and they went down the stairs together.

"He said that I've got a sister with a very strong character," Tazuko whispered into her younger sister's ear. Taeko felt ill at ease.

"Did you happen to notice," said Taeko, "that there was someone sitting next to me who looked like a clerk? What sort of kimono was he wearing, do you suppose? It was fantastically old-fashioned."

"Well, if it was the proper material," said Tazuko glancing around, "it would be Tozan cloth. But I expect it's only imitation. It's not often that one sees genuine Tozan these days."

"He seems such an old-fashioned person altogether," said

Taeko. "And then he mutters to himself the whole time while he's watching the dancing. He's somewhat annoying."

"I'd better change seats with you," said Tazuko. "You should sit next to Mr. Hoshino in any case."

This plan, however, Taeko skillfully managed to frustrate.

Tazuko Terada was staying at the Imperial Hotel. This was the first time that Taeko had realized that the Imperial Hotel had been released by the Occupation forces for civilian use. As she sat next to her sister in the car on their way to the hotel and looked out of the window at the thin spring drizzle, Taeko reflected with some surprise on the extravagant life that Tazuko appeared to be leading with such utter nonchalance.

For her part Tazuko appeared to be satisfied with the progress of her plan that evening, and she was in a good humor.

"He's a very masculine young man, isn't he?" she said. "And quite smart too. What did you two talk about?"

"Well, we didn't have any real conversation," replied Taeko. "You see, I did almost all the talking myself."

"They think a lot of him at the bank where he works. And he has a very nice home. . . ."

The variegated reflections of the streetlamps played on the shining surface of the paved road and the headlights of the car illuminated the minute raindrops. It occurred to Taeko that if she were to meet Mr. Hoshino again on the street, she would not even be able to recognize him.

"How long will you be staying in Tokyo, Tazuko?" she asked in an effort to change the subject.

"Well, it looks as if I'll have to go back tomorrow. But we'll talk about all that at the hotel. . . . Don't you suppose Uncle Soroku has returned to Kamakura today?" she added.

"Are you waiting for him to get back?" asked Taeko, looking straight at her sister's face. "That uncle of ours, did you know he used to charge interest on the money he advanced to Akira?"

Tazuko turned her face toward the window, which was clouded over with raindrops. "Yes, I dare say," she said after a while. "He's different from most people."

"All the same," said Taeko, "I can't help liking him in some strange way. I wonder why he doesn't get married again. He must be lonely living there all by himself."

"Why don't you ask him?" said Tazuko, who was glancing in the mirror of her compact and arranging her make-up.

As the car drew up at the hotel, Taeko noticed that on the water in the square pond at the entrance young lotus leaves were floating, gently wetted by the raindrops.

"The lobby is the best place to sit," said Tazuko.

In the large lobby Japanese and foreigners were sitting in separate groups around the scattered tables. The sisters found two empty chairs and sat down. They were aware that it had been a long time since they had sat together face to face.

"Would you like some tea?" said Tazuko, after glancing around at the other guests.

"No thanks. I don't feel like any."

"Well, then, we can go ahead with our little conversation."

"I'd rather not, you know," said Taeko with complete composure.

Tazuko looked serious. "Why not?" she asked. "What's your reason?"

"Reason?" said Taeko. "I don't have any special reason. It's just that I haven't got the feeling for that sort of thing."

"You should try to be more feminine, you know." said Tazuko. "When women work as you do, they change without even knowing it."

"I think I am feminine in my own way," said Taeko, and as she laughed gently the youth seemed to shine out of her eyes. "Don't you agree, Tazuko?"

"Women grow old rather quickly—without even being aware of the fact." It was the conventional warning of an elder person. "How old are you now, anyhow?"

"Some time ago I stopped believing that people become one year older each time that a year goes by," said Taeko smiling lightheartedly. "It may strike you that I'm being a bit willful, but I really don't see why we all have to be tied to the calendar to exactly the same degree."

"That's rather cocky of you, isn't it?"

"But, Tazuko, you're resisting age pretty well yourself, aren't you? No one who saw you could possibly guess your age."

"That's not the point at all," said Tazuko with an intractable look on her face. "There's a right time for marriage as well as for everything else. It wouldn't matter so much if it only concerned yourself, but—"

"But what's to say that I should behave just like everyone else? If I'm going to get married later than some people—well, all right, let it be later!"

"Is that how girls become when they work on their own?" said Tazuko.

"It's got nothing to do with that," said Taeko. "Perhaps I was born to be easygoing. I just happen not to feel yet like trying to avoid the icy winds by putting myself in the shelter of some man for the rest of my life. And the truth is, Tazuko, that you're just the same. There's something about you that makes me feel right away that you're not by any means completely at ease with your husband."

"You have a very glib tongue," said Tazuko.

"Yes," said Taeko, "I do."

On her ingenuously smiling face there flashed a look of vigor, so natural as to seem almost animal-like.

"I'm not like you," continued Taeko. "I don't keep quiet. I say what I think. You're very subdued, aren't you, Tazuko? But I know you. In the case of your husband, you look straight at him and make your judgments accordingly. But you don't let any of it show on the outside. Is that really the way things should be between husband and wife?"

"Look here," said Tazuko, with recrimination in her eyes, "it's you we're talking about, not me." Her seniority in age and her dignified role as an elder sister were both reflected in her attitude. "I can't help feeling, Taeko, that you're drifting away from Father and the rest of us. And it worries me. I saw the letter you wrote him the other day. What an utterly cold letter it was!"

"Well, I didn't have anything special to say," replied Taeko ingenuously and with an air of finality.

There was a weary look on Tazuko's face; the conversation seemed to have tired her. Then, as if she had suddenly been reminded, she said: "Oh yes, I should have put in a call to Kamakura."

"For Uncle?" said Taeko.

"Yes," said Tazuko, "he must be back by now."

She looked around for the porter, but not seeing him she went out by herself to the telephone booth. Taeko glanced round the large lobby. There were still a few people left. She felt strangely isolated. The architecture was indeed original: the stone-tiled pillars looked stunted in comparison with the enormous ceiling, and she had the feeling of being in a cellar. For a moment she tried to imagine why her sister so eagerly awaited the return of their uncle to Kamakura, and she was aware then of a heavy shadow in her sister's superficially bright life.

6 · DIM LIGHT

TAEKO gladly agreed to her sister's suggestion that she stay with her for the night. The room was conveniently equipped with twin beds. The two sisters washed their faces in the bathroom. Taeko noticed that her sister had lined up a complete set of toilet articles on the shelf in front of the mirror, even though she would be here only for such a short time.

"I've put on a bit of weight, haven't I?" said Tazuko, as she changed into her nightgown. Taeko, who did not have a nightgown, stretched herself out full length on the bed in her slip.

"Not in the slightest," she answered. "While I was looking at you now, I was just thinking how slim you were. . . . Doesn't your husband mind your staying away from home all this time?"

"On the contrary, he's probably finding it very comfortable to be alone," answered Tazuko, taking off her *tabi* socks and climbing into bed.

"Do you want the light on or off?" said Taeko.

"Either way," answered her sister.

"In that case, I'll turn it off. The lights from the garden reach right in here." She pushed the switch on the wall above her head, and the room became dark. The light seeped in through the lace curtains of the window that faced on the garden. One could see the reflection of the tree branches.

"I'm rather tired, you know," said Tazuko, changing the position of her pillow and making herself comfortable. "I can't help feeling," she continued after a few moments, "that you're rather selfish the way you make me worry so much."

"But Tazuko, that's completely unreasonable. You've never asked me to do anything before. It's I who has always had to do everything for myself."

"Look, Taeko, you don't want to catch a cold, do you? At least put a blanket over yourself."

In the dim light Taeko stretched her naked arms up in the air. The darkness made her feel happy and seemed to awaken within her some vague impulse to movement. It was really a long time since she had slept like this next to her sister—in fact, the last time must have been when she was still a little girl not yet old enough to go to school. It all seemed very cloudy in her memory, no doubt because of the war years that had come between.

"He's a gentle sort of person, isn't he?" said Taeko, suddenly starting to talk about Mr. Hoshino. The words she wanted to say began to puff up like clouds in her mind, but she realized that they would probably sound unkind to her sister and decided not to continue.

"The trouble is that I'm no good," she said. "I'm a terrible shrew really. I don't suppose I've really been very nice to you about the whole thing, but I can't help it."

"How about seeing him once again tomorrow morning and having a talk with him? You might have tea together somewhere."

"It's no good," answered Taeko bluntly.

Tazuko turned her back to her sister and prepared to go to sleep. Taeko pulled up the bedclothes and settled down. But after a while Tazuko began talking: "What about Uncle Soroku —do you think he might lend me some money?"

Taeko lay silent with her eyes fixed on the ceiling.

"I need some money whatever happens," said Tazuko, and turned round in bed to face her sister. "If I start thinking about it, I can't get to sleep."

"Are you really all that hard up for money?" said Taeko.

"Yes, really. My husband's clinic seems to bring nothing but expenses these days. It's not easy, you know. And then he's a bit of a fop—that costs money too. He's always had rather extravagant ways, and that doesn't seem to change with the years. I just don't know what's going to happen if things go on like this." She paused for a while. "Then there's the fact that we don't have any children. If we had children, perhaps it might make him settle down a bit. Some time ago I thought of trying to do some work on my own, and I made plans to open a shop dealing in imported luxuries. I paid all the necessary commissions, rented the shop, got the representation rights from the different producers—and then the money ran out. Now I'm absolutely stuck."

"I'm sure if you set your mind on it you'll manage all right," said Taeko. "That's the way you are." She did not intend her words as a compliment; it was simply that Taeko looked at her elder sister in this way. "Your husband ought to help you with the finances," she added.

"But you see he was against the whole thing from the outset. He said if I wanted to go ahead, it was all right by him, but that he wouldn't have anything to do with it. That's what he told me when I'd already got myself deeply involved in the whole scheme. The trouble is that things aren't really going well at the clinic. The patients are all right, but my husband's had a terrible time getting new equipment. Everything's changed since the war. Right near our clinic there's a young graduate from Osaka University who has opened his own clinic equipped in the latest American style. We can't afford to relax for a minute. Our income's gone down because of the national health scheme, but our expenses are ten times what they were before. We've been in practice for a very long time, and our reputation is still pretty good. But we certainly can't rest on our laurels. It's a hard situation, you see. It's no fun for my husband either. That's why I thought if I could get the shop going and start making some money, this would be a help for the clinic also. But the whole thing has stopped halfway."

Taeko realized that it went against the grain for her sister to speak openly of her affairs this way. Perhaps it was the darkness of the room that had opened her up and made her re-

veal these confidences. Taeko regretted now that she had teased
her sister by not taking the affair of Mr. Hoshino more seriously.

"I see," she said. "So that's how it is. Yes, it's a difficult problem." Taeko turned around and watched her sister's pale face
in the dim light. "What about borrowing the money from the
bank?" she said.

"I've borrowed up to the hilt," said Tazuko. "That's why I
thought of Uncle Soroku. He's the only person who can help
me now." Then, as if remembering what Taeko had told her
earlier, she added: "I don't mind paying interest on what he
lends me. But if I don't have that money soon, I'm going to be
in real trouble."

The next morning Taeko got up early, as was her habit. As
Tazuko was still sound asleep, her face to the wall, Taeko tip-
toed into the bathroom, washed her face, and got ready to go
out. Her office was only ten minutes' walk from the hotel; it
gave her a leisurely feeling compared with the usual rush of
travel from her room in Omori on the crowded trolley.

Tazuko sat up in bed. She looked as if she still hadn't slept
enough.

"Ring the bell for the boy," she said, "and order some coffee
or something. I'm going to sleep a little longer myself."

Taeko would very much have liked some tea or coffee, but
instead she decided to go out by herself somewhere and have a
glass of milk. The story that she had heard the night before
about her sister's predicament seemed to lose all reality in the
clear light of morning. Taeko opened the window and looked
out at the garden. Carp were swimming about in the shallow water of the pond. Around the edge of the pond grew regular rows
of anemones and hyacinths, their pretty blossoms supported on
narrow stems.

"Well, Tazuko, I must be off now."

Tazuko raised her head from the pillow and nodded. Then
abruptly she said: "Depending on the results of my phone call
today, I may be returning home by the night train. In that case,
I should be very grateful if you would handle the matter of
Uncle Soroku for me."

The electric lights were burning in the corridor, even though it was full daylight outside, and Taeko felt she was walking through a tunnel. On the way she passed a cleaning-woman who was carrying a broom. There were no guests in the lobby; one of the boys was cleaning the carpets with a vacuum-cleaner.

After the rain of the previous night it was a lovely clear morning. Taeko was struck by the bright color of the sky between the deep green of the trees in Hibiya Park, which was directly opposite the hotel. Crowds of men and women were hurrying along the streets on their way to work; others stood in long queues in front of the trolley-stop. Under the limpid sky the air had the softness of a late spring morning. The fresh green of the trees that lined the Imperial Palace moat stood out brilliantly against the gray of the stones. Taeko felt like walking through the park. Although she lived in Tokyo, she rarely came here, and an early-morning walk in the park was something that one would never undertake in the normal course of things.

The dewdrops still clung to the roses in the flower garden—some of them brilliantly reflected the morning sun. A dragonfly shot through the air like a stone missile. As Taeko stopped and looked at the flowers, she could hear the continuous sound of the passers-by, the footsteps and the voices of people taking a short cut through the park on their way to work. She looked at her watch and resumed her walk.

Soon she passed tennis courts where a number of men and women were busily playing. Taeko enjoyed hearing the hard twang of the balls as they hit the rackets. In the center court a blond young man who looked like an American was dashing about. As Taeko approached the court, she noticed that the man he was playing with was a familiar-looking Japanese. She could not see his face clearly, but she recognized the slender body and the powerful shoulders.

She felt strangely happy when she realized that it was Ryosuké Tsugawa, whom she had met the other day in Kamakura. As he stood waiting alertly for the ball his opponent was about to serve, she could see the perspiration shining on his freshly shaved face. The morning sun shone straight onto the court; Tsugawa was not wearing a hat, and he seemed to be dazzled by the bright light.

Quite a few people had stopped to watch, not simply because it was a game between a Japanese and an American, but because they were attracted by the lithe, energetic figures of the two young men. Judged by an amateur, Tsugawa seemed to be the stronger of the two players. Taeko watched him as he glided in pursuit of the ball, and she noticed the strength of his arms as he hit it back over the net. Taeko looked at her watch and wondered whether Tsugawa had noticed that she was there. She felt her face flush.

Taeko left the courts then and there and returned to the main road. The rose garden, which had previously been half in the shade, was now basking fully in the morning sun.

Her day at the office was the same as usual. Taeko soon forgot about her experiences at the hotel and in the park; now she was conscious only of her fingers as they moved rapidly across the keyboard of the typewriter.

During the lunch break she went for a stroll with some of the girls from the office. People were pouring out now from all the offices, making the fairly broad pavement seem narrow. It was the daily routine of Taeko and her friends to examine the window displays in each of the shops.

"Oh, they've sold that tie," said one of the girls. "I was going to make him a present of it they next time I had some money."

Taeko remembered the tie in question, but she knew that since "he" was simply a figment of the girl's imagination, she would not have bought the tie however much money she had: the girl lived with her invalid mother.

As she walked up the stairs to her office, Taeko recalled seeing Tsugawa that morning, and it occurred to her that she might easily have run into him in the noontime crowd. She thought of the things that she had seen in the store windows. Almost all of them were for men: light gray felt hats for spring, rattan walking-sticks, smart leather toilet-cases for traveling, suit materials. . . . She imagined herself presenting Tsugawa with something from one of the shops. She felt herself blushing, yet she did not want to reject the image or the light flutter of excitement that accompanied it.

The afternoon work started. It was a hard day's work; by evening she was tired and thought of stopping somewhere or her way home for a cake. Just then the office boy came to her desk and announced that someone by the name of Tsugawa was asking for Okamoto-san. Taeko's first reaction was that the boy must have made a mistake and heard the man's name incorrectly. But when she went out into the corridor, she found that it was really Tsugawa standing there in his light gray suit and gazing out of the window. He looked tall in his soft spring hat, and there was a youthful air about him.

"I happened to be passing in front of your office," he said. "I remembered that you worked here, so I dropped in."

Listening to his calm voice, Taeko forgot her first shock of surprise. She remembered the scene on the tennis court that morning.

"You leave the office at five o'clock, don't you?" he asked.

"Yes. But today I'm going to be kept a bit later because of some work."

"I have a ticket for the ballet tonight. It occurred to me that you might enjoy going, so I've brought it with me."

Without waiting for an answer, Tsugawa put his hand into his pocket and produced the ticket.

"To tell the truth," he said, "I was going to give it to you this morning . . . you know, when you were watching the tennis."

Taeko's face reddened. In her mind's eye she could see the ball bouncing back strongly from the back net.

"Did you notice me there?"

"Yes indeed," he said laughing. "I was going to talk to you, but then I found you'd already gone, so I didn't have a chance. In fact, this ticket was in my jacket which was lying right there on the lawn. . . . Well, I do hope you'll go this evening. If you can't, give the ticket to someone else—not to a man, though, you'd better give it to some pretty girl."

"What about you, Tsugawa-san?" asked Taeko instinctively. "Aren't you going yourself?"

"Well, I've only got one ticket," said Tsugawa, "and if I was able to go tonight, I wouldn't be giving this ticket to anyone, not even to you. To tell the truth, though, I'd much rather go to the movies and see some cowboy film than sit watching ballet."

"Thank you very much for the ticket," said Taeko with a formal bow. "I accept it with pleasure. It's wonderful for me, you know. I hardly ever have the chance of seeing something like the ballet, however much I want to."

Without thinking, she glanced at her wristwatch. Tsugawa, who was getting ready to leave, noticed her gesture.

"It starts at seven o'clock," he said. "In the meantime, what about going somewhere for a bite to eat?"

Taeko glanced at Tsugawa with surprise. "You mustn't go to all that trouble," she said.

"What do you mean?"

Taeko was thinking of the expense that the young man would be incurring. "No, really," she repeated, "I don't want to trouble you."

"On the contrary," said Tsugawa with a masculine disregard of the conventional phrases, "you *should* trouble me! Actually, I'm fairly flush at the moment—just like Mé used to be at the beginning of the school term. We had a bet on that tennis game this morning, you see. I told the American that he needn't bother to pay me, but he has a strict sense of duty and insisted on my taking the money. It's just about enough for our dinner."

Two days after their return from Niigata Sutekichi telephoned Professor Segi's home from the school where he worked. The professor's wife answered and said that her husband was at the university. Sutekichi was curious to know whether the man whom the professor had picked up in Niigata was still at his house. "Picked up"—yes, it was a strange expression, but it really was true that they had picked the man up, just as one might pick something up off the street. Soroku Okamoto had stuck with them all that evening; then he had taken the train with them; and at dawn the following morning when they arrived at Ueno Station, he had given no sign of being prepared to leave them. If it had indeed been an object that they had picked up, they could quite simply have left it on the train, but being a living creature, he was equipped with legs and was therefore able to tag along of his own accord.

"Well," the professor had said at the station with a wry laugh, as though trying to overcome his own doubts, "it will probably turn out all right. At least it's better than coming home from some house of ill fame with a pimp in hot pursuit trying to dun one for money. We've done nothing wrong, after all. I shall enter the house with my nose high in the air like Cyrano de Bergerac. Even my wife won't be able to say a word."

The professor evidently had been trying to convince himself.

"Would you like me to come home with you?" Sutekichi had suggested.

"Oh no, I don't need any assistance," Segi had answered with a grin. "It will be more peaceful if I come back by myself. There really shouldn't be any trouble." Then turning to Okamoto, who was standing there with a startled expression on his face, he had asked: "You're coming home with me, aren't you?"

Okamoto had behaved perfectly the whole time and had obeyed the professor in every detail. There surely could be no danger from this quarter. This man Sutekichi had reflected, was unable to take any action whatsoever unless stimulated from outside; without being prodded, he would remain in a permanent state of apathy. Sutekichi had remembered hearing of a similar case during a lecture on experimental psychology.

"If anything should go wrong," he had said, "just phone me and I'll be right over."

When Sutekichi was leaving the professor and his charge at Ueno Station, to take the local electric railway to his school, the professor had invited Mr. Okamoto to get into a taxi. Sutekichi had noticed Okamoto stepping in with a look of complete nonchalance. If Sutekichi had been in the professor's place, he would have given the driver some fictitious address and let Okamoto go off by himself to whatever fate might befall him. In fact, Okamoto would no doubt have acquiesced and stepped gently into the car, like some wooden statue. It had been early morning, and even the workers had not yet begun to appear on the streets.

Later it had occurred to Sutekichi that Okamoto's name might be in the telephone directory, and during a break at school he asked the porter to fetch him the book. The directory covered the entire Tokyo area, yet he had been unable to find any trace of a Soroku Okamoto.

The day after his return to Tokyo Sutekichi had been busy preparing his lectures, and in the evening a friend had come to call on him. Accordingly he had not been able to telephone the professor's house until the following day.

"Is the gentlemen the professor brought along from Niigata still with you?" he asked when the professor's wife answered.

"Oh yes," she said without hesitation, "he's still here."

"What's he doing?"

The question sounded strange to Sutekichi himself, but Mrs. Segi seemed to accept it as quite normal.

"Until just now he's been looking after little Taro."

This reply came to Sutekichi as something of a shock. Yet when he pictured Mr. Okamoto playing with the professor's little grandchild, he was surprised at how peaceful the scene appeared to him; it gave him a mellow feeling.

He mentioned the story to his mother, and she seemed to be quite moved by it. "Yes, that's the professor for you all right," she said. "No one else would go to all that trouble."

Old people feel for other old people, Sutekichi had reflected. His mother was certainly of the old-fashioned type—and so, by and large, was Professor Segi.

On the whole, the professor's academic connections with the Hongo University were slight. He gave his lectures, to be sure, but his own isolated type of research did not really fit in with the system at Hongo, and it made him seem rather unorthodox. Professor Segi came from a family of specialists on Chinese literature. His own field of study was paleography. His sober research in this recondite field had little connection with the modern world around him and in society at large the professor attracted very little attention. Even academic circles gave scant heed to his existence. This was largely because in his school days he had been known for his sports activities and for having a good time. At the university he had never been a bookworm, but instead had spent most of his time drinking *saké* and patching up drunken quarrels. He was a well-known figure in the student circle—but not for his academic achievements.

It was a very long time before his friends found out about his untiring studies in the field of paleontology. Even then reaction was that an idle fellow such as Segi could only have chosen such an obscure subject after entering the History Department because so few other students took it and it was therefore relatively easy. A cunning application of economic principles was also discerned; for when there were few students in any particular department, the staff of that department would value them accordingly and rarely fail them in the examinations.

During the war one of the professor's former classmates had given a party to celebrate his appointment as cabinet minister. Someone had mentioned the name of Segi, and the new minister had said; "Oh, you must be talking about that jiujitsu fellow who was always getting into brawls at the boarding-house. Don't tell me he's become a professor!"

For his part, the professor, upon hearing of this man's appointment as cabinet minister had commented that Japan must really be losing the war if a "genius" like that was given high political office.

As far as his academic work was concerned, the professor was widely criticized for his dogmatism and his occasional errors.

"Yes, I make mistakes, all right," he used to admit. "All the others are too frightened of making mistakes. It's a good thing that there's someone like me in the field. Otherwise there wouldn't be anyone to criticize, and all the other fellows would be out of work!"

After his telephone conversation with Mrs. Segi, Sutekichi decided to go and look for the professor at the university. He was no doubt either in the History Documents Section or in the library. Hongo University, where the professor had spent his student days, was now his real stamping-ground. He was popular at the university because of his good nature and because even after his graduation he had continued to take an active interest in the sports department. It was typical of the professor that whenever he visited a barber, he always made a point of going to the out-of-the-way shop in the Hongo area of his student days. The man who had owned the shop in those days had died, and his place had been taken by his son. The professor still remembered the latter as a red-faced boy—though now he was elderly and nearly bald—and whenever he saw him, he addressed him: *"Boya,* my lad!" regardless of who happened to be present.

"But really, Professor, I'm not a child any longer," the barber would protest.

"Well, that's the only way I have to call you," answered

Segi. "I can only remember you as the little boy in clogs who used to go round sweeping the hair from the floor of the shop. Do you want me to start calling you 'General' now just because you've turned bald? After all, if you were a general, you should have been arrested as a war criminal!"

"Really, Professor, you are the limit!" the bald-pated barber would say, and as he started to brush the professor's hair, there would be a wry smile on his face, for he was aware of the subdued titters of his young assistants. The professor's hair also was thinning at the roots.

In the university grounds rows of maidenhair trees were beginning to don their summer dress, and newly leaved branches were piled one on the other. Each year the shadows of the trees seemed to spread further, and to Sutekichi, who had only graduated three years before, they already looked appreciably larger than when he had left. As he walked now under the trees, he looked up at them nostalgically. It was strange, he thought, that when you were a student, it never occurred to you how beautiful these trees really were. No doubt the reason one noticed the beauty only after graduating was that in one's mind the trees had become inextricably blended with the memories of one's youth.

Sutekichi could find no trace of the professor in the library, but as he walked down one of the side streets, he spotted him sitting with another man at a table in a small tea house frequented by students.

"Hullo!" shouted the professor, as he noticed Sutekichi. "What brings you here?"

The professor's companion was a middle-aged gentleman in a spring coat. As Sutekichi approached the table, the man stood up and said: "Well, Professor, I must be going now."

"I see," said Segi. "In that case, thank you very much for all your help. I know how busy you are, and I shan't try to keep you any longer."

"There's absolutely nothing to worry about," said the man, and under his rimless spectacles his gentle eyes seemed to smile. "If there should be any trouble, I'd try that shock treatment. I think that would do the trick. Of course, from the layman's point of view it's a pretty drastic remedy, so if possible I'd hold off for about a week and see how things go."

"Right," said the professor. Sutekichi noticed that there was something unusually subdued about his manner. "As a matter of fact, I can think of three or four people among my own acquaintances on whom I wouldn't mind using that shock treatment."

"Well, really!" said the man.

"It's quite true," pursued the professor. "I can think of quite a few people who could do with a bit of shock treatment. To begin with, all the members of the Diet and the Cabinet—those fellows certainly need it once in their lives. It would be a very good thing if we could pick them off one by one in order of the precedence they hold at the Imperial Palace and give them each a dose of shock treatment. It would do them good—and help the public too!"

The man in the spring coat laughed. Bowing politely, he put on his hat and hurried out into the street. He looked as if he were running away.

"What was all that about?" asked Sutekichi.

"Well, that gentleman was Professor Waki of the Psychology Department. He's been telling me about how they use the shock treatment in cases of severe depression. The patient has to bend backward while they apply the electrodes. They stretch his body out like a sardine being grilled over a strong fire. Then they turn on a terrific current. So far as the patient is concerned, there's no question of endurance or showing his character. He's up against something quite impersonal—electric power. Yes, it's the thunder god in action, all right!"

"And you say that should be done to politicians?"

"Right. One after another, in the order of their precedence at the Imperial Palace," repeated the professor, evidently pleased with this particular formula. "You see, they must be made to remember that there's such a thing as shame in this world. They're all suffering from chronic amnesia. What they need is a tremendous shock to bring them back to themselves with a jolt. Then, if they have anything to be ashamed of, they'll remember it. Don't you really think it's a pity to let such a convenient and delightful appliance as this lie moldering in the medical science department?"

A young girl, the daughter of the proprietor, who had evidently just returned from school, came in with a dish of Chinese fried rice and set it in front of Professor Segi.

"You'll have some, won't you?" said the professor.

"No thanks."

"Do keep me company," he pursued, but seeing that Sutekichi was adamant, he picked up his spoon and started to eat his rice slowly, stopping every now and then to sip some tea.

"Professor, about that man . . . I hear you're still taking care of him."

"That's right," said Segi, and burst out laughing. "As for my old woman, I introduced Okamoto to her as someone who'd looked after us while we were in Niigata. She's taken it quite seriously and is under the impression that the reason he's so reserved is that he's from the country."

"Really, Professor!" said Sutekichi, feeling rather resentful on behalf of Mrs. Segi. "And what do you plan to do?"

"I think he'll come round to himself before too long, you know," answered the professor lightly. "As I understand, it's only his memory that is confused. Apart from that, he's quite an ordinary person. And a very gentle one, too. He's taking very good care of my little grandson."

"He is?"

"Yes, I've got an idea that he has children of his own. He's got clumsy, masculine hands, but you can tell that's he's used to looking after children and that he loves them. He's taken the little boy out, carrying him on his back, and bought him a whole stack of toys. It's really quite amusing. He must have bought him a whole cartful. Of course, I was extremely obliged to him. At the same time I had an idea that the bill hadn't been paid, and I sent someone to the shop to find out. It turned out that the bill had been settled in full. He must have made quite an unusual customer at that toy shop!" The professor laughed and added: "Yes, he's fond of children, all right."

"But hasn't he started talking about his own home or children yet?" asked Sutekichi.

"Not yet. When the little boy Taro isn't there,.they tell me he just sits by himself lost in thought. He never says a word and never looks at a book or a newspaper."

"Doesn't he ever talk at all?"

"Only about the immediate present. If we ever ask him any-thing about the past, it comes out vaguely in bits and pieces. It's obviously painful for him to use his memory, and at such times we really feel sorry for him. Yes, he's in a strange way. When I look at him, I feel deeply sympathetic. There's no certainty that you or I couldn't become like that some day. When that hap-pens, we'll probably set out to buy whole truckloads of toys!"

Sutekichi said nothing. He was aware of the warmth of the professor's heart.

"Today I called on Professor Waki at his university office and asked him for a consultation. He tells me that this amnesia is a temporary phenomenon, and that if we just leave things as they are, his memory will return one of these days of its own accord. It would be a different matter if he'd hit his head somewhere when he jumped off that boat. Waki says he can't be sure until he's made a direct medical examination, but he mentioned that there are often cases like this in which people who've tried to hang themselves or something of the sort can't remember any-thing at all for about ten days after. You see, their minds have been concentrating completely on the idea of wanting to die, and in the end the idea of death becomes fixed in their brains. One might almost say that they believe they are dead. Then it's as if all past memories withdraw for the time being."

There was a calm smile on the professor's face. Sutekichi felt that there was something buoyant about the blood that ran through this old man's veins.

"In one way I suppose it's a good thing," he continued. "It's different for you young fellows, but when people have lived sixty years or more as I have, there are things in our lives which are disgusting or shameful even to think about. When they sud-denly come to us at night, we try to force them away by groan-ing to ourselves or giving out a dry cough. . . . To go back to this Mr. Okamoto, it's very hard for us to put ourselves in his place. For someone whose mind is completely tensed toward death, there's really no room for normal, mundane thoughts to enter from the outside. That's why we have a situation like this, in which the mind has jumped into the land of the dead, even though the body itself has been rescued."

Outside the window Sutekichi could see the spring dust swirling about above the street. The late afternoon in the students' quarter seemed to mingle with the meager tulips on the table to give an air of quietness.

The professor said that he wanted to visit a second-hand book-shop in front of the university, and Sutekichi agreed to ac-company him.

"That's an old shop too," said Segi. There was deep emo-tion in his voice, as though his distant student years had suddenly come back to him.

"You know, in those days we could have a good Western-style lunch of cutlets or curry-rice for only fifteen *sen*. We could get a steak for twenty *sen*. Of course, in our boarding-houses we only paid six *yen* a month for our rooms, and three meals a day cost us only twenty *sen* altogether. So to pay twenty *sen* for a steak was something of a luxury. Come to think of it, the stu-dent's life in those days was pretty pleasant. We'd make one of the restaurants—the Tenjin Yama or the Ippaku Sha—into our regular meeting-place, and we'd all go to the same place year after year. Even if we didn't order anything to eat, they'd let us sit at the table for as long as we liked. There used to be a spacious room on the first floor, I remember, with old-fashioned gas lamps hanging from the ceiling."

The shop was the same one that the professor had fre-quented in his student days, though the owner was, of course, of a different generation. The second-hand bookshops in the Hongo district had flourished for a while after the war owing to the almost complete destruction of the Kanda area by bombing. But before long Kanda had been built up again, and it resumed its traditional role as the center of second-hand bookshops. At this stage Hongo, lacking in a similar tradition, had been doomed.

"Extraordinary!" said the professor. "I couldn't believe it, but it's true. They've gone and built a *Pachinko* parlor right here. In Paris or London I'm sure they wouldn't allow such an abomination right in the middle of their student quarter!"

Then he began to reminisce: "In July and August there was something very special about the silence of the student quarter. You used to feel quite awkward wandering through the de-serted streets when all the students had scattered to different parts of the country for their summer holidays. The doors of the lecture rooms were all tightly closed, and all you could hear was the occasional cry of a cricket. It was fantastically quiet. Then autumn would come, and people began to return one by one. I remember how happy I used to be to see familiar faces re-appearing on the streets in ever-increasing numbers. What fun it was to run into old friends again!" The professor's aged face was gleaming. "Now I'm told the students don't go to the country during the holidays; instead they stay in Tokyo all summer and do odd jobs to make a bit of extra money."

"Yes, that's become the normal thing now," said Sutekichi. "The woman in that restaurant was talking about it a while ago. She's really sorry for these young students of today. Only about once a month can they afford to go to a restaurant for a meal. It seems that in the present day and age it's impossible for most of the students to eat their fill and take their ease over a nice meal. Everyone keeps on telling them to study hard, but for some of these stupid fellows who don't have any will power I don't see how that's possible."

As they entered the bookshop, the middle-aged man who was in charge noticed the professor and greeted him courteously. The shop was almost deserted. Segi raised his spectacles and be-gan scanning the bookshelves systematically. After a while a man in a bright blue suit entered the shop and also began looking round the shelves. When he saw Segi, however, he stopped as though astonished, removed his deerstalker cap, and exclaimed: "Oh, Professor! Do you remember me, sir? I'm Ono who called on you once or twice."

"Oh, it's you," said the professor, putting back his glasses. "How are you getting along? Have you come across any inter-esting books recently?"

"Books!" said the young man, and laughter spread over his pallid face. It was the same man who had sat next to Taeko at the performance of classical Japanese dance at the Kabuki Theater. "To tell the truth, sir, I just today missed landing a rather large fish. I spotted a splendid specimen in the Kobunso catalogue—a handwritten manuscript of Oyamada Kokiyo's ram-blings through Setagaya. I was determined to get hold of this book, and so I rushed over to the shop. But, alas, they'd already sold it this morning."

"Really?" said the professor. "Oyamada Kokiyo's journal of his travels."

"That right. But there's nothing I can do about it now, so I plan to visit the man who bought the manuscript and ask him if he'll let me copy it out. But it really was a pity. I should have gone in the morning, but unfortunately I had some errands to run for my shop."

The young man evidently enjoyed talking and seemed reluctant to leave the professor.

"Are you going home now?" said the professor to Sutekichi, as the two of them emerged into the street some time later. "As a matter of fact, I'd better be getting back myself or Mr. Okamoto is going to start fretting!"

Sutekichi realized that he now had the same feeling toward the professor that his mother had expressed the previous evening. He could no longer oppose the elder man's will. In the first place, of course, it was quite possible that Soroku Okamoto's mental aberration would be cured of its own accord, as Professor Waki had suggested. But even more, Sutekichi was now deeply struck by the love that dwelled in the heart of his elderly friend—a love that seemed to operate irrespective of the object to which it was directed.

"That fellow we met in the bookshop," continued the professor. "He's an odd chap, all right."

According to the professor, the young man worked in a shop in Nihombashi that specialized in bags and pouches. From his earliest days as an apprentice, he had liked books and devoted himself to literary studies. Not only had he become versed in printed books of the Edo Period, but also he had begun to collect diaries of Japanese classical and Confucian scholars. Then he had taken an interest in records of travels in the ancient environs of Edo and embarked on geographical studies of the period. Whenever he was unable to decipher some manuscript, he would bring it to Segi's house and ask for an opinion.

"Yes, he's a rare bird," continued the professor. "Of course, a young fellow like that shouldn't take such an interest in an old fogy like me. Still, he's full of enthusiasm." The professor was obviously appreciative of the young man's labors. "He's chosen a good field for himself—one that very few other people have studied. To be sure, his formal education is pretty sketchy. He went to Commercial School, and I'm not sure that he even graduated from there. But by studying on his own and going around asking people about points that aren't clear, he's made quite a scholar of himself. I dare say he could compete with any average university graduate. Of course, it's a tradition in the old commercial section of Edo that dilettantes like that should emerge every now and then, and I'm glad to see this tradition is still being kept up after the war. As for his work at the shop, that's just become a means of earning his living."

"You say he's studying ancient records of travels?" said Sutekichi.

"That's it. He goes around collecting old manuscripts in which famous people and also unknown people give their accounts of journeying about Tokyo in the Edo Period—Meguro, Totsuka, Setagaya, mostly places which still exist in the modern city. He goes everywhere himself to see exactly what places are being described in the manuscripts. It's quite hard work, I should say. Yes, he's a queer fellow—there's no doubt about that."

Their talk was interrupted as the professor noticed a friend of his walking along the same street. He went over to say a few words to him. Sutekichi was struck by what a large circle of acquaintances the professor had.

Soon they were walking side by side again, but now Segi had complete forgotten about the hard-working young man in the bag shop.

"Do you really think that Okamoto is going to return to normal of his own accord? What about giving him some of that electric treatment that Professor Waki mentioned and shocking him back to his senses?"

"Well, we could do that," said Segi. "We could give him the shock of his life. . . . But I really don't see why it's necessary. If insanity is agony to a person, then I should try using electricity or atomic energy or anything else to treat him. But in the case of such a gentle madman, why force a cure on him, why thrust him back willy-nilly into this painful world? Even partially to forget things is one of the joys of life. That being so, imagine how delightful it must be to forget everything completely. How nice it must be to be able to say: 'Who on earth was I?' I should love to be able to say that to my wife. I wonder what sort of a face she'd make. She'd probably try beating me."

The grandchild on whom the professor doted was six years old. He had now begun imitating the older children in the neighborhood by playing at baseball, and his grandfather had bought him a glove and a rubber ball. Besides that, Segi used to play with him, and frequently a visitor would see the old professor in his sitting-room, where the walls and doors were all hidden by books, serving as a catcher for the little boy.

"When this fellow grows up," Segi used to say, "and starts throwing a proper ball, I'll really have to do something desperate!"

Because the professor managed so easily to catch the ball as it came flying, you could tell that he had taken an active part in sports during his youth. The boy used to protest that his grandfather caught the ball too easily. He particularly resented it when the professor sat on a cushion and nonchalantly caught the ball with one hand, and Taro would make him stand up like a real catcher and use both hands.

When the professor returned, he saw that Soroku Okamoto had been obliged to take his place as catcher. He could not help feeling sorry for the man as he noticed the unpracticed way in which he was standing and the look of serious concentration in his eyes. Obviously he was desperately anxious not to drop the ball. There was a good-humored smile on his face, but the expression in his eyes did not match this at all. It made the professor rather uneasy to think of the irregularity of this man's brain. Yes, Soroku Okamoto was a good man. As a catcher he was extremely awkward, but it was clear that he was used to the company of children, and this sort of thing did not seem to tire him.

"He used the name 'Akira' in speaking to Taro," Mrs. Segi told her husband. "It rather puzzled me, but he soon went back to calling him Taro."

Often Okamoto would get out a picturebook and start good-naturedly reading the boy a story. It was quite obvious that he loved little children from the bottom of his heart.

One evening the professor returned to find Okamoto and

Taro deep in a picturebook. "Oh, you're at it again!" he said. There was a calm, settled quality about the scene. Taro sat on Mr. Soroku's lap.

"And what did the monkey do then?" Taro asked, impatient at the interruption.

"He got his bottom burned!" put in the professor, taking off his tie. Taro's mother came in to help the professor change his clothes.

"You're a bad man, Grandpa!" said the child, looking up at Segi with his cheerful, innocent eyes. Then he added, as though it had suddenly occurred to him: "Damned old man!"

The professor burst out laughing and called back: "Damn you, Taro!"

"Really, Grandfather!" said the young Mrs. Segi with an air of mild astonishment. "You shouldn't teach him such bad words."

The professor removed the trousers from under his kimono and threw his wallet on the table.

"It's all right, my dear," he said. "He's going to learn all those words outside the house anyway. That being the case, his grandpa is going to teach them to him systematically. When I was Taro's age, there was no one in the whole town who could compete with me in foul language!"

Segi had obviously managed to absorb a certain amount of saké before coming home; his face was flushed and good-humored. He now made himself comfortable in his Japanese clothes, tied the *obi* round his hips, and put all his Western-style clothes aside.

"Please bring me some tea," he said. "And you might let Okamoto have a cup too. Also I think it would be a good idea to take Taro away now. It's probably getting on our guest's nerves to have him here so long."

Young Mrs. Segi returned to the room after ordering tea and began to tidy the clothes that the professor had taken off.

" 'I exhort you to do all those things in the world that are said to be bad,' " pronounced Segi, with a cigarette in his mouth. "I've just remembered those words. They are contained in a letter which the great Master of Tea Ceremony, Prince Matsudaira Fumai, wrote to his son. Rather wonderful of him, I think. I don't suppose there have been many parents who've told their childen to do everything bad. Don't you agree, Mr. Okamoto?"

"What . . . do you mean?" answered Soroku calmly.

"Prince Fumai, you know—the lord of Sesshū Matsue. He wasn't simply a practitioner of the tea ceremony but a Master of the art. Ordinary practitioners are in ample supply, but only a great Master could have told his child to do all those things in the world that are said to be bad. To hell with etiquette, I say!"

"But, Father, you can't really let children do bad things, can you?" asked Taro's mother.

"Well," said the professor, "if the child turns out to be really depraved, you have to disown him. Even the great lords had to disown their children occasionally. If they hadn't, there'd have been some awfully stupid lords. But the real point is that if a fellow can't do anything bad in this world, he also can't do anything good. Human beings aren't meant to consist just of style or appearance. We shouldn't become like mosquito-larvae bred in lukewarm water under the sun. Prince Fumai obviously realized that if his son was going to turn out like that, there wouldn't be any point in letting him inherit the family name. You've heard how the lion kicks his newborn child down into the valley. He wants to bring up only the cubs that have enough guts to come crawling up again by themselves. One mustn't always be fussing at children, saying you can do this and you can't do that. They should do as they like. And if in the process they turn out badly, well then, they aren't one's own children—just like the father lion. Let the useless ones be kicked down into the bottom of the valley. No lukewarm methods! We don't want the sort of fellows who just have conventional civilized educations. We need people with chips and cracks, twisted in ways, but with uncommon characters. You see, Prince Fumai felt all this because he was a Master of Tea Ceremony and spent this life discerning value in commonplace things. He was a great man." The professor had never appreciated the conventional "great men" of history.

"By the way," said the professor, "please give me some tea."

"Right away," said young Mrs. Segi.

The professor planned to have a final smoke before going to bed and settled himself at his desk facing Mr. Okamoto. Normally he would have asked his guest how he was feeling, but now instead he looked at him sympathetically without a word. There was something different about Okamoto this evening that attracted his attention. The professor noticed this particularly after Taro had been taken off to bed by his mother. An unusual expression had come over his normally emotionless face. His posture had lost its normal serenity. Something had stirred him, so that it had become agony for the man to remain calm. This was the first time that the professor had seen him this way, and as he looked at his inscrutable companion, he felt as if he were peering into the turbid water of some well without being able to see whether it was deep or shallow. Until now there had never been the slightest glimmer of real will in the man's behavior. He just moved this way or that as if swayed by the wind, and there was no way of telling whether his heart was in his actions. The professor and his family had judged the man to be both good and gentle, but this judgment itself was a completely arbitrary one, based as it was on purely superficial observation. The essence of Okamoto's nature was as impenetrable as the blank look on his face. Of course, he had occasionally taken some action, such as buying Taro all those toys. But even in these instances you could not tell what inner forces had motivated him.

This evening it was clear to the professor that something was stirring beneath the unruffled surface. It was still impossible to discern the man's true character, but something was clearly moving or trying to move. Soroku's face was more flushed than usual. It was an early summer evening and not yet sultry. The sliding screendoors were open to the garden, and you could smell the green leaves.

"I can hear the frogs croaking," said the professor as though talking to himself.

Soroku raised his eyes, and with a certain look of astonishment answered: "Yes."

"It's probably begun to rain. They sound like green frogs."

"Oh!" exclaimed Soroku, and he looked as though for a moment he had suddenly returned to himself. "You mean frogs?"

The professor was used to this sort of reaction by now and was not surprised. Ever since they had sat together in the *sushi* shop at Niigata he had noticed how words from the outside seemed to impinge on Soroku's vacant consciousness, like a pattern being dyed on a piece of blank material. When he repeated the words, it was a meaningless echo. Then Soroku suddenly became agitated.

"Well . . . what I want to say is . . ." he began, looking at Segi, as though his mind was working at full speed.

The professor was at first unable to grasp the drift of his words, but then he noticed that Soroku had fixed his eyes uneasily on the wallet which still lay on the table where he had thrown it some time before.

"You must put that away, or else—"said Soroku.

The professor glanced in surprise at the wallet. He noticed that his bankbook and some banknotes that he had withdrawn that afternoon in order to pay the rent were tucked conspicuously in the wallet.

"You must be careful about money," resumed Soroku. There was a new tone of remonstrance in his voice.

The professor held his cigarette in his mouth without smoking.

"There's not enough there to call it real money," he said.

Soroku fell silent, and a gloomy expression passed onto his gentle face, the expression of someone whose will is hopelessly thwarted. The professor was puzzled.

"Money is the one thing you must be careful about," resumed Soroku after a while.

He was becoming rather insistent now, and the professor pulled the wallet over to the corner of the table where he was sitting. He could not help feeling that Soroku was addressing him as if he were a child.

"Money is valuable," persisted Soroku. "All sorts of troubles come from money, you know."

"Well, well," said the professor gently. Soroku looked uncomfortable, as if he felt that his companion was not taking him seriously.

"I understand," said the professor. "I'll be careful."

"I hope you don't think I'm being rude," said Soroku with an apologetic air. "But it's just as I say."

Segi got up and went to the bathroom. He was still feeling the effect of the saké he had drunk, and Soroku's glum face suddenly struck him as comical. "How strange to be told off by Okamoto!" he thought, chuckling to himself, as he looked out through the window at the darkness of the May evening. He washed his hands and returned to the room.

"Well, it's about time for bed," he said, closing the shutters. He put on his night clothes and began to climb into his bed, which was placed next to his guest's in the neighboring room. His eyelids felt heavy.

"Professor, Professor!" said Soroku, who was still sitting at the table. "You really must put that wallet away."

"Oh, please forget about it," said the professor, whose sleepy head now rested on his pillow. For a moment he wanted to add that if anyone stopped him from sleeping at a moment like this, when he was just about to doze off, then sleep would not come to him again for a long time. Instead he said: "If any robber bothered to break into this house, he'd have to be an utter imbecile!" He turned over in bed and faced the wall away from the light in the next room. "If a robber should decide to visit us, he can have the wallet! Now let's go to sleep. It's late."

The professor was vaguely aware of Soroku turning out the light and getting into the other bed. Soon the professor was pleasantly asleep. He did not know how much time had elapsed when he awoke to the sound of Soroku clearing his throat. He opened his eyes slightly and noticed that his companion was sitting on the edge of the bed.

"What's wrong?" he asked.

"Nothing," answered Soroku, as though confused, and immediately lay down again with his head on the pillow.

The professor tried to forget about the matter and to doze off at once. He heard the dog next door going out into the street and barking: someone must be walking by at this late hour. He wondered what time it could be. At night in one's own familiar house, one is aware of the outline of things even in pitch darkness. From the sound of Soroku's breathing, he could tell that the man was still unable to sleep. Once again he heard Soroku getting up and sitting on the edge of his bed.

"Having trouble getting to sleep?" he asked.

"Oh no," said Soroku at once. "It's nothing like that." The man let out a deep sigh. The professor thought that from now on he would be quiet, but instead he heard him suddenly standing up.

"Professor," said Soroku, "I'm really sorry to trouble you, but won't you please put that wallet away?"

Segi calmly raised his head from the pillow.

"Does it bother you all that much?" he asked.

"I'm sorry I had to trouble you while you were sleeping so well."

He was in the presence of a very sick man, thought the professor as he climbed out of bed.

"All right," he said, "I'll put it away."

"Do forgive me, but it's been bothering me for a long time."

The professor staggered sleepily into the next room and turned on the light. The bothersome wallet lay on his desk.

"Yes, I'll put it somewhere where no one can get at it except me."

He walked up to the desk, which was hidden from Soroku by the bookshelf and the screen, placed the wallet on top of the bookshelf, and returned to bed.

"You really ought to buy a safe," said Soroku.

"A safe, you say?"

"Yes, then you can really feel secure."

What on earth could he ever put in a safe, wondered the professor, aware that from one point of view the whole thing was an absurd joke.

"Now let's go to sleep," he said, and climbed into bed. "There's nothing to worry about. Do try to sleep."

But he himself was unable to sleep properly. He dozed off for a while, and when he awoke he saw that Soroku was sitting again at the edge of his bed. He was breathing heavily, as if in pain, and was muttering something constantly under his breath. The professor decided to ignore him and tried to doze off again. He made a deliberate pretense at being asleep, but still sleep would not come. Then he heard Soroku get up and walk toward his own bed. This was no longer a joke, thought the professor, sitting up in bed with an automatic scowl.

"I'm really most sorry," said Soroku with an embarrassed air. "Is it morning yet?"

"No, I don't think so," answered the professor.

"I see," said Soroku gently, yet with an underlying restlessness. He now came back to sit at the side of Segi's bed, but gave no reason for his action.

"What's happened, Mr. Okamoto?" asked the professor, sitting cross-legged and with his arms folded. "I've safely put away the money that was bothering you so much. I wish you'd try to calm down and get some rest. Can't you sleep?"

"Forgive me for troubling you," repeated Soroku, raising his head. "I've been a great nuisance, but as soon as it's morning, I should like to leave at once."

"What did you say?" retorted the professor.

"I thought it was morning already. I want to go home at once when it gets light."

The professor stood up and tried to reach for the light switch.

"You say 'home,' Mr. Okamoto. Do you mean your own home? Do you understand what you're saying?"

"Yes," answered Soroku.

"Wait a moment. Where on earth is that light switch?" He hopped about on the floor by himself, searching for the elusive switch. He remembered now what he had heard from Professor Waki about people who had lost their memory and who suddenly returned to themselves on being confronted with something that reminded them of their past life. There were even cases of people who had recovered on hearing a familiar piece of music.

"Really? You really are aware that you have your own house?" said the professor excitedly. He hurried into the next room, turned on the light, and returned at once to have a look at Soroku's face.

"I really feel sorry when I think of all the trouble I've caused you," said Soroku with an unexpectedly quiet look on his face. "I myself don't understand exactly what's happened. For a while now I've been wondering why I was putting you all to such trouble here when I have my own house in Kamakura. Then when I thought about it carefully, I realized that it was only just now that I remembered having a house in Kamakura."

The professor stared quietly at Soroku. He felt as though he were handling some fragile article. From the first he was slightly dubious about this story.

"You say that your home is in Kamakura?" he asked.

"Yes, that's right," answered Soroku nodding.

"Well, in that case, I probably know something about it. My wife's father lived there for a long time, you see." It was as if he was reeling out the thread of his own thoughts. "Whereabouts in Kamakura is your house?"

The answer came promptly: "Near the Hachiman Shrine. Not far from Nameri River, you know." He spoke in a low voice, but there was something in his tone that left no room for doubt.

"I suppose your wife and children are there too?"

"No," answered Soroku in a faltering voice as a lonely shadow moved across his smiling face. "There's nobody there any longer."

As the professor stared at his companion, the latter continued: "When I go home, there'll be nobody there at all."

"I thought you had children, you see. When I watched you playing with little Taro, I got that impression. My wife thought so too."

Soroku lowered his head and answered softly: "He was killed in the war." At the same time violent emotion suddenly appeared on his gentle face, as though it were being roughly scratched by nails. Emotion had gushed forth from within this man, whose face had hitherto been an expressionless, callous mask. The professor was both astonished and moved.

"He died in the war, did he?" he said. Soroku nodded quietly, and tears shone in his eyes.

"He was my only son," he murmured. For some reason he turned up the palms of his hands, which rested on his knees, and scrutinized them.

"Yes," he continued all of a sudden, "he's dead and there's no use my complaining about it. Until today I haven't ever mentioned him to anyone. But . . ." He let out a heavy sigh. "My loneliness, you know, is something indescribable. Nothing can alleviate it. It gets worse and worse as the days go by. It does no good talking to people about it. Something must be wrong with me. Well, I really don't know how to thank you for all you've done for me."

"It's nothing."

"Oh yes it is. To you, Professor . . ." He broke off and, lowering his head, was choked with sobs.

As soon as it grew light outside, Soroku left the house, despite all the professor's efforts to stop him. In his hand he carried the suitcase which he had had ever since the Sado boat. He did not wait to see the other members of the household.

When Sutekichi heard what had happened, he visited the professor. Segi took him for a walk and good-humoredly described the latest development.

"It was a bolt from the blue. I had no idea that he had returned to his right mind. It was all very confusing."

Sutekichi could not help laughing as he pictured the final scene.

"The whole thing was a bit of a false alarm, wasn't it? Anyway, Professor, you behaved splendidly."

"Well, you know, when I went to see him off at the corner, I was worried about what would happen later. Perhaps it would have been rather better for him not to have been cured and to have held back his memories, at least partly."

"In that case there really wasn't any point in jumping into the water to save him, was there?"

"Well, it's a very good and healthy thing for human beings to forget things that aren't necessary to them. Of course, I should like people to have the courage to live through all their experiences, but if they don't, forgetfulness isn't such a bad thing, you know. In this world we all of us have hard things to put up with, and what I can't bear is to see people going about with sullen faces as if they had to bear the whole weight of the world by themselves. Nor can I bear the so-called intellectuals who take a murky view of everything. If I should happen to come across such a fellow trying to hang himself, I shouldn't mind helping him by giving a good tug on his legs. Why fill the world with gloomy ideas? Anyhow, most of those fellows don't really have the courage to die when it comes right down to it. But as for people who go round spouting extravagant nonsense about not wanting to live—well, I don't see why either democracy or humanism imply any obligation to be concerned for such weaklings. One mustn't spoil people. The purpose of humanism is to elevate human beings, not to provide them with some sort of sentimental relief. You see, we aren't automatically endowed with certain moral rights just because we happen to be born. What sort of rights do cows and horses and dogs and mice have, for instance? Seen from God's point of view, I'm sure there's no essential difference between any of us—fleas, lice, or human beings. After all, human beings, who created the atom bomb with all its large-scale cruelty, are really far more hateful and sinful creatures than those little things who prick our rumps and steal a minuscule amount of blood. 'Don't let's get too conceited over the simple fact that we're human beings!'—that's what I'd like to tell some of these intellectuals."

The professor paused for a while.

"Yet at the same time," he continued, "I still can't dismiss this whole other matter like you young people would. That man who was here had become so tormented in himself that he had resolved on death. And now we've let him go back with all the same reasons for wanting to die—whatever those reasons were— still intact."

"You mean that he might try to do it again?" said Sutekichi.

"I really don't know," answered Segi. "But I can't say that the possibility doesn't bother me."

"Do forget about it, Professor," said the young man with a smile. "You've done quite enough already. You really have no further obligations."

"Yes I do," said the professor calmly. "Suté, the reason I asked you to call today was that I thought you might go to Kamakura and have a look at him for me. You may think it's unnecessary, yet it's our business to give that man courage enough to live." They had reached the front of the local post office, and as the professor was about to enter, he added: "You can take little Taro with you. For some strange reason Mr. Okamoto seemed to be very devoted to him. Possibly Taro can help him in some way."

It was already summer in the city, and the sun glared on the surface of the road.

7 · ISLAND OF FIRE

It was close to noon. As Taeko moved about the room alone getting ready for departure, she could hear the sound of the waves. Across the pine forest you could see the ocean. Now and then, when you had forgotten all about the sea, it would suddenly roar and the broken waves would come scrambling up the sand, as though spreading a curtain of white lace. The air was torpid with the weariness of a summer noon, and the roaring of the water seemed to be transmitted to your body from below the earth. Taeko faced the dressing table. Here in the Izu Peninsula the season was considerably more advanced than in Tokyo. The sea was clouded by a shining vapor, and its color was the sleepy, vague blue of an eggplant. Each time that the white lace of the waves shone on the beach and spread toward the hotel, the sound of the water would roar across the forest.

The shadow of Oshima Island, which in the morning had stood out clearly, revealing every hollow of the mountain, was now simply a vague, monotonous blur. In the middle of the previous night Taeko had been able to see the volcano of Miharayama. It had been like looking at fireworks: a small, red flame had sprung out into the dark night air.

The hotel was newly built, and the garden was simply a grass field that ran parallel to the sandy beach. Above the yellow blossoms of the evening primroses the dancing butterfly had a desiccated look. Since it was noon the hotel was quiet, like a large vacant house, the other guests except for Taeko and her companion all having left on the morning bus for the beach. The maid, who was cleaning the guestroom downstairs, had for some time been singing a popular song with unrestrained verve. Now and then Taeko would hear her say something in her local accent. These sounds made the place seem quieter than ever, and Taeko was overcome by a languid feeling.

"The master says he left his watch in the drawer of the dressing table," said the maid, coming into the room. Taeko had, however, already found the watch and put it in her bag; she informed the maid accordingly. The maid took Ryosuké Tsugawa's suitcase and started to leave the room.

"Do come again, Madam," she said, as she stood by the sliding-door. "From now on it's fairly empty here, you see. This place is harder to get to than Atami or Ito, and I suppose that's why we don't have all that many guests."

Taeko felt her face redden as she was addressed "Madam," and her reply stuck in her mouth.

"But in your case it doesn't matter, Madam, because you've got your own car. Really, do try and come again some time."

"Yes, I shall," said Taeko with a smile. "By the way, did you say that the car was ready?"

"Yes, your husband's waiting downstairs. He says he wants to start at once."

Taeko went downstairs and into the entrance hall, where she saw Ryosuké Tsugawa standing by the door, smoking a cigarette and chatting with the proprietress. The car was parked at the entrance, ready to leave.

"Really?" she heard him say. "It's hot like this in the daytime, and then you have a heavy dew at night. I noticed that the earth was white and dry just where the car had been standing." Taeko began to put on her shoes.

The car was one that Ryosuké had borrowed from a friend. "Would you like to sit next to me in the front?" he said.

Taeko climbed in next to the driver's seat and sat there absently, like a doll, while the hotel people came and waved good-by to them.

As they drove along, Taeko noticed Ryosuké's strong arms holding the wheel. Now and then their shoulders touched lightly. Since the night before Taeko had felt as though she had been walking through misty scenery. She wasn't particularly aware that any change had occurred in herself during the past twenty-four hours; in her mind, whatever she might have experienced, she remained herself. After all, what she had done she had sought to do herself, and there was no need for uneasiness.

"Not a bad road, is it?" said Ryosuké in his open tone of voice. "I think we might go a little faster."

The thick green grass that bordered the white road on either side began to fly backward quicker and quicker. The seat creaked under her, and she felt her legs bouncing. Unconsciously she put her hand on Ryosuké's arm. Then she tried to take it away, but the movement instead seemed to tighten her clasp. She was aware of the resistance of hard muscles, and the rough feeling of the man's skin spread through her body.

Ryosuké glanced up at the mountains that towered above them on the right side of the road.

"There may be a shower," he said. "You can see clouds coming over those peaks."

"But the sea is clear, isn't it?" said Taeko, and she suddenly wished that there would be a heavy downpour of rain. The dusty road and all the grass seemed to demand rain. The earth was dry, and the bushes and trees were covered with dust thrown up by the passing buses. Occasionally a tiny village would appear, as if jumping right out at the car, only to disappear immediately behind them. They sped down a hill, rounded a curve, and suddenly in front of their eyes the ocean appeared.

The island of Oshima still floated on the horizon like a shadow. The sea shone a sort of blurred purple color.

"Couldn't you possibly get away from your office tomorrow also?" asked Ryosuké suddenly. "My friend's gone off to Hokkaido, and I don't have to give the car back for another three or four days. If we should run out of money, we could always sleep in the car instead of a hotel."

Taeko was overcome by temptation, and there was a sense of suffocation in her heart. Until this very moment she had forgotten entirely about her office—not only her office, in fact, but also everything connected with her everyday life. And that indeed was the essence of her present happiness.

"Then where shall we go?" she asked.

Ryosuké did not answer; perhaps he was trying to think of some suitable destination.

"If I stay away from my office without permission, they'll certainly give me the sack." She regretted the words as soon as she had spoken them. In view of what all this meant to them, it was, she felt, right that she should put office work out of her head completely.

"Well," said Ryosuké, "we can wait till this evening to decide."

The road began to twist, and Ryosuké slowed down to take the curves.

"There's the money problem, of course," he said, "but that can be settled somehow or other." His face seemed to brighten up, and he glanced at Taeko with laughing eyes. "You see, I didn't think things were going to turn out like this, so I came without making any special preparations."

Taeko felt her face burning, and looking at Ryosuké, she noticed a glow on his cheeks.

"I don't care if we don't have any money," she said. "I'm used to it. Sometimes I don't even have enough for lunch."

"What makes you so hard up?"

"It's because I support myself by my job."

"I hate the idea of being poor," said Ryosuké. "It's a terrible thing to be short of money."

Neither of them felt inclined for a serious conversation. At each moment the scenery was changing. The lush trees that covered the hill on their left looked as if they had burst into a flame of green. There was a wonderful energy about these trees as they clustered thickly together, jostling each other all the way up to the distant hilltop. Taeko almost felt that the trees were shouting out triumphantly.

Ryosuké pulled down the sunshade in front of the window, as the sun was now shining directly into their eyes.

"It's really going to get hot," he said. "It might be a good idea to stop in some cool place and have a rest until the worst heat has gone."

"Deep in the woods, you mean?" said Taeko cheerfully. "Or somewhere by a lake?"

She felt that she would like them to go to some mythlike place where one might hope to see nymphs or the figure of Pan. She was reminded of the sylvan figures in the ballet to which Ryosuké had given her a ticket. They had played in the fields and disported themselves in the cool waters of the river; then when they were tired, they had lain down to sleep in the shade of the leafy trees. Yes, thought Taeko, there would be water lilies growing by the shores of the lake. She did not want to be separated from the feeling in which she had lived since the night before—of walking through some misty scenery—a delicious feeling in which distance or time did not seem to matter in the slightest. It was rather like looking through the window of a flower shop in early spring when the air outside is still cold and a soft shade of steam seems to blur the various colors.

"There should be a turning somewhere here for Kawana," said Ryosuké.

Eventually they managed to get the necessary directions from a passer-by, and they turned off from the main road. The dirt road became narrower as they drove along. On either side were yellow cornfields and occasional vegetable patches, cultivated on a ground of volcanic ash. The ocean was clearly visible. They stopped and listened to the sound of a cuckoo from a distant forest.

"Cuckoo, cuckoo!" they called out in imitation of the bird.

Then they drove off again. Before long they could see the Kawana golf course spread out before them by the edge of the sea. The well-tended lawn was a vast green carpet, its soft color made one want to walk over it barefoot. Here also one could hear the distant cry of the cuckoo.

The figures of a few players were visible in the distance near the cape. Far beyond the pine forests Taeko could make out the volcanic peak on Oshima Island.

"I wonder if it's busy," said Ryosuké. When Taeko asked, it turned out that he was referring to the number of people who might be staying at the golf hotel.

"What a lovely lawn!" exclaimed Taeko. Here and there

were dotted small wild flowers, and she could even make out feathery dandelion balls perched for flight.

Ryosuké stopped the car, and the two of them walked toward the shade of the thick forest. Taeko shouted as she noticed a squirrel running away from them. The squirrel scampered up a near-by pine tree and settled on a fairly low branch. It seemed quite at ease, though it was obviously on the lookout for danger. The sea breeze blew through its bush tail and rumpled its fur. Taeko walked below the tree, careful not to frighten the squirrel. She felt as though this little animal also was her companion.

"Let's go down to the beach," said Ryosuké. He was obviously bothered by the heat. "This grass gives off terrific steam, doesn't it? Quite oppressive. Even the shaded places are hot. You don't feel it when you're playing golf, though."

"Do you play golf?"

"Yes," he answered with a laugh, "but very badly. When it comes to gambling, though, they tell me I'm quite a player!"

"There must be lilies in bloom somewhere near here," said Taeko, looking around. "I've been noticing the scent for some time now."

Just then the smell vanished, and the air was filled with the fragrance of the sea. Then the smell of the lilies returned distinctly. All these things existed for *her*, thought Taeko happily. Being happy, she was aware of happiness in everything that she saw. That lily which was growing somewhere near by was the symbol of a bride, it was as though the flower were responding to the fragrance in her own heart.

Ryosuké went down to the sea for a swim. They found a narrow, rocky beach where the cliffs screened them from the direct glare of the sun. Taeko picked an armful of lilies and said that she would take them back to the car later. The sea was clear, and you could see the sunbeams shining underwater at the base of the rocks.

"Can you swim?" asked Ryosuké, beginning to undress.

Taeko laughed and shook her head. In fact, she could swim, but she had not brought her bathing-suit along.

She sat in the shade of the rock watching Ryosuké swim out to sea. In the blue sea only the heels of his feet shone white.

Her feeling of happiness did not change. It had lasted now

for a whole day, and with time it only seemed to gain in extent and depth. She was conscious of this happiness within her own body, and it filled her with an ecstasy as though she had been overcome by the fragrance of the lilies she now held in her hand. She had passed through a gate in her own life. Taeko acknowledged this without the slightest regret. She made no effort to look back on the route which had brought her here. It was, she told herself, something that she had sought herself; there was no need for any doubts. Although in one way she felt as if she were wandering through a mist, she was strongly aware of Ryosuké's guiding hand, and her eyes were bright and open. She had wished all this for herself, and whatever came in the future, she would receive it gently.

She knew that this was a very special day. Some restraining force within her had been loosened, and now she was eagerly waiting for her real self to emerge, waiting for the storm that would bring her completely out of herself. The power that was to liberate her from all the self-imposed restraints of custom was even now opening up within her body. All that she needed was a little more courage.

She looked at Ryosuké as he came out of the ocean, his wet body gleaming in the sun, and she smiled at him. "What a big man you are!" she wanted to say, but instead she asked: "Is it cold?"

"No, it's just right. Gives you a good feeling." He shook the water vigorously out of his ears. "It's different here from Kamakura and thereabouts. The water is wonderfully clear."

They were both quiet as they looked out to the open sea. Their hearts were satisfied. The roughness of the sea's surface particularly attracted Taeko. She was not entirely conscious of this, but the desire for that roughness moved up dully from the bottom of her heart.

"It's quiet, isn't it," she said.

"Yes," answered Ryosuké, and looked up at the cliff behind them. It was as if a great screen of rock had been built there, protecting them from the gaze of any passers-by.

"No one could possibly disturb us here," added Ryosuké casually. The words burst into flame, and their warmth spread to Taeko.

"Shall I have a swim too?" she asked.

"An excellent idea," said Ryosuké.

She no longer considered the fact that she had no bathing-suit with her. With an engrossed air she began to remove her stockings and unhook her dress. She was full of the joy of liberation. When she was standing in only her thin slip, her movements seemed to betray a certain hesitation. Now only her thighs were covered; her shoulders and her full white breasts caught the wind from the ocean.

"Please go in first, Ryosuké," she said.

To hide her breasts from his eyes, she held the bunch of lilies close to her body.

Ryosuké stood up.

Taeko carefully placed the lilies in the ledge of the rock. As she stood there quite naked, her skin had an utterly pure look, as if she had been newly born.

"Be careful as you walk," said Ryosuké. "It's full of rocks here."

It was still light when they reached the entrance of the hotel, after having driven some way along the winding road. They were shown to their room, and they took a bath to wash the salt off their bodies. Then Taeko was in Ryosuké's arms. . . .

Outside the window one could see the clear silhouette of Oshima Island. It caught the western sun, and on the side of Mount Mihara the small glass window panes of a building glittered brightly. The evening light encompassed both land and sea. As she arranged her hair, it occurred to Taeko that the cuckoos and squirrels must by now have gone to sleep.

"I'm going down to the hall ahead of you," said Ryosuké.

Everything was different here from the Japanese-style hotel where they had spent the previous night. Now Ryosuké stood in front of a full-length mirror and arranged his clothes.

"It's really quite comfortable here," he said. "Places where golfers stay usually are."

He pushed a switch on the wall, as if he had just noticed it, and light flooded into the room. Taeko realized that they had been in the dark until this moment.

"Come down as soon as you can," said Ryosuké as he left the room.

Taeko, who had left Tokyo thinking that she was just going

for a short drive to the country, had not brought along any change of clothes, and she noticed now with some dismay that her only dress was badly creased from the long hours of sitting in the car.

She was suddenly startled by the ringing of the phone. It lay on a small table between the twin beds.

"Hullo hullo!" called a voice as she picked up the receiver. It was the voice of a young woman. "Is Ryobei-san there?"

For a moment Taeko thought that the woman must have rung the wrong room. "Whom did you want?" she asked.

"Oh!" said the voice, as though astonished. "Oh, it's all right, I've just seen the person in question. Sorry." The self-assured voice broke off, and there was the click of the receiver being replaced. No, thought Taeko, there had definitely been no mistake. Taeko had not the faintest idea as to who might have been wanting to speak to Ryosuké, but obviously it was someone staying at the hotel. How did this person know that Ryosuké was here? There was an overfamiliar, almost insolent quality about the way in which she had said his name. Ryobei—Taeko had had no idea that Ryosuké was given this nickname.

As soon as she had left the phone, the bell rang again.

"Do come down quickly." This time it was Ryosuké's own voice. "How soon will you be ready?"

"I don't have any real way to get ready," said Taeko after a pause.

"Well then, come right away," said Ryosuké.

"There's someone down there with you, isn't there?"

"Yes, I'll introduce you when you come down," said Ryosuké, and in the background Taeko could hear the voice of the young woman who had spoken on the phone a moment before.

"I'll be down right away," she said and replaced the receiver.

After a quick glance in the mirror she left the room. Along the corridor was spread a thick carpet. All the doors were closed, and it was utterly quiet. Even the sound of her shoes as she walked seemed to be absorbed by the carpet.

As she started walking down the stairs, Ryosuké came up to meet her. Taeko wondered whether it was because he had been worried about her.

"Who was it?" she asked.

"Oh, it's someone I know from my work," he said. "She helps me occasionally with my business. I think she's come here for a bit of golf. She's with an American buyer who looks as if he used to be here as a soldier."

It occurred to Taeko that they would probably join these people, and immediately the prospect upset her. All that she wanted was to spend a quiet evening together with Ryosuké.

"Where have they gone?" she asked.

"They're in the bar. But we'll go to the dining-room ourselves." Taeko was delighted.

The large dining-room was still fairly empty. They sat down opposite each other at a table near the dark garden. Once again Taeko was delighted as she noticed that a vase of purple and white clematis was decorating their table.

Her eyes sparkled as she said to Ryosuké: "Do you remember these flowers?"

"No, I don't," said Ryosuké.

"Oh, really! I was carrying these flowers the first time that I met you—in Kamakura. Even the color is the same as the ones I had then."

"I don't remember them."

Taeko smiled happily, thinking how typical this was of Ryosuké.

"That's just like you!" she said. "But you must have seen those flowers I was carrying."

"I doubt it. I was probably far too busy looking at you. Flowers are all just the same to me. . . . But I remember that afternoon well. You went to call on Mé's father, didn't you? You went to see that greedy old man who used to extort interest from his own son."

"But he wasn't at home," said Taeko. She did not want to pursue this conversation. "I don't care a rap about Uncle. Tonight I just want to think about us."

The waitresses were all wearing identical Japanese *kimono* with wide *obi* tied round them. One after another they brought in dishes covered with silver lids. Involuntarily Taeko began wondering how much this luxurious meal would cost. But then she resolutely dismissed such thoughts from her mind.

"Is it good?" asked Ryosuké.

"Oh yes, it's delicious," said Taeko.

"That's because we went swimming."

"Yes, I know."

Just then Taeko noticed a woman entering the dining-room. She was wearing a conspicuous red jacket, gay and so bright that it seemed to be on fire. At first Taeko thought that she was a foreigner, despite the fact that she was rather short, but a second look showed that she was, in fact, Japanese. She had evidently not come in for dinner, for she remained standing at the entrance. She was wearing a pair of gray trousers, like a man's and she held her hands in her pocket. When she saw Ryosuké and Taeko from the distance, she raised her arm and made some sort of a sign, then wheeled round and walked away from the dining-room together with the foreigner who had been waiting for her outside.

"Is that the woman?" said Taeko, giving a surprised look at Ryosuké.

Ryosuké nodded.

"She's pretty, isn't she?"

"She's a woman who's talked about a lot."

"What's her name?"

"Mrs. Iwamuro. Her first name is Kaoruko, if I'm not mistaken."

"Is she married?"

"Yes, to a former baron or something of the sort. She herself is the daughter of some industrialist."

Taeko had the impression that Mrs. Iwamuro had come to the entrance on purpose to have a look at the girl with whom she had spoken on the telephone.

"I wonder how she knew you were here."

"She must have noticed my name in the register at the desk."

"Are you very friendly with her?"

"Oh, she brings some work my way occasionally."

"Is she working herself?"

"I'm not really sure. I believe she's trying to do something. During the Occupation she used to have quite a few connections with the Americans. There were lots of rumors about her."

"Is her husband with her?"

"Why do you ask so many questions about her?" said Ryosuké.

Taeko blushed on hearing the slight tone of reproach in his voice. After all, she remembered, it was she who had been so anxious for them to get away from people.

"What did you tell her about me?" she asked.

"I said you were my fiancée."

Once again Taeko felt herself blushing.

"That makes me feel awkward," she said.

"Why?"

"Why didn't you say we were married?"

"It comes to the same thing." Ryosuké threw out the remark in an unexpectedly casual tone. "In any case, she's the sort of person who'll understand. She's a real society woman, you see—in fact, one might almost say a diplomat."

"I'm not so sure that I want that sort of person to 'understand,' " said Taeko, and she was aware that there was a feeling of excitement within her as she spoke the words.

"You see," she went on after a while, "I don't want to notice the knowing look on people's faces as they draw their own conclusions about me. For the time being I want only you to understand. After all, no one else except you really would understand anyway."

Ryosuké was obviously impressed by the honesty of Taeko's tone.

"Of course," he said, "I feel that way too. You're a good person, Taeko."

When she heard this, Taeko was suddenly filled with love, and for a moment she thought she might burst into tears. She was aware now of a weakness in herself whose existence she had never suspected before.

"I'm sorry," she said in a small voice. "I suppose this is how one feels when one likes someone. I don't know anything about such things, you see. I've been by myself—away from my father and sister—for so long. I never thought it would be so disturbing."

Her voice was quiet and suppressed, as though it were burning in her heart.

When they went out into the sunporch by themselves after dinner, Mrs. Iwamuro appeared.

The high-ceilinged sunporch stretched out into the garden.
On three sides it was entirely surrounded by glass, like a hot-
house. Had it not been for the lights, one could have seen the
sea stretching out clearly in front. It was a moonless night. At
the bottom of the undulating lawn one could here and there pick
out the lights of the fishing-boats as they set out to sea. The
porch was lit by indirect lighting, and the potted plants seemed
to be softly tinted. Taeko glanced around at the rubber trees
with their bright leaves and at the many-colored pots of summer
flowers.

Taeko and Ryosuké lowered themselves side by side onto
a couple of rattan chairs. They were long comfortable chairs on
which one could stretch out at full length as if in bed. Taeko
stretched herself out luxuriously, resting her head against the
part that corresponded to the pillow, and looking up at the ceiling, felt that she was bathing in a sea of happiness.

A massive foreigner in a bright-colored suit was sitting near-
by reading an English newspaper. He gave much the same impression as the American who had been with Mrs. Iwamuro. The
entire front part of his head was bald, which made his forehead
seem enormous. It was impossible to tell how old he was. Red
amarylis were blooming in the flowerpot next to him.

Another tall foreigner came in and sat down next to the bald
man. He addressed him laughingly, and the first man then
folded up his newspaper and leaned over to hear what his companion was saying. Both men wore suits of flashing brightness,
one a sharp blue and the other a garish brown that could almost
be called red. No Japanese could possibly have worn such suits,
for it would have made them feel conspicuous. Even these large,
pallid men looked wrong in such suits: the strong colors seemed
to separate themselves from their bodies and give a restless impression. Only a little child with smooth fair skin could possibly
wear such colors with good effect; on adults they seemed quite
unnatural.

When Mrs. Iwamuro appeared at the entrance to the sunporch, she was wearing a quiet Japanese *kimono*, and for a moment Taeko thought that she was someone else. Then she had
the sudden feeling of having been greeted by something with a
strange luster. The woman, who a while before had been wear-

ing men's trousers and had given the lively impression of a foreigner, now had on a dark blue summer *kimono*, which from the
distance looked as if it had no pattern at all. Round her slim
waist was tied an *obi*, and there was something very tight and
fresh about her figure.

The two Americans stood up from their chairs and wel-
comed her formally. Mrs. Iwamuro responded cheerfully to their
greetings and then turned her pale face to Taeko and her companion. As she smiled, she seemed to have thought of something, and now she approached them. Seeing her close at hand,
Taeko could not help being dazzled. Mrs. Iwamuro had evidently had a bath on returning from golf and had just put on her
make-up. Her slim features and the delicate texture of her skin
had a cherry-blossom glow which Taeko immediately associated
with the beauties of Kyoto.

"Can one see the Mihara-yama volcano?" said Mrs. Iwamuro
to Ryosuké. In her cheerful voice there was the lively, single-
minded passion of a child. She looked out into the darkness as
though she were pressing her face against a windowpane.

"All you can see are the lights of the fishing-boats," answered Ryosuké.

"What a disappointment! I came here specially to see the
fires from the volcano."

"Even Mihara isn't always puffing out flames, you know,"
said Ryosuké and he too got up from his chair.

"I really love fire," said Mrs. Iwamuro. "Come to think of it,
I've loved it ever since I was a child."

Her eyes were turned straight at Taeko. There was a fragrant
quality about her smiling face.

"This is Taeko," said Ryosuké, introducing the two women.

Mrs. Iwanuro greeted Taeko and then smiled again.

"You're a very pretty girl," she said, and seemed to wrap
Taeko up with her eyes. "I'll join you both later. We're going
in to have dinner now."

The two Americans, who had been waiting quietly, now
stood aside to let Mrs. Iwamuro leave the room ahead of them.
Taeko followed her with her eyes as her back disappeared in
the direction of the dining-room. She noticed that her *kimono*
was delicately embossed with a Saga embroidery of tree branches;

the background was a dark-tinted indigo. Her *obi* of figured bro-
cade was decorated with vertical stripes of dull yellow, red, and
blue.

"Is Mrs. Iwamuro from Kyoto?" asked Taeko abruptly.

"Quite possibly," said Ryosuké.

There was an elegance about this woman's face which reminded one of the dim light of a sea shell. The outline of her
features was lightly shadowed giving a soft, hazy impression.
Taeko remembered a friend of her sister's whom she had known
in Kyoto as a girl and realized that she had been in some way
similar to Mrs. Iwamuro. There had been rumors that this girl
was the illegitimate daughter of a Court noble, and ever since
her childhood she had always represented for Taeko the Kyoto
type of beauty. The indigo color of Mrs. Iwamuro's *kimono* was
of a special shade which Taeko had seen on Chinese ceramics
—a color that made the skin of the wearer look outstandingly
white. Taeko did not try to conceal the sense of surprise in her
heart at this woman's beauty.

"She looked lovely now, didn't she?" she said.

"Do you think so?"

Taeko realized that the reason she had been so particularly
impressed by the taste of the woman's colors and the freshness
they produced was that a moment before she had been looking
at the brash, unharmonious colors worn by the American men.
The *obi* had been exceptionally smart; yet there was nothing conspicuous about it, simply an air of tasteful repose. Taeko did not
quite know why, but she felt deeply moved—as if she wanted to
take deep breaths. That there should exist people in this world
who were profoundly interested in making themselves look
beautiful was in itself nothing surprising. This woman was so
utterly different from anyone that Taeko saw in her everyday
life, that the strangeness of it disturbed her.

"What is her husband like?" she asked.

"It may not be too polite," said Ryosuké with a laugh, "but I
should say that he just looks insignificant. All he seems to have
is the distinction of having formerly been a peer. I'm told that
he used to be well known for his stamp collection, but they say
that he sold it to the Americans after the war. He's a nice man, I
suppose—a gentleman anyway."

"And so Mrs. Iwamuro goes and has a good time on her own?"

"No, she's probably standing in for her husband. She isn't having a good time now. She's working," answered Ryosuké nonchalantly. "Lots of the Americans, you see, are particularly fascinated by peers. Perhaps it's because they don't have any in their own country. After all, democracy is only a system. It doesn't change people's real feelings. And Americans seem to be particularly addicted to titles. They make a tremendous fuss over them. Besides she's a very attractive woman."

He paused for a while, and it occurred to Taeko that he was speaking rather harshly.

"When they come to this part of the world," continued Ryosuké, "what interests them is, of course, the things they don't have in their own country—the novelties. All the things you see in those souvenir shops on the Ginza—they're all novelties for them. Now Mrs. Iwamuro is a rare beauty, as you see. And there are a number of people in Japan who make use of beautiful women like her, just because to the foreigners they're a novelty. Big businessmen and political bosses—they're the type who find such women as Mrs. Iwamuro quite useful when it comes to dealing with foreigners. And so far as she's concerned, I suppose, it gives her a new social position, or a profession, if you like, and brings in a nice income."

Taeko was divided between the desire to return to their room and the hope that Mrs. Iwamuro would soon return from the dining-room. The charm of this woman was such that it could readily be felt by people of her own sex. She wondered what Ryosuké really thought about her.

Taeko lay back in the rattan chair and listened to the Chopin piano concerto coming from a long-playing record. Lying here peacefully in a full-length chair and listening to music amid red tropical plants—this too was something that Taeko never experienced in her little rented room.

"I'm sorry I've kept you both waiting," said Mrs. Iwamuro. Immediately Taeko felt glad that she had not left the sunporch. In Mrs. Iwamuro's smile there lay a sunlight capable of warming people's hearts. Through the thick silk that she was wearing she exuded a delicate softness.

"Shall we join you?" she said.

The two Americans were introduced. Taeko felt quite at ease in their company. She was pleased to notice that Ryosuké seemed to know how to get on with foreigners and that he could converse with them in English, however inaccurately. There was, in fact, a certain blunt directness in his manner, but this did not seem to bother him in the slightest.

They all went down to the basement bar together. When it came time to pay for their drinks, Mrs. Iwamuro suggested that they play dice to decide the victim.

"You're the only guest here, Taeko," she added, "so it's all right if you just watch us. You'll see. Ryosuké is bound to win and get out of paying before anyone else."

"Nothing of the sort," protested Ryosuké. "It's all a matter of luck anyway."

"Well, that may be," said Mrs. Iwamuro, "but I'm sure it'll be one of our American guests who ends up unluckily. Our Ryobei-san is a very strong player!"

Taeko watched as the other four began throwing the dice. The first to win and thus escape paying was the obese, ruddy-faced American. On realizing his victory, he laughed with innocent heartiness, like a child. Now it was up to the other three.

"This time Ryobei-san will go out, I'll warrant," said Mrs. Iwamuro.

"Enough of that!" said Ryosuké, laughing and shaking the leather dice-container. "You only inhibit me when you say that sort of thing. I just can't seem to throw the dice I want. . . ."

But Ryosuké managed to win after all. The final contest was therefore between Mrs. Iwamuro and the thin American.

"It's turned out just as it should," said Ryosuké as he watched them. It was his turn now to be the onlooker and to make fun of the players. "Just as it should," he continued. "the bill will be paid by one of our two wealthy friends here!"

After three throws Mrs. Iwamuro won.

"I'm sorry," she said, and bowed with a charming smile to the American who had lost. "It is very kind of you. You favored me because I am a woman."

She spoke in broken English, yet there was something very attractive about her accent. The thin American made a great show of dismay, then laughingly produced his wallet and placed two thousand yen notes on the counter of the bar.

Taeko left ahead of the others and returned by herself to the bedroom. Ryosuké had said that he would join her right away, but he was evidently detained by the excitement of the dice game, and Taeko sat waiting in her nightgown for some time. When she lay down on the bed, she dozed off without meaning to. It was a deep and comfortable sleep. She was more tired than she had realized.

When she awoke, she noticed Ryosuké getting ready to go to bed. She felt as fresh as if she had just been born, and sat straight up in bed with a bright look in her eyes.

"I didn't hear you come in," she said, stretching out her hands to Ryosuké. He sat down on the bed and took her hands gently between his own, as if they were objects of immense value.

"It's a good thing you went to bed," he said. "If one stays on with those people, there's no end to it."

"But she's such a nice person!" said Taeko emphatically, and in her mind sprang up the fresh image of Mrs. Iwamuro. "Yes, she's a splendid woman. In fact, as that American would say, 'wonderful'!" She spoke the word in mocking imitation of Mrs. Iwamuro's companion and then burst out laughing, like a child. "Everything was 'wonderful,' wasn't it? Even when the dice rolled on the table, that was 'wonderful'!"

Ryosuké bent over and covered her mouth to make her silent. "Let's go to sleep now," he said tenderly. If you start getting worked up at this time of night, you'll never get to sleep!"

"What time is it?" said Taeko.

Ryosuké hesitated for a moment and looked vaguely at his wrist. "Well," he said doubtfully, "it's just about midnight."

"Please lend me your watch," said Taeko, stretching out her hand. "The moment it gets to be midnight I'll go to sleep. Till then let's talk. I shall keep an eye on the time."

It was an innocent request, but for a while Ryosuké did not answer. Then suddenly he said: "I haven't got the watch."

"Why?"

"I lost it in the dice game."

Without saying a word Taeko raised her head from the pillow and looked at Ryosuké.

"That's the sort of thing that happens, you know!" said Ryosuké, laughing nonchalantly and drawing the blanket over his body. "Don't worry. I'll get it back tomorrow."

Taeko sat up in bed with a surprised look.

"Who from?" she said.

"Well, from Mrs. Iwamuro, as a matter of fact."

"You mean that she would do a thing like that?"

"Definitely," said Ryosuké, and there was a certain hardness in his voice. "That's what gambling is, after all. If one loses, one's got to pay up! I'm not quite sure why, but tonight I lost."

Taeko noticed the manly smile on his face which so appealed to her.

"Now let's go to sleep," he said, and stretching out his arm, pushed the switch of the bed lamp. The room was plunged into darkness.

Taeko was about to pursue her questions, but she stopped herself. She was anxious to understand the real truth. She still couldn't believe that Mrs. Iwamuro was the type of woman who would take someone's watch away from him because of a gambling debt and then not return it. To Taeko there was something inexplicable and unpleasant about the entire incident. Yet she knew that if she talked about it, she would risk annoying Ryosuké. At the same time she felt uneasy at the knowledge that all this might somehow dispel the happiness of that wonderful day, like a shadow trembling over the water's surface. It would be better for her to continue believing in Ryosuké, rather than asking him childish questions.

Taeko lay in the dark room with her eyes open. Then in her heart, which she thought was occupied only by Ryosuké and herself, she heard voices assuring her of the contrary: "You're mistaken, you know. We're here also." And she felt as though the shadows of various people had entered between her and Ryosuké. That Mrs. Iwamuro should be one of these shadows was only natural; but there were also the figures of the girls with whom she worked, her sister in Kobe, and even her father. Her heart began to feel heavy. Yet, she told herself, she must not think about these things now. She turned over in bed and faced Ryosuké. Perhaps looking at him would give her the courage she needed.

"Can't you get to sleep?" said Ryosuké.

"No, it's all right," answered Taeko calmly. Then suddenly her previous thoughts emerged in words: "Do you like playing dice and that sort of thing?"

"Yes, I like it," replied Ryosuké stiffly. "There's nothing specially bad about gambling, you know. It's a game like any other. Americans are very keen on it."

"Yes, I remember. You had a bet over that tennis game, didn't you?"

"Are you worrying about it?" asked Ryosuké tenderly. "I'll get that watch back, never fear. Actually it wasn't the sort of watch I'd very much mind parting with. As a matter of fact, I'm usually pretty good in games."

"No," said Taeko, and all of a sudden she was able to speak distinctly. "I'm not very fond of gambling, you see."

"You mean I should give it up?"

"Well, I wouldn't say such a thing now. But I don't like it at all."

"That's rather unlike you," said Ryosuké, stretching himself out comfortably in the bed, "and not at all modern."

"The fact is," he continued after a while "I like games of chance. I think it gives a certain tone to one's life. You should play for a stake to make it interesting. But even without a stake, there comes a moment when you suddenly feel your nerves straining. That's when the fun begins. There is something very gallant and attractive about that feeling. And something pure also."

As Taeko listened, she could not help feeling that Ryosuké was expressing now the very essence of his character.

"Aren't you sleepy, Taeko?"

"No, not in the slightest."

The dimness that filled the room seemed to awaken her senses. She could feel not only the light of the stars up in the sky, but also the heavy thickness of the sea stretching out in the distance.

"They managed to drag me into the war, and I took part in the Sensho campaign," said Ryosuké suddenly. "I dream about those days even now. I remember how at one point the enemy split into two separate forces and deliberately allowed us to march between them toward our objective. In retrospect, of course, it's clear that they were being very clever by avoiding our attack and waiting till we had passed them. All our officers could think of was to get through to the objective as quickly as possible. Well, before long we found ourselves occupying a huge area of country. Just as we were thinking that we had won the day, the enemy began to open fire on us from both sides. We couldn't see them, but it was clear that we were caught right between them. It was dreadful. We knew that if we didn't advance rapidly, we'd all be shot down in short order. The Chinese managed to mow down an entire squad that wasn't more than ten yards away from ours. All of us were as pale as ghosts. Some threw themselves frantically on the ground and lay there rooted to the spot. Others shot blindly. If we stopped shooting we were terrified. This went on for two whole weeks, day after day. At that time I got the reputation of being brave. When the enemy attacked I was one of the few who held their ground instead of running away—so people thought that I must be endowed with some special courage."

Ryosuké paused for a while.

"But the truth was," he continued, "that I wasn't especially brave at all. I had simply decided that rather than continue with the present agony, it might be a good deal better to get killed. Another thing that occurred to me was that when one is under heavy fire, it doesn't do the slightest good to run away or to hide, because your bullet will get you all the same if it's fated to. So when the others rushed off and frantically hid by the roots of trees or under the walls of demolished houses, I stayed on the spot. In other words, I felt just as if I were playing dice. If I was going to die, I'd die; if I was going to come through alive, I'd come through. Heads or tails—there was nothing I could do to decide the outcome, so I might just as well stand there. Near me, I remember, there lay a Chinese pillow. I can still see it quite clearly now as it lay there on the ground. It was a red pillow with some sort of a pattern. When the bullet hit it, it moved and let out some kind of a sound. It wasn't more than two yards away from me. Later when I examined it, I could clearly see where the bullet had pierced the pillow."

"How horrible!" said Taeko.

"Yes, I was afraid all right. And at the time I wondered: why on earth did that bullet hit the pillow and not me who was so near by? It occurred to me then that the whole thing was just like gambling. That was all I could think. Gradually we advanced on Sensho. When we emerged at the banks of the Yangtze River they began shooting at us from the opposite shore. The bullets ricocheted against the walls of the houses on our side. They made a special sort of dry sound, and each time there would be a little cloud of dust. It's very special—the sound that a bullet makes when it hits a hard object. I remember it so well. At those moments too I felt that I was gambling. And this thought somehow calmed me down."

In the darkness Ryosuké's memories seemed to emerge clearly. And the more he spoke about the past, the more strongly the impressions crowded in on him. Then he stopped and turned around in bed. "The war's over now," he said. "When I think about it, I always feel as if I'd graduated from some special course. Sometimes it all comes back to me very suddenly. I remember how that red pillow jerked on the ground when it was hit by the bullet, like some living creature, a dog, for instance. And as I think of the pillow, I remember the dry dusty earth in the interior of China and the color of the tree branches burned red with shellfire and the houses of which nothing remained but the broken walls. We never had enough water to drink during our marches through that dry country. Even now I can remember exactly what my thirst at that time felt like. . . . After the war I went on a mountain-climbing trip to a place where I had once been with Mé. Suddenly a flock of martins whistled past me. Immediately my body seemed to crumple up, as though the enemy had started firing in my direction. At the same instant my previous ideas about gambling came to my mind. I was either going to be hit or not—it was all in the throw of the dice, you see."

Taeko nodded silently.

"Certain impressions stick in my mind like burs. If only I could forget them just once. But when you go through such an immense experience as a war, memories don't leave you very easily. It's a matter of time, I suppose. One thing is particularly queer: though I have never suffered so much in my life as during that time, I sometimes can't help thinking of it with nostalgia. Sometimes I find myself thinking quite fondly about the little country village where we were stationed. There was an earthern castle wall with a stream round it and ducks swimming there. Needless to say, we ate all the ducks right away. I recall a five-story pagoda built on the edge of a completely bare mountain behind the village. How could they ever have dragged the materials up there to build the pagoda? There was a primary school with a walled-in garden. Tall old willows were growing there. When we went into the classroom, we found a blackboard, and all the soldiers were reminded of their own primary schools."

"I wish you could remember only the happy things," said Taeko.

"Yes," said Ryosuké, "that would be a good thing. . . . Life to me is like a continual gamble. If I have my watch taken from me, I can't get awfully upset. After all, I can always get it back again. When I was dragged into the war, however, I was gambling with my one and only life!"

The next morning while Taeko was in the bathroom doing her toilet, Ryosuké sat up in bed and telephoned Mrs. Iwamuro's room.

"Who is it?" said Mrs. Iwamuro.

"You sound sleepy," said Ryosuké with a laugh. "You weren't still asleep, were you?"

"It's still early, you know," said Mrs. Iwamuro with a slight touch of peevishness.

"I'm sorry," said Ryosuké in a gentle tone. "It's a shame, you see, but I haven't got my watch on me, and I therefore have no idea what time it is."

"Oh, your watch," said Mrs. Iwamuro, evidently suddenly remembering about the previous evening. "Of course. I'd forgotten all about it. Well, your watch is right here, Ryobei-san."

"I feel rather sorry about that," said Ryosuké. "Would you mind looking and telling me what time it is?"

"Do you intend to phone me each time you want to know what time it is? That's going to be rather a bore!"

"Well, it can't be helped so long as the watch is in your

room. If you consider it bad manners for me to phone for the time, I can always come and knock at your door and ask you directly."

"What a threat! There's a large clock on the wall by the front desk. And if you don't want to go there, you can telephone the operator, and she'll tell you the time right away."

"Thank you but I have no use for any other time pieces except my own. You see, I'm used to only looking at my own watch."

"Well, things must be very inconvenient for you now," said Mrs. Iwamuro, and then, as though she had just thought of something, she began to laugh gaily. "Guess where your watch is now, Ryobei-san."

"What do you mean?"

"I mean guess in what part of my room your watch is lying at this moment."

"Don't tell me," said Ryosuké, "that my poor watch is in the wastepaper basket!"

"Well, I'm afraid it isn't getting too good treatment. I must have been a bit tight last night. I don't even remember doing with the watch—what I did with it."

"How very puzzling! May I come and have a look."

"As you like," said Mrs. Iwamuro.

"Apart from the watch," said Ryosuké, "I have a favor to ask you. You see, I plan to leave the hotel this morning, and there's just one thing I must ask you."

"Well, come along to my room. But I'm afraid you're going to be disappointed, Ryobei-san."

"I'll be along right away—at least, as soon as I get up, get dressed, and wash my face."

Taeko came out of the bathroom while Ryosuké was still on the phone. She stood quietly in front of the mirror. Ryosuké put down the receiver and climbed out of bed.

"I'm going over to see Mrs. Iwamuro for just a moment," he said.

Taeko realized that she had no particular reason to stop him. Yet after he had left the room she had a queer feeling.

Ryosuké went down to the bar where they had been the night before. No customers were there now—only the slanting light from the windows and a young boy wiping glasses.

"Would you mind lending me that dice box for a while?" said Ryosuké. "I'll bring it back right away."

The boy gave it to him, and he put it in his trouser pocket. Then he hurried upstairs and along the corridor, looking at the brass numbers on the doors for Mrs. Iwamuro's room. When he saw her number, he knocked lightly. She answered at once, as if she had been expecting him that moment: *"Entrez!"*

Ryosuké opened the door and walked in. At once he saw that Mrs. Iwamuro was sitting up in bed.

"Is it all right?" said Ryosuké, slightly taken back.

"As long as you don't mind seeing me in bed, it doesn't bother me." She looked at him with a cheerful, childish expression on her face. "So far as I'm concerned, it's still midnight. There's no reason for me to get out of bed just because a guest has come."

"I'm sorry I woke you so early. May I sit down?"

"Certainly."

Mrs. Iwamuro wore a thin nightgown. The gown was not the ordinary cotton kind provided by the hotel, but obviously one that she had brought with her from Tokyo. There was an innocent sort of happiness about her and a sense of utter composure.

"You said you had something to ask me," she began gaily. "What is it?"

"I should like to borrow a little money. I'll definitely let you have it back when I return to Tokyo."

A vague expression of annoyance passed over Mrs. Iwamuro's face.

"It's rather sudden, isn't it?" she said.

"Yes, it is sudden," answered Ryosuké with a youthful lack of hesitation. "You see, I'm in a spot of trouble."

"Well, I'm not in any trouble. Whatever it may be, it doesn't concern me, does it?"

"I'm not joking," said Ryosuké. "I'm in trouble, and so I've come to ask your help." He was speaking seriously now. "If you can't lend me any money, I shan't be able to pay my hotel bill."

"About how much do you want?" said Mrs. Iwamuro in a resigned tone. "You see, I don't know if I'll have enough myself."

"I don't mind deciding the matter by playing dice for it."

This new proposal seemed to shock Mrs. Iwamuro.

"What a strange man you are! I thought it was a bit brazen of you to ask me to lend you the money. And now you want to take it off me by gambling! You're a very wicked fellow!"

Mrs. Iwamuro suddenly became quiet, and for a moment Ryosuké felt that his effort had already ended in failure. Yet she still did not seem to have lost whatever it was that had made her so cheeful.

"What about that girl?" said Mrs. Iwamuro after a while. "Taeko-san, wasn't she called? Doesn't she have any money?"

"She's only an office girl," answered Ryosuké frankly. "And besides—"

"And besides what?" said Mrs. Iwamuro, gazing at Ryosuké with a playful look.

"Well . . . as a man I really can't talk about these things."

"What a gentleman you are! Well, all right. But it's a bit unfair of you, you know. You don't mind putting me to trouble, do you?" She turned over in bed and lay on her stomach, looking seriously at Ryosuké. "It's very nice," she said. "A couple of lovers! Are you going to get married?"

"Yes, of course, I mean to."

Mrs. Iwamuro stared intently into Ryosuké's face, her eyes flashing light and dark, like a cat's.

"Well, how splendid!" she said. "Let me congratulate you."

As she spoke, she stretched out her arm, took her bag, and unclasped it.

"About how much do you need?"

"If you could let me have ten thousand, I should be most grateful."

"Well, I know that people sometimes give out advice at the same time as money, but I'll dispense with that." She laughed delicately. "But it's really true that you're going to get married, is it? You mustn't deceive me about that. Being deceived is the one thing I can't stand."

"I wouldn't do a thing like that," said Ryosuké laughing.

"Then I won't say any more. Here, take this."

"You've really rescued me!" Ryosuké blurted out the words ingenuously. "If I hadn't met you here, I was going to leave the car with the hotel as security. I suppose they'd have accepted that."

"What a fool you are!"

"But I felt certain that you'd understand."

"Why?" asked Mrs. Iwamuro, and looked at him seriously. Ryosuké hesitated for a moment, not quite sure how to answer.

"If you don't mind my saying it, you have the character of an adventurer. You don't like commonplace things, do you?"

"Well, I'm not really sure."

"I'm sure I'm right," said Ryosuké. "There's something very daring about you. Or perhaps I should say courageous."

"No, it isn't like that really. At least it isn't the sort of courage a young fellow like you imagines. It's a courage that almost all women have. They may seem quite ordinary on the outside, but there's a certain strength underneath. Your Taeko-san—I'm sure she's like that. On the other hand, the women you refer to as being adventurers—they're the ones who usually have something weak about them. As to myself . . . well, I don't want to think about it, or it will surely make me feel weak."

"You're born strong," said Ryosuké. "Whatever you do, there's a strength about it."

"None of your impertinence!" said Mrs. Iwamuro with a smile. "There's no need to become personal just because you've got the money."

"I'm sorry," said Ryosuké and made to leave the room. "You've really rescued me. I'm extremely grateful."

"How serious you are," said Mrs. Iwamuro, turning around in bed again. She rested her head flat on the pillow, and as she lay there looking straight up, Ryosuké was aware of the slender, pretty bridge of her nose.

"Ryobei-san," she said playfully, "do you know where your watch is?"

"Oh. I'd forgotten all about it," he answered with a strained smile. "Where is it?"

"Well, you'll have to guess. If you guess right, I'll let you have it back."

Mrs. Iwamuro raised the upper part of her body and stretched her legs out under the bedclothes. Her head seemed to be supported lightly from behind; her arms rested on the sheet in an open position, the elbows bent. She looked extraordinarily like Goya's painting of the Maja. Because of her golf, her arms had been tanned by the sun to a delicate color of wheat. But in her present position Ryosuké could see the under part of her arms, which the sun had not reached, and they were white like the color of peeled onions.

"You've got it in one of your hands."

"No," she said with a laugh, and opening her fingers, held up her hands for inspection.

"No, it's nowhere like that," she said, and her face seemed to be flushed with victory. "I'm afraid you won't be able to guess. It's all right. You'd better hurry back to Taeko-san, or she'll get worried."

"Do let me have it back, It's an awful nuisance not having the thing."

"I agree, it must be most inconvenient. But I won it according to the fair rules of dice, didn't I? Though really you needn't have given such a valuable thing as a pledge."

"I can assure you that I'm more keenly aware of that fact than you are," said Ryosuké with a bitter smile. "If you let me have it back, I'll give you something else for it one of these days —as a compensation."

"What a cunning young man! But I can't let you have it. It'll only make you angry if you find out where it is."

"Very strange," said Ryosuké, and he pretended he was racking his brain to guess the watch's whereabouts. "I certainly won't be angry," he remarked after a while. "Wherever it is, I promise not to mind. Do take it out."

"You won't be angry?"

"Definitely not."

"I wonder."

"You shouldn't keep me in suspense like this."

Then Mrs. Iwamuro's excitement seemed to drop, and she returned to her normal composure, as though she no longer cared about the watch. Now she was like a shell that has closed itself, refusing all intrusion. There was a hidden nobility about her manner, an air of aristocracy.

"I must have been very drunk last night."

"You didn't look it."

"No, I was really drunk. Else I shouldn't have done such a mischievous thing. When I woke up this morning, I'd completely forgotten about it. Even though by all rights the watch was mine after I'd won it, it didn't deserve such rude treatment!"

"How disturbing! Do tell me where it is."

Mrs. Iwamuro's expression became serious, and she did not answer. Silently she changed the position of her body and slowly drew out one leg from under the eiderdown. It was a white naked leg, beautifully shaped. Around the slender ankle the watch was fastened like an anklet.

Mrs. Iwamuro's movements had become stiff and constrained. Ryosuké's eyes were fixed on her face, and he was unaware of her coquettish ruse. Mrs. Iwamuro's black eyes, which gazed straight into Ryosuké's, were shining.

When she realized that Ryosuké had not seen the watch, the stiffness in her body began to disappear. Softly her body loosened, like a half-blooming flower. She lowered her beautiful legs onto the carpeted floor and stood up. Ryosuké looked at her body with fascination. He saw the color and texture of her skin, which glimmered under the thin nightgown like mother of pearl. Involuntarily he averted his eyes, as though moving his hand away from something hot. He did not see the watch. He was aware of a strange pressure in his breathing.

"How obstinate you are," said Ryosuké. "Well, now I give up."

"Yes, you'd better go back to your room," said Mrs. Iwamuro, sitting down on the bed and putting her legs slowly under the covers. Her excitement had suddenly cooled and given place to disappointment.

"I'll get the boy to bring you the watch later," she said.

Ryosuké moved toward the door. "You don't need to go to all that trouble," he answered.

Before she had time to say any more the telephone by the bedside rang shrilly.

"It must be your American," said Ryosuké.

The main purpose of his visit to Mrs. Iwamuro had been accomplished, and now everything else seemed secondary. He opened the door and returned to his own room.

Mrs. Iwamuro's phone call informed her that her partner had arrived at the hotel as planned.

"I have already met Mr. Smith and his companion," he told her courteously. "Thanks to your attentions, they're in an excellent mood. They said this was the nicest time they've had since they came to Japan. I hear that you also beat them at golf. They say that you're a very accurate player. In fact, they were both praising you to the skies."

"Did you get on to the subject of business?" asked Mrs. Iwamuro. After all, this was the reason that her elderly partner had asked her to entertain the two Americans.

"I'm going to do that by and by. If I show them that I'm in a hurry, I'll lose out. But I can tell that they've already changed their attitude completely since I saw them in Tokyo. I'm quite sure they're going to be co-operative. One of them asked me if the Baroness was an executive in our firm."

Mrs. Iwamuro laughed with an air of satisfaction.

"What did you reply?"

"Of course, I answered that you were. One more favor from you now: won't you come down and have some breakfast with me?"

"You must excuse me in the mornings. I'll be with you at lunch."

After putting down the receiver, Mrs. Iwamuro lay back in bed as if she was weary. She felt very pleased that the job she had been asked to undertake was succeeding. The company for which she had entertained the Americans was a well-known heavy-industry firm. Mrs. Iwamuro laughed to herself as she remembered that the young secretary in the office had told her that the managing director (the man to whom she had just been speaking on the telephone) used to polish his bald pate each morning before taking his bath with the white of an egg and a small bag of rice-bran. She was very satisfied with her job, and the more success she had, the more she liked it. She had now already forgotten completely about her recent bold plan with all its voluptuous implications. Like a child, she would become enthusiastic over some new scheme, but then with equal rapidity she would forget about it entirely if things did not turn out as expected.

8 · THE GUEST

WHEN Sutekichi looked up from his book, he saw his host, Soroku Okamoto, come into the corridor with a Panama hat in his hand. Sutekichi rose from the straw mat on which he had been lying.

"Are you going out?" he said.

"Yes," answered Soroku.

His Panama hat looked remarkably old. It was obviously of fine quality and closely woven, unlike the present-day hats. But from its shade one could tell that it was a long time since it had been to the cleaners.

"It still seems to be quite hot," continued Soroku. "I'm just going to the barber, and I'll be right back."

For a moment Sutekichi thought of seeing him off at the front gate, but then it occurred to him that this would give the impression that he was some sort of a student dependent.

"Good-by," he said, and returned to his recumbent position on the straw mat. As he took up his book again, he heard the outside door open, and he listened as Soroku called for the old housekeeper to bring him his clogs. Then as the door closed again a cicada suddenly started to cry by the near-by plum tree. Sutekichi looked up. The shadows were beginning to lengthen in the garden. What a change it was after Tokyo to be in this house where there was a cool breeze all day long. The trees here saved one from the unbearable heat, and also there were no pavements to reflect the torrid temperature. The sea breeze seemed to follow the course of the Nameri River and to freshen the atmosphere even as far inland as this house.

Sutekichi had been reading a translation of a novel. But now that his attention had been distracted, he had trouble regaining the thread of his interest. As Soroku had gone out, he decided that he need no longer hesitate to strip to the waist and make himself really comfortable. The western sun beat down on the corridor. A dragonfly settled down on the floor. Evidently dragonflies didn't mind the heat, for this one was resting its wings in the very hottest place. Sutekichi thought of how steaming hot it would be in Tokyo from now until the evening. He thought about his little apartment and realized what a delightful boon it was for him to be able to spend even a day or two in this spacious house in a large empty room and to escape the terrible heat in Kamakura where one was right next to the sea.

Soroku Okamoto had now returned to normal, and Sutekichi could no longer recognize the slightest touch of strangeness in him. He had become just like one of the hundreds of people you see riding in the streetcars—an elderly man with a certain shadow of weariness on his face, but with no particular worries about his livelihood.

"Tell me now," Professor Segi had once suddenly said, "doesn't Okamoto seem to be unusually methodical and particular about money matters?"

"Well, I haven't had much occasion to observe anything in that line," Sutekichi recalled having answered.

"I see. To tell the truth, I've been wondering why his memory all of a sudden came back on that evening. I can't help thinking that my throwing that money on my desk served as some sort of a stimulus. Apart from that, nothing special happened that evening, you see. The other day I called on Professor Waki to thank him for his trouble, and I asked him whether this could in fact have provided the stimulus."

The professor had paused. There had been a smile on his face, but his eyes looked serious.

"Well, Waki wouldn't commit himself one way or another, although he admitted that it could have been the sight of the money that cured him. In any case, I myself have decided that that was the reason. I can think of no other stimulus that evening, so it must have been the money. I remember that when I spoke to Waki earlier about the matter, he told me that if one single clue comes along to help one recover one's memory, all sorts of other memories begin to come back one after another—like pulling at the vine of sweet potatoes in the ground. That way one recovers all by oneself, you see. The same thing might have happened if he'd chanced to walk along some street that he recognized or to bump into some old friend. After all, you know it often happens that we normal people forget something that has happened to us and then it suddenly returns to us because of some vaguely related circumstance—the sight of a blossoming plum tree, or something of the sort. It was the same with Okamoto. There isn't that much of a gulf between normal and abnormal minds. Simple common sense is at the bottom of it all —and scholarship rarely contradicts it. Old Okamoto returned to himself when he spotted the money I'd thrown on the table. That's how it was."

The Professor had seemed rather proud of his conclusions. As usual, his conversation had jumped quite arbitrarily in the direction that pleased him, as if it had suddenly taken wings.

"Professor Waki is still quite a young fellow," Segi had continued, "and he had a rather literary way of looking at things. He mentioned that sometimes people suffering from amnesia come back to themselves by hearing a snatch of music. Just a couple of bars—and all their memories come flooding back. Imagine: you could have a man sitting there with a dull, wooden look on his face, his mouth hanging open. Then you play him a bit of Beethoven's "Fifth Symphony," and all of a sudden his face becomes alive and all his past memories spring back passionately. It would make a good story for a film. Very romantic indeed! Every young girl in the audience would be completely captivated. Perhaps a symphony would be rather noisy, though. Let's make it one of Chopin's piano pieces—one of his nocturnes will do for the time being. Something subdued, you see. Our hero, whose mind has become an utter vacuum to the extent that he can't even recognize his girl-friend, hears the music, and gradually his memory comes back to him. With a start he recognizes his girl-friend's face directly in front of him. Then they both cry. In the audience, meanwhile, handkerchiefs are furiously being whipped out of pockets—out of the pockets of those modern raincoats that look like cake-wrappings. I suppose young girls nowadays bow to etiquette at least to the extent of carrying pocket handkerchiefs, don't they?"

"Yes indeed," Sutekichi had said, laughing at the professor's fancies.

"Well, I don't know if the girl-friend is called Mary or Hanako. But whoever it is, he remembers her name and becomes excited. 'Mary!' he calls out, or 'Hana-chan!' as the case may be. There's a happy ending for you. But in the case of our Mr. Okamoto we were deprived of such delightful saccharine effects. What brought him to his senses was the sight of someone else's purse. How indescribably prosaic! Perhaps in his previous life he was a professional thief. You and I may not be poets, but compared with our prosaic Mr. Okamoto, we're oozing with lyricism!"

Now, gazing out at the garden and its full summer life, Sutekichi vaguely recollected the professor's face. Although Segi was an elderly man, his blood coursed gaily through his veins, and he was always looking for a chance to poke a little cheerful fun at someone. From that elegant white-haired countenance, the rollicking Edo accent would suddenly pour forth, laced with some amusing irony. The professor had always been like this, even in the lecture halls, where things usually tended to be so dry. For this reason the less benevolent students used to look forward to his lectures, saying that they would soon be hearing one of Professor Segi's *rakugo* (traditional comic stories) again. Also the theory became established that it was impossible to fail in one of Segi's examinations.

This particular theory, however, had no foundation, being based purely on the general impression that the students derived from Segi's personality. Once eleven of his students cheated in an examination, all presenting identical papers. Professor Segi saw to it that every single one of them failed the course. The students paled on hearing the results, for it meant that they would have to take the entire year's course over again.

Yet when the new term started all eleven students appeared on the very first day in Professor Segi's lecture hall. They could perfectly well have chosen some other subject and avoided Segi entirely. The other students at the university were most impressed by this story. Professor Segi greeted the delinquent students from his rostrum with a merry smile.

"How very nice," he said. "Other fellows might have tried to rush through this course in a year. But you've decided to take your time and do it thoroughly in two years. This is really something. It's important, you know. Long after all this is over, you'll remember this and you'll realize that it's been a very good thing for you."

One of those students became an outstanding expert in paleography, the serious and unremunerative field that Segi professed, and followed up his research work. The other ten went ahead in their own vocations, but none of them was able to cut himself off from the professor. Now, years later, the students and their former teacher were able to talk nonchalantly about the cheating incident, and even to feel a certain nostalgia for it all.

"You know," the professor used to say, "I only had to glance at those papers of yours, and it was as clear as daylight that there'd been some funny business going on. They all contained exactly the same mistakes. And not in one place only, but in two separate places. You'd even written the characters incorrectly —disgraceful for university students. I couldn't have let you get away with it, even if I'd wanted to."

The ex-students thought back happily on the past. Yet they could not help feeling a bit embarrassed whenever the incident was mentioned—they remembered how completely they had been defeated by the professor.

In the same examination Segi had passed another student although he had a mark hardly better than zero. He had been an industrious student, but not particularly bright.

"He wasn't going to specialize in the subject," the professor had explained. "As far as he was concerned, a subject such as paleography might just as well never have existed."

In other words, it was not because the students were unintelligent that the professor had made them fail, but because he loathed cheating. And this fact remained engraved on the minds of the eleven students.

As for Sutekichi, his interest in the professor was by no means a form of blind devotion. He felt a great gap between them. There was the immense discrepancy in their ages. The elder man belonged to the good old days when many of the anxieties that trouble young people nowadays did not exist. This was the source of his optimistic nature and his special type of courage, which Sutekichi could not help envying.

Despite all their differences, Sutekichi was greatly attracted by the personality of his old teacher. It was not simply that he had a pleasant disposition. Sometimes Sutekichi even felt a certain antipathy to Segi's speech and manners; yet after he had been separated from him for a while, he would once more become attracted.

One thing that puzzled Sutekichi was the professor's love for his little grandson, Taro. From an objective point of view, you could not even say that Taro was an especially nice child. He was self-willed and wild; his face was fat and stubborn. When he asked for something impossible and was thwarted, he used to hit his grandfather. Then the professor would seem to shrink as he tried to soothe the little boy. From an outsider's point of view it all seemed wrong and undisciplined. Sometimes when Segi wasn't there Sutekichi felt like forcing the little tyrant to surrender even if it meant shouting at him.

Segi seemed to believe that Taro made a pleasant impression on other people. This evidently was the reason that he had asked Sutekichi to take him along to Soroku Okamoto's house in Kamakura. On the streetcar Taro had become tired, and although the car was packed with people, he had wanted to sit right next to the window so that he could look out, even if it meant pushing other passengers aside. The little boy gave nothing but trouble. Whether Soroku had been as glad to see Taro as Segi had expected was questionable. To be sure, the child had been a good companion while they had been at the professor's house. But it was different when Taro was no longer on his own territory. He was shy with strangers. And finding things different from what they were at home, he at once had begun whining that he wanted to go back to Tokyo.

Soroku had taken all this spoiled behavior very well. He had shown the little boy the pigeons at the Hachiman Shrine and the Great Buddha; he had also taken him along to the beach. It had been obvious that Soroku was doing his best; but he had been awkward and seemed to get tired early. To a small child this change of mood on the part of the older man had transmitted itself immediately. And accordingly Taro would start to pester him even more than before.

"It's hard playing with a child of that age, isn't it?" Soroku had said with a smile. Sutekichi could not help feeling sorry for the man. "Taro is a special case," he had said. "The professor has spoiled him terribly."

Soroku, however, had opposed this view.

"When he grows up, you know, it's going to be a delight for the professor to see how he turns out. And the fact is, this is the dearest age of all." He had spoken calmly in the manner of an old man. "You wouldn't understand about a thing like this unless you'd had a child of your own. There's really something very dear about them."

They had been sitting on the sand of the crowded beach. Sutekichi had glanced around at all the young men and women in their bathing-suits. Soroku had seemed very out of place in his formal clothes; his age, too, made him incongruous. Taro had been wearing bathing-trunks, but he would not go into the water unless Sutekichi accompanied him. He had run away from the waves as they moved in, then followed them out a short way into the sea. Once he had stumbled and almost fallen over.

"Oh, do be careful!" Soroku had shouted in an alarmed tone and jumped to his feet. Then, he'd noticed that Sutekichi was surprised at his excitement, and his face had reddened.

"I also had a son," he had said. "When he was just this age, I often used to take him out here. He was an incorrigibly naughty little boy. I couldn't afford to take my eyes off him for a minute. I was always wondering how he'd turn out when he was grown up, you see."

"Is he the boy who died in the war?" asked Sutekichi.

"Yes, he was," Soroku had answered. An exhausted look passed over his face, and he became dead quiet.

．　　．　　．

Since the visit Soroku Okamoto had really returned to his normal state of mind. In particular, his attitude to Segi and Sutekichi had revealed an uncommon degree of kindness. It was not simply a conventional form of kindness; it was only after hearing that Sutekichi lived in a small apartment utterly unsuited for studying that he had asked him to come and stay at his house in Kamakura during the summer holidays and to bring along his books.

"I, on the contrary, live in an enormous house," he had said, "and I don't know what to do with half the rooms. If you feel like it, please come and stay. But I'm afraid that I can't promise you much in the way of entertainment."

Sutekichi himself was still at the age where it did not particularly worry him that he might be putting other people to some sort of trouble, and he took the invitation at its face value. He had not lost the habit of mind from his school days, when he had visited the houses of his friends, of somehow assuming that young people had a special right to be treated kindly by their elders. Food served at other people's houses, even if it was exactly the same as he had at home, had always tasted much better. And so after he had gone out to Kamakura one Saturday to call on Soroku, he had not hesitated to come again and stay during the hot summer weeks. The master of the house himself certainly was pleased to have him and appeared to enjoy the company of young men.

"With a young man like Mr. Ata staying here," he had suddenly said at dinner, "we can feel nice and safe."

No longer could one detect on Soroku's face the slightest trace of the despair of a would-be suicide about whom the professor had been worrying.

When Segi had heard that Sutekichi was to be staying in Kamakura, he had remarked: "It's a well-established tradition for students to impose themselves with perfect composure on other people's hospitality." And he had given a sardonic laugh. "Just because the other people happen to be their seniors, they feel they have a perfect right to call on them—even though they may be strangers—and even to stay for dinner. I would have imagined that this custom had vanished during the wartime food shortage, but evidently not."

"Don't you think you ought to try and stop him?" Mrs. Segi had said with some concern.

"No, it's all right. Mr. Ata is not a thoughtless young man. In fact, he's quite sensitive, and he'd be the first person to stay away if he really thought he wasn't wanted."

As it was, Sutekichi and his elderly host got on very well. No serious talks arose between them to mar the comfotable atmosphere. Sutekichi had no desire to delve into Soroku's innermost heart, and he consciously kept himself aloof. Nor did Soroku ever try to start a serious conversation. It was hard to tell what he was really up to, as he walked about the rooms of the house or in the garden. To Sutekichi he seemed a very lonely man. When their eyes met, Soroku would give a faint smile. Sometimes they would go out for a stroll together. It was the height of the summer season at Kamakura.

"I haven't been walking about much outside," Soroku had said, almost apologetically.

As they strolled along side by side, Soroku never seemed to pay any special attention to what they passed on their way.

"Shall we go this way?" Sutekichi would suggest, and Soroku would merely answer: "Well, yes," and he would follow Sutekichi in the direction that he had proposed. He hardly seemed to look outside himself at all, but to be pursuing his own inner thoughts. Sutekichi had no idea what kind of shadows might be moving about in the older man's mind, and he had no intention of probing.

The cicada were still singing. Sutekichi looked up at the sky which peeped between the branches of the trees in the garden. The sky was blue—a really clear blue. What exactly was this blue color called? Sutekichi remembered having seen it in some Western painting. Could it have been a painting by Coubert, he wondered, though not caring particularly to know the answer.

Sutekichi had completely given up reading now. Stripped to the waist, he gazed out at the sky. He had discovered that sky this afternoon. Perhaps, he thought, it was a bit of an exaggeration to say that he had discovered it, but since he had found something that had not existed in his mind before, it really was a discovery so far as he was concerned.

Glancing out at the garden, he noticed that the dog had come out and was sitting on the lawn looking straight at him, as if he expected to be spoken to. Sutekichi knew that the dog's name, Friday, was the same as the day of the week in English, but he had no idea why the dog had been given the name. He had no particular fondness for dogs.

Above him the red sunset began to color the garden as if the entire air had been dyed, and the evening glow radiated on the clouds above the mountains to the east. Sutekichi felt that he himself would like to go out there and be dyed by that crimson color.

"Friday!"

All of a sudden Sutekichi heard the voice of a young woman and started with surprise. The dog rushed in the direction from where the voice had come. Taeko bent down and patted Friday's head. Sutekichi saw her, then realized that he himself was sitting there almost naked.

"Where is Uncle?" Taeko said to the dog, as if he could possibly provide her with an answer.

Sutekichi emerged onto the veranda.

"Mr. Okamoto has gone to the barber," he said.

Taeko pulled herself up straight, looked at Sutekichi, and made a formal bow.

"Will he be back soon?" she asked.

Noticing the bright look in her eyes, Sutekichi was unaccountably moved and as a result answered rather brusquely: "I imagine so."

He did not know exactly what to do and merely stood there looking at the girl opposite him. Taeko was immersed in the beautiful tints of the evening glow. The green of the lawn shone brightly, and to Sutekichi's eyes Taeko's complexion, as she walked over the grass in her dress of heavy white material, was dazzling.

"Do you have some business with Mr. Okamoto?" he asked awkwardly.

"No, it's just that I haven't been calling as much as I should recently."

She sat down on the veranda. What could this man be doing in the house? she wondered.

"Uncle's all right, isn't he?" she said. "The other day when I came here to visit Akira-san's grave, I dropped in, but he was away on a journey."

"Why don't you come in?" said Sutekichi. "I arrived from Tokyo yesterday myself. I've been invited to stay."

"How nice for Uncle to have someone staying with him. By the way, do you know Akira-san?"

"No, I don't. But I've heard about him. And the dog—do you know him?"

"Oh, indeed," answered Taeko with a laugh. She stretched out her hand to the dog, who was sitting by her feet with a serious look on his face.

"What a beautiful evening glow," she said. At such moments the feeling of elation which she kept in her heart would scatter about her like some special fragrance or brilliance. Looking up at the sky, her face assumed a new beauty.

"Who on earth gave him the name of Friday?"

"Oh, that was Akira-san," said Taeko immediately.

As soon as her uncle returned, Taeko could see that he was in a good mood. His freshly cut hair looked neat. He was a man of few words; yet as he spoke, one was aware of no effort on his part to keep other people at arm's length. He seemed happy that Taeko had visited him. Perhaps this was because he had a stranger in the house and was anxious to please him in any way possible.

"Did Tazuko come to see you?" said Taeko, suddenly remembering about her sister in Kobé.

"She came," said Soroku briefly, and an expression passed over his face as if he had thought of something unpleasant. Taeko judged that her sister's efforts to raise some money had not proved too successful. This was one of the reasons that she had come to visit her uncle today. An even more important reason was that she wanted to ask his assistance in regard to her marriage, but this was the sort of matter she could hardly discuss in front of a stranger such as Sutekichi.

"I've been seeing quite a lot of a schoolfriend of Akira-san these days. The other day when I came to visit Akira's grave, he was there also paying his respects. He was sweeping the tombstone with a temple broom. It's full of dead leaves there, you know."

Soroku listened silently to what she was saying. Clearly the reference to Akira had moved him.

"What is his name?"

"Tsugawa-san," said Taeko. She felt her face glowing and had to make a special effort to control her feelings. "He came to visit the grave. He told me he's been in this house several times and that he knows you too. But that was quite a while ago—when he was very young."

"Really?" said Soroku. To Taeko it sounded like an automatic answer, as though her uncle had not been really listening to what she said. Yet evidently she was mistaken, for suddenly Soroku said: "Isn't he one of Akira's mountain-climbing friends? You know, he used to do quite a lot of mountain-climbing. In the cupboard in his room I found a lot of equipment, though I have no idea of what exactly each thing is used for."

"Yes, that's right," said Taeko cheerfully. "Tsugawa-san has gone on with his mountain-climbing since the war. I remember how he once told me that he suddenly saw a whole flock of birds flying past him on the mountain."

"Really?" said Soroku, and once more he seemed to have lapsed into utter indifference, as if the person about whom she was talking was a perfect stranger.

Then after a moment he turned to Sutekichi, who was being left out of the conversation, and said; "Ata, do you go in for mountain-climbing too?"

"Mountain-climbing?" said Sutekichi. "No."

In Sutekichi's life there had been no scope for activities such as mountaineering.

"No," he repeated, "I've never done any. In fact, I don't even think I'd want to."

"Didn't you ever do any sports at all?" asked Taeko.

"Well, once I went out into a vacant lot with some of my schoolmates and played baseball with a rubber ball. And that was only because they got me to come along as they didn't have enough boys to make up a team."

He was aware himself of the bitter quality of his answer, and in a strange way he felt lonely. He had never particularly disliked sports, but it was simply that having been raised all alone by his mother, he had never acquired the habit of enjoying his youth or his life.

"The only time that Akira ever kept a diary was when he went out mountain-climbing," said Soroku. "I looked through his papers, but there are no diaries from any other period. When he used to go mountain-climbing, he kept a diary for two years running."

"Akira-san," said Taeko in a natural tone. And it occurred to her that her cousin was the one thing that her uncle could not banish from his mind for a single moment. Although it was almost eight years since Akira had died, Soroku still retained the rather cold, strict look of a father.

"It was terrible about Akira-san," said Taeko.

Soroku looked up at Taeko and answered calmly: "There was nothing anyone could possibly do about it."

"But it's lonely without him," said Taeko.

Soroku said nothing. Life without Akira was indeed far too lonely for him to want to hear anyone mention the fact. A shadow of loneliness passed over his face, and he looked like an old man.

"That is something no one can understand," he said. "People may have their own idea about it, but they can't really understand." Then, changing his mood, he looked at Sutekichi: "Haven't you ever done any mountain-climbing?" he asked.

"No, I haven't."

Soroku did not seem to mind the rather cold tone of the reply, and smiling gently, he said: "Well then, let's go on a mountain trip together somewhere, shall we? I haven't done any mountaineering either. It would be nice if we two amateurs went out together."

Taeko could hardly take this seriously. "You couldn't possibly do that, Uncle," she said.

"And why not?"

"Well, it might be all right for Mr. Ata. But it would be an impossible strain for you. You might manage it if you could find some low mountain somewhere, Let me see. I seem to remember hearing that quite elderly people manage to get themselves up Mount Fuji. But the sort of place that Akira went to was in the Japanese Alps."

"Well, I haven't decided yet which mountain I'll climb,"

said Soroku seriously. "You treat me as if I was a really old man. But, anyway, I'm sure that even if I was in my sixties or seventies, I could climb the Alps or anywhere else so long as I went about it the right way. I wouldn't try to go up in the same way as the younger men, mind you."

"In that case I'd advise you to take Ryo-san along as a guide," said Taeko.

"Who?" asked Soroku.

"Oh, a mountain-climbing friend of Akira's. If you get to the point that you can't walk any further, he'll carry you on his back at least!"

Tonight was the first time that Taeko had ever slept at her uncle's house. Perhaps it was because his rupture with her father had unconsciously been reflected in his attitude toward the daughter, but he had never before asked her to spend the night at his house. Taeko couldn't tell when this new attitude on the part of her uncle had started. She had already realized that there had been a definite change in the traditions of the house when she had seen that the young man Sutekichi Ata had been asked to stay.

Next morning Taeko woke up earlier than usual. Looking out of the window, she saw the morning light slanting its way across the green leaves in the old garden and making the branches of the trees and the lawn stand out clearly in relief. She felt happy.

When she emerged onto the open veranda, the dog Friday trotted along with a tinkling of his collar and a wagging of his tail. Taeko was moved by the beauty of the early morning. Then she was reminded of the morning when she had seen Ryosuké playing tennis in Hibiya Park. The green of the grass had now become even greener than she had seen it on that morning.

The night before, she had told her uncle casually about Ryosuké; this was when Sutekichi Ata had gone to have his bath and they were alone together.

Taeko had introduced the subject by announcing: "I'm planning to get married soon."

Soroku looked at her and said: "Well, congratulations to you."

He had said no more, and it had therefore been hard for her to go into details. With her strong-minded nature. it was not easy for Taeko to come out and say that she wanted to ask her uncle for his help.

"I haven't told anybody about it yet," she said. She wanted to specify that she had not mentioned her plan to her parents or to her sister, but instead added: "Not to Kyoto and not to Kobe."

Soroku looked up at her again.

"You mean they don't know about it at your home?" he said with evident surprise. Taeko nodded vigorously. Perhaps because her uncle did not want to interfere he refrained from asking anything about her decision or about the man she was planning to marry.

To cap her previous announcement, Taeko said: "He's an old friend of Akira's."

Soroku looked astonished.

"How old is he?"

"Thirty-one, just the same age as Akira would be."

Soroku turned toward the garden. Emotion showed on his profile. "Would he be that old now?" he said quietly.

"Yes indeed," said Taeko. "He was a good friend of Akira's. You will meet him one of these days, won't you?"

Now in the morning Taeko could hear the sound of someone pumping at the well in the garden. From the sound she could tell that it was a man and not the old housekeeper. She looked out and saw that it was Sutekichi Ata.

He seemed to her to be a gentle, quiet fellow. Now he approached the veranda and lay a wet towel down to dry in the sun. He had on a pair of trousers and an open-necked shirt. He was standing gazing seriously across the garden. He did not realize that Taeko was looking at him, and she could not help smiling at his pensive air.

After they had said good-morning to each other, Sutekichi announced that he was going out for a walk. Taeko felt like taking a walk herself, but she thought that Sutekichi lacked all the cheerfulness which one expected in a young man and that he would not make a very gay companion for a morning stroll.

The housekeeper had just got up. There was time to spare before starting preparations for breakfast. Her uncle was still buried in sleep.

After Sutekichi had left, Taeko heard the sound of the latch clicking on the outside gate. Abruptly she stood up and ran after the young man.

"Do you mind if I come with you?" she said.

He looked surprised, but nodded in assent.

"Where are you going?"

"I haven't decided yet."

Taeko glanced back at the gate to see if Friday was following them. As she stood there, Sutekichi started to walk. He was clearly a rather odd character and Taeko began to feel a certain interest in him.

"Do you always take walks without knowing where you're going?"

"Yes, that's right," said Sutekichi, but at the same time he was thinking of where Taeko might like to go.

He took the road by the mountain side in the opposite direction from the town.

"The walks people usually take when they come to Kamakura are extremely uninteresting," said Sutekichi in the positive manner of a young man. "Most well-known places and historical locations are artifical, and in any case, they are all thoroughly vulgarized by sightseers." Taeko did not dispute his words, and he continued: "Even the Hachiman Shrine is like that, isn't it? It really is a letdown to see how they've started renting boats on the Gempei Pond. Whenever a place begins to get popular, greed enters into the picture."

"Do you have a job, Ata-san?"

"I'm a teacher."

"Then I'll be your pupil," said Taeko with a frank cheerfulness. "Please teach me anything you like."

A bitter smile passed over Sutekichi's face as he walked up the mountain road, his body bent slightly forward.

He spoke very little, but occasionally he would look aside. They were coming now to the top of the hill. There were no more houses, and by the roadside there were graves.

Suddenly Sutekichi stopped and looked back in the direction from where they had come.

"That's the Hachiman Shrine," he said.

"Which do you mean?" asked Taeko, looking in the direction to which Sutekichi pointed. The hills were covered with green foliage. Right in the midst of this green she could see the two-storied vermilion gate of the Hachiman Shrine. It was a side view, and the gate appeared to be lifted up as though it were resting on a shelf. The gate and the roof of the shrine made a mass of vermilion color against the green of the hills. The roofs of the other houses were low and sank into the summer green-ery as though into an ocean. Only the two-storied gate stood out clearly.

Sutekichi looked into the distance with a proud expression on his face.

"This is the place to see the Hachiman Shrine from," he said. "There's nothing vulgar about this view. It's magnificent, isn't it?"

Taeko nodded. This really was an original angle from which to view the famous shrine. The two-storied tower stood there by itself, as if it were a vermilion-lacquered ship floating clearly on a sea.

"It's because you can't see any people that it looks so noble," said Taeko.

"Well, that might possibly be the reason," said Sutekichi, evidently not wishing to agree too thoroughly with his "pupil."

"Ata-*sensei*," said Taeko suddenly, "are you a teacher of philosophy?"

"Me?" said Sutekichi with astonishment. "What makes you think that?"

"Oh, I just had that impression."

Sutekichi blushed. "No, by no means," he said. I'm just a plain history teacher."

"You like studying, don't you?"

"Very searching questions!" said Sutekichi, blushing again. "Yes, I admit I do like it."

"That's the feeling I had."

Sutekichi fell into silent embarrassment. He had become a teacher in order to make a living—not that he wasn't interested in educating his pupils, but the need for a salary had become more important than all his studies.

The mountain road looked as if it collided head on into the

mountain, but then suddenly they came to an open-mouthed tunnel.

"This tunnel comes out at Yato," said Sutekicho. "Would you like to go through, or shall we go down to Hikakugaya?"

"Wherever you say," answered Taeko. "I'm your pupil, you see."

"But there's really nothing I can teach you," said Sutekichi, suddenly becoming very serious. "My students are all of high-school level. You're too old for me."

In the tunnel it was dark and the drops of water falling from the roof had made the road muddy. Their voices, echoing on the rock walls sounded louder than normal —not like their own voices at all.

"If it were possible," said Sutekichi, "I'd work on my own speciality rather than teach children. I don't really feel that I have the proper qualifications for teaching yet. But things haven't turned out as I had hoped."

He was silent for a while, then continued with a sudden access of youthful excitement: "I had an idea of what life should be like. One thing I very much wanted to do—walk along the route that Alexander the Great took when he marched from Europe to attack India. There are all sorts of remains along that route and any amount of interesting material waiting to be excavated. I used to think that I might continue my studies by making my way along that route. . . ."

When they emerged from the tunnel, the sun shone dazzlingly in their eyes.

"I didn't want to learn everything from books; I wanted to see with my own eyes famous places in Persia and Afghanistan."

"Do you like traveling?"

Taeko's question acted as a sudden dampener on Sutekichi's enthusiasm.

"I don't mind it," he blurted out in an almost angry tone.

What he had been telling her was a dream that had rested in his mind since his youth, and now he regretted having let it slip out of his mouth in such a way as to give the impression that he was very confident of his own abilities.

The Englishman Sir Aurel Stein had, he recalled, made his way along the route taken by Alexander the Great, and German scholars had also examined it thoroughly. Sutekichi was also familiar with the research conducted by an English university on the remains of the ancient city of Taxilla situated in modern Pakistan and knew that their findings were soon to be published. How stimulated he had been to hear of this work! It had intoxicated him in his younger days to think of setting off by himself on an expedition over the route—an expedition that no Japanese scholar had so far been able to undertake—and he had pictured himself returning to write a book, a real contribution to world history.

But he had to make a decent living, and his dream had begun to languish. Then he had read about a party of students crossing Central Asia in a Citroën, and later about a group of American scholars mounting a large-scale expedition to the Victory Memorial that Darius the Great had left on a great stone wall in the desert. The Americans had been equipped with large quantities of color film and the most modern measuring instruments, and it had struck Sutekichi that the days of Marco Polo or of the Priest Sanzo, when people walked thousands of miles on foot to make their discoveries, had really passed. Now expeditions and surveys of this type could be carried out with relative ease. It was regrettable that his country and he himself were unable to participate in any of this work simply because of the expense. The great ambitions of his youth, which had seemed quite dreamlike in their impossibility of realization, had now become utterly reasonable—if only he had the money.

Sutekchi's research projects required as their first condition the ability to pursue work on the spot. He had studied under Professor Toshiki Imai and had engraved on his mind the idea that history must at no point be separated from geography; according to Imai, no historical research was orthodox unless it was accompanied by investigations on the actual site.

Sutekichi guided Taeko down the hillside through the grass where the cicadas were crying. As they reached level ground, they came to rows of houses standing side by side: even in this remote spot few places were left uninhabited.

Taeko noticed golden-banded lilies blooming on the cliffside.

"Oh, look at those wonderful lilies!" she exclaimed. Sutekichi stopped and looked up. But it made little difference to him whether lilies were blooming or not. Taeko, as she looked at them, was reminded of the glitter of the ocean under the cliff at Izu that evening when she had held the lilies in her arms. Also she thought of Oshima Island, misty in the offing, asleep in the dark sea.

"Do you swim, Ata-san?" she asked.

"I hate swimming," replied Sutekichi rather curtly. "I don't mind when there aren't any people about, though."

"I see," said Taeko cheerfully, thinking that this was the first time she had really agreed with the young man. She looked up at his face and suddenly realized that she was at a loss for what to say. Her face was beautifully shaded, and she felt supremely happy.

"I wouldn't want to go swimming at Yuigahama, either," she said, "with all those crowds of people."

"I agree," said Sutekichi. "Now if it were the River Indus, I'd gladly go in, even if there were crocodiles swimming about in the water!"

Taeko was not aware that the Indus was the river that Alexander the Great had traveled to on his expedition.

That morning Taeko returned to Tokyo. She had taken the day off from her office and could certainly have stayed on in Kamakura. But her uncle said nothing to detain her and so she returned to Tokyo in the midst of the summer heat, mentioning something about an appointment with a friend.

Before leaving, she had a talk with her uncle about the money her sister from Kobe had tried to borrow.

"Tazuko told me she would call here again. But please tell her I absolutely refuse to lend the money and that she'll be wasting her time if she comes here. Once I've refused something I'm going to go on refusing it, however many times she asks me."

Until now Taeko had felt fairly indifferent about her sister's problem, but after hearing her uncle's categorical words, she could not help feeling sorry for her.

"It's a shame," she said, sighing unconsciously. Then, all of a sudden collecting her courage, she added: "Uncle, please try to help Tazuko in some way. If you don't, she'll be in great trouble."

Soroku evidently chose to ignore this plea and remained silent.

"That's really so, you know," pursued Taeko.

"You mustn't speak about things that don't concern you," said Soroku severely. "When Tazuko came out here last time, I was utterly exhausted. She got on my nerves, and I may have given her rather a curt answer. But the fact is, I wish she wasn't always asking for things for herself."

"It's because she considers you her uncle," said Taeko.

"It's just a nuisance, that's all, " said Soroku with an air of annoyance.

In view of her uncle's pique, Taeko did not broach her own affair. It was clear to her now that in dealing with this man, who had charged interest on money he had given his own son, financial matters were taboo, and she was determined not to touch on such things if she could possibly help it.

After Taeko had left, Soroku relaxed in the company of Sutekichi. Inevitably the subject of Taeko came up in their conversation.

"I don't quite know what to say about her," began Soroku, "except that she's a rather unfortunate girl." Sutekichi looked up with interest.

"It's a private matter," continued Soroku, "and not very pleasant to mention. But actually she's the child my elder brother had with a maid who was working at his house. My sister-in-law more or less took her over, but all the same she's different from the other children."

Sutekichi was started at the indifferent manner in which Soroku mentioned this matter—a matter which, he felt, should certainly not have been revealed to an outsider.

"I don't like her father," continued Soroku.

"He's your elder brother, isn't he?" said Sutekichi.

"I don't regard him as my elder brother," answered Soroku bluntly. His tone seemed quite unsuitable for his gentle personality. "We don't have anything to do with each other. But his children occasionally come and visit me. Perhaps because I don't like my brother I'm rather inclined to favor the daughter who was born as the result of his misconduct."

Sutekichi said nothing. He did not like hearing private matters concerning other people's families.

"Well, it's not of much importance," said Soroku, looking out at the garden. "It looks as if it's going to be another hot day, doesn't it."

"Yes indeed," said Sutekichi, breaking into a smile.

The matter of Taeko was still in Soroku's mind. He could not help comparing her with her elder sister.

"Her sister, you see, was brought up to be selfish and extravagant," he said after a while. "What a difference between her and Taeko, who since she came to Tokyo has been making her own living as an office girl, or a typist, or whatever it is. I didn't think she'd be able to manage, but somehow she gets on all right without receiving the slightest help from her family. Perhaps circumstances have taught her how to fend for herself, or perhaps she'd been planning for a long time to leave home and was prepared to look after herself. In any case, she seems to be managing very well on her own."

It occurred to Sutekichi that there was no trace in Taeko of the type of childhood that Soroku had mentioned. She was as gay as a flower in the field. There must be something very exceptional in the character of a girl who, despite such an unfortunate birth, could remain cheerful and innocent and without the slightest bitterness.

When Soroku had left the room, Sutekichi set himself to the task of reading the proofs which Professor Segi had given him so that he might earn a little extra money during the vacation. The proofs consisted of a collection of *samurai* letters from the time of the civil wars. It was dull work and, because of the frequent use of unusual characters, extremely laborious. Some of the letters were by famous warrior-statesmen such as Oda Nobunaga—hardly a companion whom Sutekichi would have chosen for a hot summer day. After working for a while, he looked at his watch. Not two hours had elapsed since Taeko's departure.

All of a sudden Sutekichi felt that he disliked being in Kamakura, and he became anxious to return to Tokyo, even though here it was pleasantly cool and in the city suffocatingly hot. He had not noticed it while she was here, but now that she had left, there was something strangely empty and boring about the atmosphere of the house. He put aside the proofs and went out. This feeling of vacancy would surely pass over, he told himself, if he could only get his mind onto something else.

He walked down to the beach and onto the cape. There were no swimmers here. He settled himself on a rock that jutted out into the sea and gazed at the blue water as the wind blew on him. His vacant feeling had disappeared now, and in its place, Taeko had entered his mind.

The story about her birth which Soroku had inadvertently mentioned had moved Sutekichi, and he could not forget about it. The noon sea glittered, expanding and contracting the deep blue shadow of its surface. He could see the reflection of the rock on which he was sitting. Water insects were jumping in and out of a little hollow on the rock. Apart from them, there was only a little child playing with a fishing-net.

The sun shone strongly, and the breeze from the ocean blew pleasantly on his dry skin. The wide summer sky was as bright as if a tube of paint had been dissolved over its surface. It was quiet. This was real happiness for Sutekichi—to sit here on a rock by himself thinking his own thoughts with the wind blowing on him. That his thoughts should be occupied by a young girl such as Taeko was, however, most unusual.

The tide was coming in and, before he knew it the waves had started to wash high on the sandbanks where the child was playing. The water splashed against the rock, making a peaceful gurgling sound. Even the little hollow on the rock was filling with water, and the insects moved away from it in a group.

Taeko and he had quite a lot in common, thought Sutekichi. For one thing, they were both engaged in work that they did not like and which they had to pursue regularly if they wanted to make a living. But Takeo, who as a woman was supposed to be the weaker of the two, could put up with it and remain cheerful and gentle.

Sutekichi looked back at his troubled life. What had become of his ambition to trace the eastward route of Alexander the Great? He could not remember exactly when it had begun to vanish. Of course, it had all been a chimera—a mere childish dream, like wanting to become a pirate who roams about the world, or, in the case of modern boys, a famous baseball player.

Yes, his hopes had shrunk since then. Apart from the process of growing up, the social uneasiness of the postwar period was responsible for this shrinking process. The age of individualism had come to Japan too late. It was an excellent thing, of course, that the dignity of human rights had finally come to be respected. But at exactly the same time Japan had entered the age in which it was considered essential, in order to eliminate social injustice, that people suppress their egos and submit themselves to a system of centralized organization. In these conditions Sutekichi had come to realize that scholarly research was virtually out of the question for a young man who was born poor. And, after all, what meaning was there in delving into research on Alexander the Great and such subjects when people were dying of starvation by the roadside.

Young plants anxious to grow up in their individual ways soon atrophied in the poverty and atmosphere of these times. It was different for a solid personality, like Professor Segi, deeply rooted in the earth. He was an old well-implanted tree. But the roots of young scholars were shrunken, and in the strong gales of the postwar world it was hardly possible to cultivate noble spirits imbued with the desire for patient research. The existence of Alexander the Great—about which there was, of course, no historical doubt—had, it occurred to Sutekichi, become thin and shadowy, as though he were merely a hero in a fairy tale. This was the reason that the young man had lost his courage. The thought came to him that if he had been born fifty years earlier, or in the world that would exist fifty years from now, things would be different. He was not aware that human beings in whatever age they live always belong to a period of uneasy transition from the past to the future. That the agony of the present world should become the totality of the human problem was only natural for a young man.

Yet, despite all these doubts, Sutekichi's feelings today were different from usual. When he returned to Soroku's house and was informed by the old housekeeper in the kitchen that Taeko had left her compact in the bathroom, he said: "I shall bring it to her myself. I'm going back to Tokyo."

9 · THE STAIRCASE

THE SETTING sun glared down on the streets, but within the stone building the lights were on in the corridors and offices, and it seemed to be nighttime. According to the middle-aged receptionist, Taeko had already gone home, since the time had come for the office to close. Sutekichi noticed that some of the men were still sitting at their desks working. They had taken off their jackets, but looked very hot nevertheless.

"What time does she come in the morning?"

The woman replied in a tired and not too friendly tone: "At about nine o'clock. If you want to see her, you'd better come about noontime."

Sutekichi thanked her and started down the stone staircase. The compact that Taeko had forgotten was still where he had put it in his coat pocket. It was not a particularly valuable article, and he could just as well have left it for her at the reception desk. But he had no such thought in mind. He intended to come to this place again himself.

In his absence from the city a special-delivery letter from Professor Segi had been left for him at his flat. In it the professor asked him to meet him at the usual place on the Yuraku-cho at eight o'clock that evening. This was a small drinking establishment where he usually stopped on his way back from conferences.

It was still too early to go there, however. Holding Taeko's compact in his pocket, Sutekichi stopped by the side of the street, and wondered where he might go and wait until eight. An empty taxi was moving slowly along the road, looking for a customer. Thinking that Sutekichi was a likely prospect, the driver drove close to him and looked into his face. He was just about to open the door when Sutekichi flurriedly waved his hand in refusal and started to walk off.

The offices were all closing and the pavements were crowded. The shopwindows, which had now been illuminated, were hidden from sight by the throngs of passers-by. The thick wall of people's bodies stopped any breeze and made the air even more sultry.

Sutekichi found a slightly less crowded street and began walking along it. He had no special purpose in mind. He had intended to invite Taeko out and to talk with her for a while over a cool drink; for this he had brought some money with him. But his plans had gone awry. Between some pleasant-looking little restaurants and teashops he noticed shopwindows in which antiques and imported goods were displayed. The idea came to him that he could please Taeko by giving her some present when he returned the compact. It was like a sudden rise in the temperature of his body, and he could not get rid of the idea. "Of course, I'm rather poor, but . . ." However inebriated he might be by his plan, he would not forget these introductory words. It was by no means impossible, he thought, that he should give Taeko some modest present suitable to his purse. He felt happy to think that she would accept a present from him, however small, so long as she knew that it came from his heart.

He walked up to one of the shopwindows which displayed foreign goods, but felt embarrassed as soon as he started to look. Each of the articles on display seemed threateningly luxurious to him. Evidently it was not customary to attach price tags to them, and Sutekichi was quite unable to distinguish the quality of the articles from looking at them. He had no idea of what they were for. There were some unusually beautiful ornaments there, too.

It was all right to look at the things from the outside this way, but he was sure that he would be put to shame if he should enter the shop and that he would blunder hopelessly.

What about a book? he suddenly thought, and became more cheerful. Yes, indeed, what could be more suitable as a first present? Books never went out of fashion, like ornaments. Besides, they were incomparably cheaper, and also very elegant. Finally, he had no doubt that Taeko liked books.

He came to a new shop where Western books were on display and entered. He had no idea of what sort of a book he would buy for her and thought that he would decide after looking about the shelves—perhaps find some fairly simple book about Alexander the Great. But things in this world do not go as one expects. There was not a single book about history in the shop. The only books available were about the present, and there was nothing of an authoritative nature. Sutekichi's heart began to beat joyfully, however, when he came on a collection of English poetry. Yes, a book of poetry would make an attractive present. But when he looked at them, he found that he didn't know the name of even a single author. He had read very little in the way of literature, but he knew that the more modern the poet was, the harder his writing was to understand. He could not imagine that any of these ultramodern poems would be suitable for Taeko. Then once more he cheered up as he noticed an attractively illustrated book of fairy tales for children. But, after all, would Taeko really be pleased to receive a book just because it was pretty? Wouldn't she feel that he was making light of her? If it came to that, he might as well give her a pretty box of chocolates. Once more he felt disappointed. He was determined to select the right thing, even if it were only a small present.

"Have you got any Japanese postcards?"

A clear feminine voice came from across the shelf where Sutekichi was standing.

"No, I am afraid we don't, Madam," the shop attendant answered politely.

"Then what about a photo album that would be suitable to send abroad as a gift? Lots of publishers must have brought out albums like that."

Sutekichi glanced up at the speaker and then opened his

eyes wide. She was a Japanese lady, but wearing an evening gown, and, looking at her from behind, he saw that her pretty neck and shoulders were daringly exposed. She was dressed in an impressive style that one would never see on the street, but only in the movies.

Mrs. Iwamuro laughed and, turning around, spoke in English to the Westerner who was accompanying her.

"They don't have any postcards, but they do have photo books."

Her companion too was elegantly dressed in evening clothes. He turned his healthy-looking face and began to examine one of the albums.

"Don't you have any scenes from Nikko? The Toshogu or the sleeping cat or something like that?" asked Mrs. Iwamuro, interpreting the foreigner's words. Beneath her long white skirt, with its beautiful pleats, one could see a pair of slim silver shoes. Her necklace was of white pearls. In the brightly lit shop Mrs. Iwamuro's outstanding looks showed up strikingly. Outside the window passers-by had stopped and were peering in, but evidently this woman was used to being looked at, and her manner remained composed and natural. Her splendid figure seemed to have come directly from some extravagant soiree or dance; now it moved along one of the bookshelves. She stood in front of a number of magazines spread out near Sutekichi, picked up one of them, and, opening it quickly, glanced at it.

"Jimmy!" she called loudly to her companion. "Is this a baby penguin? How sweet! I must buy this."

Sutekichi looked at the magazine and recognized it as a well-known geographical magazine published in America.

The young man was aware of the word "lady," but until then he had never seen one in the flesh. Her lipstick, to be sure, was rather dark and garish, but this made little difference to him. Yet he could not restrain a certain scholarly smile when he saw that she had taken that geographical magazine to be simply something about baby penguins—not that the magazine itself was such a very scholarly thing. Not only was Sutekichi rather surprised at this display of ignorance, but also he could not help feeling critical.

A woman as gorgeously dressed as Mrs. Iwamuro could certainly not have arrived on foot. And indeed a modern car of the finest color and design stood waiting on the street outside. Her foreign companion escorted her to the car and helped her get in. Then they glided smoothly away into the beautifully illuminated summer evening.

"I see," said Sutekichi to himself, smiling sardonically, while at the same time admiring the car. "Well, if she had walked down the Ginza looking like that, and not come in a car, she would have looked like one of those decorated floats in the festivals."

He set about looking for the present he had temporarily forgotten during Mrs. Iwamuro's presence in the shop. Then he bought a collection of poems and left the place.

Evening had begun to flood the city recklessly with fluorescent and neon lights. It was not yet night, and the dim light of the summer evening modulated the green of the trees along the street. When Sutekichi looked at his watch, he noticed that there was still quite a lot of time until the appointed hour. But time did not seem very long when he started to think of Taeko.

"How noisy and crazy it is—a town full of people like this!" he thought; at the same time he remembered that he had not known how to answer when Taeko had seriously asked him in the morning in Kamakura whether he was studying philosophy. If he really wanted to carry out those studies, he could do it, he told himself emphatically. Yes, he could even explore the road that Alexander the Great had trod, if he did not let himself become overpowered by the hardships of life. Of course, Taeko must agree with his plans. Indeed, not only must she agree, but also she must passionately encourage him. He immediately saw himself as the leader of a well-equipped expedition setting out by airplane for the starting-point in Athens. Yes, it would be a task with great scholarly significance—not like climbing the Himalayas.

Though it was still early, Sutekichi went to the small drinking-place. It was on the second floor of a building near the Yurakucho market; from a narrow entrance one climbed up a flight of wooden stairs. Directly opposite the building, the trolley tracks crossed a bridge, and the trolleys were constantly running to and fro. Each time that one of them passed, the roughly constructed building shook as if there had been a small earthquake. When the customers had had a few drinks, however, none of them bothered about this in the slightest. The noise of the passing trolleys made it necessary for even Professor Segi to raise his voice to a high pitch. According to the professor, having to shout while one was drinking made the wine take effect rapidly; he accordingly praised the place for its cheapness.

Segi had settled his broad frame by the wooden partition in the shop and was talking to the owner while waiting for Sutekichi's arrival. As usual, he had become heatedly interested in what he was saying, and his face was shining.

"Hullo!" he shouted simply when he saw Sutekichi enter. Then, lowering his voice as if to say something confidential, he fixed the owner of the shop, who stood there in his cook's clothes, and who had started to leave on seeing Sutekichi, and continued with his story: "And so you see . . ."

So the professor was off again, thought Sutekichi, and felt a smile come to his face. The owner of the shop had been chosen as the victim because there was no one else there.

"Yes, the artificial eye he had swallowed passed through his stomach, down through the intestines, and finally appeared at the terminus, "the professor was saying.

"Yes, to be sure," said the owner of the shop, fully aware that he himself was an uneducated man, and he listened respectfully to the story, since it came from a university professor.

"When children used to swallow coins accidentally," continued Segi, "their mothers made them eat sweet potatoes. That was in the old days, or, rather, I should say the days when we still had copper coins in Japan—in other words, not so long ago as all that. Nowadays, of course, a real copper coin is quite a valuable thing in itself. . . . Well, that man I'm telling you about—he had quite a shock, and suddenly he remembered about his mother, though, to be sure, he had not been a very dutiful son. So he had someone go and buy some sweet potatoes for him, and he munched away at them. It didn't help in the slightest. Next he used a purge, but the false eye still remained where it was. So he called the doctor."

"Yes, I see," said the proprietor.

"Well, the doctor immediately started to examine him. But suddenly he turned pale and rushed out carrying his bag. People followed the doctor and asked him what had happened. That

man was staring at me through his buttocks!' said the doctor.
'Quite terrifying!' "

The first person to burst out laughing was the professor himself, but for a moment the proprietor did not realize that the
story had been a joke.

"Ha, ha, ha! How do you like that?" said Segi.

At last the proprietor understood and burst out laughing.

"You really are a rascal, Professor," he said. "I was honestly
worried about that poor man and was wondering what on earth
would happen to his false eye."

The professor returned to a more serious demeanor.

"You know the Japanese expression: 'to look at someone
through one's buttocks,' meaning to look at him disdainfully,
don't you?"

"Really, Professor!" said the proprietor.

"But it's quite true: if one swallows a false eye, one's bound
to glare at someone through one's buttocks. Now I don't know
whether this particular eye was made of glass or some plastic
material, but in any case it goggled at the poor doctor. However
experienced a doctor he may have been, he could hardly help
being shocked at such a sight. Ha, ha, ha!"

The professor turned to Sutekichi. "Do sit down," he said.
"Thank you for doing that proofreading."

The proprietor left the room laughing, and the waitress
brought in some saké and a saké cup for Sutekichi.

Sutekichi looked for somewhere to put his book, but finding
no suitable place put it on the table.

"Oh, so you've bought a book?" said the professor. "I envy
you."

Before Sutekichi knew it, the professor had stretched out his
hand and picked up the book, which was still in its wrapping.

"You don't mind if I look at it, do you?" he said. "What sort
of a book is it?" Not realizing that Sutekichi was blushing, the
professor undid the wrappings and read the title.

"Oh, a collection of poems. How very tender!"

The professor removed his glasses. A cheerful, mischievous
smile seemed to play on his eyes. He leafed through the book
with a look of admiration. Sutekichi had chosen as a present for
Taeko a collection of ancient and modern love poems, and it
was for this reason that he was blushing.

"Very nice," said the professor with a sigh. "Although I look like this now, there was a time when I used to enjoy reading such poems. Of course, that was before I began to bury myself in musty documents. Then I was a handsome boy whose heart beat to the poetry of love. That's how things degenerate in this world—it's a case of handsome boy turning into a fusty old professor, isn't it?

"Yes, it's very nice," repeated the professor after a pause.

Sutekichi recognized these words as a sort of danger signal, and he tightened himself up in preparation. Something bad almost always happened after the professor said: "It's very nice."

Segi put down the book. "Ah," he said, picking up his saké cup and urging Sutekichi to join him in a toast.

"Let's drink to your good health," he said.

"Why that, all of a sudden?" asked Sutekichi, smiling shyly.

The professor only said "Hmm" by way of answer, and, picking up the collection of poems once again, looked at it seriously.

"Shall I read you something, Suté-san? I see they're all translated into Japanese. All right?"

> " 'If I compare how I felt before I met her
> And how I felt thereafter,
> Then I must say that in former days
> I knew naught of tender thoughts.' "

The effect of the saké could already be seen on the professor's cheerful face as he recited the poem.

"It's very nice, Suté-san, isn't it?" he said.

"Is that poem included in the book?" asked Sutekichi.

"Yes, it must be here somewhere. If it weren't included, you really couldn't call this an anthology of ancient and modern poems. Well, what's happened? Have you begun to have tender thoughts like that?"

The question came as a surprise to Sutekichi, and he felt confused.

"No, I, you see—" he stammered.

"Don't try to hide things. It's splendid to have tender thoughts. Since the war young people have become completely incapable of really having such thoughts. . . ."

He interrupted his remarks and lifted the saké cup to his mouth once more. He was clearly in a good humor.

"It isn't really a matter of their having adopted the American style," he continued. "Rather, I'd be inclined to call it the Japanese-American style. Things go wrong in the process of translation from the American into the Japanese. If you look round in a trolley, for instance, you're quite likely to see Americans who really do have tender feelings. There's something tender about the way they give their arms to a girl. But when a young Japanese man does the same thing, it's all unutterably false. If you want to look at it in a sympathetic way, I suppose you can say that they simply aren't used to these things. But really, it's so affected that I find it quite intolerable. It's all just a matter of appearances—a sort of etiquette, you know. I can't stand it. What can be worse than pure etiquette without any spirit behind it? I can very well see that if we have to send some newly made representatives abroad we have to give them pamphlets on etiquette to take along, so that they'll know how to behave themselves in foreign countries. Otherwise they might be a national disgrace. But at home in their own country I don't see why they have to try to imitate Americans so much. And why can't our young people have tender feelings? In any case I'd like you, Suté-san, to have such feelings. Ah, let's have a toast. To your amour!"

Something the professor's rambling remarks struck Sutekichi's heart directly and aroused a defensive attitude in him. Yet the poisoned dart that the professor had released also unexpectedly cheered him. Sutekichi even felt a desire to become drunk on saké, which did not fit at all into his usual serious character.

"The fact is," said the professor, "in Japan it's only ugly old men like me, isn't it true, who can afford to be pleasant to women in front of other people?" His remarks had once more assumed a general tone. "I'm not trying to blow my own trumpet, or anything of the sort. But it seems to me that that's how things are. Now, by nature I'm inclined to be unkind to women myself, even if I'm asked to be nice. . . . Perhaps it's all because Japanese people aren't really made to take things in an easy way. At any rate, as soon as a young Japanese man feels he has to do something, it becomes strained and deliberate. They're making a conscious effort, you see—like poor people when they begin spending money. They can't do it in a natural way, so they become self-conscious about it. 'Look at me spending money!' they seem to say. And thereby they lose. Because, without knowing it, they make themselves conspicuous—just like pickpockets or thieves. Now these young men who force themselves to behave in a special way in trolleys and other public places, they're a kind of thief themselves. If things go wrong, they're the type who will turn on others with a revolver."

The professor paused for a moment. "Now a thing like modern love," he continued, "isn't it just like robbing the other person by cheating him? It's the same on both sides—men and women. Come on, Suté-san, drink up!"

"I don't mind," said Sutekichi. "But are you sure it's all right for you to drink so much, Professor?"

"You mean that I may get drunk?"

"Well, I'll see that you get home if you do."

"You needn't worry about my difficulties," said Segi with a proud air. "You think I'm an old man, don't you? But I still have a heart that's capable of throbbing when I read love poems."

"Really, Professor?" said Sutekichi.

"The only trouble is, it's become a nuisance. You see, I'm plagued by the thing called understanding. That man Musei Tokugawa is a real rascal, you know. The other day, when I met him again after a long time, he asked me what I enjoyed doing most in the world apart from my work. I thought about it carefully and gave him a completely honest answer. 'Well, let's see,' I said, 'I'm most happy when I'm sitting on the veranda of my house and dreamily looking at the plants in my garden.'

"When he heard this, he gave out a rather disagreeable grunt. 'Have you reached the point of liking stones?' he said.

"I told him I didn't have any special interest in things like stones.

" 'That's a good thing,' he said. 'When people start taking an interest in stones, it means that they've got an affinity for tombstones. You're quite safe until you reach that point.' Then he kept on repeating, 'So you've got to liking plants, have you?' After a while he asked me: 'What about beautiful women? There are fewer of them about these days, aren't there?'

"Without thinking, I answered him honestly: 'Yes, there don't seem to be many left.'

"Then old Musei's straw-colored face broke into a smile. 'Oh, I see,' he said with a knowing look.

"When I thought about it afterwards, I realized that he'd baited me. Because, by saying that there weren't any beauties left in the world, it really meant that my heart was rarely moved nowadays when looking at women. In fact, I was admitting that I had approached the state of cold stones and dried-up trees —that I had become an old man, in short. I'd known this when he asked me, I should have answered: 'Oh yes, I'm forever being bothered by seeing beautiful women!' Damnation! That chap Musei tricked me completely, didn't he? Ha, ha, ha, Suté-san. But it's very nice at your age. Even a woman who looks as if she's come out of a cage in the zoo strikes you young fellows as the fairest of the fair. They look like Yang Kuei Fei or Cleopatra, don't they?"

Then the professor asked Sutekichi about Soroku Okamoto. Their journey to Niigata had been aimed at finding some ancient literary documents that were still held by old families and temples in Sado. Their harvest, however, had not been as rich as they had expected; instead of valuable manuscripts, they had picked up Soroku. He had by now become a pleasant topic of conversation when they talked about the past.

"Well, have you seen our Mr. Okamoto since the other day?" said the professor.

"Yes." Sutekichi's cheeks, already slightly flushed with alcohol, became redder still. "I just came back from seeing him yesterday."

"Is he all right? You didn't notice any bad symptoms, did you?"

"There's nothing to worry about. He's back on his feet."

But you could not always tell these things just from the outside appearance, warned the professor. "Human beings, you see, are constructed in a remarkably complicated way. Very often they do not show their real feelings at all. And you can't take them apart, like watches or radios, to examine them. . . . When people are thinking very intently about something, they often become silent. They instinctively want to avoid making contact with the world and jogging their nerves. So they turn away, they become taciturn and expressionless. When you see Mr. Okamoto, does he talk a lot?"

It was hard for Sutekichi to answer one way or the other. There were times when Soroku chattered away pleasantly, but it also happened that he fell into complete silence.

"On the whole he's not too talkative," said Sutekichi.

"In fact, he's just like me," said Segi with a composed look. "Yes, he's the very image of me. He's tender and gentle by nature. However, I don't want to commit suicide—not that I'm a Christian, but I simply don't want to do such a thing."

"I don't think you need worry about that, Professor."

"You shouldn't be quite so sure about that. When you dismiss the possibility so easily, it really stirs me into wanting to do it. But if I should decide on such a step, I'll carry it out in a really spectacular way—in a way that no suicide has ever planned before, since the beginning of history. By the way, does Mr. Okamoto read the newspaper properly every morning?"

This struck Sutekichi as being something of a loaded question, not unlike the ones that Musei Tokugawa had asked the professor.

"Yes, he does."

"Does he read the gossip column and the sections on current affairs?"

"Yes indeed."

"Well, that's a relief. If he was at the stage of not reading newspapers, one really might have to worry about him. People who are interested in finding out what critics have to say about the new films for the week aren't likely to go hang themselves. It's safer for people to stay worldly!"

"But you rather dislike the newspapers, don't you, Professor?" said Sutekichi with a slightly bantering air.

"Well," replied the professor nonchalantly, "I read them all the same. What I don't like is to be controlled by the newspapers. As long as they don't try to control me, it's all right. And it isn't only newspapers. I hate everything that tries to control human beings, whether it's the government or the military or the Communists."

"Come to think of it," said Sutekichi, "Mr. Okamoto doesn't only take the ordinary newspapers, but special papers concerning stocks and shares. And he reads them with the greatest interest as soon as they're delivered."

The professor stared at Sutekichi, then suddenly stretched

out his arm and seized the young man's hand firmly.

"Ah, in that case he certainly isn't going to die. When people have such desires, they're quite safe."

"He has a big house, you know. He'd be delighted if you visited him once, Professor."

"Would he really?" The professor removed the saké cup from his mouth and looked up. "If Mr. Okamoto saw my face, he'd remember the suicide incident, and he wouldn't feel a bit happy. In fact, it would be very unpleasant for him."

"Oh no, sir," said Sutekichi with some surprise. "If you really think that, surely the same thing applies in my case. Perhaps I am an unwanted guest, for that matter."

"You're young."

"He's an extremely nice, gentle man, you know," said Sutekichi. I know how thankful he feels toward you, Professor."

"Well, that's his business," said the professor absently. The saké seemed to have taken effect, as one could judge from the sudden changes in direction of his conversation. A further standard sign of inebriation was a tendency of the professor to repeat himself. His students were all used to this particular symptom. However amusing the professor's witticisms might be, they became a cause for concern rather than laughter after they had been repeated a few times.

"Well, is that so?" he said, picking up Sutekichi's book once more. "A collection of love poems, is it? You've become like that, have you, Suté-san? A bit late in the day for you, isn't it? But perhaps you're one of those great talents that tend to mature late. I, on the other hand, graduated from the stage of love songs and collections of love poems while I was still at school. I reached the point of not needing poems or songs any longer. I managed very well without them!"

"Yes, I'm sure, Professor," said Sutekichi, looking rapidly at his watch. "It's almost ten o'clock, you know. Shall I take you home by and by?"

"Not yet. First we'll have another bottle of saké. This charming book of yours can serve as an accompaniment to our drinking. Yes, this can only happen when one is young. The stars shining in the sky and on earth the forget-me-nots blooming. What a happy thing it is! And reading poems the while. A shame we don't have any cheap stuff to drink. But let's drink this slowly. I say, Suté-san, does this book have the poem of Omar Khayyám? 'The Rubaiyat.' Of course, that gives rather an impression of aged love. The tune is a decadent one, not youthful. Let's see. I think I remember a few of the verses. Yes, I've got a good memory. Let's see. . . ." The professor closed his eyes in an effort to help his memory. "Ah, yes, now I remember:

> *'Ah, make the most of what we yet may spend,*
> *Before we too into the Dust descend. . . .'*

It's a translation by Yano Hojon. Now let's have a verse about saké. This is translated by Ogawa Ryosaku. Excuse me if I make a mistake.

> *'Ah, with the Grape my fading Life provide,*
> *And wash the Body whence the Life has died. . . .'*"

Then, turning to the proprietor, Segi said to him in a loud voice: "Old chap, when I'm reborn, I shall be coming up the stairs of this house without fail."

Sutekichi helped the professor as he tottered out into the street. Yurakucho Station was directly in front of them, but Segi said that he wanted to walk as far as Tokyo Station so that they might enjoy the evening breeze.

"I say, Suté-san, have you really got a sweetheart?"

Sutekichi was too embarrassed to answer. The professor walked along the pavement with his body bent forward and his head hanging heavily. He seemed to have forgotten his question.

Marunouchi with its large office buildings was already as dark, as if it were midnight, and there were hardly any pedestrians. The only sound was that of their shoes as they walked along the night streets under the heavy branches of the trees.

"I'm sleepy," said Segi. He looked up, stopped walking and seemed to be trying to determine where he was. When he saw that Sutekichi was with him, he said: "Oh, it's you, is it?" in a rather discouraged tone of voice and started to walk again. He appeared to be walking in his sleep. When Sutekichi took his arm, the professor let him hold it without the slightest reaction. Every now and then his gait became unsteady.

"Suté-san, let's rest for a while," said the professor, and suddenly came to a halt. He noticed that there were some stone steps in the entrance of a near-by building. Sutekichi hesitated.

"Don't you feel well?" he asked.

"Certainly I fell well! I feel too well, in fact," answered the professor. He walked up about three steps and sat down in a characteristic fashion.

"It would be sheer paradise to have a little nap now," he said.

"You mustn't go to sleep, Professor. The station is directly over there."

"Well, I feel splendid. There's a nice cool breeze here." The professor sat hugging his knees. He had closed his eyes and seemed rather more sober than before. Two cars passed, one after another, illuminating the surface of the street with their headlights, but not the area where the two men were sitting.

"Suté-san," began the professor, "there's no reason why you have to stand. Do sit down."

"I'm all right," said Sutekichi.

"It's not all right. When you stand like that, it's as if you were urging me to go home. It's no fun at all!"

"Very well then" said Sutekichi with a bitter smile, "I'll sit down." He sat down quietly on the step below the professor. They made a funny couple, he thought—teacher and student sitting like this in the middle of the night facing the street.

"Suté-san," came the professor's voice. "Your love affair—is it progressing smoothly?"

"I really don't know," said Sutekichi.

"What do you mean by 'I don't know'? Do you mean to say it doesn't matter to you if it's not going smoothly? That's wrong, you know. It isn't like that, is it?"

"Professor," said Sutekichi in an embarrassed tone, "are you trying to catch me out?"

"What good would that do me?"

Sutekichi did not answer.

"It has come to my attention," continued the professor, "that you have fallen in love with some commonplace girl. And I want to congratulate you. I'm serious, Yes, very serious—What I really want to say is, I'm on your side and please see that things work out successfully. But since it's none of my business, I shall refrain from saying it."

Without Sutekichi's noticing it, the professor had opened his eyes. His manner was calm and encouraging.

"Most young people since the war would laugh at me if I spoke to them like this. And even you, I expect, feel like saying: 'Thank you for your kind interest, but don't worry about me.' Well, that's all right too."

Sutekichi noticed that the professor was no longer bantering, but was utterly serious. It was typical of him to wander like this from one subject to another, occasionally going off the track and becoming downright rude. But his heart was always warm and kind.

"Only I . . ." continued the professor, and it was as if he had raised his thick eyebrows in the darkness, ". . . I suppose I'm a sort of relic of the Meiji Period. But the fact is that the superficial, frivolous type of love that's so common among young people in the postwar period—love that's just like one of the latest popular songs—I loathe it, it makes me sick to my stomach! I should like to be excused from the sight of this sort of thing. When I hear a friend of mine say he's in love, I want it to be such a deep feeling of devotion that in a loud voice in front of everyone I can tell him: 'Well done!' That's real love. Not the American type. Two people who come together like that never need bother the courts with a petition for divorce as long as they live. Their love goes on all their lives. This is a big thing, you know, and not something to be looked for in the ordinary course of things. And such love doesn't seem to exist much any longer. This is a period of insincerity, and people think they can get by without being sincere. And I don't mean only in matters of love. It seems to apply to everything. Now if someone's really in love, I expect him to be prepared to sacrifice himself completely. But nowadays it's the exact opposite. The young men and women of today love each other with the intention of getting something out of it. The spirit of thieves or pickpockets seems to have spread in the world. But a person in love should never want to get something out of it. It mustn't be a matter of working out one's accounts. If one is lucky enough to find a real partner, one should simply rejoice in the fact and not be looking for some advantage beyond it. There's something rather filthy, isn't there, about the spirit of collusion one so often sees between young couples? To fall in love . . . well, love you see isn't a thing that can be undertaken by just anyone. In the first place you have to be prepared for it. And in so far as you love someone, you have to lose yourself. You must be completely willing to sacrifice yourself. If love is like that, it elevates the spirit of a human being. And after that even if the love should fail in some way, there will never be any cause for regret. But when love is being sold bit by bit—well, one might just as well go to bed with a streetwalker. What do you think, Suté-san?"

"I'm listening," said Sutekichi. "I have nothing to say myself."

"Why?"

"Well, tonight I just want to hear your opinions."

"The more you listen, the less interesting it is for a young person like yourself."

"I don't think so," said Sutekichi.

"Well, all right. But if you do have someone to love, embark on it with courage," said the professor, standing up. He seemed to have returned to a condition that would permit him to walk as far as the station. "With courage, I said. I would never say successfully. Still less would I say skillfully. It's all right if you go about things unskillfully. If you have someone to love, you must be ready to risk your life for her. If you can't do that, you simply become a thief, trying to steal someone else's love. And there are lots of thieves walking about!"

Taeko's cheerful face suddenly appeared before Sutekichi and seemed to choke his heart so that he could not speak. His was not a cheerful love, perhaps because he was so conscious of his own material poverty. This was a loss to him: for Sutekichi the world's agony preceded its sweetness.

"The withered branch of Salzburg, isn't it?" said the professor, as he walked under the branches of an acacia tree. "That comes from Stendhal. Love, according to him, is a phenomenon whereby one deceives oneself, as though one were to put crystals on a withered branch and regard it as being pretty like a flower. When I look at my wife, I'm often astonished as I think that she too is a withered branch. It's only when one has woken up as I have that one sees withered branches where other people see cherry blossoms. Or if cherry blossoms sound too old-fashioned, let us say lilac blossoms. . . . Not that I want to discourage you in any way, Sutekichi. But I know that even if I pour cold water on the spirit of someone young like you, the water simply turns into a sweet scent—and I'm the one who's left looking like a fool. I know that materialism is fashionable these days, but I get my pleasure out of finding spring in an ordinary blade of grass that happens to appeal to me. The sense of the 'wonder of the world' may not exist in foreign countries. But that's no reason for us to get rid of it here in Japan. The idea that flowers may blossom on withered branches is not one that would occur to foreigners with their theoretical minds. But it is one that has often come to our ancestors. Even the withered branch of Salzburg, if it were Japanese, would have remained a beautiful thing, shining year after year with its crystals all intact. That is, if it was seen with the sincere love of a real Japanese."

The professor's eloquence had returned. His students used to admire him for the way in which he could recite old poems without forgetting a single word. Not only was his memory accurate, but you had the feeling that the flowers of the words blossomed around it. The professor's words now seemed to transform the night street and the young summer leaves. Sutekichi had the feeling that he was touching the vague scent of the flowers. Perhaps the smell was wafted from his own heart.

"I like to see fine people," said the professor, and a youthful passion could be felt in his husky voice. "Men or women, it doesn't matter which. I like to see fine, earnest people. I don't care if they're the *fin-de-siècle* type—so long as they are fine as human beings. I think that's all I really wanted to say. It's of no importance. What was I talking about?"

Sutekichi was still unable to answer. What a splendid teacher, he thought. It didn't matter whether the professor's actual remarks were correct or not. Once again Sutekichi thought about the rough, but hearty love which this man felt for his students.

"Let's drive home," said the professor, "I'm tired now." He leaned against one of the trees. "If you see a taxi looking for a fare, please stop it."

Sutekichi went to the road and began looking in both directions. First one heard the footsteps, then the black silhouette of a person would emerge out of the dark. An occasional car sped past, and its headlights seemed to make the trees or the human figures loom large. But not a single taxi came. When Sutekichi looked back, he saw that the professor was leaning against the tree: his head was bent forward and he was asleep.

I⊤ WAS a rainy morning when a luxurious car belonging to a certain synthetic-fiber company came to fetch Kaoruko Iwamuro at her house in the outskirts of Tokyo. The road was muddy from the heavy downpour, and there was a constant succession of puddles.

"Do you suppose it will be raining at the other end too?" Mrs. Iwamuro asked the young man (the secretary of the president) who was sitting next to the driver.

"Well, Madam, according to the weather forecast, it should be clearing up in the west. I expect you'll be getting some sun by the time you reach Nagoya."

"Really?" said Mrs. Iwamuro. "Well, I hope you're right."

The windows were closed because of the rain, and it was steaming hot. Mrs. Iwamuro found the constant movement of the windshield wipers strangely irritating. The fact that she had quarreled with her husband that morning about her impending trip was a further cause of irritation, although this had evaporated as soon as she left home. Now she was making a deliberate effort to cheer herself up.

"There's still plenty of time till the train leaves, Madam," the secretary pointed out politely. "So we can drop in at the hotel. Everyone's meeting there. I've packed everything I thought you'd need on your journey. I've put it all in a case in the office. Perhaps you'd be good enough to see if it's all right."

"Thanks for all your trouble," said Mrs. Iwamuro automatically. "And my sleeping pills—did you pack those too?"

"Yes, Madam, I got them at the American Pharmacy. They're packed in with the other things."

Under the low, cloudy sky the dark brick building of Tokyo Station looked even gloomier than usual. The party with which Mrs. Iwamuro was traveling arrived in three large cars. It included the head of an American company and his wife, and as a result the porters were weighed down with luggage. Inevitably they attracted a good deal of attention.

The express train "The Dove" was due to leave in fifteen minutes. They made their way through the crowds in the main part of the station and came to the platform where the train was standing. There was hardly anyone about, and the streaks of rain pouring into the empty spaces gave a cool feeling. The first-class observation car was at the far end of the train, and they had to walk a considerable distance to reach it.

Mrs. Iwamuro noticed a young girl in a raincoat on the platform. The girl greeted her with a smile. Who on earth could she be? Ah yes, it was that Taeko girl whom Ryosuké Tsugawa had introduced to her at the Kawana Hotel.

"Hullo, Taeko-san," she said pleasantly, as she noticed the expression of admiration on the girl's face. "Are you off on a trip?"

Taeko nodded.

"And where are you going?"

"First to Kyoto and then to Kobe. My sister lives in Kobe, you see."

"I'm going to Kyoto and Nara," said Mrs. Iwamuro affably. "So we'll be together on the same train, won't we?"

"I'm traveling third class," answered Taeko in a forthright tone.

"Come to our compartment after the train leaves," said Mrs. Iwamuro, hurrying to catch up with her companions. "I'll tell the conductor that you'll be along." Then, by way of an afterthought, she added: "And Ryosuké—hasn't he come to see you off?"

Taeko blushed prettily. She had arranged to visit her sister in Kobe and to ask her to intercede with their parents for permission to marry Ryosuké; the young man for his part had agreed to speak to his mother about their marriage.

"He'll be coming soon," explained Taeko.

"Yes, to be sure," said Mrs. Iwamuro lightly. "But, Taeko, there's something rather unreliable about our Ryosuké. . . . Well, the train will be leaving in a few minutes."

Turning her dark, intelligent-looking eyes on Taeko, she nodded good-by and hurried toward the first-class carriage. Through the window she could see that the other members of her party had already settled down in the spacious observation car. The attractive girl attendant, standing by the entrance to the carriage, bowed to Mrs. Iwamuro as she entered.

"Thank you in advance for all your trouble," said Mrs. Iwamuro.

Inside the car the blue-eyed foreigners* were lolling comfortably in the sofas and armchairs together with the president of the company and his subordinates who were accompanying them on the journey—they were waiting for the train to leave. Kaoruko Iwamuro was aware that their approving looks were all concentrated on her, and instinctively she made the movement of her body and the expression on her face as beautiful as possible. Her way of moving her eyes and holding her head up proudly, as though confronting an audience, revealed a definite American influence. When Japanese people observed this woman with her fine, delicate features adopting such a positive expression, they could not help feeling that there was something forced and unnatural about her. Foreigners, however, reacted in a different way; even the women were charmed by her and loudly sang her praises. "What a really attractive woman the Baroness Iwamuro is!" they would say. When they looked at her, they must have felt that a perfectly shaped doll with a magnificent, immobile face had suddenly begun to move like a human being.

* "Blue-eyed" has become a conventional epithet in Japan to describe Westerners.

The men who had come to see them off were all important business executives. They stood there impeccably dressed and, apart from the constant motion of their fans, nothing disturbed the calm of their pose.

"It wouldn't be a real party if you weren't along, Madam," said one of the men, bowing politely to Kaoruko. He spoke in a strong Kansai* accent and gave a flick with his closed fan. "You're different from the likes of us," he added. You're born to live in luxury."

The words struck Kaoruko as containing a deliberate snub to her aristocratic pride. She smiled to hide her annoyance, then deliberately turned her back on the man. The company for which these men worked not only had paid all the expenses of her lavish journey, but also for some motive that was not quite clear had given her a considerable sum of money as a sort of honorarium. Kaoruko felt sure that this man had been referring in his uncouth tradesman's way to the fact that before reaching the station the secretary had handed her a large sheaf of banknotes. Beneath the superficial politeness of his greeting lay his knowledge that, aristocratic though Mrs. Iwamuro might be, she was being paid for her services. Yes, she thought, it was far more pleasant to work for foreign clients than for her own countrymen with all their innuendos.

Looking out of the window, Kaoruko remembered having met Taeko on the platform, and she wondered anxiously whether Ryosuké Tsugawa had arrived before the train left. The young man had still not paid back the money that she had lent him about a fortnight before at the hotel in Kawana, nor had he called on her since that time. This had not worried Kaoruko, who tended to be rather lackadaisical about such matters; but her meeting with Taeko had abruptly reminded her about it.

There was the usual restless atmosphere in the compartment as the train was about to leave. Kaoruko went onto the observation platform at the back and gazed toward the spot where Taeko had been standing. The train was due to pull out in three minutes. All the passengers had settled down in their seats, and the only people standing were those who had come to see them

* The west of Japan (Osaka, Kobe, Kyoto, etc.).

off. Just then Kaoruko noticed her husband striding down the platform. She blanched. No, there was no mistaking him. The squat, stout figure was certainly that of Takabumi Iwamuro, who by all rights should now be in their house in the outskirts of Tokyo.

The train left on the second. The platform with its crowds of waving people and the rain-drenched railway line began to move slowly backward. Most of the passengers went onto the rear of the train to wave good-by to their friends, but Kaoruko Iwamuro remained in the observation car. She was, however, carefully looking out of the window as the train glided down the long platform. There was no sign now of the little man who had stood there in the rain wearing his old sun-helmet—the man whom she had instantly recognized as Takabumi, her husband. Instead she noticed Ryosuké Tsugawa, who had come to see Taeko off and who now seemed to be drawing himself up in an effort to find her among all the other passengers. But there was no time for Kaoruko to attract his attention. The angle of the platform had altered, as if it were on a revolving stage, and a moment later it was cut off from view. Tokyo Station itself rapidly grew smaller under the great rain clouds and then became invisible.

Kaoruko's eyes met those of the foreigner sitting opposite her, a member of the party, and she smiled to hide the uneasiness that was once more mounting within her. So Takabumi was on the same train, she thought. It could certainly not be a case of mistaken identity. How many people were there nowadays who would wear an old-fashioned sun-helmet? Besides, she had immediately recognized the particular helmet. It was old and sun-bleached, a relic of the days (before high blood-pressure had made her husband give up energetic exercise) when he had gone riding regularly in the Imperial Stables.

It seemed quite impossible that her husband should be taking this train. Yet the man in the helmet had stepped into a second-class compartment just three carriages away from hers.

Only that morning she had quarreled violently with him about this journey. The ostensible reason for the quarrel had been their child. Kaoruko, however, was well aware that one of his usual unmanly accesses of jealousy had made her husband try to stop her from leaving. Her knowledge that he was simply using the child as a pretext provoked an immediate reaction in her. The only thing that guaranteed the child's future in these hard times was the fact that she, Kaoruko, went out to work; it struck her, therefore, as utterly illogical that her husband should use the child as an excuse for hampering her movements. Takabumi was well aware that times had changed, and it irritated Kaoruko that he should nonetheless stick obstinately to outmoded attitudes. All that she asked of him was that he should not interfere with her activities. Since she had become a working woman, it was only natural that she should have the right to enjoy herself when the occasion arose. This was what all men, including her husband, had done in the past. Why should they begrudge women the privilege, now that their roles were so often reversed?

Kaoruko could not express herself in these terms when she was face to face with her husband, but that is what she felt in her heart. Her feelings were exactly the same when it came to the question of their child.

When she was away from her husband, the outside world sent her gusts of fresh air, and she seemed to breathe more freely. Foreigners never gave her the sense of restraint and unease that her countrymen invariably produced in her. They were free—free as air or water.

"In that case," Kaoruko remembered her husband saying as she was leaving the house, "I'm at liberty to go exactly where I want while you're away."

She had never imagined, however, that he would take the same train. Her husband's motives were really inscrutable, and Kaoruko decided that there was no point in tormenting herself about something that she could never understand. At the same time she was aware that what really annoyed her was that he should be wearing that helmet—that ancient helmet designed for a damp, steamy day in the tropics.

When the train left, the passengers settled down to various activities. Some of them started poring over magazines, others read their newspapers, still others spread out their box lunches. Taeko looked out of the window.

It was still raining, and the sky was a solid sheet of gray.

Among the clusters of dreary suburban dwellings the Japanese umbrellas carried by occasional passers-by looked surprisingly bright. The color of the grass in the vacant lots also struck Taeko as beautiful. Now they were passing an industrial area where tiny uniform houses were dotted among the sooty factories. Taeko noticed that while the owners of one house had carefully tilled their little field and had even planted dahlias and cornflowers on the borders, the field in front of the identical house next door had gone to waste and there had been no effort to make a garden—rather like a textbook illustration of how different people managed their lives. That house, where the garden had gone to rack and ruin, was probably inhabited by people who were dissatisfied with the present and who, for some secret reason, were unable to live in harmony with the world.

Then she noticed a little child with an umbrella waving and shouting at the train. The rain was pouring down everywhere, and the buses splashed clouds of mud as they rattled through the puddles.

"Are there any vacant seats in here?" Taeko heard someone ask. She looked round and saw a gentleman in a sun-helmet addressing the conductor. "I've got a second-class ticket," he was saying, "but I can't find a single seat in there, so I'd like to change to this carriage."

"These seats are all reserved, sir," replied the conductor. "But if you don't mind waiting a while, I may be able to help you. More passengers get on at Yokohama, and until we leave there I can't tell if there are going to be any seats vacant."

Hearing that the second-class carriages were full and that a passenger had actually been squeezed out of second into third, a number of people near Taeko stretched their heads to look at the man talking to the conductor. When the conductor left, the man remained standing in the aisle. He rested his arms on the back of a seat that was occupied by one of the other passengers, and his body swayed with the motion of the train. He was a stout middle-aged gentleman, and, though he was far from tall, he had the air of the ex-military man. He was evidently feeling the heat, and after a while he removed his helmet, revealing a receding hair line. He looked fairly young in his helmet, but when he was bareheaded one could see that he was considerably older. He gave a rather dapper impression, and it was clear that he paid considerable attention to preserving a dignified mien in front of people. Taeko glanced at him as he stood there by himself: there was something lonely about the man, she thought. Not having anywhere in particular to look, he stared directly ahead with a stern expression on his face.

After they left Yokohama the conductor came and informed the gentleman that there was an empty seat for him. A young man who had been sitting diagonally across from Taeko had taken off his shoes and spread himself out on two seats for a nap. Now the conductor awakened him and told him to relinquish one of the seats; he did so with undisguised reluctance.

As she looked out of the window, Taeko's attention gradually wandered from the scene outside, and soon all she noticed was that under the gray, rainy sky the fields and the hills were flowing along as if they had turned into water. When they emerged from the Totsuka Tunnel the rain started to come down with a vengeance and sluiced on the train windows in a constant stream.

"Oh, I'd forgotten!" she thought, abruptly recalling that Mrs. Iwamuro was on the same train. "I'd completely forgotten." Mrs. Iwamuro had asked her to come in for a chat, and it occurred to Taeko that, if she could talk to her about Ryosuké, she would be less painfully conscious of the separation.

It bothered Taeko, however, that she would have to go into the observation car. She was not unduly timid by nature, but having to go into a first-class compartment made her hesitate. Besides, it occurred to her, wouldn't Mrs. Iwamuro have her usual entourage of people? Ryosuké, who for Taeko had become an obsession capable of making her utterly wretched, was for Mrs. Iwamuro merely a subject of desultory conversation— something that might help to pass the time but which had no more significance in her glittering life than one of the countless little bubbles in a bottle of soda water.

Taeko looked at the gentleman opposite her. He had placed his sun-helmet in the parcel rack and had turned his balding head to the window; evidently he was examining the scenery. The young man who had been obliged to relinquish one of his seats was now sleeping soundly, whereas before he had only been resting; next to him the elderly gentleman looked extremely stiff and proper as he gazed out of the window. His features were gentle and bespoke good breeding. There was a loneliness about his profile, Taeko noticed again. She wondered whether it was the reflection of the rain outside which accentuated the exhaustion of the years. His was a strong face, but marked with deep lines of weariness.

She turned and looked out of her own window. As they approached Odawara the sea came into view. Soon, thought Taeko, they would be reaching Atami. When she next glanced at the older man, she saw that he had taken a small newspaper out of his pocket and was studying it intently—a betting sheet for the bicycle races.

Kaoruko Iwamuro had started playing bridge with her foreign companions. The company people did not know how to play bridge, and among the Japanese members of the party only Kaoruko, who had learned the game from her husband, was able to put up a good fight. Soon she had entered into the spirit of the game. She was a strong player, and she was beginning to win when the waiter came from the dining-car to take their orders for lunch. The director's private secretary walked over to the card-players and asked what they would like. Kaoruko spoke to her companions in English and translated their orders. Then she added abruptly: "But I should like to be excused, if you don't mind. I'd just like the waiter to bring me some sandwiches and tea in here."

"But, Madam," remonstrated the secretary, "if you don't go in with our guests, they'll all be very disappointed. I really must ask you to join us."

Kaoruko stuck to her ground, "I'm sorry," she said, "but I can't stand those crowded dining-cars. Besides, you know, I'm not an interpreter. I'm afraid I sound rather self-willed, but I must ask you to let me stay here quietly."

At the same time she was thinking that, if she were to go through the next carriages on the way to the dining-car, she would have a chance to walk defiantly past her husband. Even if their eyes should meet, she would deliberately ignore him.

"Oh dear," said the secretary, "I don't know what to do about this. I'd better go and see what the director says."

"It makes no difference what he says," retorted Kaoruko,

and calmly continued her game. She explained to the foreigners that she intended to stay behind in the observation car while they had their lunch. Soon they had all left for the dining-car, and she was alone.

Takabumi's decision to take the same train as Kaoruko without a word of explanation had clearly been intended to insult her, and she felt extremely provoked. Yet on consideration she realized that there was absolutely nothing he could do. Her husband's training was such that, however much ill feeling he might harbor toward her, he was incapable of making a scene in public. His regard for name, family, and reputation rendered him immobile at moments when most men would be impelled to take some drastic action. Apart from riding, the only abilities that people recognized in Takabumi were hunting and shooting. Of what practical use were such accomplishments in this modern age? Together they would not bring in even one hundred yen. If a man with so little power of economic survival as Takabumi attempted to restrict her freedom of action on the grounds that he was her husband, Kaoruko saw no reason that she should continue to put up with him. Apart from everything else, it was a simple matter of ensuring her own livelihood.

Kaoruko had no idea how far her husband planned to follow her on this journey. Obviously his only aim was to make things disagreeable for her. Probably he would get off the train at Atami or thereabouts and go back to Tokyo. No man in his right senses could possibly intend to follow her for the week or more that she was going to spend traveling about Kyoto and Nara. Besides, he didn't have the money. What on earth had made him behave like this? Granted that his action might not be sufficient grounds for divorce, it was certainly enough to constitute an insult that would justify a legal separation. The one thing which worried Kaoruko was that, despite her husband's timidity in front of other people, he was extremely strong physically. There was no telling that, when they were alone, he might not resort to force in a fit of wild anger. Suddenly alone in the observation car Kaoruko felt a tremor of apprehension, and she frowned nervously.

There were windows on three sides of the observation car, and the rainy, leaden sky was constantly in view. Kaoruko looked at the passing countryside, but the thought of her husband continued to haunt her. It occurred to her that Takabumi, if he knew she was alone, might at any moment appear at the entrance of the car.

The young girl attendant brought Kaoruko a tray with sandwiches and tea covered with a napkin. Her thick, lustrous hair was done in a permanent wave, and it moved gently under her uniform cap. It gave Kaoruko a pleasant feeling to observe the girl's pure white skin which looked as if it was still innocent of worldly troubles.

"Thank you so much," said Kaoruko, speaking with a slight lisp and deliberately punctuating each word. Then abruptly she added: "And would you mind letting me have a telegraph form?"

She lost no time in putting into effect the idea that had occurred to her. Taking a pencil out of her bag, she quickly called to mind Ryosuké Tsugawa's office address and wrote it in the space provided on the form.

WAITING FOR YOU MIYAKO HOTEL KYOTO STOP PLEASE ARRANGE COME IMMEDIATELY.

Having written this, Kaoruko wondered whether she should not give up the idea. It had occurred to her that it might be a good thing to have Ryosuké next to her when the time came to confront her husband. Though the young man knew nothing about the situation, so long as he was present her husband would restrain himself when speaking to her, and her worst fears would not be realized.

"Well now," said Kaoruko, smiling up at the girl attendant, "would you please bring me some fruit?"

"Very well, Madam. What would you like? I believe they have pears, bananas, and grapes."

"Anything will do," said Kaoruko. "Well, let's see. Let's make it grapes."

As the girl left, the secretary returned to the observation car and informed Kaoruko that everyone was still waiting for her in the diner.

"There's an empty seat," he explained, "and if you don't

join us, it will give the table a lonely look. That's what Mrs. Strauss said."

"I made my excuses to Mrs. Strauss as well as to the others," said Kaoruko.

"But, Madam, I know everyone will feel much happier if you come. Do you know that Mrs. Strauss is drinking beer too? They're good drinkers, aren't they, those Americans? Even the women."

All of a sudden Kaoruko felt cheerful. Yes, she told herself, she would walk calmly past where Takabumi was sitting. The idea filled her with enthusiasm.

"Beer?" she said facetiously. "That's a drink for horses and Germans." Then she rapidly finished writing her telegram and signed it with Taeko's name. In his present mood Ryosuké was far more likely to come if Taeko summoned him; besides, thought Kaoruko, this would be a good subject to tease him about later.

"All right," she said lightly, "I'll come. But only after I've had time to do my make-up," she added as she stood up. "You'll wait for me, won't you?"

"Of course, Madam," said the young man. He was very pleased: not only had he accomplished his mission, but he would be able to satisfy his youthful vanity by accompanying a beautiful woman through the second-class carriages, thus attracting the attention of less fortunate passengers.

"Why don't you let me give that telegram to the conductor for you, Madam?"

"Yes please," said Kaoruko cheerfully, looking into her compact mirror. "I'm trying to make a nice surprise for a young girl I know by asking her boyfriend to come to Kyoto. She's on this train."

They walked through the four second-class carriages that separated the observation car from the diner. Since the seats all faced the direction in which the train was moving, Kaoruko could see only the backs of the passengers as she passed down the aisle. She would, however, be able to identify Takabumi at once from the shape of his head. As she entered each carriage she looked carefully at the passengers expecting to recognize her husband, but he was nowhere to be seen. What could have happened? Ah, of course, she thought with a certain excitement,

he must have gone to the diner himself. She knew that the dining-car was small and that Takabumi might very well be sitting
at the table directly next to hers. In that case, thought Kaoruko,
it would be slightly embarrassing in front of her companions to
pretend to ignore her husband entirely.

"Very well," she told herself. "I'll nod to him ever so slightly.
That'll seem even more of an insult."

Takabumi, however, was not in the dining-car. She glanced
round the tables as she chatted amiably to the foreigners, but
there was no sign of him. She must have missed him as she
walked through the second-class carriages. No doubt she would
spot him on her way back when she would be facing the passengers head on. But when they left the diner and returned to
the observation car, she still did not see him.

Kaoruko was overcome by an unaccountable sense of relief.
Suddenly she felt delighted to be on a journey, and she returned to the lighthearted mood that the company of foreigners
usually inspired in her.

"Ah, it's clearing," said one of her party, looking out of the
window. They were just passing the beach near Yui. The gray
water turned blue, and everything brightened up. The road
next to the railway line was already becoming dry.

"How splendid!" declared Kaoruko, looking at a cloud scud-
ding rapidly out to sea. It was fascinating to see how fast the
cloud moved, presumably blown by the wind. The large gray
cloud as it passed seemed to shower the sea below with rain, making the surface as dark as night.

The Americans invited Kaoruko to play some more bridge,
and, as she absorbed herself in the game, she became entirely
oblivious of the long journey to Kyoto. She was in the highest
spirits and had banished from her mind all thoughts of her husband. She even forgot that Taeko was on the train and that a
few hours before she had used the girl's name to telegraph
Ryosuké Tsugawa.

At Kyoto Station they all left the observation car and stood
on the brightly lit platform. Kaoruko entrusted her luggage to
the porter from the hotel and was about to walk toward the
exit when among the crowd further down the platform she noticed her husband's sun-helmet.

There was no longer any room for doubt: it could only be

Takabumi. Automatically she walked behind the large protective frame of one of her foreign companions. She felt strangely excited by the shock. Had Ryosuké received her telegram, she wondered, and if so would he arrive promptly?

As soon as Taeko met her sister, she knew that she had come at an unpropitious moment in so far as her own problem was concerned. The money trouble, which Tazuko had gone all the way to Kamakura to discuss with their uncle, was still unsettled; also, her brother-in-law had been having an affair with a girl, much to the unhappiness of his strong-minded wife.

"I wonder why I always have to fuss and worry so much," said Tazuko with a sigh. "When all's said and done, it's better to be single, like you."

Taeko was well aware that for all her sister's strong-mindedness she was essentially an extremely good-hearted woman. As she observed Tazuko, she realized that, much as she might quarrel with her husband, he was constantly in the center of her thoughts and actions. She had been trying to scrape together enough money to open the luxury shop in Kobe not to satisfy any desire for show but to help improve the shaky finances of her husband's clinic. Her inherent good nature emerged from the fact that some time previously, when her husband had already become involved in a romantic imbroglio, she had told Taeko and others with a certain tone of pride that the young lady in question was one of the most fashionable and popular geishas in the Nanchi quarter. Though she used to berate her husband for his infidelity, she seemed to derive satisfaction from the knowledge that the girl was a geisha of high standing. Later, when the geisha had left him for a businessman who was better endowed with money and power, Tazuko, though thoroughly relieved, had expressed sincere resentment on her husband's behalf at the girl's "betrayal"—as if she too had felt betrayed.

According to Tazuko, she and her husband were obliged to live rather an extravagant life in order to hold their own among fellow practitioners. Doctors who could not live extravagantly had trouble in getting good patients. Upper-class people insisted that even the doctors who looked after their health should as far as possible belong to the same stratum of society. For this purpose Tazuko tried to act as a sort of ambassador for her husband. By opening a shop in Kobe that dealt in Western-style luxuries she hoped to gather a small group of smart women customers, who in turn would provide patients for her husband. The shop was to be no idle woman's whim but a serious business proposition which would earn enough money to buy new equipment for her husband's clinic. But so far all this had remained something of a daydream. The shop had required far more capital than originally estimated, and after the initial rental had been paid virtually nothing remained.

"I know an old family in Senba who deal in textiles," Tazuko told her sister. "I heard from a young married woman who belongs to the family that they want to sell their precious heirlooms. They want to do it privately without going through a dealer. They've got a Korin scroll, a Nonko teacup, and dozens of other extremely valuable objects that would fetch several million yen on the open market. Now the family have agreed to let me handle the sale if I collaborate with Mrs. Suzuki in Mikage. You don't know of any possible buyers in Tokyo, do you, Taeko?"

Tazuko was by far the more talkative of the two, and Taeko was obliged to listen patiently before discussing her own affairs. If Tazuko succeeded in getting a good price for the heirlooms, the family was prepared to give her a bonus and also to advance money for her shop by investing in shares. The trouble, thought

Taeko, was that all this talk had evidently been between women, and it seemed doubtful whether the various plans were quite as firm as Tazuko suggested. Besides, even if her sister succeeded in putting her plans into effect, the result would be, not to make her existence something new and more meaningful, but simply to extend her present mode of life and make it busier. There was something rather pathetic about Tazuko's constant struggles.

Taeko recalled how as a girl her sister had given the greatest attention to her dolls. Tazuko had taken lessons in the Japanese dance, and the memory of her dancing before their parents to the folksongs "Overture" and "Seven Children" remained vividly in Taeko's memory. Looking now at Tazuko, the younger girl realized how utterly she had altered since those years; yet at the same time she was aware that her sister's present feelings about the "Western-style luxury shop" did not differ essentially from what she had felt in the past about her doll in the long-sleeved *yuzen* kimono. Tazuko may have become rather more calculating in the course of the years, but Taeko had the impression that at heart she was still a little girl, standing on tiptoes, as it were, and quite unsure of herself. She lived in relatively favorable circumstances, and from most people's point of view hers was an enviable position. Yet there was something frail and weak about her. Tazuko herself was, of course, unaware of this, and she was sticking to her plan with characteristic determination.

"Surely it would be better to give up the idea of the shop," Taeko felt like saying. "Aren't you taking on more than you can handle?"

She was aware that her thoughts had once again drifted back to their childhood and to memories of how differently they had been brought up, even though they had lived under the same roof. When she considered that her own mother had been a maid, she realized more than ever how different Tazuko was from her. She remembered the quiet, smug expression on her sister's pretty face when as a little girl she had prepared to dance to the accompaniment of folk music. Her attitude had been one of complete concentration on the dance and of determination to keep everything else at arm's length—the same attitude, thought Taeko, that Tazuko had clung to even after getting married and setting out in the world, an attitude of which she herself was devoid. Taeko felt sure that this approach did not serve to give strength to her sister's life; in fact, it seemed to have exactly the opposite effect.

Well, perhaps in due course she would find that there was nothing so strange about all this. After all, she herself was still only at the threshold of life, while her sister was an experienced woman who (superficially, at least) had been favored by fortune since her childhood.

"What do you think about Uncle?" asked Tazuko. "When I was in Kamakura he told me he had no money to spare. Do you suppose it's hopeless? It can't actually be true that he's short of money."

"I don't know," replied Taeko casually. A look of annoyance showed on Tazuko's face as she realized that Taeko was not concentrating properly on the matter.

"After all," continued Tazuko, "if he really didn't have any money, how could he live the way he does—just eating and resting without doing a stroke of real work? Of course, I don't suppose he has much in the way of ready funds. Who does these days? But if he's put his money on savings account or invested in shares, there's no reason he can't use that as collateral to borrow what he needs from the bank. Why does he have to be so stingy with us? It doesn't seem to matter to him in the slightest how badly things go for us. Hasn't he heard about blood being thicker than water?"

When Taeko thought about her uncle, however, it was not his stinginess that came to mind but the indefinable aura of loneliness that hung over him. There was a certain purity about this loneliness that appealed to her.

"But, Tazuko, you can't really say that things are going badly."

"And why not, may I ask?" said Tazuko sharply.

"Well, I don't consider myself unfortunate."

Taeko was about to add that in comparison with most people she and her sister were extremely fortunate, but she realized that this argument would be meaningless to Tazuko. If it came to comparisons, Tazuko would only refer to her husband's more fortunate colleagues who had modern well-run clinics.

.   .   .

On the following day Tazuko took her sister into the city to visit the "shop," which was conveniently situated near the toll road. It was part of a recently constructed block of buildings. The shops on either side were already open for business, but the place that Tazuko had rented was completely empty, although it had elaborate gold lettering above the show window. The interior was redolent with the smell of varnish from the walls; the remains of boards and timber still lay about on the concrete floor.

"It looks awful," said Tazuko with a sigh. "If only I could get things started inside!" Then with characteristic enthusiasm she began describing to Taeko how she was secretly dreaming of decorating the bare interior. She had obviously exerted the greatest ingenuity in planning the cases where the goods were to be displayed and even the exact shape of the chairs on which the customers would sit.

"Everything has been ordered. But I'll have a terrible time paying for the things if they're ready too soon."

Taeko was amazed at her sister's improvidence; at the same time she felt sorry for her. The worst of it was that, even if Tazuko should succeed in opening the shop, all sorts of things would be bound to go wrong and her dreams would almost certainly be betrayed.

"I wish you could manage to bring Uncle from Kamakura to have a look at the shop," said Tazuko. "It's beautifully situated, isn't it? It's very near the station, you see, and there are lots of dance halls and movie houses further down the street. Now on this side of the shop I'm planning to put a sofa and a couple of chairs—just enough so that my customers can relax over a cup of tea. And if they want coffee or ice cream, it's no trouble at all —they'll deliver it from that shop down the street."

When Taeko asked about the key money, Tazuko explained that this had been covered by part of what she had contributed to the building expenses. It occurred to Taeko that the sensible thing for Tazuko to do would be to cut her losses and sell her rights to someone else for a good price; but she realized that her sister was far too enthusiastic about her plans for such a suggestion to be of any use.

After leaving the shop, the two of them strolled down the Motomachi shopping street. They had no particular destination in mind, and when they reached the end of the street they turned round and started walking back. Then Tazuko suggested that they go and have a snack at a near-by teashop owned by a friend of hers. The friend was a married woman, like herself, who lived in the suburbs of Kobe. She was running the teashop on her own in order to make some extra money. It was a tiny place, surrounded by a wooden wall and situated on a narrow, tunnel-like alley. Because it was lunchtime, the shop was full of customers.

"Atsuko-san has really made a success of this place," said Tazuko. Taeko detected a wistful note in her sister's voice. "She serves alcoholic drinks only in the evenings, but even so she manages to dispose of dozens of cases of beer every month. Her wine merchant's bill comes to tens of thousands of yen." It was clear from Tazuko's detailed knowledge of the shop's finances that there were no secrets between her and her friend.

A waitress brought them a plate of meat sandwiches. They had been neatly decorated with lettuce and tasted extremely good.

"Well now, Taeko-san," began Tazuko abruptly, removing the lettuce leaves from her sandwich, "about the conversation we had last night. I'd like you to wait a little longer before doing anything."

Taeko flushed as she realized that Tazuko was referring to her request that she should speak to their parents about Ryosuké. Tazuko picked up a sandwich with an elegant movement of her delicate fingers and popped it into her mouth. There was a finality about her last remark, and for some time neither of them spoke. Even at noon it was dark in the little teashop, and the lights were on. Tazuko wore her hair up, and Taeko noticed how the light picked out the hairline on the nape of her sister's neck.

"Oh yes, Taeko-san, there's something else. You remember Mr. Hoshino, don't you? Well, I told him on the telephone that you were coming to Kobe. He was very pleased and said he'd like to see us. I do hope we can all have dinner together this evening."

Taeko had completely forgotten about Mr. Hoshino, the young man whom Tazuko had forced her to meet at the Kabuki Theater in Tokyo with a view to an arranged marriage.

Now she remembered him, and for a moment she was taken aback by the peculiar callousness of her sister who could calmly broach this subject after she had already been told about her relationship with Ryosuké.

"Mr. Hoshino hasn't given up, you know," continued Tazuko. "In fact, he's very serious about you."

"Please forgive me," said Taeko, automatically falling back upon an expression that she had been in the habit of using years before when she was still living at home, "but I've never given Mr. Hoshino a moment's thought. Besides, I can't come tonight. I've already arranged to go to Kyoto."

"I'm sorry," said Tazuko, "but I've already phoned Mr. Hoshino, and he said he'd come this evening."

Taeko seemed to pick up spirit at her sister's words. "Look, Tazuko" she said, "when are you going to speak to Father about what I told you?"

For a while Tazuko did not reply. Then in a decidedly high-handed tone she said: "Taeko, would you mind not mentioning that matter any further? I really think you should give up the whole idea before you go and make some silly mistake. Father and Mother certainly wouldn't approve if you decided such a matter on your own. Now in the case of Mr. Hoshino it's entirely different. He comes from a secure, well-established family. But how on earth do you think you'd manage in a household consisting of the widow of a government official?"

"Those things really don't matter to me, Tazuko," replied Taeko with a smile.

"And why, may I ask?" said Tazuko, fixing her sister with a serious look. "Marriage isn't something to decide for oneself, you know. After all, Taeko, you don't consider yourself to be one of those *après-guerre* girls, do you? You still have some respect for your family. Now to return to that friend of yours—does his family have any means?"

"I haven't given the matter a moment's thought." Taeko shook her head, and the youth of the girl seemed to sparkle from her hair. "You see, Tazuko, I'm marrying a man, not a sum of money. I've never even asked him about his financial situation, but I'm sure the answer to your question is: 'No—his family has no means to speak of.' Still, that doesn't worry me in the slightest. As I said before, it's the man I want to marry, not what he owns. I suppose it sounds funny, but there it is. And somehow I can't believe that my attitude is wrong."

Most of the customers had left, and the teashop was nearly empty. Taeko still spoke softly; but her face was flushed with emotion, and she felt as though a typhoon had stirred up inside her. Tazuko, however, seemed to feel none of her sister's excitement, and she gazed impassively at Taeko with her calm, cool eyes. Her love of etiquette and order had come decisively to the fore. If there was anything in the world that people like Tazuko detested (people, that is, who enjoyed a secure life and an established position), it was the disruption of the *status quo*. Though Taeko might appear to be entirely unrelated to her, thought Tazuko, the girl was nominally her sister; and if Taeko decided to throw caution to the wind, the disgrace would inevitably reflect on the entire family, including herself.

"I see," said Tazuko after a pause. "And if he has no means, what do you intend to do if things go wrong and you end up on the streets as a beggar?"

"Me—a beggar?" said Taeko, flushing violently. She felt that she could no longer afford to dismiss her sister's remarks as a joke. "I've been managing to earn my own living perfectly well until now, haven't I? And even if things should turn out in the absurd way you suggest, I'm sure I can take it in my stride."

"So you are going to become a beggar, are you?" said Tazuko, and there was something essentially cruel about her clear Kansai accent. "I understand."

She must not let herself get angry, Taeko realized. It required all the self-control she could muster to remain calm, for her heart was full of Ryosuké and everything she wanted to say was about him. She forced a smile to her face and tried to think of some way to change the subject. But her thoughts kept on slipping back into their original groove. As bad luck would have it, a new customer appeared just then in the teashop with a tennis racket under his arm. He had evidently come directly from the tennis court, and Taeko was immediately reminded of Ryosuké as she had seen him that day in Tokyo slamming the ball powerfully across the net so that it raised a cloud of white dust on the base line. The carefully contrived smile froze on her face, and she looked wretched enough to burst into tears.

"This is delicious," she said with a deliberate effort at lightheartedness which would have been obvious to anyone. "It's very well cooked—and this Kobe beef is so tender, isn't it?"

"Look, Taeko-san," said her sister, "do you really think I'll get nowhere with Uncle? Won't he do anything to help me even if he hears that things are so bad for me that I'm thinking of killing myself?"

"When I get back to Tokyo, I'll talk to him about it again."

"But you must be really serious about it, Taeko. It's terribly important."

"Yes, I intend to," said Taeko with a nod, before her sister had even finished speaking.

"Intending isn't enough," said Tazuko. "You've got to get results. This is a matter of life and death. . . . Oh yes, about those Nakazoe heirlooms—the Nonko teacup, the Korin scroll, and the rest. I do hope you'll find me a good buyer in Tokyo or Kamakura or somewhere."

Taeko was so overcome with misery that, if there had been no other customers in the shop, she might easily have knelt down before her sister and pleaded with her. She knew very well that since the balance of financial power in the family had altered, her parents in Kyoto had come to leave all important decisions to Tazuko and that, if she wanted to get their permission, it would be essential to have her sister's prior consent.

Although she had heard Tazuko's last remark, she had completely forgotten it. She smiled by way of reply and nodded vacantly. She must insist more strongly, thought Taeko; after all, this was why she had taken the train all the way to Kobe. She had been mistaken in thinking of her sister as being kindhearted and well disposed toward her. She had always known that Tazuko was a strong-minded woman, but now she realized that in her innermost nature there was something as hard and unyielding as a rock. What could it be? Perhaps it was connected in some way with the candidate for marriage whom Tazuko had recommended and whom she was trying to have Taeko meet again that evening. In that case, there would not seem to be too much cause for alarm. The young girl still did not understand that what really actuated her sister was far more deeply rooted. It was a loathing of any tendency on Taeko's part to violate the etiquette, form, custom—the entire structure of quasi-morality that she, as an elder sister, considered to be paramount.

When they left the shop and walked down the street, the two sisters made an extremely attractive pair, and several passers-by turned around to look at them. In the setting of the harbor town of Kobe with its mixture of the old and the new one could detect something special in these two young women— a certain refinement, perhaps—which had taken a long time to develop.

"Goodness, how hot it is!" said Tazuko. Walking gracefully under her parasol, she seemed to be addressing the world at large rather than her sister. Then she turned to Taeko and said: "So you will come and meet Mr. Hoshino for me, won't you?"

Although Taeko's mind was now made up, she smiled as though she were resigned to obeying her sister's wishes.

"All right, if it's just a matter of meeting him, I don't mind. But that's all."

After they had walked a little further, Tazuko turned to Taeko and asked with a sudden access of sisterly warmth: "You haven't gone and done something hasty with your friend, have you, Taeko-san? It's terrible what young girls do these days."

In order not to offend her sister, Taeko spent the evening with her and Mr. Hoshino, the young man who worked in the bank. They dined at one of the restaurants in the residential part of Kobe which had survived the wartime incendiary raids. From the veranda one could look down on the sea and the city lights. In the garden the sweet oleander grew as profusely as bamboo in a grove, and you could see their red blossoms in the moonlight.

Mr. Hoshino turned out to be more pleasant than Taeko had expected; his behavior toward her was natural and certainly did not suggest that he had any ulterior design. Of the three of them only Tazuko seemed to evince any particular enthusiasm about the meeting. Mr. Hoshino's manner was completely relaxed, and Taeko had the feeling that he was not nearly so eager as her sister had intimated.

As they ate their dinner, Taeko recovered her composure. For once and all she had given up any idea of depending on her sister. The road that she must follow was now clearly fixed in her mind, and she realized that her hopes of obtaining her family's consent merely represented an effort to act according to an established worldly routine—a routine to which she was not necessarily tied. If her parents refused their consent, she would simply have to go ahead on her own; and Taeko believed that she was capable of doing so. Her sister and she had from their earliest childhood been completely different, she thought—and this idea, in which there was not the slightest trace of girlish sentimentality, seemed to restore her composure.

"Would you like me to take you dancing somewhere after dinner?" said Mr. Hoshino to the sisters. Tazuko accepted promptly, but Taeko declined the invitation.

The three of them went down the hill to where Taeko and her sister had walked that morning. With its night illuminations it looked like a completely different street.

"Are you going to Kyoto directly?" asked the young man. "If so, let me take you to the station."

Taeko was embarrassed. "To tell the truth," she said, "there's something I want to discuss with my sister."

"What a charming reply!" said Tazuko, laughing brightly, yet with a reproving note in her voice. "You know, Mr. Hoshino, I really don't think I can recommend a girl like that as a wife."

"It's all right," said Mr. Hoshino gaily. "It's perfectly all right." Partly owing to the beer that he had drunk during dinner, he sounded so merry that one might well have expected him to start whistling at any moment. Then he continued in a forthright tone: "I'm afraid it may sound rather rude, but I'm beginning to think that if I did go and marry this young lady she'd only be a burden. I realized this while I was talking to her just now."

"Oh, you're quite mistaken," put in Tazuko.

"Well, I've been making my calculations," continued the young man. "Not because I'm a banker, mind you, but because one really has to think clearly about these things. And I'm quite sure there's a happier way for both of us. Really there is."

Taeko did not know what her sister thought about these remarks, and she did not want to know. All she felt was that her own face was glowing in the evening twilight, and as she gazed at the young man she had the impression that she was climbing toward some ineffable happiness.

"Well, Miss Taeko," said Mr. Hoshino, "will you shake hands with me?"

Without a word she nodded vigorously and put out her hand. Between the two of them there was an undisguisable brightness and a straightforwardness that only youth can know.

"I should like to shake hands with you and say good-by here," continued Mr. Hoshino. "Just a moment, please," he added, putting his hand into his pocket and extracting a handkerchief. "I'm a gentleman, you see, and I must do things properly."

With an exaggerated gesture he was about to wipe the perspiration from his right hand when several round, glittering objects dropped out of his handkerchief and fell onto the pavement with a patter.

"Dear me," said the budding bank manager, "my *pachinko* balls!"

The car speeded pleasantly along the well-paved road, taking Kaoruko Iwamuro and her companions back to Kyoto from their excursion to Nara. The road followed the embankment above the Hozu River, and they had an uninterrupted view of the splendid wide riverbed. The river had long since left the mountains and now, like a great *obi*, it flowed through the plain past sandbanks and clusters of reeds, sometimes reflecting the clouds on its pellucid surface, sometimes glittering in the sunlight. As they were driving across open country, there was a pleasant breeze, and after the heat of Kyoto it was like a different world.

All that they had seen during the heat of the day in Nara was the Great Buddha in the Todai Temple, the Kasuga Shrine, and the deer in the park—to which, perhaps, should be added the stuffed deer that the photographer had produced when taking a souvenir picture of the party. The Americans, being businessmen, were thoroughly bored at being shown Buddhist statuary and the like. In Kyoto, too, they had been bored with all the temples, although the large scale of the architecture had impressed them.

"Our American guests are only interested in things that move," Kaoruko warned the guide as he started conducting them along the standard sightseeing route. As a matter of fact, she herself was much the same in this childish preference for moving objects. When they came to the Chion Temple the Americans noticed a large beetle that had fallen on the steps; one of them knocked the beetle over on its back, and they all stood for a long time watching with great enjoyment as the insect struggled desperately to right itself. Occasionally they would walk into a little shop in the town; they were invariably surprised at the worthless goods on display and laughed heartily at the frugality of it all. In Kyoto they had been taken to see the *maiko*, the apprentice geisha, in the Gion district. At first they had admired the girls with great cries of, "Isn't she something?" but after a while they evidently tired of the immobile faces with their thick white make-up. It was the same at the Japanese dinner party to which they had been invited. The Americans had all looked extremely bored until it was announced that several cages of fireflies had been brought from Uji and that the incandescent insects were going to be set loose in the garden. Thereupon they all rushed out to the veranda with the greatest glee.

"The Americans say that tonight they don't want to go anywhere," Kaoruko told their host, the director of the company, who was sitting next to the chauffeur. "They just want to stay in the hotel and play bridge." She noticed the slight admixture of white hair on the director's strong neck; he was wearing a finely woven Panama hat.

"We reserved a room for dinner at the Hyotei restaurant," he said, turning around. "Don't they want to go there?"

"Mrs. Strauss says she's tired," replied Kaoruko. "I expect it's the heat."

The director valued Kaoruko's opinion. She seemed to have a keen understanding of what American people felt and her recommendations were invariably correct. Although she had never set foot in the United States herself, her plans for entertaining Americans never failed to please the guests. She was considered extremely intelligent, but at the same time there was something instinctive about her knack of handling American visitors; or perhaps it was that in the course of time her own disposition had come to resemble that of the foreigners themselves.

"Driver," she called out boisterously, "isn't there another road back to Kyoto? It doesn't matter if it's a bit longer. It's a shame to take the same road both ways."

There was a road from Hino and Daigo which came out at Yamashina; it was a good road without too much traffic. Although it took them a little out of their way, it was far more pleasant than the main Fushimi thoroughfare, where the huge sightseeing buses seemed to squeeze them and where the children played in the narrow lanes. Here they passed peaceful scenery with ricefields and bamboo thickets, much to the delight of the foreigners, who had not had a chance to see much of the Japanese countryside at close range.

The drive along the well-paved highway gave them a pleasant feeling. It was not at all tiring, for it made one's blood circulate vigorously without producing the muscular fatigue associated with rough, crowded roads. They expected that it would be hot when they got out of the car at Kyoto, but the sun had lost its earlier force, and inside the hotel, which was built on the side of the mountain, the air was agreeably cool.

They had just stepped into the elevator when a page boy ran up to Kaoruko.

"A message for you, Madam," he said, handing her a small envelope.

The door closed and the elevator started to move. As she opened the envelope, Kaoruko was surprised to hear water running inside the wall of the shaft.

"What on earth is that?" she asked the young girl in uniform who was operating the elevator. "It sounds like water."

"Yes, Madam," said the girl. "It's the rain from the day before yesterday coming down the mountain side."

"It sounds as if it's on this side of the wall," said Kaoruko. "I thought it must be a broken pipe or something."

"Yes, when it rains heavily the water gets into the shaft. They're trying to mend it, though."

"Isn't it going to wash the entire hotel away?" Kaoruko was about to ask with deliberate exaggeration in order to make the girl laugh; but at that very moment she noticed the writing on the message, and she silently knit her brows. It was from her husband, who had come to the hotel while she was out.

"Well," said Kaoruko to the Americans as the elevator reached their floor. "I'll be seeing you presently."

"Yes, Ma'am," answered one of them. "Have a good rest now." They got out of the elevator and walked down their respective corridors.

As soon as Kaoruko reached her room, she opened the message and read it. Takabumi had called at half past three—an hour and a half earlier; he would, said the message, visit her again that evening. Kaoruko hurried over to the door and put the key in the lock. Perhaps because she was upset, she had trouble in getting the key to fit, and she became more and more nervous until she finally managed to lock the door securely.

Locking the door, however, would not stop Takabumi from coming to her room. "Well, there's no reason I should see him even if he does come," she told herself defiantly. She threw her bag on the table and, unhooking her dress, walked over to the bed. Perhaps a bath would make her feel less tired, she decided. The drive in the car had not tired Kaoruko, but Takabumi's message had somehow taken all the strength out of her. She felt thirsty and rang for the waiter. When there was a knock on the door a few moments later, she completely forgot having rung and turned around with a start.

"Who's there?" she said, hastily covering her bare shoulders with her nightgown. Then she remembered having called for the waiter. "Yes, come in," she said. "It's all right."

Since the door was locked, she had to go and open it. The exaggerated carefulness of her movements bespoke her inner confusion. She ordered a soft drink and some iced water, then threw herself on the bed. She tried to relax by emptying her mind of all thoughts, but somehow she could not settle down. The sun was hidden behind the trees that grew on the mountain close outside the window, but the red evening glare managed to shine through the branches and made Kaoruko's room extremely hot.

The setting sun cast the shadow of the trees onto the paved road. Although it was evening, the day was at its hottest. The

smell of asphalt drifted through the heated atmosphere. Beside
the modern road there was something rather shabby about the
row of old-fashioned Mushiko style wooden houses. They were
all little shops, but often it was hard to tell what they were selling. If a passer-by stopped to look, he would find that one shop
specialized in fans—and that a set of ancient fans was unobtru-
sively displayed in the window, while the next shop, in which
the owner was nowhere to be seen, dealt in utensils for the tea
ceremony.

Takabumi Iwamuro walked aimlessly through the streets of
Kyoto, duty streets that looked as if they had been thoroughly
pressed down by the crushing heat until there was no life left in
them. He was wearing his sun-helmet, but the surface of the
road threw up unbearable clouds of heat. For several years he
had been suffering from high blood pressure. Recently he had
been forcing himself not to think about it, since worrying only
made matters worse; but now he became uneasy at the thought of
dragging along his corpulent body under the scorching sun. He
had been informed that a cold winter was far more dangerous
for people with high blood pressure than any summer, but he
felt that something might very well happen to him in this over-
powering heat.

On being told at the hotel that his wife was out (what, he
thought, could be more preposterous than having to visit one's
own wife at a hotel?) he had left a message and once more ven-
tured into the torrid Kyoto streets. He was hungry, but he hesitated to have a proper meal since he was short of funds—so
short, indeed, that the purpose of his visit to Kaoruko was to get
some money from her. After a while he noticed a little shop
with a long, red, dust-capped lantern hanging outside. What
could it be? Ah yes, it was an *udon** shop. He decided to go in.

The proprietor addressed Takabumi in a thick Kyoto accent.
His tone seemed peculiarly cold, but since Takabumi had missed
his lunch he was far too hungry to pay any attention to delicate shades of feeling. In Tokyo he had hardly ever visited an
udon shop, and he was amused to see a sign announcing "fox
udon" and "badger *udon*," unfamiliar names used to describe different varieties of the dish.

* Thick buckwheat vermicelli.

"What's the difference between the fox and the badger *udon?*" he asked the shopkeeper absently. The man turned his sullen face to Takabumi and in a characteristically offhanded manner replied: "There's starch on the badger."

Takabumi ordered both types of *udon*. He found that there was fried bean-curd floating in the fox *udon*. The badger *udon* seemed to be a finer dish, and had a thick arrowroot broth poured over it; it was, however, only slightly more expensive.

When he had eaten his fill, Takabumi sat back and reflected pleasantly that, since there were such dishes as fox *udon* and badger *udon*, there would be nothing strange in weasel *udon*. At the same time it occurred to him that if his friends knew that he, Baron Takabumi Iwamuro, was having his supper in a little *udon* shop on a noisy street, they would really feel that times had changed.

He went into the street and sat down under the trees. Removing his hat, he wiped the sweat from his forehead. He had been perspiring profusely, and the back of his coat showed damp marks. He had said that he would return to the hotel in the evening. It was now almost evening, but he doubted whether his wife was back yet from her drive.

After a while he stood up and started walking. This time he went down one of the back streets and came to the side of a river where the drainage water was flowing. Takabumi was looking for a cool place to rest when he was surprised to hear a strange, primitive cry. There was a zoo on the other side of the river. "I wonder if it's a fox or a badger," he muttered in an effort to amuse himself; but he did not succeed in laughing.

There were some steps leading down the stone embankment of the river, and Takabumi noticed that a man on the bottom step had thrown a net into the water. It was hard to imagine what fish one could hope to catch in this place. The man was dressed like a laborer, and Takabumi wondered whether his net-throwing represented business or pleasure.

As Takabumi crossed the little bridge, he noticed the way the iron railing was bent outward. The white dusty road at the other side looked as if it led to some temple. The pine-covered mountain ahead approached him as he walked away from the river, and the cry of the cicadas seemed to come from within its depths. Takabumi looked around to make sure that he would find his way back along the unfamiliar road. As he did so, he noticed the hotel on the hill where he had visited his wife earlier. One part of the building was lit up by the setting sun; the remainder was hidden by the hills. Takabumi took out his watch and saw that not even an hour had elapsed since he had gone to call on Kaoruko. How long they were—these summer days!

The telephone on the bedside table began ringing, and Kaoruko picked up the receiver. She had lain down after her bath, but had been unable to go to sleep. The darkness was seeping into her room, and she had not yet turned on the light. Kaoruko glanced at the mirror and noticed her own white figure clad in nothing but a thin slip.

"This is the front desk, Madam. There's a Baron Iwamuro here to see you. Would you like him shown to your room, Madam?"

"No," she replied firmly. "Please have him wait in the lobby. I'll come down at once."

There was no reason for her to hurry, thought Kaoruko, and she remained sitting on the bed for some time. Since they were meeting in the hall, there would be other people about, as well as members of the hotel staff, and her husband and she would maintain a polite reserve toward each other. Just then she heard the elevator stopping at her floor and the sound of footsteps coming along the corridor. With a start she pulled the heavy bedspread over her knees. She suddenly felt as if she were naked, and her heart started to pound.

The footsteps, however, were not Takabumi's. After they had disappeared down the corridor, Kaoruko turned on the light and started to dress. Not only at home, but when traveling, she always used to change into Japanese clothes in the evenings. Even among the well-dressed Kyoto women Kaoruko's kimonos invariably attracted attention. That evening she was wearing a new kimono that Takabumi had not yet seen. It was indigo blue with a fine pattern. Her under-kimono had a neckband of a bold color—a fashion that Kaoruko adopted only when she was on a journey and that she had never once shown her husband. She could not help feeling pleased with herself when she looked in the glass and saw the vermilion neckband, which contrasted sharply with the sober kimono and which might well have been worn by a young girl. There was something strong and sensitive about the line of this brightly colored neckband; at the same time it had an antique elegance that reminded one of paintings of women from the Meiji Period. Although Kaoruko liked striking new styles in her Western wardrobe, she preferred a more old-fashioned type of chic when it came to Japanese clothes. There was a voluptuous fullness about her body, but when she wore a kimono she looked as slender as a fashionable geisha.

Kaoruko walked down one flight of stairs to the lobby and saw her husband at the entrance of the terrace gazing into the darkness outside. Although he had his back to her, she recognized him at once from his characteristic posture. Several people were scattered about the hall in little clusters. Only her husband was by himself, and he stood out from all the others. Kaoruko walked up to him.

"Sorry I kept you waiting," she said in a normal tone of voice as if there were nothing out of the ordinary in their meeting.

Takabumi wheeled round. "What a splendid view!" he said, seemingly reluctant to take his eyes from the scene beyond the terrace. "That's Mount Yoshida over there, and that must be the Kurotani Tower."

Kaoruko had never had the slightest interest in the temples of Kyoto, and she looked without expression in the direction in which her husband was pointing. She felt that his only aim was to smooth over the initial awkwardness of the meeting. Since the hotel was at a considerable elevation, she could see the hills and mountains far into the distance. Indoors it was night, but the summer light remained outside even though the sun had set; the green of the hills and the brown-green of the trees stood out clearly, interspersed here and there with the pinpricks of lights from the low, flat city of Kyoto.

"Wouldn't you like to sit down?" said Kaoruko.

"Hm," he said, and walked slowly toward a chair, as though irked at having to tear himself away from the terrace. As Kaoruko sat down opposite him, she was annoyed to notice his sun-helmet lying on the table between them. Now that they were together she realized that she had nothing to say to her

husband, but, looking at the helmet, she abruptly remarked:
"It's got very dirty, hasn't it?"

"Hm," said Takabumi, looking at the hat. There was a
twinkle in his eyes. "It's old—just like our marriage."

"What a disagreeable remark!" said Kaoruko.

"Excuse me. Please don't read any irony into what I said.
That's certainly not what I intended. Far from it—you're still
very young. And I may add without flattery that you're prettier
than ever." Until then he had not seemed to pay any particular
attention to her, but now he looked carefully at his wife's elaborate make-up. Seeing Kaoruko for the first time in her splendid
evening clothes, he was dazzled by her elegance—as, indeed, any
man would have been, whether or not her husband.

"Red still suits you, doesn't it?" he said, referring to the neckband of her under-kimono. Kaoruko found Takabumi's flattery
unbearable and felt like leaving him then and there.

"You're making fun of me," she said.

"Oh, you mustn't take it amiss. I'm quite sincere in thinking
that you look lovely. What's wrong with saying so? I, on the
other hand, have grown old—just like my hat. And besides, I've
come down in the world."

"Well, you've done so of your own free will, haven't you?"
said Kaoruko.

Takabumi smiled wryly. "I should never have allowed myself to fall into such circumstances," he said with a self-mocking
laugh, "but times have changed. With the way things are now
in the world, a man doesn't know what to do with himself. It's
better to be a woman. Especially a woman like you, who knows
how to keep her looks."

"Even if one doesn't feel like it," said Kaoruko, "one should
always take good care of one's appearance. Otherwise one can't
make a living."

"Yes, but let me tell you that a time comes when one can't
do anything about one's appearance, however much one may
want to."

Though Takabumi was careful to preserve decorum and not
to let his tongue run away with him, a familiar harshness had begun to emerge in his speech. He wanted to take back what he
had said and to direct the conversation into more pleasant channels, but, owing to his ambiguous nature, he only succeeded in

making matters worse. "The fact is," he continued, "I'm unmanly and sloppy. People always used to say that this particular combination made one inferior even to women and children. Looking back on it all, I can see that there's nothing really new about my present troubles. In the old days a man of my type could enjoy a better life than most people simply by sticking to his privileges as a member of the nobility. It's really quite strange to think that such a system was generally accepted in the world. Now such a man is a decayed house whose foundations have been removed. It's only natural that such a house should lurch over and collapse. Of course one can say: 'Why don't you try getting a job and doing some work like everyone else?'" Takabumi looked up and peered into his wife's eyes. "That's what you've advised me to do, isn't it? Well, the answer is that there's a law of gravity and that the force pulling one downward is stronger than anything else. All one can do is to fall."

He paused for a while, then continued clearly: "And that doesn't apply only to me." There was a certain sadness in his gentle expression. "We're all the same—everyone in our circle. You too. We're all falling. It's no use saying it isn't so, because it is. Such are the times we live in. And the future will be the same. You see? It's only a matter of who is falling faster."

"What's the good of talking like that?" said Kaoruko.

"Good?" said Takabumi, deliberately assuming an expression of complete impassivity. "It's no good. Still, it's probably better to see things clearly and not to deceive oneself. I sometimes wonder whether it isn't because we were lucky enough to enjoy a pampered upbringing that we are now incapable of understanding despair in its real sense, however bad things become for us."

Takabumi was purposely speaking against himself, but, looking at his wife, he realized that she was not taking it in that way. "Let me put it this way," he continued. "Even though we are fully aware that things are bad for us and will continue to be bad, we somehow feel that we'll manage to pull through. This easygoing attitude, this false optimism of ours is an essential part of our nature—a congenital disease, so to speak."

"And," continued Takabumi after a pause, "only those people who, unlike us, know what despair means are capable of living in this world—of really living, I mean. Our own class is so constituted that until the very end we can never understand what despair means. And so we go through our lives without knowing how to live. After the war our class fell on hard times. But were we really unfortunate? I have my doubts. Of course, we all complain about how terrible conditions have become for us. But I wonder whether people who can still complain should really be called unfortunate. Real misfortune in this world makes it impossible for people even to talk about it."

"That's enough," put in Kaoruko. "I never thought that I should hear such talk from you."

"Since we don't have a home any longer," said Takabumi with a cold smile, "we can't very well talk about rice-bran pickles and such charming domestic details. That's true, isn't it? It's been a long time since we discussed whether today's cucumber pickles tasted good. Only couples who are happily settled in their home can talk about such things. You and I are beyond the stage of discussing our food and meals. We can't talk about anything that concerns home. So we might as well change to general topics that have nothing to do with our roles as husband and wife. Once the conversation turns to abstract matters, there's no question of our hurting each other."

"You hate me, don't you?" said Kaoruko.

"Do you really suppose I have the energy for that? One aspect of having been a peer is that I don't. And, apart from anything else, what good would it do to hate you? You're immortal, you see, and nothing can really upset you. It's a strange strength you have—that ability of yours to get along however circumstances change. It's something that only women seem to be endowed with. . . . Tell me if I'm hurting you and I'll stop."

"No, please go on," said Kaoruko. There was a cool expression on her face, but inwardly she felt that this was her opportunity to bring to its necessary conclusion a matter that until now had been allowed to remain in an ambiguous, halfway stage. She had felt this ever since Takabumi declared a few minutes before that they no longer had a home. "Please continue," she repeated.

Takabumi, however, chose this moment to change the subject. "I'm rather thirsty," he declared. "Would you mind ordering me a whisky or something? And I expect you'd like one yourself. You've become quite a drinker of late, haven't you?"

Kaoruko felt that she could stand no more. "I can't sit here with you indefinitely, you know."

"Really?" said Takabumi. "Ah, to be sure, you have work to do, don't you? Still, I'm sure you won't mind inviting me to a glass of whisky. I'm sorry to say so, but I haven't had a decent drink for ages."

When Kaoruko called the waiter, Takabumi calmly gave the order himself. He asked for the most expensive Scotch available and ordered a double. Then, disregarding Kaoruko's objections, he added: "And please bring the same thing for my wife."

When the drinks came Takabumi picked up his glass and drank a good part of it. One might have expected that the strong whisky would do something to soften his mood, but from his youth Takabumi had never allowed alcohol to modify his stiff manner.

"When I was walking round outside just now," he said, sitting bolt upright, "I came across a man fishing by himself in the canal. He didn't catch anything, but he kept on throwing in his net. People who are acquainted with poverty, you see, tend to become very patient. I'm a poor man myself, but I still couldn't carry patience to the point that he did. The trouble with me is that I'm only halfway there—I still believe that somehow things are going to work out."

Kaoruko had no intention of listening to her husband's gloomy ramblings, and she drank her whisky in a deliberate effort to let the alcohol cheer her up. Now that it was night the hotel was full of people. Several of the men had brought along geishes from the Gion district, and the merry sound of conversation filled the large hall. Only the table where Kaoruko and her husband sat facing each other was subdued, as if suspended in a vacuum.

"And what brought you to Kyoto?" asked Kaoruko casually, as though it were some gratuitous question that she might just as well not have asked.

"Hm," said Takabumi, smiling into his glass. "Perhaps to keep an eye on how you were behaving yourself."

Kaoruko was annoyed. "Are you joking?" she said crossly.

"Of course, I am," said Takabumi. "How could I supervise you—even if I wanted to?"

"I'd rather you showed me a little more respect, if you don't mind."

"I don't think I've said anything to make you angry. Anyhow, I've decided not to interfere with your life in future, whatever happens. What good does it do, after all? And now that we've broken up like this, things should be a little easier between us, don't you think?"

"Are you sure you mean what you're saying?" asked Kaoruko.

"Certainly I do."

"In that case wouldn't it be better if you and I made a clean break?"

"I'd rather put that off for a while," said Takabumi, and his smiling face assumed a severe expression. "If we separated for good now, I'd be the loser. As for our child," he added, "I'd rather we didn't mention him. We'd better keep all this ugliness between the two of us without bringing the child into it."

"I see," said Kaoruko. "You want me to go on working indefinitely while you live in idle comfort."

"It was never my idea that you should work," said Takabumi. His manner was as stiff and correct as ever, but one could see from his eyes that the whisky had taken effect. "It's a shame," he continued. "By the way, if I were to ask you now to give up your work, would you agree?"

Kaoruko did not reply.

"No, of course you wouldn't. You like it. You're happy doing what you are."

Kaoruko looked back at her husband with a hard expression and replied emphatically. "Yes, I am. If I said I didn't enjoy it, I'd only be lying. I feel I can breathe more freely now than when I stayed at home and kept house for you."

There was a strange sound, and Kaoruko looked up. Takabumi had crushed his glass of whisky, and the pieces lay scattered on the table. Takabumi gazed directly into his wife's eyes with a hard, frozen look. There were trickles of blood between his fingers. Without the slightest change of expression he silently wrapped his hand in a handkerchief. Noticing that his wife had turned pale, he quietly apologized.

"Not enough self-control, I'm afraid," he said. "Or rather, it's a matter of virtue disappearing in the face of poverty, as the

proverb has it. That doesn't apply to people who have never had
anything all their lives, but it's certainly true of you and me."

"Would you mind excusing me?" said Kaoruko.

"I see. So you're going to throw your husband out *à la
Américaine*. Let's talk quietly for just a few more minutes.
What about telling the waiter that we've had a slight accident
with the glass and ordering another drink?"

He spoke in an extremely subdued voice. Kaoruko glanced
at the people sitting around the table directly next to theirs:
they were chatting away cheerfully, apparently unaware that
Takabumi had crushed his glass to smithereens.

"Don't you need a bandage or something?" she asked.

"Don't worry," said Takabumi, glancing perfunctorily under
the handkerchief.

"Let's go to my room," she said.

Takabumi looked up at his wife. He was evidently amazed
at her suggestion, but his expression did not change.

"You mean you'll share your bed with me?" he asked impassively.

Kaoruko felt the blood coursing through her veins, and she
was overcome by an entirely irrational sense of confusion. A
slight flush came to her pale face, and she broke into a smile.

"What on earth are you saying, Takabumi? What a terrible
man you are!"

"So you won't sleep with me? You won't put me up for the
night? Well, I have my own room at an inn, so I won't press
the point. The only thing is that I'm rather low in funds. I'd
intended to pay for my journey by playing the bicycle races,
but instead after a couple of days I've gone and lost the lot."

"Do you mean to say that you go in for betting on bicycle
races?"

"That's about all I'm good for now. So far as I'm concerned,
you see, it's a matter of floating or sinking."

"You certainly have taken up some plebeian occupations,
haven't you? Really, Takabumi! Bicycle racing, of all things!"

"No, I think you're wrong about that. In any case, please
let me have some money. Then I'll be off. I have no intention
of bothering you any further. 'Pathetic!'—that's what you'd like
to say, isn't it? Well, this is how people act when they've come

down in the world, and no one has any right to condemn them. With some cash in my pocket and a bit of luck at the race track, things may work out in the next couple of days so that you won't be sorry I came here. Just let me have some money, and you can do exactly as you want from now on."

"I see," said Kaoruko offhandedly. "But still I'd rather you hadn't come."

Opening her bag, she extracted some money and, without counting the amount, quickly handed it to her husband, taking care that the people at the next table should not notice.

There was a proud look on Takabumi's face.

"I won't say thank you," he stated confidently. "I'm glad to see that I still have some rights as a husband."

"So you'd sink to making remarks like that, would you? I shan't forget what you've just said."

"Now that I've got the money everything is all right. I'm quite a mercenary fellow at heart, you see. Well, shall we go to your room?"

"Allow me to decline your charming offer," said Kaoruko with an icy smile.

"Hm, I see. It wouldn't really do, would it? I suppose it's only natural that you should dislike me. All the same, what about one more whisky?"

From the expression on Takabumi's face one would imagine that he was smiling at his circumstances as he continued his monologue. "I used to think—though rather vaguely, to be sure—that husband and wife were traveling companions for life. But we seem to have drifted apart halfway through the journey. We couldn't go back now to where we were even if we wanted to. Don't think that I'm blaming you! It's no one's fault. I wonder if our original sin, so to speak, didn't arise ineluctably from the luxury-loving class to which we both belonged. Come to think of it, it seems as though all the couples in our circle had a draft blowing through the walls of their marriage. By means of forbearance and mutual dishonesty they managed to put up a good front and not to let any of the cracks appear on the surface. The unhappier they were, those couples we used to know, the more they tried to keep up appearances. One might have imagined that if husband and wife were both aware of each other's unhappiness this would serve in some pro-

found way to bind them together. But it doesn't work out like
that. . . . I didn't want to bring him into the conversation,
but the truth is that the only thing that held our marriage together was our son."

There was a frozen look on Takabumi's face as he threw
out his words. Then abruptly he retracted what he had said.
"No, to bring Takamasa into this would only be cowardly.
There's no need to pollute someone who is utterly innocent.
Let's keep the mud-slinging between ourselves! To be sure, there
was a time when we were in love with each other and people
actually envied us."

"I do wish you'd stop," said Kaoruko, and there was pro-
found sorrow in her voice as she repeated the words, "Do please
stop."

When he noticed this, Takabumi's tone became even
harsher than before. "It was always my habit in the past," he
said, once more looking directly into his wife's eyes, "to stop halfway in our conversation. Either I'd give up in the middle, or I'd
lose my temper. But I wonder if it wouldn't be a good idea to
continue for once until the very end—and not to mince my
words while I'm about it. Yes, I think it would be a very good
idea. Now, you and I were never a couple in the proper sense
of the word, were we? What we really were was a pair of ornaments whose aim was simply to assume some superficial sort of
pose before the world. You were an extremely attractive woman
whom any husband would be proud to introduce into society.
And what you liked in me, I'm sorry to say, was the position and
title to which I was born. It's not true to say we loved each other.
There was really only the shallowest connection between us."

"Are you trying to hurt me?" asked Kaoruko in a voice husky
with emotion. Her features no longer looked beautiful. "You,
who let me work—while you live in complete idleness yourself."

"Work, my dear, isn't quite what you seem to think it is,"
said Takabumi. "Have you ever worked till you were wet with
perspiration, till you were too tired to stand up straight? No, of
course you haven't. What you call work is just another form of
play. I suppose you're still really a child. You've never grown out
of your childhood simplicity."

Takabumi's voice was blurred, and his eyes seemed to be
shining with tears. His voice had become gentle and quiet.

"Women don't really understand the meaning of what they do. After the war when I lost my special position in society I was no longer of use to you. Then it was the Americans who came to occupy a special position in Japanese society. I don't want to sound envious, but that's how it was. And so, like a bee that has found a new supply of honey . . ."

It was the same exchange that they had gone through time after time in the past. Kaoruko was thoroughly accustomed to her husband's arguments and had learned to turn a deaf ear. But this evening there was something new in Takabumi's expression. Since they were sitting in a hotel surrounded by strangers, he spoke as calmly as possible. But in this very calm she could detect an icy hardness. It bewildered Kaoruko, and at the same time it provoked a sharp antipathy in her. Her outer bearing was one of cool indifference, as if to suggest: "Say what you have to say, and I'll hear you out." But inside she was reacting violently to her husband's ill-natured remarks.

Kaoruko felt that they had now reached the decisive stage. At that moment she became aware of the scent that came from a flower arrangement in another part of the hall, and she breathed in the aroma intently—the smell of ginger. Kaoruko knew that for the rest of her life whenever she saw a ginger plant she would be reminded of this fierce evening—this evening which, she felt sure, would be the last with her husband.

"You can think exactly as you like," she said calmly. "It's all the same to me." Her face was as white as a sheet of paper.

Her husband picked up his sun-helmet and left the lobby—with what destination she neither knew nor wanted to know. As soon as he had left, Kaoruko walked back along the deserted corridor to her room. Her breast was seething with fury.

"Well, take care of yourself as best you can"—Takabumi's parting words still echoed in her ears. "But then, I don't suppose you really know what you're doing." She had sensed something strangely manly and gentle in his voice. And the deep, moist look of Takabumi's eyes as he gazed into hers conveyed a forgiveness and an entreaty that seemed to contradict everything that he had been saying to her that evening. At this thought Kaoruko was overcome with a new distaste for the man. He struck her now as a poor servile creature who was prepared slugglishly to endure all his present dissatisfactions rather than make a clean break.

When Kaoruko returned to her room, she felt thoroughly soiled. In particular, Takabumi's old sun-helmet had aroused her strongest aversion. On an impulse she strode into the bathroom and turned on both taps fully so that the hot and cold water splashed loudly into the basin.

As she stared into the mirror and started to do over her make-up, the water poured fiercely into the basin and a few moments later it was flowing over the edges. Kaoruko felt it lapping at her feet. She hurriedly stretched out her hand and turned off the taps, at the same time making an effort not to get herself wet. She could not help smiling at her own confusion. She felt like a naughty child who has been playing with water. The bath mat was thoroughly drenched, and it occurred to Kaoruko that she ought to inform the maid. Just then the telephone rang. No doubt it was the young American that had accompanied her from Tokyo who had been making vague declarations of love since the outset of the journey.

Kaoruko picked up the receiver.

"Hullo," she said in her usual cheerful tone.

"It's me," came the reply in Japanese, and Kaoruko was momentarily taken aback. "Yes, it's Tsugawa."

"Oh, Ryobei-san." She had completely forgotten about the young man and was amazed to hear his voice. "Where are you speaking from?"

"I just arrived on the train. I'm at the same hotel as you. I noticed in the register that you were staying here, and so I thought I'd try phoning you."

Kaoruko suddenly remembered the telegram that she had sent from the train. She felt like bursting into laughter, but she had to pretend not to know anything about the matter.

"What a strange coincidence!" she said. "Who are you with?"

"I'm alone," he replied.

Hearing his youthful voice, Kaoruko was reminded of the young man's pleasant, rough-hewn manner, and she was pleased to have a companion with whom she could feel so completely at ease.

"That's perfect," she said. "Are you in your room now?"

"Yes, I am. I've only just arrived, you see."

"In that case, why don't you go down to the bar on the second floor, and I'll join you at once."

"What about coming to your room instead? It's on the same floor as mine, and the porter told me that it's almost next door."

"Well, well," said Kaoruko with a laugh. "Oh, I suppose it's all right. Come along."

She had hardly put down the receiver when there was the sound of footsteps outside her door. Ryosuké knocked and came in. Sitting by the mirror, Kaoruko turned to greet him. There was an easygoing rough quality about the young man that pleased her. He stood there smiling pleasantly, and it amused her to think that he was utterly unaware of the hoax that had brought him to Kyoto.

"Good evening," he said. Instead of looking directly at Kaoruko, he glanced round the room. "A big room, isn't it? Nice and cool too."

"Is yours small?"

"Yes, it's on the small side, I had to leave in a hurry, you see, and I didn't have time to get together the money I needed. There's some waiting for me in Kobe, though. That's what I'm counting on."

He had settled himself calmly in a chair and certainly did not give the impression of having rushed down to Kyoto on the spur of the moment.

"The fact is," continued Ryosuké, "a friend of mine came down here ahead of me and should have been staying at this hotel. I got a telegram asking me to come."

Kaoruko did her best not to show her amusement.

"And wasn't your friend here when you arrived?"

"No, evidently my friend has gone on to Kobe without waiting for me," said the young man softly, as if speaking to himself. He stood up, walked over to the full-length mirror and examined his face.

"I need a shave," he muttered. "Oh dear, I wonder if I forgot to bring my razor."

Kaoruko was suddenly overcome by a fit of laughter, and she had to make the greatest effort to control herself. Her cheeks were flushed, and it seemed as if the whisky that she had drunk with her husband during their recent turbulent encounter was abruptly taking effect.

"What's so funny?" said Ryosuké.

"Nothing important. I'll tell you later," said Kaoruko. "Well now, Ryobei-san, since you're here why don't we go out together somewhere? Let's see what Kyoto looks like at night!"

"Yes, I'm afraid I did forget that razor," said Ryosuké, continuing his own train of thought. Like most young people, he tended to be absorbed in himself; the words seemed to bubble forth naturally from his great body without any regard for the people about him. "And I expect that the barber shop in the hotel is closed."

"A bit of beard won't matter," said Kaoruko. "On the contrary, it'll make you look even tougher, and you'll be a more effective bodyguard. That's important, you know, if one's walking at night through a strange town."

"No, no, I have to look my smartest. After all, we are in Kyoto."

"Come on, Ryobei-san," said Kaoruko. "It really doesn't matter about shaving. At least you washed your face after getting off the train, didn't you?"

"As a matter of fact, I didn't. I came directly to the hotel, and then I was rather put out when I didn't find my friend waiting for me. I forgot all about washing. If we're going out together, let me wash in your bathroom."

"All right," said Kaoruko with a slight air of impatience. "I'll wait." She took a pack of American cigarettes out of her bag and started to smoke. Presently she heard Ryosuké's voice above the sound of running water in the bathroom.

"I'm using your face lotion. I hope you don't mind."

With the cigarette in her hand Kaoruko picked up the telephone and asked the clerk at the front desk to order a car. Then she sat back and imagined how she would spend the night—a free night, very different from her usual evenings. All of a sudden she remembered Takabumi and nervously looked at her watch. She was not particularly worried about running into her husband when she went out. The recent stormy parting from Takabumi, however, remained vividly in her mind and filled her with bitter hostility toward him.

"We'd better hurry, you know," she called out to the young man. "Would you mind locking the door when you leave? I'll go ahead."

Kaoruko hurried along the corridor toward the elevator. There was still no one about. When she passed the porter's room she had the impression that someone was in the back, but no one seemed to be looking out. It occurred to her that, having now obtained some money, her husband might on the spur of the moment have decided to take a room at the hotel. It was just the sort of ironic move that he would make. On his journeys he had always preferred Western hotels to Japanese inns. Then Kaoruko recalled the violence with which he had crushed the whisky glass in his bare hand, and a shudder ran through her body.

Without waiting for Ryosuké, she pressed the button for the elevator. Reaching the lobby, she was relieved to see that the clerk was still standing at the desk.

"We want to go out for a drink somewhere," she said, smiling pleasantly at him. "Can you suggest a good place?"

"Would you mind waiting a moment, Madam?" said the clerk affably. He disappeared into a back room and after a short consultation with someone came back and handed Kaoruko a piece of paper with the name of a bar.

The door of the elevator opened, and Ryosuké stepped out. A few moments later they drove off in the car. It was dark and quiet in that part of the city, as though it were the middle of the night. The trolley lines glittered coolly along the surface of the road. "Tonight I'm doing exactly as I want," declared Kaoruko silently, and she seemed to be addressing the figure of her husband whose image remained so sharply in her mind.

"Well, that's enough," said Ryosuké. "Let's go back to the hotel." It was already past midnight, but Mrs. Iwamuro still did not want to go home. She had drunk glass after glass of whisky and was by now extremely drunk. There were still other customers in the bar, however, and Kaoruko was too well bred to lose control of herself. They had gone from bar to bar during the course of the evening. At the last place Kaoruko had started playing dice, and they had stayed particularly long. At the moment she was playing with the young woman from the Gion geisha district who owned the bar.

"A real battle between Tokyo and Kyoto, isn't it?" said Ryosuké. Indeed, the battle was not only in dice but also in drinking. Each time that one of the players lost she had to take a full drink, and Ryosuké noticed that by now both their faces were flushed. Earlier he had whispered to the waitress to fetch a taxi; the car had arrived some time before and the driver was impatiently sounding his horn. Kaoruko did not even notice the strident blasts.

"Really," said Ryosuké, "we'd better be off. We can't keep the driver waiting indefinitely."

"You can go home on your own, Ryobei-san," said Kaoruko. "Osomé-san will see me back to the hotel when I'm ready to leave."

"No, no, you've had quite enough. At this rate, it'll be morning before you know it."

Ryosuké frowned at her, but she still paid no attention to him.

The taxi-driver had decided that blowing his horn was useless, and he looked into the bar.

"Aren't you coming yet?" he said.

"Yes," said Ryosuké. "Let's be off. Come on, Mrs. Iwamuro. The taxi won't wait any longer."

The owner of the bar sympathized with Ryosuké and urged Kaoruko to leave.

"Well," said Kaoruko, "since we've got to leave, let's have just one more go."

"Yes, but only one."

"You really are a nuisance!"

Ryosuké put on his hat and stood up. Finally they got into the car. As soon as they started moving, Karouko asked the driver whether there wasn't some other bar in Kyoto that was still open. Before the man could reply, Ryosuké said: "Kindly take us directly to the hotel."

"But I don't want to go back."

"All the bars are closed by now," Ryosuké told her. "It's best to return to the hotel and ask the porter to bring something to drink."

"Well, I'm going to sleep."

The alcohol seemed suddenly to have taken effect; Kaoruko

lay down, supporting her head on Ryosuké's lap. Since he could not very well force her to sit up straight, he allowed her to lie there.

"Um," she murmured, "it feels good!"

"You drank an awful lot," said Ryosuké. "You must have a terrible head. I was really astonished to see how much you could manage in one evening."

Kaoruko lay quietly on the back seat without answering. Since her head was facing downwards, Ryosuké could feel her warm breath against his knees. Then with a gentle movement she drew his hand toward her and held it between her palms.

"Oh yes, it feels good," she repeated. "But I'm afraid the drink has suddenly gone to my head."

"That's hardly surprising, you know."

"So I get no sympathy from you at all," said Kaoruko.

She gave a deep sigh and then became completely subdued. After a few moments Ryosuké felt something warm between the fingers of the hand that Kaoruko was holding in hers. He looked and saw that her cheeks were covered with tears which were flowing gently onto her hands. It must be the effect of of alcohol, he thought. But he had no inclination to ask her why she was crying.

"We're almost at the hotel," he said.

At this, Kaoruko abruptly lifted her head from his lap, sat up straight, and looked out of the window. Then she took out a handkerchief and wiped her face.

Kaoruko did not remember how she had stepped out of the car, nor how she had made her way through the hotel lobby. When she came to herself a few moments later, she was standing in the elevator and being held up by some man. At first she thought it was Takabumi, and she made a violent effort to shake herself free. Then she saw that the face was Ryosuké's.

"Oh, it's you, is it, Ryobei-san?" she said with an abashed air. "I must have fallen asleep."

"While you were walking? Rather an achievement, I must say."

He was a tall, powerfully built young man, and when they stepped out of the elevator he had no difficulty in supporting her as she made her way unsteadily down the corridor. The hotel was dead quiet, and only occasionally the silence was broken by the sound of someone snoring in one of the rooms.

"Would you unlock the door?" she said.

Ryosuké did as he was asked and threw open the door of Kaoruko's room.

"Well, have a good sleep," he said.

"Wait a minute. You've got to take me all the way into the room."

The light on the bedside table had been left on, and it gently illuminated the spacious bed. The maid had removed the cover and turned down the sheets. Ryosuké helped Kaoruko to the center of the room and promptly turned to leave.

"Good night to you," he said.

Kaoruko tried to unfasten her *obi*, but suddenly her legs gave way, and she sat down on the carpet next to the bed.

"Look out!" said Ryosuké. "Do be careful."

"You've got to put me to bed," said Kaoruko. "I can't possibly undress myself."

Ryosuké stopped at the threshold and turned round.

"Do you want me to call the maid for you?" he asked.

"Certainly not!" she replied emphatically.

With a perplexed air Ryosuké looked around the room for a bell. Then he saw that Kaoruko, while still sitting on the carpet, had somehow managed to unfasten her *obi*. The neck of her kimono had come loose and beneath the rich silk material the young man could make out the bright red of her under-kimono and, in contrast, the white roundness of her full breasts. His momentary confusion turned to anger.

"Really!" he exclaimed. "This is going too far. It's late and I'm sleepy."

"Well then, you can sleep here."

Her face, too, had assumed a fiery expression. This did not come from any artifice on her part, but from a sensation that had begun to burn fiercely throughout her body.

"What's wrong with you anyway?" As she threw out the challenge, her dark eyes flashed and she gazed directly at Ryosuké.

The young man smiled. He also felt that some powerful force had sprung up inside him, removing all his timidity. He was firmly convinced, however, that this force was nothing but revulsion and scorn aroused by Mrs. Iwamuro's brazen behavior. The two of them glared at each other for a moment that seemed far longer than it actually was. The hotel was utterly quiet, and not a sound came from the street to break the perfect stillness. There was nothing to be heard but the gentle swishing of silk as Kaoruko removed her *obi*.

"You really are drunk, aren't you?" said Ryosuké.

His own voice sounded thin and empty to him, but Kaoruko heard in it a warm strength and fullness.

"No," she said, "not in the slightest." But the deadly pallor of her cheeks belied her words. "It's all right, you know. You can do exactly what you want."

A sudden thought of Taeko made Kaoruko feel so light-hearted that she wanted to burst out laughing. She felt her heart pounding. Ryosuké no longer made any move to leave the room. In what way, she wondered, was he different from all the other men to whom she had given herself out of a momentary whim? Yes, it was Taeko that made the difference. The existence of this young girl made Kaoruko glow with a strange excitement. She felt as if she were gambling and, already she was preparing to exult in her victory.

"It's all very well to claim you aren't drunk," said Ryosuké. "The fact is that you can't even stand up straight."

"In that case why don't you help me to stand up? Are you afraid of touching me?"

"Don't be stupid!" said Ryosuké.

He walked up to Kaoruko from behind and lifted her with deliberate roughness. The alcohol had made her body limp and heavy. Then, as he lifted her, her kimono fell open, and Ryosuké saw the white, beautifully shaped legs which he had glimpsed that morning in the Kawana Hotel when she had returned his watch to him. At the sight of their long nakedness he was unbearably aroused. For a moment the thought flashed through his mind: "She's soiled. This body of hers has been handled by Americans." But then he became aware of the rich scent emanating from the voluptuous body in his arms—the scent of a gardenia whose petals have just begun to take on a tinge of golden brown.

THE SUN was still high in the sky and it was early in the afternoon when Soroku Ōkamoto reached the Ozawa mountain hut
at the entrance to the Harinoki Pass, which runs from the
Shinshu side of the Japanese Alps to Tateyama in Etchu.

Most mountaineers would have considered it a waste of daylight hours to stop at Ozawa for the night; after a short rest
they would have pressed on and easily reached the Harinoki
hut by nightfall. This, as a matter of fact, was exactly what
Akira had done on his visit to these mountains. Consulting his
son's diary, which he carried in his pocket, Soroku saw that
Akira had spent the first night at Omachi, had passed the
Ozawa hut, and had reached Harinoki Pass in time to spend
the following night there. Soroku had originally intended to
follow the same schedule, but his legs were unaccustomed to
mountain-climbing and he had been obliged to cut down his
daily mileage to half of that covered by most climbers. Soroku,
now a man in his fifties, was obliged to edge his way forward
gingerly, like an inchworm.

When it had occurred to Soroku one day in Kamakura that

he would like to follow in the footsteps of Akira and to walk along the same mountain path that his son had climbed years ago, he had abruptly translated this wish into action. For the same reason he had previously set out on a journey to the unfamiliar island of Sado. On these occasions it was as if he were overcome by a fit, and he moved in a sort of trance. Once the idea of departure came into his head, nothing could make him stay quietly at home.

Soroku himself could not explain the real reason for this peculiar behavior on his part. All he could say was that, unless he set out on these journeys, he could find no inner peace—as though there were some shadow in his spirit that he himself could not comprehend. In olden days parents who had lost a child often used to set out on pilgrimages through the country. Soroku knew that in these modern times he could hardly imitate their example. Yet he felt that he was gradually coming to understand these parents of old and the way in which they were consumed with emotion so that their actions became a sort of prayer.

It was strange, yet by no means incomprehensible, that by journeying to unknown parts of the country, by exposing themselves to the wind and the rain, by dragging their bodies into the most desolate and wretched places, people should succeed in finding a certain peace and a surcease of their sorrow. Yet no such solution seemed possible for Soroku. He had no wife to share his sorrow. He was utterly alone; indeed, he had made loneliness an essential condition of his life. He had no traveling companion who could accompany him through unknown parts in the wind and the rain—a companion to whom he could become still closer as a result of sharing a common grief.

Of late Soroku had come to realize that during his wife's lifetime he had given her nothing but trouble; yet he wondered if he would behave very differently if she were still alive. It occurred to him that it was precisely because he was a widower and alone that he had taken it into his head to go mountain-climbing and had glibly set out on this journey.

Soroku had taken the train to Shinano Omachi and had gone directly to an inn. There he had made inquiries about a certain mountain guide whose name appeared in Akira's diary. Since it was over ten years since Akira had come to this place, there was no telling whether the man was still alive, but somewhat to Soroku's surprise the same guide was readily available. He called at the inn in the evening to make arrangements for the climb. The guide was a sturdy man, about the same age as Soroku. He looked like a typical mountain peasant who, when the climbing season was over, worked on his fields and who, despite his advancing age, somehow could not manage to tear himself away from the mountain trails.

"Mr. Okamoto, you say?" The guide scratched his head dubiously. He was not one to make a pretence of remembering someone he had forgotten.

"Yes, that's right," said Soroku. "He came here with a party of about four school friends. Surely you remember him."

"How many years ago would that be?"

"It's about ten years now."

Soroku had forgotten to bring a photograph of his son. He had no desire to force the guide to remember Akira.

"Well, sir, once a student has visited these mountains he almost always comes back. They grow up quickly, of course. Many's the time that I've not been able to recognize a customer because only a few years before he still looked like a schoolboy. Sometimes a youngster I've taken out on the mountains will come back ten or even twenty years later, bringing his wife and children along. Yes, there have been many gentlemen who've kept in touch with me year after year."

The guide mentioned the names of several of his old customers, evidently expecting Soroku to recognize them.

Well, thought Soroku, it seemed clear that from among his memories of all the young men who had come to this place season after season the image of Akira had disappeared.

"Whose group was he with, sir?" mumbled the guide, bending his wrinkled neck to the side. He used the English word for "group," and Soroku realized that he must have picked this up from the young students whom he had taken out on expeditions.

When Soroku reached the mountain hut it was early, and, since he had nothing to do, the guide suggested that they should set off directly for the near-by ravine. Soroku, however, did not feel like moving.

He thought of the trip so far. He remembered how he had left Omachi by car; as they drove along the rough road, he had gazed constantly at the mountains toward which he had been heading. When they had reached the end of the road, they had made their way on foot along a forest path, stopping for rest at frequent intervals. A group of students, among whom were several girls, had caught up with them—all efficiently equipped for mountain-climbing, and marching along with an air of buoyant cheerfulness. Soroku would have liked to attach himself to the group, but not being strong enough to keep up with them, he had been obliged to step aside and let them pass.

"Where are you heading for?" a member of the group had asked in a decisive tone.

"We'll be going from Daira to Goshiki," Soroku's guide had answered, "and then we're cutting through to Toyama."

"That's where we're going too. Is the road to the Daira hut very bad?"

"Parts of it were hit by the typhoon, but it's not all that bad."

Soroku, already exhausted by the short distance that he had walked, had sat by the side of the road and listened to the conversation.

"Where will you be spending the night?" one of the students had asked.

"At the Ozawa hut," the guide had replied.

The students had burst out laughing, and Soroku had detected a certain scorn in their expression.

"Well, you really believe in doing things comfortably!" one of them had said with an artless smile.

The students had then said good-by and started walking. Soon the sound of their steps had receded; down the open path their figures had become smaller and smaller and finally disappeared altogether behind the trees. After some time the bright sound of voices had come from the distance.

"Yoho!" they had shouted. "Yoho!" had answered someone in another group. Each time their calls had emphasized the fantastic silence of the mountains. Presently Soroku had run into a group coming down the path from the mountains. From the speed with which their legs had moved he had felt that they were almost flying. Some of the passers-by had exchanged brief greetings, others had only smiled and nodded. Their friendliness, came from the fact that there were so few people in these parts. A warmth that one would rarely find on city streets seemed to spring up instantaneously among young mountaineers, and they threw out affable greetings to each passer-by—including complete strangers.

Presently the forest had became thicker and the path narrower. Sometimes it had been completely blocked by trees that had been felled by avalanches, making it necessary either to crawl under the trunks or to find some suitable foothold and to climb over—all entirely new exercise for Soroku, and soon he had been gasping for breath. They came to some swampy ground and had to walk close to the face of a cliff. At one point they had crossed a narrow log bridge—Soroku trudging along inertly behind the guide. He had remembered with dismay that this was only the first day of the climb and by far the easiest. Upon reaching the hut at Ozawa, he had not even the strength to remove his socks, but had simply collapsed in a chair and sat there motionless.

A near-by mountain stream sounded like wind in the pine trees as it swished its way down the valley.

"Over that way," he had heard the guide saying, "the trees are beginning to thin out. It won't be so good if there's an avalanche . . . not enough protection."

The hut, however, stood safely by itself in the midst of a dense forest.

Soroku had been told that, however good the weather might be in the morning, there was no telling how it might change in the afternoon. When he woke up on the following morning, he saw that it was a beautiful day. As the hut was in a valley, it took some time for the sun to reach it, and at first the sun only illuminated the mountain peaks. The sun dyed the stone a bright red; then imperceptibly it oozed down the side of the mountains and toward the hut.

The song of the early birds filled the clear air of the valley. Soroku felt thoroughly refreshed despite his exhaustion of the preceding evening. He washed his face in the mountain water, which was too cool to keep for more than a few seconds in his hands. Then he looked up at the sky and was overcome with elation.

A group of young people had come up from Omachi on the previous evening and had stopped at the same hut as Soroku. As soon as it became dark they had lain down and slept soundly. They had still been in the hut when Soroku woke up, but they had breakfasted rapidly and set off before he noticed it.

The guide informed Soroku that he did not have sufficient equipment for the climb. He discussed the matter with the young woman who owned the hut and managed to hire the necessary items. The guide packed everything neatly into a large knapsack and a few moments later announced that they were ready to leave.

The owner of the hut, as well as the young girl from the village who worked there during the climbing season to earn extra money, came out to see Soroku off. They left the hut empty and walked along the mountain path in their ordinary clogs. They had not gone far, however, before the young woman broke the strap on one of her clogs and they had to return to the hut.

"Well, sir," she said, "have a good climb. And do be careful, won't you?"

It was clear from her voice that she sympathized with Soroku, who was so much older than most of the climbers.

Having waved good-by to the two women, Soroku and the guide set off in earnest. Soroku braced himself for the climb. Now at last, he thought, the real mountains would begin.

Although it was already near the end of August, the foliage was as green as in the early summer. The thick forest was alive with the constant twittering of birds. Gradually the trees thinned out, and through the branches Soroku made out what looked like a solid white wall—the snow that still remained in the ravine from the winter months.

"We follow this ravine all the way up to that 'neck,' " explained the guide.

Soroku examined the scene in front of him. The steep ravine extended far into the distance and ahead of it soared a great pile of rocks. This looked far easier than the rough forest road. In fact, thought Soroku, you could probably climb this part of the mountains with your eyes closed, just as if you were walking along a broad city pavement.

Presently they were standing on a grassy cliff, dotted here and there with little mountain lilies. Looking down the ravine, Soroku saw that the snow divided at a certain point and that beyond it there was a tunnel-like hollow, from which a rill poured fiercely down into the valley.

As far as he could see there was not a sign of human life. Dyed by the morning sun the mountain peaks and the ravine lay there in perfect stillness. The only sound was that of the running water. At the point where they entered the ravine the guide unloaded the knapsack from his shoulders and had Soroku sit down on a rock. He then helped him put on a pair of hobnailed shoes to stop him from slipping on the snow. Soroku sat there as obediently as a child. "I'm entirely in your hands," he thought, and a gentle smile came to his face.

"It was just about here," said the guide, "that those students from Waseda University ran into the avalanche and were all buried alive. About ten years ago, it was. It took a long time before they could find the bodies. You see over there, sir? That's where the avalanche came down. And up there on the mountain they've put a memorial tablet to mark the disaster. I was called out to help search for the bodies. You've never seen such deep snow! And the wind was blowing it all over the place. We didn't have a chance. Yes, I remember it as if it were yesterday. Even that hut we stayed in last night at Ozawa was buried up to the rafters. You had to crawl in and out through the smoke trap on the roof."

"They were young fellows, weren't they?"

"Yes, sir, they were all students."

Soroku's eyes took in the surrounding scene. It was so quiet that he felt he could hear the echo of their conversation hovering in the air for some time after they had stopped speaking. Then, as he turned his head, he had the impression that Akira's voice was calling him: "Father, Father!" He could not tell where it came from. Yes, thought Soroku, it was this very ravine that his son had climbed with his friends. In his little red diary Akira had clearly recorded his time of arrival at the ravine and the time at which he had reached the Harinoki hut at the top. As Soroku followed the guide on his first trip up the mountain, he felt that he was far from being a stranger on these slopes.

The snow was uneven and dirty. Here and there it was broken in great cracks, and sometimes the weight of his body as it pressed on the hard white surface opened up fissures as long as an *obi*.

From the distance it had not looked like a very steep climb, but now that he started up the slope he found himself trudging along with considerable difficulty; even though he had no load on his back, he had to bend forward and use his stick for support. Thanks to his nailed shoes he was able to climb without slipping. Yet he kept his eyes on the snow ahead of him and was constantly aware of his own dark shadow on the white ground.

After a while he found that at every count of twenty steps he had to stop for breath. Each time he would look up at the high mountains that bordered the ravine, like the walls of a great corridor. There was not a single cloud in the deep blue sky. On the slope above he made out the stripe-like scars left by falling stones and boulders. The snow reflected the morning sun with dazzling brilliance.

The guide noticed that Soroku was having increasing difficulty in starting after each of his rests. At one of the stops he left his charge by the side of the path and clambered up to a grove on the side of the mountain, reappearing shortly with a handful of green plants. Evidently this was some mountain herb which he intended to eat when they reached the next hut. Soroku started climbing again. He became more and more conscious of the weariness in his body. A few moments later he stopped and, leaning on his stick, looked back at the ground he had covered. He was surprised to see how steep the slope was. At the same time he noticed that he had hardly come any distance at all since the beginning of the ravine.

With the wind blowing over the snow and the sun shining down, Soroku felt hot one moment and strangely cold the next, until in the end he was no longer sure whether he was hot or cold. All he knew was that he was perspiring profusely from the effort of the climb and that his eyes were hollow with exhaustion.

He had still not reached the halfway point up the ravine.

"I've certainly dragged myself to an odd place this time!" he thought. Then he made an effort to imagine his son. Presently he was aware that not far from his own shadow, which moved sluggishly along the snow's surface, Akira was accompanying him with his young, lively gait. He even seemed to hear the boy laughing at his father's discomfiture. Though Soroku was wearing a soft felt hat in place of the pilgrim's wide-brimmed sedge-hat, he too had a traveling companion like the bereaved fathers of old, and the same sorrow as theirs was engraved on his heart.

The more I suffer on this mountain, he told himself, the more I shall be contributing to the repose of my son's soul. With a deep sigh he picked up his stick and once more started to climb.

"There's a great hollow up there called the Mayakubo," said the guide. "It stretches from one peak to the next and it's covered with thick snow." Soroku glanced directly overhead at the Mayakubo; it looked like a sort of pond. Then on the right-hand side the guide showed him the remains of the old road along which people had brought sacks of salt, loaded on the backs of cows, over the mountains from Etchu. Soroku's interest in the various sights was perfunctory. He was concentrating entirely on transporting his own aged body up the side of the mountain. He was fully aware now (though he had no inkling of the reason) that people can find far more solace in suffering and sorrow than in the pleasures of life.

"Neck" is the word the mountain people use to describe those parts of the ravine in which the base of the mountains on both sides come closer together. After they had passed the second neck, they removed their nailed shoes and started to walk along a stretch of stony hill directly below the steep cliffs.

The ravine became still narrower. The mountain stream could be seen pouring fiercely down the rocks and then disappearing beneath the eaves of the thick snow. When finally they came to the end of the ravine, it was only to approach a new one, still steeper and more forbidding than the ravine they had just left. Here the snow was even whiter than before. The new ravine was at the very summit of one of the mountain ranges, and it ran on in a straight line, seeming to touch the clear blue sky. The reflection of the sun was almost blinding.

"When we get up there," said the guide, pointing to the end of the new ravine, "we'll be at the hut."

It did not look far. Soroku put on his nailed shoes again and set off with determination. But, although the destination was clearly in sight, they had still not reached it after an hour of heavy climbing. Owing to the steepness of the slope, they could not climb straight up. Soroku's bent knees were almost touching the snow as he trudged along.

"Keep it up!" he told himself, wiping the perspiration from his face. "Just a little more effort." Then he seemed to hear the voice of his dead son directly next to him: "Yes, Father, keep it up!"

He stopped halfway up the slope and looked down in the direction in which he had come. He was astounded to see how steep it was. If he lost his footing and slipped, there was no telling how far he would fall. He shut his eyes. Then he felt his knees relaxing and his body beginning to tremble. He would have to concentrate entirely on the effort of climbing; he must look only at the snow directly before his feet; if he let his eyes stray further afield he might very well lose his nerve.

Presently two young students came down the ravine in a great cloud of snow. They were wielding their sticks vigorously and walked with such energy that they looked as if they might easily shoot down to the bottom of the valley without any further effort on their part. When they reached the entrance to the ravine, they straightened themselves up and lightly jumped over to the stony hill on the right, along which they rapidly disappeared in the distance.

Soroku's destination now seemed so close that he could reach out and touch it. He used his remaining strength to pull himself to the top of the slope, almost as though he were crawling. At each step his legs felt as if they were going to stick in the snow.

The new plateau was backed by a high snow embankment and the guide explained that the hut was sheltered behind it. Suddenly Soroku felt that he did not have the strength to take even one more step.

"A rest," he muttered and sat down on the snow. Looking

down at the slope he had just climbed, he was amazed to see what he had accomplished. From the guide's point of view, of course, this was no slope at all; noting that the bunch of herbs had fallen from his knapsack, he ran down the hill they had just climbed, picked up the herbs and clambered back to the top—all without the slightest sign of effort.

After a while they started walking again.

"Is that Toyama Prefecture over there beyond the embankment?" asked Soroku.

"Yes, sir, that's right."

When they reached the top, a great vista lay spread out before them. Range upon range of immense mountains extended into the distance, stretching themselves up to the sky. In his exhaustion Soroku could do no more than gaze vacantly at the sudden panorama.

"Yes," he thought, "there are also things like this in this world of ours."

For a while he accepted the sight absently, as though it were something entirely beyond him; then all of a sudden he realized that these great ranges, lined up together under the summer sky, were the Northern Japan Alps, which surrounded the great peaks of Yari and Hodaka-no-Mine.

The Harinoki hut nestled at the foot of the embankment. Since they had set out from the Ozawa hut early in the morning, it was still only about two o'clock in the afternoon when they reached Harinoki. Soroku had not realized that on fine days the mountain huts normally remained empty until nightfall. When he entered the little hut, there was not a soul to be seen. The floor was covered with straw matting. The stove had gone out. The space on the other side of the partition had been turned into a primitive kitchen. A rhythmical sound, like the pendulum of a wall clock, reverberated loudly in the cold still air.

"After you've had a rest," said the guide, "what about going up to the top of Harinoki? The weather's good, and you'll have a fine view of Kurobe River. It's no distance at all from the hut."

Soroku was too exhausted to have any appetite. The guide opened a can of peaches for him. After eating a couple of slices, Soroku gave the rest to the man. He walked over to the window and looked out at the view. The near-by mountain was clearly visible, from its foothills in the marshland up to the snow-capped summit. Extending beyond it, the peaks of the other mountains were lined up in an endless succession. He felt he was gazing at the turrets of some great castle, except that nothing built by human hands could ever conceivably equal this great assembly of mountains which stretched out as far as the eye could see.

Soroku realized that there was absolutely nothing for them to do in this deserted hut during the long hours until nightfall. No doubt the guide was afraid that Soroku would become bored if they stayed in the hut and had therefore suggested that they should climb to the top of Harinoki.

"All right," he said, "let's go up!"

They left the hut and started climbing. It certainly did not look very far to the top. The slope was dotted with a profusion of endearing little mountain flowers.

Now Soroku could clearly see the ridge of Mount Naru-sawa, and above it the tops of Mount Atodate and a whole row of other mountains. Their snow-covered peaks glittered like jewels in the full afternoon sun—a series of gigantic statues placed at regular intervals in a grandiose corridor.

So long as he could stand there gazing at the scene in wonder, everything was all right. But a few moments later he found himself venturing onto a precipitous slope with a tremendous drop on one side. The path was covered with scree, which crumbled under Soroku's feet and made it hard for him to keep his balance. If one slipped here, he thought, one had every chance of hurtling down hundreds of feet into the valley below.

Noticing Soroku's unsteady gait, the guide showed him how to hold his stick on the mountain side of the trail and to support the weight of his body on it. Despite these instructions, Soroku had trouble in moving efficiently. His knees bent limply, deserted of all their strength, and each step became a problem.

Now there was no thought in Soroku's mind except the danger of falling off the edge of the path. He felt trapped: whether he went forward or backward, there was no escape. The guide had so far not realized how exhausted Soroku really was, and he kept up a rapid pace.

Imperceptibly Soroku's mood approached despair. If this agony was to continue, perhaps it would be easier to fall off the mountain and have done with it all. At this thought he stopped walking and gazed down into the distant valley below. He had turned deathly pale.

The guide glanced back and, seeing his charge standing there immobile, hurried to his side. Soroku felt utterly helpless: he had cramps in his legs and he was hardly capable of talking.

"Are you having trouble, sir?" inquired the guide.

"I can't go on."

"In that case, sir, I'll find you a place where you can rest. Follow me up here!"

The guide led the way up a slope off the trail, and Soroku crawled after him toward a near-by ridge, clutching onto the sturdy creeping-pines that covered the ground. Presently they reached a small level space.

"Why don't you sit down here, sir? You must be very tired."

"Yes, very. My legs have stopped doing what I tell them."

Soroku felt unable to inform the guide that, apart from this purely physical difficulty, he had lost his nerve. Of course, he told himself, he had been completely unqualified to venture forth on these mountains. Not only was he far too old, but he had never in his life done anything in the way of real exercise.

After settling himself snuggly among the roots and branches of a creeping-pine, Soroku felt a little more at ease. He looked down. Far below he could see the great valley opening up and from its edges rose one mountain after another. The valley itself seemed to be swallowed up in the ravine that he had climbed earlier. Soroku felt that he was sitting on a shelf.

"We're almost there now," said the guide, eager to set off again after their short breather.

"I'm afraid my body just isn't up to it," Soroku wanted to say, but he did not even feel strong enough to utter the words.

The guide took out a cigarette and started to smoke. Then he noticed something on the branches of a creeping-pine. Stretching out his hand, he picked it up and smilingly showed it to Soroku. It looked like woman's hair.

"Hm," said the guide. "A bear must have passed this way. Look at that hair—it's all over the place. That's bear's hair, you know. They're always scratching themselves and dropping their hair."

It occurred to Soroku that if a bear were to emerge from between the trees at that very moment and stand before him he would not be particularly startled and he would certainly not have the energy to run away.

"Do you get quite a few bears round here?"

"Oh yes, sir. And it can be quite dangerous, too, if you happen to come on one when you turn a corner in the forest—especially if it's a mother with her young. But if they see you first it's all right. They always run for it."

Apart from being thoroughly exhausted, Soroku now felt sleepy. He turned his face to the side and looked silently at the mountains ahead. Suddenly he remembered that, when he had gone to the island of Sado in much the same spiritual condition as now, he had been struck by the thought that he could not continue any longer in his present existence. And only an instant later he had forgotten everything and jumped off the boat—not so much from a conscious sense of loneliness as from a feeling that he could not endure life any longer.

He had failed on the sea, but here in the mountains it would be childishly simple. Though he felt he was half asleep, his mind continued to work keenly on these thoughts. Then once again he was startled to hear Akira's voice calling to him.

The mountain ridges stretched out under the still evening sky. The snow-covered range of Mount Atodate sparkled with light and seemed to float in the deep blue sky. A scene to open any man's eyes. Could anything in the world, wondered Soroku, be more peaceful than this? There was not a sound anywhere.

Strangely enough, it was when he thought he was hearing Akira's living voice that his son's death came to him with peculiar vividness. It had been his intention to journey to these mountains in the company of Akira, but now he realized that his son had ceased to exist long before he set out. It was a sad thought; yet Soroku felt that in some way he was separated from this sorrow. He had utterly lost his bearings, and perhaps this was precisely because his mind had become too clear.

Now he had the feeling that he had suddenly entered a new world—a world as distinct from the other as sleeping is from waking. He was alone in this world. Akira had died and was no longer in it. And what had he himself been doing until now? What had he been doing that he should have resolved to take his own life? When he had failed in his attempt at drowning himself, he had, as he now recalled, gone through a period when all distant memories had vanished from his mind. And now it seemed as if he were suddenly being stripped of near memories.

Soroku felt quite calm at the thought. What did it matter if he did forget these things—things that were mainly concerned with Akira? There was really no harm in forgetting him. Instead of immersing himself in memories, he himself must live in Akira's place. Normally it would be Akira who would live in Soroku's place, but war with its outrageous power had reversed the process, imposing on the father the duty to live in place of his son. The thoughts came to him clearly, without the trace of a shadow; and, as if an opaque membrane had been removed from his eyes, he saw everything vividly in a new light.

Again he looked down into the valley, but he no longer had the feeling of being swallowed up in its depths. It still frightened him, however.

"Let's quit here!" he said. On the spur of the moment he had resolved not to force himself through the remaining three or four days of this painful journey.

He was able now to confess in all modesty that the mountains had defeated him. Reputation and glory did not matter to him in the slightest. He had been beaten, and why not acknowledge the fact?

"We'd better go back," he added, turning to the guide, who stood there waiting with a bored look on his face. "I know it's a pity after coming all this way, but I've really reached the end of my tether."

The guide reacted with rugged simplicity. "Is your body giving you trouble somewhere? You must be careful, sir."

"It's just that I'm not used to it."

Soroku smiled bitterly: at that moment he knew that he had finally been subdued by the mountains. But it did not matter any longer. Perhaps Akira's spirit, which had brought him on this escapade to the Alps, had some other thing to reveal to him and did not wish to take him further than the entrance to the mountains.

They returned to the Harinoki for the night. The next day they went down to the Ozawa hut by the same route as before and spent one night there before proceeding to Omachi. On their way down the ravine the guide solicitously tied a stout piece of string from the knapsack round Soroku's waist and fastened the other end round his own wrist, so that even if his charge should slip there would be no danger of his falling off the edge. This set Soroku's fears at rest. On the other hand, when he and his guide passed a group of young climbers coming up from the valley he noticed that they looked at him strangely. It would have been all right if they had a proper rope, but, being led by a string, he could not help feeling like a monkey who is out for a walk with his trainer.

Soroku counted the successive necks of the ravine that they had passed on their way up, and not until they reached the first neck did he remove the string and start walking by himself. When they reached Ozawa, the woman who owned the hut greeted Soroku with genuine concern. Since he had originally planned to cut across the mountains to Toyama, she had not expected to see him again, and her first thought was that he must have hurt himself. He lay down at once, too exhausted even to remove his socks. The woman steeped a towel in some cold mountain water and placed it on his forehead. Moving the icy towel so that it covered his eyes, he lay listening to the cool sound of the little wind bell that tinkled somewhere outside the hut. After a while the woman changed his towel. Soroku realized that the water probably came from the little stream behind the hut which was so cold that it hurt to put one's hand in. Soon he began to feel drowsy, and all the heaviness vanished from him.

On the following day the owner of the hut had a passing laborer arrange for a car to fetch Soroku from the next village. The man who had climbed to the other side of the mountains to do a job was on his way back. He had stopped at the upper reaches of the Kurobe river to catch some bull trout, and the fish lay now in a basket, neatly packed in snow.

The road to Omachi was covered with stones, and the car

shook constantly. When they reached the inn Soroku was more exhausted than ever. He had begun to suffer from nausea and felt slightly feverish. As a result of having suddenly come down from the mountains, the late August heat in the village was sweltering.

Before parting from his guide, Soroku decided to invite him to a meal at the inn, and he asked what food was available. He was told that he could have some carp boiled in bean soup. This was better than he had expected in a mountain village, and he ordered the dish for dinner. Then he lay down on the *tatami*—alone in his own room for the first time since starting on his mountain journey. His forehead felt hot, and he asked the maid to bring him a wet towel, like the one he had been given in the Ozawa hut. Down here in the valley, however, the water was lukewarm.

The inn was situated conveniently close to the station. Near by, a station restaurant had just opened for business, and a loudspeaker uninterruptedly blared forth an invitation to passers-by to come in and enjoy a large cup of saké for a special price of only fifty yen. The roar of passing freight trains added to the turmoil.

Presently Soroku heard someone coming into the garden outside the room where he was resting. He removed the towel from his eyes. The red zinnias were in full bloom, and in one corner stood a new stone lantern. A man in a chef's hat walked across the garden, carrying a bamboo basket. He stopped by the pond and slowly removed his clothes. The pond was surrounded by stones and by a mass of shrubbery.

"Are we going to eat the carp out of that pond?" said Soroku in a startled tone.

"Yes, sir," said the chef, as if it were the most natural thing in the world, and he stepped into the water.

Under the searing sun the water looked unpleasantly tepid. The placid surface started to shake, troubling the calm reflection of the zinnias.

"Do you like night clubs?" asked Taeko.

"No, I really don't think I do."

As soon as Sutekichi had spoken, he felt that he could have answered in some more effective way. Taeko, however, seemed to be entirely unaware of his awkwardness.

Sutekichi's mind was made up: come what might, he had to broach the subject of marriage that evening. It was now or never. Yet he was painfully aware of his innate tendency to bungle things and felt quite fainthearted at the thought of what lay before him.

"And you—do you like night clubs?" he said, realizing that once more he had merely parroted one of Taeko's conversational overtures.

"Well," she answered, "I don't have any strong feelings on the subject one way or another. I went to a night club the other evening, though, and it didn't seem too bad."

"I don't suppose I'm really cut out for the more boisterous enjoyments in life," said Sutekichi.

"No," said Taeko, "I suppose there's nothing very boisterous about your studies." She tilted her head to one side and smiled in the characteristic manner that so often sprang into Sutekichi's mind when he was away from the girl: sometimes it would come to him when he was in conversation with one of his colleagues, and he would almost suffocate with longing. Now that her radiant face was before him in reality, he was conscious of the latent luster of her warm pink skin, and he felt his breath coming fast. At the same time he could not dismiss the thought that, if Taeko actually should decide to become his wife and to enter the household of an indigent student like himself, the relentless demands of daily life—cooking, washing, looking after his mother—would soon deprive the girl of her beauty. Now that he was meeting her alone for the third time, determined on this occasion to disclose his sentiments, he felt his resolution wavering. It was not easy for him to clothe his infatuation in words. Though he did not try to direct the conversation into other, more impersonal channels, he still could not come directly to the point; indeed, he even seemed to be avoiding it.

A waitress brought the tea and cakes that they had ordered. Taeko and Sutekichi were sitting in a modern tearoom of a type that had become fashionable after the war. The room was smartly decorated and showed a certain French influence. The lights were hidden behind a thick glass ceiling and produced a dull, restful illumination; the walls were painted in a quiet neutral color. The decorator seemed to have been almost pathologically careful to exclude everything from the room that might remind one of the demanding, disordered world outside.

Looking round the tables, many of which were occupied by foreigners, Sutekichi observed that all the customers were well dressed and apparently affluent. There was a calm about these men and women betokening the absence of money worries. Only he himself seemed to be out of place as he sat there in his shabby mackintosh, and no doubt he gave an incongruous impression to his fellow customers. On such occasions it never occurred to Sutekichi to wish that he also had some money. His reaction, on the contrary, was to resolve to study still harder. Pure academic pursuits were unfortunately out of the question, but at least he would like to be back in his own place of work—a place more appropriate to his meager resources than the present elegant tearoom. He liked far better to sit calmly in his own modest room than to emerge into the world of excitement and luxury where he could only feel ill at ease. ("And if," he told himself, "I should succeed in persuading this girl to marry me, not only shall I be forcing things into an unnatural pattern, but I shall come to feel ill at ease in my own life just as now I am ill at ease in this tearoom.")

Taeko adroitly cut her cake with a small silver knife and put a piece in her mouth. There was an air of practiced sophistication about her movements which for a moment made Sutekichi's own piece of cake stick in his throat. ("How shall I tell her? If I don't say anything today, when shall I have another chance? And until that next chance comes I shan't even be able to read a book in peace.")

Gradually it grew dark, and it became cold outside. The lights from the shops across the street and the silhouettes of the passers-by were reflected in a large mirror that formed the far wall of the tearoom; as dusk fell, the images became blurred.

"One can't get away from chrysanthemums these days," said Taeko, looking with a smile at the flowers on their table. Then, abruptly changing the subject, she glanced at Sutekichi and asked: "Do you think I've got any thinner?"

"No, I shouldn't say so."

Taeko was silent for a moment. Then she smiled.

"So much the better," she said.

"Is there any particular reason that you be thinner?" asked Sutekichi casually.

"Yes, lots of reasons."

"But surely," said Sutekichi, "people like you don't have any real troubles."

"Now you're being rude." Taeko glowered at the young man, but the expression in her eyes was gentle.

"Rude? You sound as if you took pride in having troubles."

Taeko did not reply. Sutekichi glanced at the girl. Perhaps because of what he had just heard, he now seemed to detect a shadow about her cheeks that had not been there in the summer.

"Well," he continued, "what sort of trouble have you had?"

"Heart trouble."

Sutekichi was so shocked by her reply that he could hardly utter a word. He felt himself changing color.

"Who is it?" he asked.

"Someone you don't know. But please let's change the subject, Sutekichi."

They went out into the street. Sutekichi had no intention of saying good-by to the girl then and there.

"What about a walk?" he suggested. "It would be nice if we could have dinner together . . . but I'm stone broke at the moment."

"It couldn't matter less," said Taeko cheerfully. The young man's frankness seemed to please her.

"Well then," said Sutekichi, "let's walk together as far as Hibiya. And while we're walking, perhaps you'll tell me about him—the other man, I mean."

Sutekichi was waiting for her to say that it was all a joke; but then he noticed that a certain tension lay behind the smile on the girl's face.

"No," she said, putting her head to the side, "I'd rather not."

"Why?"

"Because it only concerns me. And, anyhow, what good would it do to talk about it?"

"Yes, what good would it do?" He echoed her words with peculiar readiness; then all of a sudden he was overcome with excitement. His face flushed, and his feelings became incoherent. "What good would it do?" he repeated. "It has nothing to do with me."

In his agitation Sutekichi bumped into a man who was walking in the opposite direction.

"Why don't you look where you're going?" snapped the man, and Sutekichi became even more flurried than before. The man, however, did not carry his annoyance any further, and a moment later he disappeared in the crowd. Thereupon Taeko was surprised to hear her companion blurt out: "Yes, yes, to be sure. The man in question is obviously not me. I must no longer flatter myself on that score. Quite so. That being the case, there's nothing to stop me speaking out openly, but . . . ah yes, would you first tell me quite clearly that I'm not the man in question?"

"No," said Taeko with an astonished look, "it isn't you, Sutekichi."

At this the awkward young man regained some of his composure. In the normal course of events the girl's tacit rejection should have made Sutekichi resign himself to returning calmly to his studies without fear of any further emotional turmoil. As it happened, however, Taeko's words had the contrary effect and made it harder than ever for him to tear himself from her.

For a while they walked along in silence.

"Let's go somewhere where there are fewer people," proposed Sutekichi. "It's difficult to have a proper conversation in this crowd."

"But I've got to leave you when we get to Hibiya," said Taeko.

"And then where do you go? Are you going home?"

Taeko could not answer, and suddenly she felt the tears welling up in her eyes. She remembered that she should have been meeting Ryosuké that evening; but in the afternoon she had received a telegram at her office in which Ryosuké had canceled the appointment and had not even said anything about another meeting.

"Let's go this way," said Sutekichi in a sudden access of resolution, without waiting either for Taeko's reply or for her agreement. "It's nice and quiet."

They walked down the street under the railway bridge that led from the Japan Theater to Yurakucho Station. After they had cut across a busy shopping avenue, along which the shop windows were gaudily studded with lights, they came to a quiet back street.

"I've never done very well where money's concerned," began Sutekichi, "and I'm afraid it's not in my power to make anyone happy in a worldly way. Money and I are always going to be strangers. So far as that side of life goes I'm utterly powerless. I can't do anything about it."

He had calmed down considerably since when they had first started talking, but now Sutekichi was annoyed to find that he was once more becoming incoherent.

"Yet I'm quite sure," he said, "that even without money a person's sincerity counts for something. Now the fact is, Taeko, that I very much want you to be happy. I'll do anything in my power to help you."

A strange ardor had come over Sutekichi, and there was even a certain fierceness in his tone.

"I really believe it," he went on. "Just now you were saying something about being in trouble. If it's a matter of your emotions, I don't suppose there's anything I can do about it. . . . But, you know, I've been terribly fond of you from the very beginning, and I do so much want you to be happy. Please don't forget this. I want you to be happy as long as you live."

Taeko made no reply.

"Lifelong happiness," continued Sutekichi, "must be a pretty rare thing in these unsettled times. That's why I particularly want this for you. Poor as I am, I'll be watching you from the distance and hoping for your happiness. And please don't think that this is completely useless. I'm not making things up, you know. And I'm certainly not trying to flatter you or to say things just to please you. You see, I have my own path to follow. The only thing I can do is to travel along it straightforwardly. You have your path and I have mine. All the same there's no harm in my hoping that your journey will be a smooth and happy one. Please allow me to do so."

"I'm very grateful to you," said Taeko. "But what has suddenly made you say all this?"

She seemed to be admonishing him for his outburst, and Sutekichi became more serious than ever. There was even a stern expression on his youthful face. He realized that he had never spoken like this before in his life.

"It's for the sake of human honor," he said. "This may strike you as an exaggerated, or even a dishonest, way of speaking. But that's how I and my teacher honestly look at things."

Taeko did not ask who Sutekichi's teacher might be; she was still far too surprised at the sudden ardor of the young man to think of anything else.

"So you see it isn't for my sake," he continued with a frank, happy look on his face. "And surely there's nothing wrong in aspiring after something not for one's own sake but for the sake of human honor and dignity. It's like a friendly greeting to the humanity of which we all form part. Now, as I said, I've become very fond of you, Taeko. But I don't intend to marry you. You've got a different path to travel, you see. You can't take the same path as I do."

He paused for a while, then continued: "If we were to get married, I'd make you unhappy and you'd make me unhappy. Our lives would both go to pieces. Of course, none of that stops me from loving you. I can't help the feelings I have for you."

For a moment he wondered whether he was right to speak as he did. Then he realized that if he did not unburden himself of his feelings now he would never have another chance. However inept he might be in expressing himself, he had to tell Taeko what lay on his mind.

"So I'm not asking you for anything. I have no request to make of you. I want to leave things between us just as they are —straight and aboveboard. Please don't think of me as an odd fellow, Taeko. I suppose I am different from most people in that I don't attach too much value to love and I don't expect too much from it. I imagine that's partly because I was born into such a poor family. But it's not only that. It's because life itself and the pursuit of learning have always seemed so important to me. In comparison with them, love is a mere wayside distraction. What really matters to me is to follow my own path. Of course, I don't have any inordinate ambitions in life. I just want to make my own journey cleanly and honestly."

He paused, and the thoughts surged through his head. "Wait," he told himself. "Aren't you saying all this because you realize that you've lost Taeko to someone else? Isn't it just a matter of sour grapes?" They walked along in silence. "No," he decided, "there's more to it than that." For some time his heart had been like a pendulum that has lost the regular rhythm of its beat, but now his feelings seemed to be slowly returning to normal. Perhaps he would suffer later on. Nevertheless, he was beginning to realize the path along which he must journey. For, even as Sutekichi spoke to Taeko, his mind had been earnestly seeking that path, and now he had begun to find it.

"I'm afraid, Taeko, I must have surprised you with all these strange remarks."

"No, not really," she answered quietly.

"I'm sorry."

Sutekichi gazed at the branches of the plane trees by the side of the road. Dimly illuminated by the street lights, they emerged, yellow and autumnal, out of the surrounding darkness. There was still something stern in his expression, and he was aware of it himself.

"I'd like to hear you talk about yourself sometime, Taeko."

"Yes," said Taeko with a smile, "sometime."

Sutekichi still felt envious of the girl.

"You are happy, aren't you?" he said.

For some time Taeko did not answer, and they walked along in silence as if their conversation had come to an end.

"I'm not being sarcastic, Taeko-san. I mean exactly what I say."

"Sometimes I'm very far from happy," said Taeko.

"But you're prepared for that, aren't you?"

After saying good-by to Taeko at the Hibiya crossroads, Sutekichi started to walk toward Yurakucho. Glancing back, he saw that the girl was standing by the bus stop waiting with a crowd of people in the glare of neon lights that came from the shop behind them. He would have liked to rejoin her and continue their talk, but it embarrassed him to go back, and, besides, he felt like being alone.

Yet, when he finally was by himself, he was overcome with loneliness. He knew that he should resign himself to his lot, yet he wondered whether all his talk to Taeko about a calm, humble life had not been so much bluff. Until recently he had been quite satisfied with the prospect of some modest happiness, suitable to his station in life; but now even this hope seemed to have disappeared.

Looking up, he saw that he had reached the side of the railway bridge. A large crowd of people, who had evidently just streamed out of a movie, surrounded him on the pavement and waited for the traffic light to change to green. Only a few yards away, he remembered, was the street down which he had helped the drunken professor to Tokyo Station, listening to the usual flow of strong-minded opinions. "Love is a desperate business," Professor Segi had said. "It's not for people who like doing things by halves."

Sutekichi smiled bitterly as he recalled the professor's words. It was his teacher's exaggerated mode of expression that had spurred him to action. "Yes," Segi had said, "it's a desperate business. But nowadays people go about it halfheartedly. And yet they're convinced that they're in love. They're only lying to themselves. How could love be such a wishy-washy thing? After all, it's what Romeo and Juliet died for, isn't it? But in this day and age young men who say they're in love behave like sneak thieves or prowlers. They handle everything very cleverly and always have an eye to their own advantage. . . ."

The leaves lay scattered on the concrete surface of the road. A moment later the traffic lights changed and the leaves were trampled underfoot as the crowd surged forward across the street. Sutekichi wondered whether the professor had put in an appearance at the little bar where he so often went in the evenings. It was only a few steps away on the other side of the station. Why not go and have a look? For a moment he hesitated, remembering that he had no money to pay for his drinks; then he decided that if necessary he could leave his watch for security, as he had occasionally in the past.

As Sutekichi started to walk toward the bar, he thought of the professor and felt that a slender ray of light had begun to pierce through his dark mood. He looked forward to being attacked by his old teacher. He might very well react against some of Segi's more outrageous views, yet the fact remained that he wanted to come into contact once more with the innate goodness of the man.

"Yes, my young friend," the professor would probably say, his eyes shining like a tiger's, "love is a very terrible thing indeed." As soon as Segi had nibbled at a good piece of bait—a rice-biscuit or some dried octopus—he was caught. From then on he would chat away happily so long as one wanted to listen. Sutekichi could hear the voice in his ears: "You're laboring under an illusion if you don't realize what a terrible thing it is. It's no niggling little emotion that comes every day of the week. No, it's love—LOVE." He would repeat the word loudly. "What makes one fall head over heels? There's only one thing that can have this effect—one blind, unabashed, bottomless thing, a thing that is constantly with one, waking or sleeping. But I suppose this sort of love has virtually disappeared from the modern world. We live in bad times, Sutekichi, my boy. These are the latter degenerate days that the Lord Buddha predicted. And if there actually were such a thing as real love left in the world, it would be so valuable that it would have to be preserved in a can and sold to the Americans."

Sutekichi walked up the creaking staircase to the bar. The place was empty, except for one table of customers by the wall. There was no sign of Professor Segi.

"The Professor was here until about ten minutes ago," said the owner. "He was with a nice-looking white-haired gentleman."

"Really?" said Sutekichi. The information surprised him, since the professor was usually accompanied by students or other young people.

"Yes," put in the waitress. "He was quite an elderly man. I him saying something about coming from Kamakura."

As she stood waiting for the bus, Taeko was still in an undecided frame of mind. Ordinarily she would have gone back directly to where she lived in Omori. For a moment it occurred to her that Ryosuké's plans might have changed and that he might have gone to Omori believing her to be there. But no, the tone of his telegram left no room for such a possibility.

For some time she had felt that he was in his office. Even if he was not there, he might have gone out for a moment on business and would be back shortly; in any case he would surely have left a message. She could not get the idea out of her head. Even while she had been walking with Sutekichi she had visualized Ryosuké arriving at his office: after hurriedly looking through some papers he would go out again into the night and she would have missed him irretrievably. The thought filled her with impatience.

The bus still did not come. Taeko stood nervously in the darkness. Behind her lay the moat of the Imperial Palace, and beyond it grew line after line of trees. She could hear the branches beginning to stir in the wind. On the other side were the railings and trees of Hibiya Park. Taeko recalled how, after spending the night with her sister at the Imperial Hotel, she had got up early in the morning, and on her way past the Hibiya courts seen Ryosuké playing tennis with a young American. She held the memory to her breast, enfolding it tightly in the joined sleeves of her overcoat. It had been a summer morning; the sun shone on the flower beds, and the lawn was shaded with the reflection of the rosebushes. Taeko looked round. A number of cars had stopped at the near-by traffic signals, and for a moment their headlights picked out the branches of the trees, dyeing them a pale yellow; then the cars moved away and the branches relapsed into darkness.

"Time has really passed," thought Taeko with a sigh. It was enough for her to see Ryosuké's face to forget everything. Yet their relationship had lost its earlier pristine quality, and all sorts of unpleasantness had come between them, so that when she was alone she felt herself weighed down by disagreeable fancies. All this used to melt away as soon as she met Ryosuké and she would once more feel gay and lighthearted. Such was the power of the young man's lively eyes and of his powerful body that without saying a word he could banish all unease and free Taeko from her oppressive thoughts.

Finally the bus arrived. Taeko got off at the Sangen Bridge and walked back a short distance into a murky sidestreet, which was full of little private companies and offices. The surface of the street was extremely uneven, and at night it was very hard to walk there in high heels. Taeko, however, instinctively quickened her pace.

Ryosuké was usually to be found in a little private office that he had rented on this street. He shared the office with a few other young men, each of whom had his desk there and carried on his own independent business. As a result, Taeko was fairly sure of finding someone in the office even at this time of the evening. As she approached the building, she saw that it was the only one in which the lights were still burning. She could make out someone moving behind the glass door.

"Mr. Tsugawa?" said the man when she asked him about Ryosuké. "Oh yes, he left some time ago."

"You don't happen to know where he went, do you? Has he telephoned since he left?"

Another man was sitting at a desk in the corner of the office; he had a green shade over his eyes. "Yes," he said, looking up, "Tsugawa said something about going to the Nikkatsu Hotel. He's doing lots of business with the Americans these days."

Taeko returned to the Hibiya crossroads where she had stood waiting so long for the bus. Although it was still not very late, there were now hardly any people waiting for the trolleys, and the place had a desolate air.

Taeko walked to and fro outside the Nikkatsu Hotel. The shutters had been lowered in the shops along the street, and the windows were all dark. The only light came from the neon signs that hung high on the walls of the buildings. Looking through the glass doors of the Nikkatsu Hotel, Taeko saw that the hall was empty. She noticed that the doors of the elevator at the other end of the hall were painted the same light gray as the walls outside. The door opened and a man came out. Taeko felt her hands go cold in her pockets as she peered across the hall to see whether she could not recognize Ryosuké's familiar over-coat. She was throbbing with impatience. Twice before she had been in the same state; on both occasions she had got up in the middle of the night and gone all the way from Omori to where Ryosuké lived in Koishikawa; after walking about for some time outside the front door, she had returned home; and she had never told him about it. It had been enough for her just to walk outside his house; after that she had been able to go home and sleep soundly, whereas if she had not gone she would have lain awake miserably all night.

Taeko walked once more past the entrance of the hotel. She was about to give up and go home when it occurred to her to go into the hall and have a look. Just then a colored gentle-man, who looked as if he might be an Indian, pushed open the door and walked into the hotel. As if he had taught her a neces-sary lesson, Taeko went up to the door and resolutely pushed it open. She followed the man to the other end of the hall and stood next to him while he pushed the button for the elevator. She expected that it would take some time to reach the ground floor, but almost instantly the doors slid open. The gentleman stepped aside to make way for Taeko, then followed her into the elevator. The doors instantly slid together, smoothly cutting off the outside world.

Since it was a new building, the elevator was of modern construction; Taeko was impressed by how silently it moved up the shaft, so unlike the creaking contraption in her own office building. The uniformed attendant faced the door and an-nounced the number of each floor in English as they passed.

"Which floor is the hotel bar, please?" asked Taeko.

"It's on the sixth floor, Miss," said the attendant.

"Well then, please let me off there."

"Sixth floor," the attendant announced in English. Taeko understood him perfectly, but for a moment she smiled and wondered whether she had not left Japan and Tokyo far be-hind her.

She stepped out and found herself in a large corridor. Considering that there was not a soul in sight, the illumination seemed unnecessarily bright. She walked over to the cloakroom, and from there she could see one corner of the bar.

"That's the bar over there, isn't it?" she inquired.

"Yes, Miss, that's right."

Then Taeko heard herself ask an entirely unprepared question. "Do you know if Mrs. Iwamuro is here?"

"Well, let's see, Miss," said the cloakroom attendant, putting her head to the side. "I'm really not sure." Taeko interpreted this as meaning that Mrs. Iwamuro was not there, and she felt unaccountably relieved.

The bar had transparent walls of glass and vinyl. Customers were sitting in groups round the little tables, and some of their chairs stretched out into the corridor. There was no sign of Ryosuké. All the customers seemed to be foreigners. A waitress in a pink uniform noticed Taeko standing by the entrance and came up to her.

"Is it all right if I sit here?" asked Taeko, blushing.

"Yes certainly, Miss," said the waitress. "What can I bring you to drink?"

"Something cool, please. What about a lemonade?"

"Very well, Miss."

As soon as she had sat down Taeko felt calmer and she started looking round. This was her first visit to the hotel and it surprised her that she was not more timid. Her table was directly next to a sort of balustrade, and she could look directly down onto the hall of the hotel one floor below. Varicolored armchairs were spread about on the light gray carpet, and almost all of them were occupied by foreigners who sat comfortably talking to each other. On the far wall hung an embroidered tapestry, and on a shelf below was a lacquered Chinese vase whose red color stood out with startling vividness against the gray background.

If Ryosuké was in the hotel, thought Taeko, he was bound to be either in the bar or in this hall. Perhaps they had made a mistake at his office. Alternatively, he might have finished his business and gone home.

"The halls of the big Tokyo hotels—that's where I meet people and that's where I do my business," Ryosuké had once told her. "I don't really need an office. All I want is a place where I can telephone and make my contacts. One table is all I need. And even that I share with a friend of mine."

Taeko had been rather discouraged when she had first seen that Ryosuké did not even have a room of his own in the office where he worked.

"Ah yes," she had said, "I suppose it works out quite well for you." Still she could not help feeling that there was something a bit forlorn and insubstantial about the arrangement.

As she started to drink her lemonade, Taeko noticed a new group of people coming into the hall. It was a party of men and women, evidently American. They sat down at a table in the middle of the room and called for the menu. After they had each examined it in turn, they gave their orders to a waiter. Presently the waiter returned, and they followed him up the spiral staircase to the floor where Taeko was sitting. She noticed that the women went ahead of the men as they walked past her and disappeared into the near-by dining-room. Their place was taken by a group of three men who looked Chinese; they sat with their bodies eagerly bent forward and embarked at once on a heated conversation.

For some reason Taeko recalled the evening early that summer when she had gone to the Kawana Hotel with Ryosuké. Memories of one detail after another sprang up vividly—the red orchidaceous plants which stood in pots on the veranda; the sound of the cuckoos from the distant woods as they had walked past the golf course on that limpid, drowsy afternoon; the exhaustion of her body after swimming in the clear water beneath the lily-covered cliffs, an exhaustion that had wrapped itself pleasantly about her all evening.

Looking down over the balustrade, Taeko felt that the hall below was like a pond filled with soft light. By association, the strangers who moved about from one part of the hall to another looked exactly like fish swimming in a pond. Then all of a sudden Taeko noticed Mrs. Iwamuro standing at the far end of the hall looking at the red Chinese vase. Taeko did not know very much about Japanese clothes, nor had she any particular desire to. Yet as soon as she saw Mrs. Iwamuro in her kimono, she was impressed by the beauty of it. The first thought that came into Taeko's head was not to wonder why Mrs. Iwamuro should still be frequenting Westernized places, like the Nikkatsu Hotel, but to admire the magnificence of her dress. For there was a striking originality about her style. The kimono was decorated with a fine gold pattern but from the distance it looked like pure white silk. Round it was wrapped a black *obi* splashed with great red leaves. With this startling contrast of black and white Mrs. Iwamuro looked no less brilliant than the vermilion vase at which she stood gazing.

Taeko had no way of knowing that when Mrs. Iwamuro had appeared in the lobby earlier she had been wearing an entirely different kimono. In the evening she had changed into white to make herself look like a moonflower that one sees on a summer night. This change in itself was enough to attract the attention of anyone who had seen her in her earlier kimono; and now she stood in the lobby, fully conscious of the impression that she was making.

While looking at the vase, Mrs. Iwamuro at the same time spotted an empty chair; she rapidly moved toward it and sat down. Then she glanced up toward where Taeko was sitting. For a moment Taeko thought that she was looking at her, and she wondered whether she ought not to make some gesture of greeting. Then she noticed that Mrs. Iwamuro was smiling with her dark eyes at a group of foreigners who were sitting at a table in the other end of the bar. The foreigners raised their hands in a signal of acknowledgment. Taeko thought they must be buyers. Presently one of them lifted his large body out of the chair and hurried nimbly down the spiral stairs to where Mrs. Iwamuro was sitting. He bent over and evidently asked her to join him and his friends at the bar. Mrs. Iwamuro shook her head with a smile, and after a few more words the foreigner returned alone up the stairs.

Then Taeko noticed that another man was standing next to Mrs. Iwamuro. Not until he turned in Taeko's direction did she realize it was Ryosuké. It was the last thing she had expected at that moment, and she felt her heart pounding with surprise.

Mrs. Iwamuro greeted Ryosuké affably, a calm smile on her face. The young man started to say something, then took an object out of his pocket and placed it on the round table in front of Mrs. Iwamuro. With a startled gesture Mrs. Iwamuro covered the object with her hand as though to conceal it. Then she gently moved her hand and brought it to her *obi*. Taeko only saw the object for a flash before it was hidden, but it looked to her like a room key. There was something flustered about Mrs. Iwamuro's movements as she put the object away; she seemed to be worried about whether anyone in the room had seen her. This made Taeko turn pale.

Ryosuké had obviously not noticed Taeko's presence on the balcony above. He sat down next to Mrs. Iwamuro and said something that made them both laugh. Then he called for a waiter and asked for the menu. After discussing it with Mrs. Iwamuro he gave some instructions to the waiter. From beginning to end his manner was one of perfect composure. Presently the waiter returned to announce that their dinner was ready. Ryosuké pulled back Mrs. Iwamuro's chair for her in the Western fashion and accompanied her up the spiral staircase.

Taeko paid for her drink and hurried down the corridor. The elevator wafted her noiselessly to the ground floor. As she stepped out into the street the clean autumn wind hit her in the face.

"Let's sit down here and have a rest," said Professor Segi to Soroku Okamoto, pointing to a near-by bench in the park. In recent years it had been a rare event for the professor to walk in the park and he hardly ever sat on a bench. Even if it had been a daily occurrence, however, this ebullient gentleman would have derived just as much enjoyment from it as he did now when it was something out of the ordinary.

"Ha, a bench, is it?" he exclaimed, peering at the wooden structure with his short-sighted eyes, and even stroking its surface as though moved with admiration by its presence. "They certainly don't advance much with the years, do they?" He stood back and looked at it for a moment as if it were some rather outrageous creature. Then he shrugged his shoulders; it was only a bench, after all. "Everything else in the world seems to get modernized by leaps and bounds. Only these poor objects stay exactly as they used to be. You know, Mr. Okamoto, they haven't changed one iota since the time of the Russo-Japanese war half a century ago. I remember the first one I saw—they'd probably imported it from England or somewhere—it went up in the middle exactly like this one, and it had exactly the same spaces between each of the boards. It's as if they'd settled every detail of the construction once and for all by law."

There was something mildly ludicrous about the manner in which the professor was so impressed by an ordinary bench; yet Soroku saw that his companion's youthfulness derived precisely from this characteristic.

"Of course," continued Segi, "one gets a pleasant sense of stability from the way the four legs stretch out at oblique angles. I wonder who first thought of this exact shape. It's the genuine article, this bench, the genuine article. Yet why do you suppose no one ever tried to make the slightest improvement on it? Why no progress? Was it because they considered that a mere park bench deserved no further attention?"

"Oh but surely," said Soroku, darting a surprised look at the professor, "these can't possibly be the same benches that were put here fifty years ago. They must have been changed."

"Well, that's another possibility," said the professor, and finally the two men sat down on the controversial bench. In front of them stretched the lawn; it was as flat as a board and surrounded by flowerbeds.

"A devilish lot of buildings have sprung up round here," resumed the professor. "One feels them looking down on one from all sides. At night, of course, one is spared that particular unpleasantness."

Soroku could not help smiling at the thought that he was sitting here in Hibiya Park on an autumn evening. He was doing something that he had often thought about but never actually tried. A sense of calm came over him, and he looked about. In the dark the trees looked even blacker than he would have expected. A cool wind blew pleasantly against his face, which was still slightly flushed from drinking.

"One can't see any stars, can one?" remarked Soroku.

"No," said the professor. "It's because of all the electric lights and neon signs down here."

"It was a magnificent sky up there in the mountains."

"In the mountains?" asked Segi, as though challenging his friend. "Which mountains?"

"Ah yes, I haven't told you about that, have I?" He did not

wish to hide his experience from the professor; at the same time
he had no particular desire to talk about it.

"Do you mean the Central Alps? When on earth did you go
there?" The professor sounded surprised—yes, decidedly surprised. "And who were you with?"

"Oh no," said Soroku quietly and smiled, "I was alone."

"I see," said Segi nodding, and it was clear from his look
that he felt what a hard thing his companion had undertaken.
Instantly he recalled his first meeting with Soroku on his return
from Sado Island. When he next spoke he had gone back to his
usual sanguine tone and to his characteristic manner of analyz-
ing things bit by bit. "And when you went to the mountains, or
wherever it was, did something good happen to you?"

For some time Soroku was silent. When finally he replied,
there was a forthright simplicity about his tone. "Yes," he said,
"something good."

"I see," said Segi, after waiting in vain for some elucidation.
"And I suppose the stars are very beautiful in the mountains."

"Yes," said Soroku with the same simplicity, "very beautiful.
Almost frighteningly beautiful."

The professor felt uneasy. His uneasiness had nothing to do
with Soroku, who sat there in his strangely calm attitude. No, it
was concerned with himself. He felt that now it was he who
was uneasy and flustered. He stretched himself out so that his
body, wrapped in its overcoat, sat firm and calm on the bench.
Through the branches he could see the vivid neon lights flashing on and off outside the park. A young couple walked past
the bench; they looked like lovers who were having a secret ren-
dezvous.

"You've changed, Okamoto, haven't you?" said the professor,
suddenly breaking the silence. "There's no doubt about it—
you've changed."

"I . . . I give that impression, do I?"

"Yes," said the professor emphatically and turned around to
face his companion, "you're a changed man. I'm very pleased to
see it."

"It's thanks to you."

"It was rather absurd of you to jump into the water, wasn't
it?" The professor's bright nature showed through his words. "It
really surprised me, you know. It surprised me that the Sea of

Japan should go on being exactly the same as it was before."

"Yes," said Soroku, "I've been nothing but a trouble to you, I know. It's all like a dream, so far as I'm concerned. But I know that I owe absolutely everything to you. I am so very grateful."

"You really don't need to thank me," said the professor politely, yet with a touch of crossness. "I'm not asking for that." Then abruptly his tone changed. It was as though he had been struck by the thoroughgoing simplicity and purity of his companion and had felt that he must give up his usual bantering approach. "It worked out all right, didn't it? But let me tell you that at one stage I was completely at sea. You see, I've spent most of my life looking through motheaten old manuscripts, and I have had very little experience when it came to handling living people."

"I don't agree," said Soroku. His face colored violently, but his tone remained as calm as ever. He sat silently in the dark until he regained his composure. "You've probably already noticed," he continued, "that I've had little experience in talking to other people. I'm a poor talker, and I have trouble in expressing what I think."

"You make me sound like a real old chatterbox."

"Oh no, I never— I didn't—" The professor's interruption had thrown Soroku into complete confusion, and he stuttered helplessly for the right words. Professor Segi felt guilty and abruptly lapsed into silence. "As silent as a clam," he thought, remembering the Western expression, "that's how silent I am." And then it vividly occurred to him how very silent a clam really was as it stuck to its rock by the seashore.

"No doubt," said Soroku in a deep voice, "it's because you're always with young students. If I may say so, Professor Segi, I really have the greatest admiration for the way you keep your youthful spirit. You seem to achieve without the slightest effort something that would be impossible for most people, however hard they tried."

"A doctor friend of mine," said the professor, emerging from his clamlike condition, "told me that I was suffering from debilitation of the cranial nerve. Of course, it was rather irresponsible of him to diagnose my brain condition considering that he's an ear-nose-throat doctor specializing in diseases of the nose. However, it's not for me to gainsay him, and I dare say he may be right up to a point. You see, I'm rather on the soft side where other people are concerned. That's how I'm constituted. I tend to adapt myself to the way things are going and to look at everything in a light vein. I admit it freely. That's why I've done so badly all these years. People never take me seriously, not even my old friends. It's not a quality that helps one to get ahead in the world."

"Really, Professor, I don't agree with you." Soroku's tone was serious, but he avoided expressing himself too openly. Talking to Professor Segi made him behave like a bashful child who is always on his guard. "If I may say so, sir, everyone looks on you with the greatest respect and affection."

"Don't be ridiculous!"

"No, that isn't just words. The humanity and goodness that you possess are things of great value which cannot be acquired by simply accumulating money. You are a very fortunate man, sir."

"Come, come, Okamoto," said the professor, "let's change the subject. If you were a woman it might be different, but for two grown men to sit on a park bench flattering each other is really rather absurd, don't you think? Not that I dislike flattery, mind you. But it really isn't done."

"I'm so sorry. Please forgive me."

Once again Soroku's forthright manner utterly disconcerted the professor, and a strained look appeared on his face.

"Let me tell you something, Okamoto. The fact that I always look so cheerful shouldn't be taken too seriously. This world is a difficult place to live in, but it doesn't do the slightest good to go about with a long face just because things may be painful and trying. It doesn't matter so much when you're alone, but in the company of other people it's a good policy never to show that one feels gloomy. That's something we can learn from the old *samurai* tradition. It's a sort of courtesy toward the people we happen to be living with."

Soroku silently bowed his head in assent.

"In my opinion," continued the professor, roused to an extent that was unusual for him, "the real scum in this world are the people who only think about themselves. It's they who make this extremely difficult world of ours even more difficult. Those are the people I thoroughly detest—the people who think that so long as they are all right everyone else can go to the devil. Yes, those are the ones I despise. And how many of them there are these days! You see them sprawling on the seats of the trolleys, acting as if they were the only passengers and not giving a damn for some wretched old woman who has to stand in the aisle. And it's not only in trolleys. The same thing goes on in every walk of society. I suppose it's because Japan is such a small country with such an enormous population that some people decide to force their way through by dint of strength and money, regardless how they may be hurting others. As I said, the world's become a hard place to live in, even if one has no special difficulties at the moment. If a man wanders about thinking that he's the only one who's unhappy, he's making a great mistake. For the fact is that there will always be numerous levels of unhappiness far worse than his own. That's what people tend to forget. You see, Okamoto, we're all living together in this world, and we should try to share each other's difficulties. To pity another person is mere presumption. We should consider his problems as being our own. Of course, we hear a lot of talk these days about freedom. Freedom, freedom! But surely freedom doesn't mean that one should do exactly what one feels like. I know it doesn't do any good to get angry, but when I see people pushing their way about and not giving a damn for anyone else I feel like having a fight—yes, even now, old as I am. I don't start using my fists, of course. But on a trolley, for instance, if I happen to see some selfish, ill-mannered lout, I go up to him, look him straight in the face, and laugh at him in the most unpleasant way. Then the poor fellow will worry himself silly wondering why I've laughed at him."

"You really don't do such things, do you, Professor?" put in Soroku.

"Oh yes, I do. When I was young I was a very wicked boy, and I used to cause my parents a lot of trouble. Among my various activities at that time was to train myself to produce a special kind of laugh at will. It was a sort of investment on which I would be able to draw in the future. You see, most people can't burst out laughing on the spur of the moment if they're told to. But I can. And I may say without undue conceit that when I laugh at someone in my special way I can make cold shivers run down his back. At such times I become a real bogyman."

The professor laughed loudly; it was a clear, bright laughter.

"I'm talking a lot of nonsense," he continued. "But you may be interested to know that during the war I used to make it my daily task to go up and laugh at military men on the trolleys. It didn't matter if they were old or young, so long as they were the strutting kind who tried to lord it over the rest of us. Human laughter is a complicated thing, you know. Even the military couldn't very well arrest people for simply laughing. The only trouble was that there were so many of them and I laughed so much that the entire area between my mouth and my chin became exhausted. Finally, although I was still laughing inside, my facial muscles simply wouldn't function. Apart from that, my whole face was becoming twisted into a sort of permanent grimace. So I decided to limit my attentions to officers of the rank of major-general and above. The trouble was that most of them avoided the crowded trolleys and went about in their own cars. This was a great disappointment. At the same time I was beginning to suffer from malnutrition and I lost my strength. In the end even I couldn't laugh. Yes, my friend, that's how it was."

The professor paused for a while, then continued: "Even nowadays the people I particularly want to laugh at usually drive about in their own private cars and manage to avoid me. Everything's becoming too damned convenient in this world. The only time I get a chance is when I'm standing waiting for a bus next to a traffic signal and one of these gentry has to stop his car willy-nilly for a red light. Then the enemy gets a good broadside of my laughter. But apart from such rare occasions, it's all very frustrating these days."

When Professor Segi ceased fire, the hum of insects became audible from somewhere near by. Soroku felt that the span of his thinking had somehow broadened while he had sat there on the bench. He was a strange man, this professor, a very strange man. At one time Soroku had regarded him with a certain awe; but this had given way to something far more intimate, and now as he sat silently next to him in the cool autumn evening he felt that his heart was being warmed by the man's presence. In the course of his entire lonely experience he had never known such a person.

"Well," said Professor Segi reluctantly, "I suppose I should be going. It's nine o'clock—time to start reading old letters by old priests."

"You're going to start work now?" he asked.

"Yes, it's a good time for work," said the professor with a smile. "That little rascal Taro won't be there to disturb me. At the moment I'm reading through various letters written by warriors and priests during the Kamakura Period, about seven hundred years ago. They got them together for me at the Kanazawa Archives in Kanagawa Prefecture. It's very interesting to get to know about the lives of those fellows. Take tea, for instance. Nowadays even people like you and I can buy it without the slightest trouble. But in those days they had a terrible time getting hold of some tea—rather like it was during the last war when we couldn't lay our hands on a pound of coffee for love or money. Occasionally someone would send a priest a packet of tea. This would delight him greatly, and he'd write an elaborate letter of thanks. Yes, it's all very interesting. In the old days, of course, people who really appreciated tea used to go to the greatest pains to grow it themselves in a corner of their own garden or a rice field. It wasn't a question then of being able to buy all one wanted in a market. It required more than money to have good tea. No doubt it was all very inconvenient compared to the present system. Yet surely there was something very elegant about picking tea leaves from one's own garden. And, come to think of it, I wonder whether inconvenience isn't really a necessary prerequisite for elegance. The very fact that things took so much time gave a savor to life. People wouldn't dream of growing their own tea nowadays, would they? And if by any chance a man should slip into doing something of the sort, it would almost certainly seem like an affectation. But there's nothing wrong about it, you know. To make something in one's own house with one's own hands and then to have it delivered to an intimate friend for his enjoyment—what could be better? One's heart is in the gift in a way that's impossible with something that's been bought in a shop. That sort of life continued in Japan until quite recently, except, of course, in the cities. As things become more convenient, people get to be lazier and lazier. No doubt it's a convenience to have plenty of money, and the Americans, who have more than anyone else, claim that they know how to enjoy life. But I wonder whether people can really understand the enjoyment of life in a country where even home cooking has become a matter of opening a few cans. The food a man most enjoys is the food he eats in his own house. But how can he really enjoy it if there's no real human effort involved, if it all comes out of cans—yes, out of the same cans with the same lettering that he can find wherever he goes? Human beings are, so to speak, slowly being forced out of business. It may be very practical. But it simply won't do. When money begins to lord it over us, there's less and less room left for real enjoyment and real feelings. I can imagine a company president who has made a fortune out of selling canned food but who secretly plants tea in his garden—Western-type tea perhaps, but nevertheless real, living tea. He sticks his tongue out at the can-crazy world about him and leads a charming, elegant life. Ah well, enough of all that! I really must be getting home."

The two men stood up and started walking side by side through the dark cluster of trees. They noticed someone coming from the opposite direction and then saw that it was a young girl in a bright red coat. They were about to pass her when she wheeled round, seized Professor Segi tightly by the arm and started walking along beside him.

"What on earth are you doing?" said Professor Segi in amazement. "Let go of me at once!"

The girl stared calmly at the professor and laughed.

"I'll get another girl for your friend," she said. "Where shall we go, Daddy?"

"Thank you for the kind suggestion," said Segi, "but we really must decline."

"Oh no, you mustn't!" said the girl. "It won't be expensive. Really it won't. I can guarantee that, Daddy."

"Look here, my girl," said Professor Segi with an extremely serious expression, "I may be an old man but I happen to hold the fifth rank in jiujitsu, and I won't have much trouble in shaking off a slip of a girl like you if I want to."

"It's all right," said the girl.

"No, it isn't all right. Kindly release my sleeve!"

Then he looked at the girl and burst out: "You're bright red, aren't you? You look like the goddess of smallpox. What a terrible fate to be bewitched by you! But, my dear girl, you really must let me off."

"No, I won't let you off," said the girl. "I mean it. I'll go anywhere you want. We can go to my place, if you like, or anywhere else."

"Please don't try to make an old man ashamed of himself," said the professor.

Soroku said something to the girl and tried to pull her away from his companion. This only served to make her abusive. "You're an old milksop!" she said. "But if you really don't want me to hold onto you, Daddy," she added, "I'll let go. I'll walk along next to you."

"I do wish you'd excuse us for this evening," said Segi. Then he looked at Soroku for the first time since their unexpected encounter and smiled bitterly. The girl trotted along calmly next to them. She was utterly unabashed, and with her plump, youthful shoulders seemed to push aside the professor's remonstrances. "What an outrageous, boorish girl!" he thought.

"It really won't do you any good to come along with us," he said after a while.

"It's all right," she said.

"Oh really," said Professor Segi, "I do wish you'd listen to reason. Look here, my girl, I'm probably older than your own father."

"What difference does that make?" asked the girl, looking placidly at her victim. Then, receiving no reply, she added: "You're a man by the looks of it. Or aren't you up to that sort of thing any longer?"

"Oh, good heavens! What have I done to deserve this?" sighed the professor with an exaggerated expression of dismay, as though the girl's imperturbability had driven him to his wit's end. "I'm going home," he added in an unexpectedly loud voice.

"Huh!" said the young girl with a nasal laugh, and followed the two men as they set off again through the park.

"You're a real greenhorn, aren't you?" said the professor. "You should look at your men, my dear. If you'd looked properly, you'd have realized that those two old codgers on the bench weren't very promising customers. You've only just come out of your swaddling clothes, and I already have one foot in the grave. We'd make a fine couple! But really, my dear, you shouldn't bother old fellows like us. When a man gets to be our age, the sight of a young woman as a rule evokes nothing but a belch. No girl could possibly induce me to do anything at this stage of the game. A lifetime of experience has taught me a thing or two!"

"You're a funny fellow, aren't you, Daddy?"

"What's that?" said the professor in absolute amazement. "Funny, you say?"

"Yes, funny."

"You put it very neatly, don't you?" said the professor, and the wry look on his face suggested that he was speaking from his heart. "Anyhow, I'm going home. I have no more to say to you."

"It doesn't matter," said Soroku, who had been silent until then. "You can leave her to me."

Segi looked at his companion. "Don't!" he said simply.

"You needn't worry," said Soroku with a laugh. "It's perfectly all right. Please go home, Professor."

Segi looked as if he wanted to say something else, but the serious expression on Soroku's face seemed to prevent him.

"Very well," he said. "I leave her in your hands. I'll just walk to the end of the path with you and then go home. Just one final word, though. It's all very well to do what one likes, but for heaven's sake, Okamoto, don't give her too much money."

"I understand," said Soroku.

A few moments later the two men parted. The girl put her arm through Soroku's. "Please let go," he said gently. The girl was slightly taken aback by his serious, straightforward manner and walked along obediently beside him.

"Well," she said after a while, "don't you want to go somewhere with me?"

Soroku could not help smiling at the way the girl repeated her offer. The listlessness about his manner toward her contrasted with the professor's acrid approach.

"Let's walk along here," he said. "It's a nice quiet path."

The girl, however, was still restless, and she kept looking inquiringly at her new companion, as though somehow beguiled by the way in which he walked silently along.

"You're a good kind man, aren't you, Daddy?" she said.

"I wonder."

"Shall we go somewhere together?"

"No, let's just walk. Don't worry—I'll give you some money."

The girl looked startled for a moment and was about to say something. Then, as if she had changed her mind, she nodded meekly and her face took on the look of a demure little girl. Soroku walked on silently. This was his first experience with a girl from the streets, but it did not occur to him that he was doing something reckless—reckless enough, in fact, to have surprised even the professor. Nor did he feel any of the scorn for the girl's position which he would certainly have experienced in the old days.

"Your mother and father are still alive, aren't they?" he said.

"I don't want to talk about them," answered the girl.

"I see."

After another silence Soroku said: "If you keep on the wrong path too long, you'll find one of these days that it's too late to turn back."

"Yes," said the girl, "but it can't be helped."

The girl had expected Soroku to contradict her, but he did not abandon his quiet, moderate tone. She found him very strange.

"Have you no real plans for your future?" he asked quietly. "I think you ought to go home to your parents." The girl did not reply and he continued: "Whatever happens, a young girl like you mustn't ruin herself. You must be more careful with yourself, you know. Of course, I'm just a casual passer-by and I can't really do anything for you. But don't you think that, so long as you don't wait too long, you can go back to where you started? No one can help you to go back. You can only do it by your own strength. And if you yourself have no such desire— well then, you're done for! Really, my dear girl, you shouldn't be where you are now. If you have a home, go back to it!"

"And who asked you to poke your nose into my business?" said the girl.

"Hm, who indeed?" said Soroku without a trace of annoyance, and he was surprised himself at how calm he was. "I just felt like telling you these things when I saw you. You're still such a young girl, and I thought that, if I spoke to you, you might think about what I'd said."

"Well, I don't want to hear any more about it," said the girl, stopping in her tracks. There was a fierce look on her child-ish face. "I'm leaving you now."

Soroku paused for a while. Then he said gently, "Let's walk a little further."

The girl calmed down again and walked along beside Soroku. But there was a mischievous look in her eyes, as if she had de-cided to get her own back by playing some trick on him.

"What do you do, Daddy?" she asked.

"Well, let's see." Soroku put his head to the side and smiled; but when he answered he spoke in his usual forthright manner. "I don't really do anything. I suppose I should feel guilty when I think of everyone else working, but the fact is that I just stay at home and look after my money."

"How splendid!" said the girl.

"No, there's nothing very splendid about it."

In the end Soroku had never told Professor Segi about the impulse that had restored his memory to him when he was suf-fering from amnesia. That impulse had simply been his anxiety on seeing the money that the professor had left unguarded on his desk one night. Remembering it now, he was so ashamed that he blushed to the roots of his hair. Yet he felt that this eve-ning he could finally make a frank confession. For his entire way of thinking about money had changed, and now he vaguely began to see that it was in fact money that had made his whole life so narrow and comfortless. Yet to tell all this to a young streetwalker whom he had casually met in the park would not get him very far. He was about to put his thoughts into words when he realized that he was like a blind man helplessly look-ing for some guidance.

"How is it—this work you do?" he said. "It must be very painful." There was something unsure about his words, as though he were handling a fragile article; yet a sincere sym-pathy shone in his eyes as he looked at the girl beside him. For a time she did not answer and there was a hard look of anger on her face.

"There's nothing painful about it," she said defiantly.

"Just think it over again," said Soroku in a cheerful tone. "I've lived in this world quite a long time, as you can see, and I've managed to learn just a little. If you twist your life out of shape, things will never turn out well for you. One gets more and more unhappy as the years go by. But if you start living according to your own true character, however hard it may be at first, your feelings are bound to get clearer, and in the end you become glad that you're alive. Life's a long business, you know. You mustn't try to hurry things at your age."

Soroku stopped walking and in the darkness extracted a large sheaf of banknotes from his pocket. He hesitated for a moment, then decided to give the girl an amount that even she would find exorbitant.

"Use this to improve yourself," he said, handing her the money. "And now, good-by."

When she saw the amount of the money, the girl became flustered. "Oh no," she said, "you mustn't give me all that."

"Take it and go home to bed," said Soroku, and left her standing by herself on the path. As soon as he had walked off, it occurred to him that the money he had given the girl might well serve to make her even worse than before. Perturbed at the idea, he quickened his step as though running away.

●

Taeko was hammering away at her typewriter when she was called to the telephone. She stopped typing. As usual she did not ask who the caller was, but she felt sure that it was Ryosuké, and before standing up she had to make a deliberate effort to calm herself.

"Hullo, hullo," came a voice, "is that you, Taeko-san?" At first Taeko did not recognize her sister from Kobe; recently she had been so intent on other things that she had completely forgotten about Tazuko.

"Oh, it's you, is it?" she said in a surprised tone.

"Yes, why? Is anything wrong?" said Tazuko. "I have something to speak to you about, but I suppose you're busy today."

Taeko knew what her reply ought to be—"Of course, Tazuko, I can see you whenever you like"—but she also knew that her sister was bound to ask her about Ryosuké, and she decided to avoid a meeting.

"Yes, I'm afraid I'm terribly busy today."

"What about tonight?" asked Tazuko.

"All right. But it may be rather late."

"Hm. What a nuisance," said Tazuko softly, as though speaking to herself into the receiver. "You see," she continued, "I was planning to go down to Kamakura this afternoon, and I was hoping that you'd be able to come with me."

"I'm afraid you'd better go by yourself, Tazuko."

"The trouble is that if I go alone it will be purely a business talk, and I probably won't get anywhere with Uncle. If you were along, you could back me up."

Taeko understood the nature of the business that was suddenly taking her sister to Kamakura; at the same time she knew her uncle's solitary nature and realized that the visit was bound to be fruitless.

"Well, Taeko-san, what about it?"

"It wouldn't do any good if I came along, you know."

"You're a coldhearted creature, aren't you? And what about that talk I begged you to have with Uncle Soroku some time ago? I wanted to ask you about that too."

Taeko felt utterly enervated. She realized how difficult things must be for Tazuko if she had to persist in such hopeless negotiations; yet in her present state of mind Taeko did not feel capable of sharing her sister's troubles.

"Please forgive me this time," she said.

"But that isn't all, Taeko. I also wanted to speak to you about your own problem. We can't leave things as they are, you know."

"Look, Tazuko, I've got some work to finish in a hurry. When I get through, I'll try phoning you."

"I may have gone out by then. I'm not here for long this time."

"Are you at the hotel?"

"Yes, that's right."

After she had hung up, Taeko felt unhappy, for her sister's sake as well as for everything else. There was a great weight on her heart. Nothing seemed to go right for anyone. It frightened her that she should be thinking like this and yet she could not help it. Fortunately there was a lot of typing to be done in a hurry, and this seemed to help her. But now Taeko was dismayed to find that she was making far more mistakes than usual. So long as the taptap of the keys continued smoothly beneath her fingers the dark thoughts seemed to stay away; but, as soon as she made a mistake and had to start correcting it, all the sad thoughts came rushing back and seemed to weigh down on her shoulders.

"It's time for the midday break," said the girl who worked at the desk next to Taeko. "What about going out and getting a little sun?"

When the tension of the work relaxed, Taeko became fully conscious of the exhaustion that resulted from her recent sleepless nights. It worried her that not only her body but also her mind itself seemed to have lost its usual equilibrium. "I mustn't rush things," she had told herself as she lay looking at the dawn light coming in through the window. "I must act calmly as if nothing had happened." But already on her way to work she had abandoned this resolution and now, as she walked down the street with her friend, she had a sudden impulse to leave her and rush to Ryosuké's office. She would have done better to go to Kamakura with her sister, she told herself. Or perhaps she ought to go somewhere far away by herself and think it all out. If things went on like this, her head would burst with pain. She felt the tears coming to her eyes and wished that she had someone to whom she could appeal.

"Now that's a very handsome scarf," her friend was saying as she gazed into a shopwindow. "It would be just perfect for 'him.' Yes, I mean it. I've been thinking so ever since I saw it here yesterday."

Taeko looked round as if she had just woken up. She heard her companion prattling away in her usual flippant fashion and became aware that they were standing in front of a shopwindow.

"You're strangely silent today, aren't you, Taeko-san?" remarked the girl.

Taeko stretched her lip in an effort not to burst out crying. "Not really," she replied.

That was, in fact, all that she could say. The misery of the past couple of nights seemed to have piled up inside her. If things were going to go on being as painful as this, she sometimes thought, it really didn't seem worth while living. Yet at other times she tried to look at everything more calmly. Perhaps it had all been a misunderstanding on her part. But in that case why did Ryosuké still not suggest that they should live together? Surely that is what he would do if he really loved her. Yes, she had been tricked. Her life had become utterly hopeless.

Even at the blackest moments, however, a slim ray of light would suddenly appear, like a candle that might be extinguished by the smallest gust of wind, yet sufficient to tell her that all was not yet lost. If only she could pry him away from Mrs. Iwamuro, there might still be hope. Perhaps she ought to meet her and have a talk. Yes of course, that is what she must do.

But why, wondered Taeko, had she become so helpless and weak-willed? Surely it was nothing within herself that had reduced her to this state of confusion in which she did not even know any longer what she was thinking. No, it was outside her, and that made it all the harder.

Yet how could something outside herself make her so despondent that she no longer wanted to live? What had happened to the real Taeko that she should be so ineluctably sunk in misery? She was no longer herself, and her feelings were no longer her own. Some outside force had so overpowered the real Taeko that she could no longer think clearly.

It was a clear autumn day, and the streets were even more crowded than usual. The light was bright; now and then Taeko smelled a whiff of chrysanthemum.

The thing to do, she thought as she walked along the crowded street, was to reject all influences that came from outside herself. Then perhaps she would be able to take a firmer view of things.

When she returned to the office and started walking up the stairs, Ryosuké was just coming down. After the blinding light outside, Taeko was not yet accustomed to the darkness of the building, and she was not even aware that Ryosuké was directly before her until he called out her name. Hearing his voice, she stopped dead in her tracks as if terror-stricken.

"What's wrong?" said Ryosuké.

Taeko glanced at her wristwatch—a reflex action aimed at avoiding Ryosuké. She did not even look at the hands of the watch; yet this little gesture of hers was just what was needed to rescue the girl from her terrible agitation.

"Oh, I'm just going out for a walk with Uiko-san," she said and, without waiting for his answer, she turned round and started walking down the stairs. Ryosuké ran down and caught up with her. As soon as he was walking next to her, she realized that however much she had tried to discipline her feelings she had been waiting for him all the time, and her body was suffused with warmth.

"What on earth is the matter, Taeko? You look as if you'd seen a ghost."

He turned round and laughed. No, thought Taeko sadly, she could never bear to lose this man. Already her exhaustion had vanished, and she felt the blood coursing pleasantly through her veins.

"A lovely day, isn't it?" she said calmly.

"Hm, I suppose so," replied Ryosuké in his usual easygoing manner. "Unfortunately I never have time to wander about and enjoy the time of day."

"Have you been very busy recently?"

"Yes," he said with a smile. "There's no rest for the poor, as they say. But things will work out for me somehow or other. What about lunch? Have you eaten yet?"

"Yes," said Taeko with a nod.

"I wanted to invite you."

"I'll keep you company, if you like, but I won't have anything myself."

"Oh, surely you can have a bite of something light."

"No thanks. I don't have the slightest appetite."

Taeko was thoroughly confused about what to say. She was terrified of annoying Ryosuké or putting him in a bad mood. She found her own pusillanimous attitude to him quite unbearable. With a deliberate effort she turned round and looked Ryosuké in the face. As soon as she really saw him she was overcome with relief and vainly wished that he could make all her doubts evaporate in the air.

She smiled to cover her confusion. "It was terrible," she said. "I had no idea what to do."

"You are a hotheaded girl, aren't you?" he said, calmly accepting her words. Then immediately he changed the subject. "I'm awfully hungry," he said. "Where would you like to go?"

"What about the dining-room of the Nikkatsu Hotel?"

Ryosuké gave her a dubious glance. "I've gone and said it!" she thought and waited nervously for the outcome.

"Why the Nikkatsu Hotel?"

"You go there quite often, don't you?"

"Yes, that's true." Taeko noticed a shadow pass over the young man's cheerful face. "It's a sort of office for me."

Taeko waited for something else, but it did not come. Instead, Ryosuké tightened his lips and said with a rather severe expression: "So that's where you'd like me to take you?"

"No, I really don't want to go there at all."

"Why not?"

"Why not, indeed!" answered Taeko. But she was frightened of coming any closer to the point and said plainly: "I don't want you to spend too much money. It worries me."

Ryosuké accepted her simple reply at its face value.

"I spend money when I've got it," he said. "But when I don't I have to give up all luxuries, though it's hard at times." Taeko listened silently. The young man laughed and went on: "Of course, there are times when I've got to go in for a bit of extravagance even when I'm broke. Sometimes it's essential for business. That's how one builds up credit."

They found a small, unpretentious restaurant near by and went in. Ryosuké ordered a simple dish of curried rice and set to with a good appetite. As she watched him munching away, Taeko felt her heart melting. The very size of the young man's healthy body gave him a special childlike innocence. Yes, thought Taeko, he really was hungry.

"I don't care how modest it is," said Taeko. "I'd be perfectly happy with a simple life together. Couldn't you find some work that would make that possible for us?"

"Me?" said Ryosuké, looking up at the girl.

"Yes."

"I can't fit into such a pattern," said Ryosuké.

"In that case," said Taeko, "I'll get more and more discouraged wondering when we're ever going to be able to live together. Surely it would be better to make up your mind now and find a place, however small and simple, where we could move in together without waiting all this time. It would make all the difference for me, you know."

Ryosuké smiled. It was a youthful, manly smile, but Taeko detected in it a nuance of bitterness. He took out a cigarette, tapped the end lightly on the table, and slowly brought it to his mouth.

"Give me a free rein just a little longer," he said. "Things are going to turn out all right before long, and then I'll show you how much money I can make! If I draw in my horns at this stage of the game, there's no chance of ever getting ahead."

The smoke moved along his clean-shaven face and drifted off to the side. There was a twinkle in his eyes, yet at the same time a touch of haughtiness. "Things have changed since the war, you see. These aren't normal times. But I'll manage to break through, don't worry. If you don't have a certain amount of capital these days, you either work to death or the people on top manage to bleed you white. To tell the truth, I'm a bit late in the game, but I've still got a good chance. If I can just make a foothold for myself and get a little recognition, I'll be able to launch out on my own. At the moment I'm naked, you see. If I come a cropper now, I'm really done for. But don't worry, Taeko. I've always been a good gambler. And I've still got plenty of spunk left. It's all a big game, you know. And it's by winning and losing that we become real people. That's what's meant by having spirit. And besides . . ." he hesitated for a moment, "and besides, I was born with a strong will to come out ahead. I've always hated the idea of being poor. Perhaps it's because I had a comparatively good life when I was small. There's no getting rid of those habits, you know. They stick to one all one's life. Perhaps it's just that side of me that made you like me."

Yes, thought Taeko, he was probably right. Yet there was something dangerous about that part of Ryosuké's nature. How should she tell him?

"I've always imagined that happiness was something more peaceful," she said. "Something that lets one put one's mind to rest."

"Not for me, it isn't," said Ryosuké with a lively expression. "No, not for me. I prefer being shaken about a bit to resting peacefully as if one were asleep. There should be some excitement in life. After all, the whole world's shaking nowadays. There's no point in growing like an old potato."

"Yes, but—" began Taeko, not knowing quite how to express her thoughts. "But surely work is one thing and life's another. Even you have to rest sometimes, don't you? And then—"

She hesitated again. Ryosuké was smiling at her. No doubt he was thinking that her point of view was typically feminine. Yet, typical or not, Taeko was speaking from the bottom of her heart. She knew that, come what might, she could never leave this man, and so she had to tell him what she really thought. The question was how to tell him without arousing his resistance.

"For us women," she said, "real life is something peaceful, something that rests the heart."

"Well, I have nothing against that," said Ryosuké with a laugh.

"No, but you act as if you were constantly engaged in some sort of a gamble. I don't know how I'll manage to live with that."

"By believing in me," said Ryosuké, stretching out his well-formed hand and gently holding Taeko by the arm. "By believing that I'll win. Don't you think so, Taeko?"

"Yes, I do." Taeko was flustered, and the feel of his warm flesh against her almost brought tears to her eyes. "You see, my dear, I understand your nature now. I'm not asking you to do everything just the way I want. But I know there are bad things in the world as well as good things. That's what worries me. If it weren't so, I wouldn't be left waiting like this."

Ryosuké drew back his hand and looked Taeko in the face.

"Don't worry," she continued, "I want to go on believing in you. That's what gives me the greatest pleasure in life. That's what gives me the strength to go on living even now that I've gone against my own parents and my sister."

"I'm sorry," said Ryosuké in a subdued voice. "You've had a hard time. But I'll arrange everything soon, believe me."

"Why soon?" said Taeko. "Why not now?"

"I'm afraid that's impossible. At the moment I'm shifting as best I can. I still don't have enough funds to make a go of it."

"That's not what I mean," said Taeko.

"What then?"

"If we lived together . . . yes, I know we'd manage all right, and it would be like entering a new world."

"But at the same time you'd be killing me. Do you realize that?"

"Killing you?" said Taeko. "Why should I? What do you mean?"

"You'd take away my freedom of movement." There was a cold, severe look in his face which Taeko had never seen there before. It suggested a nature that in time of crisis could become extremely fierce. The expression did not show will power or courage, but potential brutality. It was an expression that one often saw on former military men, who had acquired the habit of being merciless to those in their power.

"And that," continued Ryosuké, "happens not to suit me."

"I don't mean that," said Taeko. "Look, Ryosuké, you have a fundamentally good nature. I'm sure of that. But if you go on as you are now, it's going to be ruined by the influences round you. That's what worries me. However lucky you are, you're bound to lose at times. It happened that evening at the Kawana Hotel, didn't it? Well, if the same thing happened to you in your work, on a really big scale, you'd be in a terrible state. All the more terrible because you're so sure of winning."

Taeko was excited, and every now and then she had to make a deliberate effort to keep her equilibrium. Yet she had not been too upset by the new aspect of Ryosuké's nature that she had just discovered. Whatever unpleasant qualities he might have they were part of the man, and she accepted them as she accepted the whole of him.

"I'm sorry," she continued, "I suppose I've said something rather unpleasant. Scold me if I'm in the wrong. But sometimes I get so worried. That's why I had to speak."

Ryosuké looked uncomfortable. "Yes," he said, nodding his head, "very unpleasant."

"Yes, I suppose so."

If everything, thought Taeko, was a matter of winning or losing, it was clear that she had not won in this discussion with Ryosuké. When she had envisaged their talk, she had felt that, if the worst came to the worst, this was how things would turn out. Yes, she had lost.

And then, of course, there was the question of Mrs. Iwamuro. How should she broach this, she wondered, glancing up at Ryosuké. Then she saw that the look on his face had turned into a harsh expression of defiance. Yes, that was it. He had stood calmly on the field of battle surrounded by enemy fire with exactly that expression. The bullets had hit everything round him, but he had been spared. And now he lived in the belief that this luck would continue to get him out of every critical situation. Every fiber of his taut young flesh seemed to express the belief. He was a magnificent statue, thought Taeko; the fragility and the evanescence of it awoke a strange vibration in her heart. Only for a second did she see him thus—just the time it took her to place her coffeespoon on the saucer.

"How pathetic!"—the feeling came to her like a gust of wind that has blown imperceptibly into the room. She looked at the chrysanthemums on the table; the air was redolent with the aroma of coffee. And in her mind's eye she could see her mother working in the kitchen—the pathetic figure of her mother who had always sacrificed herself for others.

"In all games," she said, "there are winners and losers, aren't there? But there are always lots of losers and usually very few winners—one, or perhaps two. Of course, Ryosuké, I pray from the bottom of my heart that you'll win. But I find myself visualizing all the losers of this world. And I can see you among them."

"I wish you'd stop," said Ryosuké.

They were both silent. Taeko was terrified of loud voices.

"Let's forget it!" he continued. "There are better things to talk about." Then in his usual way Ryosuké calmly changed the subject and said in a pleasant tone: "Couldn't we go to your place for a while?"

This was what Taeko had been longing for him to say; indeed, it was what she herself had been wanting to suggest. Yet she could not give him an immediate answer. First there was a barrier that had to be surmounted.

"Have you met Mrs. Iwamuro recently?" she asked, looking up at Ryosuké.

"No," he said, "I haven't seen her for some time."

Taeko sat speechless and looked at the wall opposite.

When Tazuko Terao called on her uncle, he was lying on a deckchair in the garden enjoying the pleasant afternoon sun. The old house was full of light. A number of books, evidently new publications, lay on the straw matting in the sitting-room.

"So you grow clover here, do you?" said Tazuko, looking around the garden.

"Yes, so it seems," replied Soroku, turning round in his chair and glancing in the same direction. "I always forget what plants we've got. But when the right season comes along, they appear and greet me, and then I'm reminded of them like old friends."

The purpose of Tazuko's visit, of course, was to borrow money; but she had great difficulty in deciding how to broach the subject. Her uncle was well aware of this fact. As soon as they had left the garden and gone into the sitting-room, he took the initiative himself. "I suppose you've come about the same old business."

"Yes, Uncle, I have," said Tazuko, darting a quick glance at Soroku to judge what mood he was in. "But that's not the only thing. I also want to talk to you about Taeko. Has she called on you, by the way?"

Soroku shook his head. "She came down during the summer, but she hasn't been here since. As a matter of fact, I wish she'd come more often."

"And didn't she discuss the question of her marriage with you?" asked Tazuko.

"Let's see now. I do seem to remember she said something on the subject. But what was it? I'm getting awfully absentminded, you know."

"Taeko tends to be a rather self-willed girl. She seems to think it's all right to decide everything for herself."

"Well, since she's the one who's concerned," said Soroku seriously, "why on earth shouldn't she decide for herself? Even if I were consulted I shouldn't be able to give any opinion one way or the other. Nowadays girls of that age are much more sure of themselves than they used to be in the old days. They don't need any comments from the sidelines."

"But really, Uncle," said Tazuko with a disgruntled look, "you've got the wrong idea about freedom. I was awfully worried about Taeko living by herself so far away from the family. Even my husband mentioned the matter. He said I should ask you to keep an eye on her."

Soroku smiled. "That's no good," he said flatly.

"Why not?"

"I can't manage my own life properly. How am I going to look after someone else's?"

"What do you mean, Uncle?" said Tazuko, fixing Soroku with a look of mild indignation. "You've got your life so neatly organized."

For a while Soroku looked silently at the garden. Then his serious face was creased with a smile. "Neatly organized, you say? In what way, may I ask?"

"In every way! You've got your own life so well organized that you don't care about anyone outside—not even your own family."

Soroku looked up at Tazuko. Then slowly he said: "Well, I wish you'd leave it like that—our relationship, I mean."

Tazuko looked open-eyed at Soroku. "Please, Uncle," she

said in a quiet tone of supplication, "please do something about my request. Really, I beg you."

"What?" said Soroku, as if he had suddenly been brought back to himself. "Are you referring to your own affairs now? I was thinking about Taeko."

"Oh yes, I'm also asking your help about Taeko."

"Well, I heard she'd found someone she wanted to marry. How have things turned out?"

"I was against the marriage," said Tazuko. "Since then she hasn't been to see me about it."

"Why were you against it? Did you have any particular reasons?"

Tazuko's real concern at the moment did not lie in the question of her sister's marriage. Yet she could not help being struck by her uncle's interest in the matter.

"He's only a young fellow," she said, "but already he's mixed up with some sort of brokerage work."

"There's nothing wrong with being a broker if one does one's job properly. Anyhow, the important thing is the man himself, not what he does for a living. I seem to remember hearing that he was a classmate of Akira's."

At this, Tazuko felt that she had understood what was really going on inside her uncle's mind.

"Really!" she exclaimed. "Taeko never mentioned it to me. That puts quite a different complexion on the matter."

"Well," said Soroku after a pause, "that in itself doesn't mean that everything's going to go smoothly. In any case, I'll have a good talk with Taeko."

"Ah, that's splendid!" said Tazuko, deferring entirely to her uncle. "If I can leave the matter to you, we can all put our minds at rest about Taeko."

"It isn't that simple," said Soroku brusquely. "For one thing I'm not used to this sort of business. I'll never really get to understand people. If Akira had lived, I'd no doubt have run into this problem of marriage. And, in that case, I'm sure I'd have let him do exactly as he wished. On the other hand, it would have been his responsibility if things went wrong."

"Well, I feel a load off my shoulders," said Tazuko with a sigh of relief. "We were really worried, you know. Not that I've thought for a moment that Taeko would go and do something irresponsible."

"Well then, please tell her to come and see me some time."

To hear her uncle, usually so cold and isolated, make this suggestion (unenthusiastic though it was) was to Tazuko a real surprise. She even seemed to detect a note of affection in his voice as he continued: "I don't suppose it will do any good, but at least I can hear what she has to say."

Now, thought Tazuko, was the time for the conversation to turn to her own problem. She was wondering how to begin when Soroku himself broke the ice. "Well now, about your question."

"Yes."

"You won't get anywhere with me, however much you go on about it. So please don't let me hear any more about the matter."

"What are you saying, Uncle?" asked Tazuko, a look of deadly earnest on her face.

"I'm just asking you to leave off," said Soroku gently. "It's I who am asking you a favor this time: please leave off."

"But, Uncle," pleaded Tazuko. She felt as if she had suddenly been turned adrift, and all her earlier composure vanished. "I'm in terrible trouble. Please listen to me at least."

"I do wish you'd stop talking about it."

"But there's no one else I can possibly turn to."

"Please don't make me say too much, Tazuko." The expression on Soroku's face was as frank as his words. "If I start talking, I'm bound to attack your entire attitude to life. And then the question will arise as to what I've done with my own life. What's the use?"

"All I'm asking of you is some money," said Tazuko earnestly. She put her hands on the straw matting where she was kneeling and bowed to the floor. "I'm really in trouble, Uncle. I don't know how I'm going to manage."

"In trouble?" said Soroku. "That doesn't sound like you, Tazuko. Well now, you'd better leave."

"I'm going to hold this against you for the rest of my life," said Tazuko.

"Oh, that's all right. You can hold it against me as much as you like. It won't worry me."

"So you really won't help me, even though you've got the money?"

"Hm. No, I don't deny that I have money."

"If you want interest, I'll pay you at whatever rate you say. I've come here prepared to pay a stiff rate."

"Don't be silly!"

"But surely, Uncle, you don't mind making a profit."

"No, it's no use." Soroku's face was flushed, but he was still not angry. "I'd be more inclined to listen to you if you were a perfect stranger rather than a member of the family. I'd never lend money to a member of my family."

"Yes, Uncle, that's precisely why I suggested paying interest —just like an outsider. You can handle the whole thing on a completely businesslike basis. I don't mind."

"What an unreasonable woman you are!" said Soroku, and for the first time he showed signs of irritation. "It may be fashionable nowadays, but the fact remains that what you're trying to do in Kobe is utterly superfluous. Even if a shop like that could pay its own way, there's no reason that you should have anything to do with it. Now, if you were a war widow, for instance, and you had to earn a living, I'd be on your side and probably even put some money into the shop. But, since you're doing it purely for your amusement, I dare say it would be better if the whole thing fell through. Under such conditions I can't advance you a single yen however much you pester me."

"Is that all the sympathy you have for me, Uncle?"

"What an awkward question!" said Soroku with a smile. "Now if it's a matter of your finding it difficult to wind things up down there, it would be perfectly simple for me to go and arrange it for you. But I don't suppose it's come to that yet, and no doubt you'll manage so long as you don't attempt the impossible."

"No, Uncle, I've run up debts all over the place."

"That's no problem," said Soroku. His voice was soft; but, as he sat on the floor hugging his knees, his body, thin as it was, suggested all the immovable strength of a wall. "It's simply a matter of paying back what you've borrowed."

"But I haven't got the money," said Tazuko, smiling at her uncle.

"What? That's child's play! If you do as I suggest, I could

have someone go down to Kobe for me—or I could even go my-self and do a bit of sightseeing at the same time—and we could settle the whole matter in no time. But it's so easy that you can perfectly well manage it yourself. I gather that you've al-ready decorated the place as a shop, so the thing to do is to sell the rights to someone else and pay off the debts with the money you get."

"If that's all there was to it," said Tazuko, "I shouldn't have come all this way troubling you for advice."

"Well then, go ahead and do as I say."

"But really," said Tazuko, looking aghast at her uncle, "there's such a thing as my reputation to consider."

"You shouldn't worry too much about that, Tazuko. If you start something that you aren't used to, it's no disgrace when you make a failure of it. You live for yourself, don't you, not for other people? You've gone and started this shop to give yourself some extra pleasure. There's no earthly reason that you should worry about what other people may think now that it's gone badly. As soon as you realize that a thing is more of a burden than a pleasure, you should cut your losses and get out of it. What's the use of carrying a burden that gives you no pleasure and does no one else any good?"

"But everyone knows that I've got a well-to-do relative. They're all wondering why I'm having such trouble when I've got an uncle who is in a position to help me."

Soroku was silent for a while, and it was evident that he was making a great effort to keep his temper. "Why on earth should I come into the picture?" he said. "I've long since stopped working, and I live entirely on the interest from my investments. In a sense I could be considered a burden to the world—producing nothing and only consuming. What appears to be my fortune doesn't really belong to me at all. It's merely something that the world has given me to keep in custody dur-ing my lifetime. That's what it means to acquire money. Some-times one knows quite clearly to whom the money must be re-turned and in such cases one pays it back when the time comes. That's how I feel about it. The trouble is that I don't know who I'm meant to pay my money back to. Still, if I were to have my money taken from me, I wouldn't be able to eat any longer. So I dawdle along, carefully looking after the money that's been entrusted to me. At some time or other I shall return it to society and thus settle my accounts in full. Even if Akira had lived, I don't think I'd have given it to him. I'd have wanted him to work and make his own living."

There was an excited flush on Soroku's face. He had not been elaborating an excuse to avoid making Tazuko a loan, but had been sincerely groping for an answer to the entire question of money; and now he was confident that he had arrived at a reasonable conclusion, or at least very close to one. "Strangers . . ." continued Soroku, half thinking aloud, "no, I mean to say that money does not really belong to one. It is entrusted to a person for his own use. He has no right to throw it away. I certainly can't use my money to help you wipe up your mess. Can't you understand that?"

"But I said that I'd pay you back with interest." Tazuko had turned pale, and she had an empty sensation inside. At first she had felt like smiling as her uncle babbled away about his money, but gradually she had been overcome by a stifling sense of oppression.

"Rather than let you have the money," said Soroku, "I'd throw it by the roadside for the first stranger to pick up. If I wouldn't even give it to Akira, do you really suppose that you have a chance?"

●

────────────────────
════════════════════
────────────────────

"Really?" said Ryosuké, putting his head to the side and smiling. "Isn't it getting a bit cold for ice cream?"

He opened the door of the teashop but, instead of standing aside for the two women who were with him, strode in ahead to find an empty table. One could tell from his tall, resolute figure that he was used to leading the way.

Taeko sat next to her sister and faced Ryosuké across the table. She had just introduced him to Tazuko and was pleased to see how easily and naturally he behaved. A promising beginning, she thought with relief.

At first she had been rather worried, realizing how many things required an explanation. She really did not know how she and her fiancé would reply to her sister's inquiries. It was not simply a question of the main problem, which hung now like a dark shadow between Ryosuké and herself; she was not even prepared to answer ordinary, everyday questions—questions such as when they actually intended to have their ceremony.

Ryosuké, however, seemed to be quite impervious to all this.

"Hang it!" he exclaimed, slapping his knee. "There was a football game today. I even went and bought tickets."

"If you don't want to miss it," said Tazuko solicitously, "please go ahead."

"Oh no," said Ryosuké. "In any case I've got an appoint-ment. And they're going to win this year even if I don't go, so it's quite all right."

Taeko was surprised. "Do you mean that you were on the team yourself?" she asked.

"Yes, Taeko, that's the general picture." Ryosuké addressed her in a familiar way that made the girl blush in the presence of her sister. "I thought that if I went and sat in the special section reserved for former members of the team, the young fellows would see me and it would buck them up."

"He was at the same school as Akira-san, you know," put in Taeko.

Tazuko nodded.

"Mé didn't go in for football himself," said Ryosuké. "He was quick on his feet all right, but there was something weak about the fellow. He didn't have much fight in him. And then I don't suppose that father of his would let him go in for any rough games."

"By the way, Tazuko-san," said Taeko, picking up a spoon-ful of ice cream, "have you been down to Kamakura yet?"

Tazuko's face clouded over and she seemed hesitant to reply.

"Ah yes," said Ryosuké with a smile, as if to cover up the embarrassed silence, "that reminds me. I suppose I ought to put in at least one appearance there myself. I haven't seen Mé's old man for years and years, but from my childhood impression I think of him as a rather formidable creature."

"Oh no," said Taeko, "he's a fine gentleman." She looked innocently at her sister as though to get her confirmation. "Though, to be sure, Ryosuké tells me that when he lent Akira money he always used to charge him interest."

"He's got the money, all right," said Tazuko, finally break-ing her silence. "And since Akira was his son, the boy at least managed to get some of it out of him by paying interest. But when it comes to the likes of us, Uncle treats one like dirt." She looked as if she was going to burst into tears of mortifica-tion. "Do you know what a terrible thing he said to me? 'If I had to give you money, I'd rather throw it away on the road for the first passer-by to pick up'—that's what he said. I've never been spoken to like that in my life, not even by a perfect stranger. And he meant what he was saying, mind you. He's a real fiend!"

Taeko looked up in surprise and saw that her sister had turned dead white.

"Uncle must have been in a nasty mood, that's all. He's not as bad as all that, you know."

"No, he's a fiend—a fiend in human form. This time he's thoroughly convinced me of the fact. I knew he'd broken with Father and Mother, yet I kept an open mind about it all. But now I realize the sort of man he is, and I can see there's no coming to terms with him. He's quite impossible."

"It's strange," said Takeo. "Uncle may be difficult where money is concerned, but I'm sure he's not as heartless as you seem to think."

"That's because he's nicer to you, I suppose," said Tazuko. "Perhaps it's that you live nearer him than I do. Anyhow, you seem to be the only member of the family who's in his good graces."

In a rather peculiar way the conversation was beginning to turn to Taeko, and the young girl tried to parry further remarks of the kind by laughing with simulated gaiety and saying: "Well, Tazuko-san, why don't I have a go at him about money? Then perhaps I'll come a cropper too!"

"It's no laughing matter," said Tazuko. Her earlier agitation was giving way to an air of quiet dejection. "I've made one useless trip after another from Kobe. Completely useless . . . Well, Mr. Tsugawa, perhaps I shouldn't be talking so openly about these family affairs, but since you evidently know Uncle yourself, I don't suppose it matters. Of one thing I'm quite certain—I have no desire to meet that man again."

"All the same," said Taeko softly, "it's a shame you couldn't have seen Uncle about something else."

"It's no good," said Tazuko, "no good at all. What can one expect from such a Shylock?"

Taeko looked at her sister. She knew that her underlying nature was optimistic and that these fits of distress never lasted for very long. She looked wretched at the moment, but her misery had no real roots, and by the time she returned to Kobe she would be in just as sanguine a mood as if she had never gone to Kamakura at all.

"I'm sorry," said Taeko to Ryosuké. "We shouldn't keep talking about our family matters."

"Oh, it's quite all right," said the young man. He looked at the two sisters with a cheerful air of animation as though totally unconcerned with their recent conversation. "What splendid weather we're having! This is the best season of all, though it's still a bit warm for football."

"You seem to have a lingering attachment for the game," said Tazuko. "Are you sorry you gave it up?"

"Good heavens, no! I don't have time for that sort of thing." He glanced at his watch. "I'm afraid I have an appointment at four o'clock. I hope you'll excuse me if I leave ahead of you."

"Where are you going now?" Taeko heard herself asking. "To a hotel?"

"No, back to the office." He casually put his hand in his pocket and extracted a small packet. "I'm sorry that it isn't wrapped properly."*

As though bending over the table to examine something, he placed the packet on Tazuko's lap. It was a bundle of thousand-yen notes secured by a piece of brown tape.

"Goodness me!" exclaimed Tazuko.

"You may be needing a little spare cash on your trip," said Ryosuké. "Perhaps this will come in useful. I hope so." He put on his hat and sprang lightly to his feet. "Well, if you'll excuse me, I really must be off."

Tazuko made a confused effort to turn down the young man's unexpected offer, but it was clear from the outset that she would end by accepting it. Taeko for her part was amazed that Ryosuké should show such kindness to her sister; she was strangely elated by his gesture, and she felt herself flushing. Ryosuké's openhearted nature seemed to be revealed in this artless action of his.

"No, no," he was saying, "it's quite all right. Please use it for whatever you need."

---

* Gifts of money are traditionally wrapped and tied in a special sort of paper with special string and knot; cash gifts are far more common in Japan than in the West.

He was blushing himself now and seemed to be in a hurry to leave.

"Well," he said, "I hope we meet soon again. Please let me know if you have any free time before you go."

"Really," exclaimed Tazuko. "I don't know what to say."

She looked at her sister as if hoping to find an ally, but already Ryosuké had left the table, and they could see his sturdy figure striding toward the door.

"I wonder if it's all right," said Tazuko. "I really shouldn't let him do this."

All of a sudden Taeko began to realize what lay behind this action of Ryosuké's that had taken place so quickly and smoothly. She knew that it was an essential part of his temperament to take some bold step on the spur of the moment.

There was no telling the amount of the money without counting it, but judging from the size of the packet there must have been at least one hundred thousand yen.

"He seems to be quite well off, your young man," said Tazuko with a smile, tucking the money into her bag. Her ill humor had entirely vanished and now she was ready to purr at anyone, including her young sister. "Of course I'll pay it back, but for the time being I'm going to accept his kind loan. I don't mind telling you it's really saved my life. I didn't even have enough to settle my hotel bill, and I was going to have to phone Kobe. Of course, you needn't let him know that, but I do hope you'll thank him very warmly from me."

Taeko smiled at her sister, but her feelings seemed to be gradually freezing inside her. Clearly Ryosuké had done something rash, and he would regret it later. She could no longer look at it in any other way. His gesture had certainly been one of kindness; and indirectly it was kindness to her rather than to Tazuko, for his aim had obviously been to make some slight improvement in Takeo's position at home. This being the case, she should accept the gesture for what it was and refrain from useless reflections. All the same, she could not prevent a growing sense of uneasiness as she thought of the difficulties that Ryosuké might have as a result of this.

When they stepped into the street, it was a beautiful autumn day.

"Where shall we go now?" asked Tazuko cheerfully. "I'd like to buy you a little present to thank you for your help."

"Oh no, you mustn't," said Taeko, dejected rather than angry. "Anyhow, I've got to get back to the office."

She felt that there was a slightly bitter ring in her reply, and she very much wanted to be alone. She walked with her sister as far as the Owaricho crossing and there said good-by.

At first she set off toward the office, then suddenly changed her mind and decided to follow Ryosuké to his office and have a talk with him.

She turned around, wondering whether her sister had noticed. Tazuko was on the sun-drenched pavement, surrounded by crowds of people. Taeko watched her as she crossed over to the opposite pavement and stood there for a few moments, uncertain which way to go. Then she evidently decided to return to the other side of the road and visit the near-by department store. If one watched people from the distance, thought Taeko, when they were off their guard like this, there was something strangely lonely and pathetic about their movements. That is how her sister lived, Taeko told herself, her bright-spirited sister who was now once again crossing the street with all the other people.

When she reached Ryosuké's office, she found it in a very different state from when she had first visited it in the evening. All the desks were occupied. Some of the men were talking loudly to their visitors, others were busily writing. Though it was full daylight outside, the electric lights burned brightly.

Taeko stood by the entrance and looked in. There was no sign of Ryosuké. She thought that she recognized his desk, but there was a stranger sitting there reading the evening paper. He was smoking a cigarette, and a hat was perched on the back of his head. She was just wondering whom she could ask when one of the men stood up and started to leave the room.

"Could you tell me if Mr. Tsugawa is here?" Taeko asked him.

"Tsugawa?" he said, looking round the office. "No, he doesn't seem to be here." The man examined a blackboard on the wall. "And he hasn't left any message." Then, turning around, he called out to the occupants of the office, "Has anyone seen Tsugawa?"

Just then a corpulent middle-aged man appeared at the entrance behind Taeko. "I've got some business with Tsugawa too," he declared. His breath reeked of saké. Taeko glanced up at him. He was wearing an old overcoat. It was unbuttoned and shabby. The man gave an air of general dilapidation. Yet there was a solid, respectable look about his forehead with its receding hairline; it reminded one of a company director and made his poor clothes seem strangely incongruous.

"He showed up this morning," said someone from the rear of the smoke-filled office, "but he went out later and hasn't been back since. He did say that he'd be here this afternoon, though."

Taeko recalled that Ryosuké had said he was going back to his office.

"Oh, so he's out?" muttered the stout gentleman, looking at Taeko. "Well, if he's said he's coming back, I might as well sit and wait." His slightly blurred speech revealed the effects of saké. "Are you going to sit and wait too, young lady? I say 'sit and wait,' but this place doesn't seem to boast any seating arrangements."

Taeko decided to go back to her own office and to try again later. She nodded briefly to the gentleman, as if trying to avoid something dangerous, and edged her way past him into the alley outside. Her body did not actually brush against the man, but as she passed him he lost his grip on the hat he was holding, and it fell to the floor. It was a hard sun-helmet, and it made a great clatter as it rolled over. It stopped directly in front of Taeko and lay there, like a pot that has been turned upside down.

Taeko picked up the hat and handed it to the man.

"Merci, Mademoiselle," he said. "Je vous remercie infiniment."

At first Taeko did not know what he was saying, then she realized that he was thanking her in French. There was a gentleness about the man that even managed to show through his exaggerated drunken gestures.

"Ah, my chapeau," he said, carefully extracting a handkerchief from his pocket and wiping the helmet with an air of reverence. "No doubt, my young lady, you consider it rather odd that I should be sporting a sun-helmet in this cold weather." He smiled at Taeko with his eyes. "And you're quite right to think it odd. This type of headgear, as you correctly surmise, is designed to shield one from the sun in the hot weather. It is meant for tropical places, like India and Africa. One wouldn't need a hat like this in Japan even at the very height of the summer heat. And yet I go out with it even in the autumn and the winter. The fact is that my wife can't stand it, and that brings out all my most perverse instincts." He laughed loudly. "Under our new Constitution the Emperor is designated as the symbol of the people. And now I have my own symbol— this old sun-helmet. I wear it as a badge of honor. It is a symbol of my utter uselessness in this world."

He was really extremely drunk, thought Taeko, and she tried to hurry away.

"My dear young lady, please excuse my bad manners."

Even in his present state there was a certain decorum about the man. There was something familiar about him. "To tell the truth, I've been drinking some of that ambrosial fluid known as saké. It's not I who is being rude, it's the drink! But what about old Ryobei? Isn't he coming back?"

"I really don't know."

"Hm, I was depending on him for something." He looked straight at Taeko. "Forgive me for asking, but why have you come to see him?"

"Well, really I don't . . ."

"No, I'm sorry, I shouldn't have asked you. No doubt you're seeing him on business."

Taeko wanted to get away from the man, but she could not go very fast on the narrow unpaved alley that led to the main road, and somehow she found herself walking next to him.

"Well," he continued, "there's only one thing I wanted to see him about—and that's money. I'm afraid it's all rather sordid, but the fact is that I've gone to the dogs . . . yes, gone to the dogs. I was having a drink in that place over there—you see that place that looks like an old barracks—but after I'd finished I felt I hadn't had quite enough. A very unsatisfying feeling, you know. So I decided to ask our Mr. Tsugawa for a little money so that I could go on drinking. It came to me all of a sudden, this brilliant decision of mine. When Tsugawa sees my face, he'll fork out the money. He's got to, you see. He's under a moral obligation."

Taeko walked along silently.

"Now don't get the idea that I won't pay him back," continued the man. "If I don't actually repay him myself, my wife will pay for me. The trouble is that he isn't in his office. He's a lucky fellow, our Mr. Tsugawa. He's got off easily this time. Yes, indeed. He has no desire to see my face. If he meets me on the street, he runs for it. But when I find him in his office, he's properly caught!" Once again the man burst out laughing. "It's saké that endows me with this amazing wisdom. I'm a real glutton when it comes to saké. But do tell me, my dear young lady, what is your connection with Tsugawa?"

Taeko hesitated for a moment, but the vague antipathy that she had begun to feel against this stranger prompted her to answer him point-blank: "We're getting married."

The man was struck silent and gazed at Taeko with amazement. His small sunken eyes, surrounded by a sea of wrinkles, opened to an extent that one would hardly have believed possible.

"I see," he said in a voice that was scarcely more than a whisper. "In that case I'm afraid I've been very rude—suddenly putting you a question like that. I'm drunk, of course. But still I shouldn't have been such a fool."

Taeko glanced at him. She noticed that the collar of his shirt was frayed and dirty. But his manner had altered completely, and the effects of alcohol seemed to have worn off. In a flash he had become a different person—well mannered and self-controlled.

"I'm afraid I've behaved disgracefully," he said. "Please don't think too ill of me. To think that I should speak like that to someone I've just met for the first time!"

The time had finally come, Taeko thought, for them to go their own ways. At that moment she remembered how rudely the man had spoken about Ryosuké. At first she had dismissed it as part of his drunken babbling, but now she felt vaguely worried by what he had said.

"Do you happen to know a woman called Kaoruko Iwamuro?" asked the man, all of a sudden raising his head, which had been sunk in the collar of his overcoat.

Taeko looked up at him. The man had taken her by surprise, and she turned her face so that he could not see her expression. But her answer was forthright.

"Yes, I've met her." Then, as though a light had flashed on her, not from outside but from within, she retorted: "Is she your wife?"

Takabumi Iwamuro nodded vigorously without saying a word. At the same time a cold sad look came into his eyes. It was some time before he spoke.

"But only for appearance's sake, mind you, just a matter of form," he said. "Though, of course, a young girl like you can't be expected to know about such things."

A slight smile played on his face—an unshaven face, engraved with the exhaustion of age.

"Oh well, it's of no consequence," he said, and again lapsed into silence. Taeko had the impression that he was deeply agitated but doing his best to suppress his feelings.

"The world's a very nasty place, isn't it? Yet some people manage to live splendidly. They may seem weak, but they don't give up. Take the *pan-pan,* for instance, the young streetwalkers one sees all over the place these days. People despise them and keep them at arm's length as if they were lepers. Yet this is the easiest way for a girl from a poor family to make a living, and I don't see why they should be condemned out of hand. The worst one can say is that they're poor ignorant creatures. One can't laugh at them. Who in the world is so perfect that he has nothing on his conscience? Who can afford to throw the first stone at these girls? The really impure people are to be found elsewhere. They are people, men as well as women, who have all the advantages of knowledge and education, yet who lose their sense of shame just as easily as these *pan-pan* girls. They may keep up appearances, but their actions are exactly the same. I'm one of them myself, you know.

"If you put some bait in front of me, I can't help snatching at it instantly. Yes, I've reached the ultimate in slovenliness!" He laughed again. "I'm drunk, of course. Please don't mind what I say. To tell you the truth I had a drink at that wine shop just now—in fact rather more than one drink. I was drinking

some stuff called *shochu*. It tastes pretty foul, but it's cheap
and it's effective. It's the stuff the workers drink. Well, all sort
of fellows came in while I was there. And you could tell from
looking at them that not one of them was a weakling like me.
That type of man doesn't drink to drown his miseries, you see.
Saké fits neatly into his normal pattern of living. He works
out exactly how much money he's earned that day by the sweat
of his brow, and then he drinks what he can afford. In other
words, he knows when to stop. There was one fellow, for instance, who said that he'd like another drink, but that if he
had one there wouldn't be enough money left to feed his wife
and children. So he paid for what he'd drunk and hurried home.
There was nothing demoralized about this fellow, you see.
He was a simple, honest chap who wasn't trying to give himself airs or to make any particular impression. He kept his feet
firmly on the ground and clearly spoke out what he thought in
front of everyone. Those are the sort of men I watch as I stand
there by myself drinking my *shochu*—solid men with a solid
sense of responsibility. I'm completely different, of course. I
don't feel there's any future for me. That's why I've let myself
go and drink all I can get hold of. But, much as I want to drink,
I haven't got the money. That's the real trouble. Where can I
get the money? I've sunk pretty low, haven't I? And then—"

"Look here," interrupted Taeko, unable to stand any more
of it.

"I'm very sorry," said Takabumi, recovering his dignity as
though he had suddenly returned to himself. "Yes, I've been
extremely rude. But let me ask you one more thing. Won't you
meet my wife some time? I'll come with you, if you like. I think
it would be a good thing to get Tsugawa away from her."

Taeko had expected to hear something like this, yet she
was at a loss for a reply.

"What would she say, do you suppose?" continued Takabumi. There was a puzzled look on his face, as though he was
searching for an answer to his own question. "Don't get the
idea that I only think of her as a bad woman. I realize that
men and women are quite different. Men tend to be governed
by a single set of circumstances, but women change like
chameleons. At the moment she's doing rather well for herself.

Yet sometimes I can't help feeling sorry for her. I . . . I've lost all power of action. It's a great misfortune."

A sorrowful shadow passed over his aristocratic features. There was an apologetic tone in his voice.

"But she isn't aware of this misfortune. Because things are going so well for her. By relying on her own strength, a strength she should never have had in the first place, she is able to keep herself in a good humor." Takabumi's eyes darted about nervously. "When all's said and done, women are very different creatures. They always feel they're on a stage—a magnificent stage where everything glitters and sparkles. It never seems to occur to them that it's all a sham, that the scenes are made by sticking bits of old newspaper together. Take my wife, for instance. She goes on acting happily. That's it—it's an act. It may be the part of a beautiful woman, or some flashy modernistic part, but she's always acting. Even when the curtain comes down and she has to go back to her cold gloomy dressing-room, she's still as happy and excited as if she were on the stage. Why should she care about her husband? For she's determined to see herself as a princess, and if her husband should appear on the scene it reminds her of their poor humdrum life together, and the beautiful dream is shattered. From one point of view it's all rather pathetic. There's always someone to flatter her into taking some part. Of course, it's foolish of her to dance to other people's tunes. But not for a moment does she realize that she's being put through her paces like a monkey who's led about by a showman. The world's a frightening place. I know all about what goes on behind the scenes, in the dressing-rooms. If you go on using them, the time's bound to come before very long when you get pushed down and trampled mercilessly underfoot. Yes, I know all about it."

The conversation had wandered from what Taeko had been expecting to hear. This was not simply a result of the saké, she felt. Mr. Iwamuro had purposely changed the subject. Having briefly broached the idea, he had prudently dropped it. Taeko wondered what he had really wanted her to say to his wife. The idea that she and Mrs. Iwamuro should meet may have been an irresponsible notion induced by his drunken state, yet Taeko could not stop herself from hoping for precisely such a meeting. A feeling of unhappiness welled up in her like a great cloud that covers the sky before a typhoon.

With a deliberate effort she made herself look at the matter in a new light. No, she must not let anyone else's opinion enter into something that concerned only her and Ryosuké. In her distress she had often felt like appealing to someone else for help, yet so far she had managed to avoid mentioning the matter to anyone and she had kept the problem entirely to herself.

"I'm afraid that I should have nothing to say to your wife even if I did meet her," declared Taeko. She felt herself weighed down by an almost unbearable burden, but managed to get the words out with a smile.

Takabumi nodded vaguely in agreement. "I don't like people to be unhappy, you know, and yet I manage to make them unhappy. I suppose it's because I'm floundering about myself and don't really know what I'm doing. Well, I'd better be off. I'm afraid I say all sort of things that shouldn't be said. But now I'll leave you. I've spoken like a fool ever since we met."

Ryosuké closed the window next to the driver's seat—not that it was particularly cold, for the car was a new model and had an efficient heater, and besides, he had Taeko sitting snugly next to him.

This was the first time that they had been out of Tokyo together since their trip to Izu early in the summer. "We'll have to come back to Tokyo the same day," he had told her when suggesting the drive. "I've got to hand the car over to the man I sold it to." Despite the hurried nature of their journey, this clear winter Sunday had all the charm of a festival for Taeko.

They had agreed to drive to Lake Hakoné and back. Ryosuké was a skillful driver. As soon as he sat down in front of the steering-wheel, he seemed to be filled with the joy of living; the very fact of holding the wheel appeared to give him a special pleasure. After they had left Totsuka on the Tokaido highway the road improved, and it was possible to drive along at a good speed. When they came to the old-fashioned bridge at Yumoto, there was a sharp curve and the extremities of the arches made the road even narrower, so that it was a tight squeeze for any large car.

"What a damned stupid bridge!" said Ryosuké in a scornful tone. "It would be a terrible bore if I went and damaged the car now after I've gone to all the trouble of selling it."

So saying, he put his foot on the accelerator, and they shot up the mountain road at a speed that made Taeko terrified. The road was beautifully paved. It ran along the edge of a deep valley, and one sharp curve followed another until, before knowing it, they were high in the mountains. Some of the mountains were dazzlingly bright, others were sunk in shadows. A vivid green forest of cedars on one hill would border on another hill that was covered with the bright red leaves of a copse; and no less beautiful were the stretches of dry grass high up on the mountainside.

"I always imagined that mountains in the winter would be dark and gloomy," Taeko heard herself saying, "but these are so fantastically bright."

"We're a bit late for the red maples," said Ryosuké, putting a cigarette in his mouth. "The red leaves move steadily down the mountain, you see. They'd already passed Yumoto, hadn't they? I think they must have gone all the way to Odawara by now."

Taeko smiled at the young man's amusing way of expressing the progress of the red autumn foliage. He made it sound as though the leaves were sentient creatures who deliberately made their way from the top of the mountains down to the sea. Perhaps, she mused, they actually entered the sea and that was how coral came to be formed.

On their way along the coast the sea off Izu had been a clear deep blue. The silhouette of Oshima Island had been visible in the offing, and Taeko had thought nostalgically of the time when she had seen it during their journey to Kawana —the journey that had turned out to be their honeymoon. She had climbed down the side of the cliff where the lilies bloomed and she had walked into the glittering water and Ryosuké had taken her by the hand. Despite herself she sighed deeply. It was a happy memory, to be sure, yet there was something painful about it all that made her extremely restless. There was so much that she wanted to say, and she had to make a great effort not to let it come to the surface. Looking through the windshield at the hills and at the valleys buried in their green cedars, Taeko had determined that for this one day she would banish everything from her mind except the beauty of nature. But already, she realized bitterly, that seemed to be impossible: other thoughts kept crowding in.

Presently they reached a little village called Ai no Yado with houses of thatched roofs and mountain flowers in the gardens. The trunks of the trees were in the shade, but the winter sun shone peacefully on the branches. After they had passed the village, Taeko turned around and looked back. Moments such as these could never be found in the crowds and turmoil of the city. No sooner had Taeko thought this than she recalled her meeting with Takabumi Iwamuro; at the same time she remembered Mrs. Iwamuro and also her elder sister who had now returned to Kobe. Her happiness clouded over. Human affairs, if one could express it in a single phrase, seemed to be fearfully confused. To relax one's guard for a moment meant being tripped up and knocked about severely before one knew what had happened. Taeko would have given anything to be able to feel at ease about Ryosuké.

In the end it had turned out as she had feared: Ryosuké was unable to give her what she was really seeking. On top of this another shadow—a shadow that she loathed—had thrust itself in from the side. It appeared that it was impossible in this complicated world for people to cultivate their own pure feelings; external lights and shadows always seemed to enter, so that one lost one's original focus.

Just before entering Moto-Hakoné Ryosuké stopped the car and they looked down at the lake. Perhaps because they had been driving along a cold desolate plain, the lake looked particularly bright, as if someone had placed an ancient mirror in the midst of the wintry mountain landscape. It was cold and forbidding, yet there was a beauty about that brilliant water.

They drove between the rows of pine trees that lined the old Tokaido highway and soon reached the Hakoné Hotel. From the garden they could see the white slopes of Mount Fuji. Now that they were directly next to the lake the water looked even colder. There was a slight wind, and the waves lapped against the shore.

There was hardly anyone in the dining-room. As they were finishing their lunch with some fruit, a pleasure boat stopped at the near-by landing and a group of tourists stepped off. For a while the tourists swarmed around the pier, but presently they melted away as if they had never been there, and nothing was left but the large pole on which a flag fluttered forlornly in the breeze.

"It's really too quiet here," said Ryosuké.

"Yes, but it's nice," said Taeko with a smile. "I certainly prefer this to the crowds of Tokyo." She paused for a moment, then added: "There's something I want to talk to you about."

Ryosuké looked up. "What is it?"

"It's about us."

"You mean what we talked about the other day?"

"That's right. But it's not only that." Taeko shook her head and smiled; she had become completely calm. "There's something else too."

Ryosuké said nothing for a while. Then he called for the waitress, asked for the bill, and paid.

"Let's go into the lobby," he said.

"Very well." Until now Taeko had retained her self-control. She had realized that once she gave free rein to her womanly instincts there was no telling how wrought up she might become, and she had been obliged to keep up a secret battle with herself in order to hold her feelings in check. But now at last she was confident that she could speak out, without saying anything either ugly or hurting.

"Well, Taeko, what do you want to say?"

"Let's have our tea first," she answered, smiling playfully. She picked up her cup and drank. She had resolved to break the ice by broaching the most difficult subject first. "Do you think we'll stay together all our lives?" she said.

A concentrated look appeared on Ryosuké's face, as though he had unexpectedly been confronted with the full earnestness of Taeko's spirit.

"What do you mean?"

"That's what I'm asking," said Taeko. "What do *you* mean?

Am I really indispensable to you, Ryosuké, now and always?"

"Yes, that's the general idea. And what about you?"

"Do you need to ask?"

"Well, I suppose. . . . But really, Taeko, you've taken me by surprise—bringing up this sort of thing all of a sudden."

"It's because I feel so uneasy." She was able to say the words quietly and in the same controlled tone as before. "I don't think you really understand what I'm going through."

"But I've asked you to wait, haven't I?"

"It only seems to get worse by waiting."

"What do you mean, worse? Can't you trust me?"

"I'm afraid that's what it looks like. And it seems to be getting harder and harder."

"You don't really understand people, do you?" said Ryosuké, looking reproachfully at the girl.

All at once her various grievances against Ryosuké started to race around inside her mind. Yet she knew that if she mentioned so much as one of them, all the others would come pouring out uncontrollably. After all the unhappiness she had gone through she still knew that she did not want to cause Ryosuké the slightest suffering. If anyone was to be hurt, she thought, let it be herself. On no account must she start making accusations.

"No," said Taeko, "perhaps I don't understand people. I'm a woman, and no doubt there are many things I don't understand. I suppose that's why everything seems so bad to me."

"What worries you," said Ryosuké, "is that I still haven't done anything about our being together. That's it, isn't it? No doubt it's been selfish of me. Yes, I admit it myself. But it simply couldn't be helped. At present I don't have the resources that would allow us to live together. We've got to wait. I have no intention of deceiving you, Taeko. There's another difficulty. It's hard for me to mention it, but you'd better know. Mother is against the marriage. She's an old-fashioned sort of woman, you see, and she greatly dislikes the idea that you've got a job of your own. I'm sure the time will come when I can have my own way, but for the present I can't possibly desert Mother. She's alone in the world, you see, and I'm her only child. When it comes to this sort of thing I suppose I'm on the old-fashioned side myself. Even if I were to leave home, I'd always have to look after Mother. I could never leave her in the lurch. It's not just a matter of my livelihood. I'm incapable of deserting my own parent. That's how I'm made."

A terrible sadness came over Taeko. She thought of her relationship with her father and of many other things besides. The impenetrable barrier that she had always felt at home now seemed to have emerged starkly before her eys. The fact confronted her ineluctably: she was the daughter of a housemaid, while Ryosuké was a son of good family.

"You must always have been a great favorite at home," she said in a downcast tone, "ever since you were a little boy. But you see, Ryosuké, I had been hoping that your mother would become my own mother too, and that idea made me very happy."

"It's not your fault, Taeko, or mine. The trouble is Mother."

"And if your mother should accept me, will everything be all right?"

"We've got to wait. I wouldn't get anywhere if I spoke to her about it now."

What if he left home as she had done, thought Taeko. Now that things had come to this she felt capable of making the suggestion. There seemed to be no other way to escape from the pressure that hung over them.

She was about to speak when Ryosuké looked up and said: "I've had another idea. I was very unhappy about the way things were turning out, and I decided there was another solution." He paused for a while as though searching for the right words. "Who lay down the rule that a husband and wife have to live in the same house? What's to stop a married couple from getting on perfectly well even if they aren't actually living together?"

Taeko was struck by a sense of loneliness, as if she had been irretrievably betrayed. There was something coercive about Ryosuké's tone as he continued: "Of course, it would be rather unconventional for husband and wife to live apart. But I really don't see why it's such a silly idea. The time is undoubtedly coming when it'll be quite the normal thing to do. I don't know too much about ancient history, but a friend of mine mentioned to me the other day that it was the regular thing in the Heian period* for couples to live apart and for the husband to visit his wife at her place. So there's really nothing all that strange about it, is there? Of course most people feel that everything has to be done in the conventional way, and that since it's normal nowadays for husband and wife to live together every other system must be wrong. On the other hand there are some strong people in the world who aren't afraid of breaking the established rules. Such people see nothing wrong in couples living apart. There's a terrible housing shortage everywhere, and for ordinary people who have no savings it's a real problem to find a decent place to live. And then there's the matter of raising money to buy furniture and all the rest of it. And there's no rule that one has to go through all this agony. It's just a matter of custom, of blindly following the established convention."

"Yes," said Taeko, "but surely there's the pleasure of sharing a home together."

"Please don't think that I'm telling you this to shirk my responsibilities. It all came to me because I was in such a difficult position and I wanted to find some way to make things seem better. It was a matter of consoling myself, so to speak. That's why I didn't mention what I'd been thinking even to you. To tell the truth, even I have some respect for wordly conventions. I don't for a moment believe that I'm strong enough to have my own way regardless of what other people think. But I was in a difficult position and this seemed to be the best solution. Being in trouble, you see, is stronger than conventions or anything else."

"It doesn't work like that for women."

"Who decided that? If a woman is strong enough, she can adapt herself perfectly well. When economic conditions become difficult, you see, one shouldn't make them even harder by sticking to outmoded old customs in the teeth of every difficulty. I know that I give the impression at times of being rather flush, but the fact of the matter is that I'm only just managing to get by. I could hardly be any poorer if I tried! Don't you think it would be rather stupid of me to attempt the impossible

---

* The classical period of Japanese culture, ninth to twelfth centuries.

by insisting on doing everything according to established form?
If we are strong, we should follow our own paths. Don't you
agree? And if the bond between us is so weak that we can't
make a go of it under the present conditions—well, we should
do our best to strengthen that bond. Of course, the real trouble
is my family. If Mother were younger she'd probably be able
to understand how things have changed in the world. Unfortunately she still lives in the past, and she's got the idea firmly
embedded in her mind that the marriage of children is a matter
for the family to decide. Nothing could change this—not even
war or financial ruin. That's why I decided that I must find
some system that would let us stay together without going
against Mother's wishes. The way I hit upon may be rather
unusual, but after all we live in a time of extremes. You can regard it as being a temporary arrangement that will only last so
long as Mother is alive."

What bothered Taeko most was the glibness of Ryosuké's
suggestions; she found it intolerable.

"Why not cast off your old way of looking at things?" continued Ryosuké, noticing Taeko's crestfallen expression. "Try
looking at it like this: you and I will be giving birth to a new
way of living." He paused for a while, then went on. "When
all's said and done, I'm a child of the war. During the Occupation years I got into the habit of barging into any house that I
happened to feel like visiting. This came to seem quite normal
to me. You see, Taeko, all those ideas about the sanctity of the
home and having one's own house for one's own family—they
belong to settled normal times. I'd like to have a house of my
own—who wouldn't? But the fact that I can't have one doesn't
strike me as being out of the ordinary. Everything in the world
is topsy-turvy these days."

"The only exception, I suppose, being your mother's home,"
put in Taeko.

"She belongs to another age."

"Yes," said Taeko, "but it's not only your mother. All
women have an old-fashioned side. Whatever you say, I still
want my own house. Really, Ryosuké, I so much want to have
my own house." Now her feelings had come to the surface, and
she felt the tears welling up. "I think I told you about it once,
didn't I? I've had parents, but I've never had a real home. Per-

haps that's why I'm so anxious to have my own house. I want a place where I can be with you. I want to plan a home by myself, and I want to create it with my own hands. I don't care how small it is, so long as it's a place of our own where I can always feel at ease."

"You mustn't give way to emotions," declared Ryosuké. "You should use your brain a little more. And why, I wonder, are you so eager to shut me up in a cage?"

There was a spitefulness about his words that shocked Taeko deeply, and she could feel that her face had turned white.

"I've never had any such idea. But if there's any cage involved, I want to shut myself up in it too. But Ryosuké, I don't want to restrict you in any way. All I want is to be able to live in the same place as you. Is that so very unnatural?"

Ryosuké had an uncomfortable look on his face. It was the honest, indignant look of a little boy who feels that he has been treated unjustly. He wasn't telling lies or making evasions, thought Taeko. Rather, it was as though, confronted by the realities of the world, he had been confessing his own weakness and cowardice. Thus as a sort of self-vindication he had evolved the abstract notion that a husband and wife should live apart.

"We'd be behaving differently from other people," continued Ryosuké. "I'm fully aware of the fact. But I see absolutely no harm in trying. We might even be setting a fine example to the rest of the world. As long as we understand each other perfectly, I'm sure we can have a happy married life even though we happen to be living apart. All that we need is love and trust. Then everything will go beautifully, I'm sure of it. You may say that it isn't natural, but surely there are many more unnatural things happening in the world that people would never dream of questioning. After all, 'natural' is only a theoretical concept that people have laid down arbitrarily. Things that seem unnatural may in fact be much more in accordance with the new conditions in the world. You see, Takeo, we're living at a turning-point in the world's history, and many things that would have seemed abnormal in the past will soon become quite commonplace. To put it in a slightly exaggerated form, there's no telling whether even such stability as exists in the world today may not all be swept away tomorrow. It's all in the luck of the draw!"

"If I'd read that sort of thing in a book," said Taeko all of a sudden, "I think I'd understand it. But surely, Ryosuké, all we need is a tiny bit of courage. What we want to do is something perfectly commonplace, something that almost anyone can manage."

Taeko felt that the conversation was diverging from the main point. What they were talking about now seemed completely superfluous. In any situation, she thought, it was always possible to produce as many "good reasons" as one wanted. She had no need for them whatsoever. She wanted to throw them all to the wind and to concentrate on building up their own private world—hers and Ryosuké's. When it came to this, neither the opposition of Ryosuké's mother nor his theories about living apart mattered in the slightest. There was one simple problem and one alone: was Ryosuké being sincere with her or not? What Taeko sought was Ryosuké's heart, not his words.

Yet, simple as it appeared, she was unable to get to the root of the matter. The trouble was that she did not want to lose Ryosuké. At the same time she could not hide from herself the suspicion of his insincerity. He spoke of a new form of marriage in which husband and wife lived apart; yet she felt that he lacked the positive, deliberate qualities that would enable him to settle down to it and put the plan into practice. If his suggestion had sprung from a sincere belief, surely he would have presented it to her in a more forceful way, in such a way that she could not refuse. Instead it had emerged as a form of self-justification, as if he had merely been explaining his own position rather than planning their future life together.

"You know," said Taeko, "when you gave that money to my sister, I was extremely grateful, of course, but at the same time I couldn't help thinking that if we had that money ourselves it would have allowed us to set up house together—on a small scale, perhaps, but at least together. And as for Tazuko she could have managed perfectly well without it." She paused for a moment, then went on: "There are many couples in this world, Ryosuké, who have never managed to accumulate that

much money in all their lives yet who still succeed in having a
house of their own where they can live together in a normal
way."

"Their ideals in life are different from mine," said Ryosuké.

"No, it isn't just a matter of acquiring a certain amount of
money. Don't you see what I mean?" She looked directly at
Ryosuké as though appealing to him. "You've often told me
that you hate poverty. But I really don't know what you mean
by poverty. When, according to you, does one cease to be poor?
And when does one become rich? It's all relative, you see, and
some people can never be satisfied, however much they may acquire. I wonder if money wouldn't always be escaping us, running away from us. Perhaps I shouldn't say so, but I have a
feeling that you will never be rich. However much you have, it
will never be enough. And it seems to me that it's quite normal
in this world for people *not* to make money. There's something
wrong about the very way in which money is made. If one
makes up one's mind from the outset that it's impossible to
count on this sort of thing, I'm sure one can live far more easily.
One doesn't have to be cowed by poverty. One can endure it
perfectly cheerfully. I'll show you that it's possible—this kind
of cheerful poverty. It may be hard at first, but don't you think
it's rather splendid? Instead of living on riches, we can both
work. If we work, we can demand pay. That is our right, after
all. We shan't be expecting any unreasonable stroke of luck,
but at the same time we shan't have to endure any unreasonable
poverty. We may be poor but we'll feel wonderful. We'll look
down on our poverty and laugh at it. That'll be easy so long as
we're together. Things may be hard for a time, but we won't
find them hard, and we're bound to pull through. I'm sure
we'll manage. Yes, I'm quite sure. If only we make up our
minds to it, we'll manage easily. We may be living in a small
house, but this won't worry us. 'Oh, what a ridiculously small
house!' we'll say."

When they left the lake it was still light, but by the time they
had reached the foot of the mountain and were once more
driving along flat country the short winter day had drawn to
an end. A chilly mist had settled over the cold, naked-looking

rice fields. The headlights of the car picked out the vegetables in the fields by the road. They were vividly green—more green than one could possibly have imagined.

Ryosuké switched on the radio and manipulated the knob until he had found some dance music. He evidently wanted to relieve the tedium of the long drive, but Taeko found the music intolerable, and after a while she asked him to turn it off.

"But why?" asked Ryosuké. "It's nice and lively, this music."

Taeko preferred the whistling of the air against the windshield to the wail of the saxophone. In the distance across the cold wintry fields she could make out a farmhouse, then a factory, which moved slowly backward till they disappeared behind the car. The road ran through the country without any turnings; occasionally they passed an oxcart on its way back to a farm, and Taeko was reminded that for all its modern paving this was still the Tokaido highway that had carried travelers of old between Kyoto and Edo.

Ryosuké had still not given any satisfactory answer to Taeko's question, and she herself hesitated to force things to a conclusion. She had an uneasy feeling that they were approaching dangerously close to the brink, and she was anxious to avoid an irretrievable mistake. Ryosuké for his part was clearly taking advantage of this hesitation by keeping the conversation as vague as possible. It made Taeko extremely impatient, and she had to exert the greatest effort to control herself. It was a trying task, yet she could not afford to do otherwise.

"Yes," said Ryosuké, "she really doesn't run too badly."

He was referring to the car, Taeko realized; and as he drove he seemed to be straining every nerve to note how the various parts of the engine were behaving.

Taeko edged closer to Ryosuké; her body pressed against his but she was careful not to impede his freedom of movement. Now she could let herself believe that their two bodies had become one, and instantly she was able to forget her unhappiness; this close physical contact was a sedative that put all her worries to sleep. But it was a sad feeling. She felt like a little child who is being lulled to sleep by a cradle song, yet who is still awake and who keeps on crying for some reason that she cannot quite understand. The vibration of the car was making her drowsy, but she was wide awake to her forlorn sense of sorrow.

"Sleepy?" said Ryosuké gruffly. "Go to sleep if you want."

She shook her head and at the same time she felt the tears coming to her eyes. Just when she most wanted Ryosuké to be gentle with her, he had assumed a harsh, rather frightening tone. She shut her eyes but sleep would not come; instead, as if in a nightmare, she kept on seeing the elaborately adorned figure of Mrs. Iwamuro.

"Are you cold?" asked Ryosuké.

"No."

"We're just passing the avenue of pine trees at Totsuka. The way this car runs we'll be at Yokohama Station in less than ten minutes." He paused for a while, then added: "This is the sort of car I'd like for myself, you know. The fellow I'm delivering it to has made all his money since the war. He's a young chap, too—just about my age."

Taeko opened her eyes and abruptly asked: "Tell me, Ryosuké, do you like Mrs. Iwamuro?"

Ryosuké turned around with an astonished look. "What's that?" he said.

Taeko's voice was so quiet that the sound of it made her feel even more doleful than before. "Won't you leave her for my sake? I know it shouldn't worry me, but it does—terribly."

Ryosuké sat next to her, sunk in silence. Then he shifted his position with a jerk and turned the steering-wheel sharply to avoid a bus that was coming at them head on with its lights glaring brightly.

"What a strange thing to say!" he remarked in a matter-of-fact tone, finally breaking the silence.

"No," said Taeko, and compressed her lips tightly so as not to reveal the powerful emotions that were surging up in her. "Please do that for me."

"But look here, Taeko, it's thanks to her that a lot of this business comes my way. Take this car, for instance. It's she who arranged for me to get it from an American at Washington Heights."*

Taeko said nothing, and Ryosuké continued: "This is the

---

* Large American military base in Tokyo.

third one I've sold. It's out of consideration for Mrs. Iwamuro that they let me pay afterward. For someone like me who has no capital it's the only way to do business. I'm not in a position to pay for things in advance."

"Do you mean to say," said Taeko, "that if you broke with her you wouldn't be able to go on with your work?"

"I wouldn't go quite that far. But it would certainly limit my activities. But anyhow, why are you so against her? She may have a rather shady reputation, but there's absolutely nothing bad about her."

"Yes, I'm sure," said Taeko. "The fact remains that I don't like her. Is it wrong of me to say so?"

"But why? What earthly reason can you have to dislike her?"

There was something very distressing to Taeko about the way in which Ryosuké expressed himself.

"I really don't know myself. Perhaps it's because I don't find her pure."

"Not pure?"

"That's right. There's nothing clear or transparent about her nature, you see. I may be mistaken, of course, but it seems to me that there must be something wrong about a woman who gives the impression of being so completely unclear. It's what is known as feminine instinct, I suppose. And usually it's correct."

"You're imagining things," said Ryosuké.

"I try not to imagine anything. But I'm so worried that I can't sleep at night. It's stupid of me, I know. Perhaps I'm ill. Please be patient with me." She stared out of the window. "When you say that you can't carry on your work without her, it makes me realize that she's using you too, and I can't bear the thought."

"No," declared Ryosuké loudly. "There's nothing like that in it. Ours is a relationship between two equal people. It's all a matter of business. In business you can't always choose who you're going to deal with. It's like that for everyone. Business is business, however much you may dislike the other person."

"But do you dislike Mrs. Iwamuro? Is she just 'another person'?"

Taeko was doing her best to preserve a light tone, but now

her true feelings were breaking through, and she felt herself being cornered by the earnestness of her emotions. The lights of Yokohama poured in through the windshield like so many stars. Ahead of them a red moon rose in the sky directly above a large factory area.

"I'm always praying that nothing will come between us, Ryosuké. And it worries me terribly that I can't see through your feelings at all."

"I'm sure it's all a misunderstanding," declared Ryosuké, gazing straight ahead.

Taeko lapsed into silence. She felt utterly battered by what Ryosuké had said. Time after time she had told herself that she should speak out fearlessly, but she had failed to do so. By being less than frank with herself, by not telling Ryosuké all that she knew, she had forced him ineluctably to be deceitful with her. It hardly seemed likely at this late stage that Ryosuké would expunge all the lies that had accumulated over the past months. Essentially he had a good character, she felt, but he only gave free rein to his good qualities when he was so inclined; at other times he could be both evasive and deceitful. Even if she were to force the issue, could he really be expected to wipe out all his previous prevarications in a sudden access of honesty? Taeko lacked the confidence to put it to the test. She was terrified of making him angry. She could not bear the idea that their hearts might drift apart. Until now she had always acted with the greatest care, as though she was dealing with something very fragile. In practical terms this meant that she had invariably given in to Ryosuké. But she no longer knew how to handle the situation. One lie seemed to lead inevitably to the next. Gradually Ryosuké had come to assume a completely different attitude; it was as if he had put on a suit of armor to cover his true personality.

They were now crossing the long Rokugo Bridge. It was only a short distance to the Omori suburbs where Taeko lived in her rented room. She was in a quandary as to whether she should ask Ryosuké to let her out at Omori or whether she should accompany him to the center of the city. Their conversation seemed to have reached a dead end. All of a sudden she realized that precisely because of her feelings for Ryosuké, feelings so powerful that she would have been prepared to die for him, she was also capable of leaving him for good when the situation became impossible. Taeko hardened her heart. She knew that things were beyond repair.

They passed Omori and approached the center of Tokyo. Takeo roused herself from her thoughts and decided to change the subject. "Where are you taking the car now?" she asked.

"To the garage of the Nikkatsu Hotel. There's a huge garage in the basement of the building. One drives directly from the street down a sort of ramp."

Once more the resplendent figure of Mrs. Iwamuro flashed before Taeko's eyes.

"Would you mind letting me off before we get there?" she said.

"Why?" asked Ryosuké, glancing up at her.

"Because I don't want to risk meeting Mrs. Iwamuro"—the words were on the tip of her tongue, but once more she did not utter them.

"I was thinking we might go somewhere for a bite of dinner," said Ryosuké. "Just to round off the day, you know." He was concentrating now on maneuvering the car through the heavy traffic, and he spoke in a casual manner.

They turned right at the Hibiya crossroads and pulled up at the entrance of the Nikkatsu garage. Taeko got out of the car and watched Ryosuké driving it down the ramp. As soon as he had disappeared into the depths she walked off by herself along the crowded street. This was the only form of protest left to her. She had no destination in mind.

"Look here, Miss Okamoto, would you mind going over to the American Pharmacy and buying me a few more of these tubes if they have them?" The director of the office where Taeko worked held out a small glass tube that was used for absorbing nicotine. He was worried about his blood pressure and recently he had taken to smoking a nicotine-free pipe. "A friend of mine told me that they're selling these tubes there."

Taeko removed her overcoat from the hook on the wall and got ready to go out. It was still early morning, but when she was out in the street she found that the sun was shining brightly and that it was a beautiful winter day. As she crossed the Yamashita Bridge she noticed the carrier pigeons from the near-by newspaper office circling overhead; their reflections skimmed over the surface of the water.

She soon reached the Nikkatsu Building and was walking along the covered pavement that led to the pharmacy when she noticed a woman standing there in a gray overcoat. Something about the woman's back made Taeko's heart pound. Just then the woman turned around. It was Kaoruko Iwamuro. She had a black kerchief round her head, designed rather like the veil worn by nuns in the West, and this seemed to accentuate the whiteness of her skin. There was an elegance and fascination about her beautiful smooth face with its aquiline nose which made passers-by turn around despite themselves. The color of her overcoat harmonized perfectly with the black kerchief and the strikingly white skin.

Before Taeko could get away, Kaoruko noticed her and smiled affably. There was nothing for it but to return her greeting.

"Everything all right, I hope?" said Kaoruko in her usual graceful tone. "I'm waiting for a car myself."

Taeko noticed for the first time that they were standing close to the entrance of the underground garage where she had left Ryosuké on their return from the drive to Hakoné. The concrete ramp curved around at a gradual incline; it was like a tunnel and even in the middle of the day it was illuminated by electric lights.

"Where are you off to, my dear?" asked Kaoruko.

"I'm going to the pharmacy."

"Ah yes, the American Pharmacy."

Taeko was anxious to get away as soon as possible, and she shifted her feet nervously. As usual Kaoruko's beauty failed to suggest any aura of sin. She had the complete self-confidence and composure of her class and age. It was clear that she looked down on Taeko as her inferior and even felt vaguely sorry for her. At the same time she always seemed to be teasing her in a way that made it impossible to put up any resistance.

"I'd just like to ask you about something, Taeko," said Kaoruko, toying with one of her gloves and suddenly assuming a familiar manner. "What's happened to Ryobei-san?"

Taeko wanted to say that she did not know, but she was

overcome with sorrow and only had the strength to return Mrs. Iwamuro's smile.

"Our Ryobei-san is really too irresponsible, you know," continued Kaoruko. "He promised to come and see me about some business but he didn't show up. I've telephoned him time after time but they always say he's out. If you see him, please tell him, won't you? It's almost a week now."

The glare of headlights shone out of the cavernous garage and with it came the harsh sound of a horn. The front of an elegant new car slowly emerged up the ramp, and the two women looked up. The rest of the car came into sight, and Taeko noticed that the driver was a foreigner in a loud sweater who looked American. This was evidently the person Kaoruko had been waiting for; as soon as the car stopped she went over and said something to him in rapid English. Then she returned to where Taeko was standing.

"I think I'd better tell you what's happened," she said. Kaoruko had lost her earlier composure, and her words gave Taeko a strange impression. Her usual gentle air seemed to have disappeared.

"Ryobei-san is a good fellow at heart," began Kaoruko. Now that she had a serious expression on her face she looked very much older. "But he's awfully sloppy when it comes to money matters. I'm a friend of his, so I tend to take a rather lenient attitude. I've warned him about this in the past, but it's water off a duck's back."

Evidently in accordance with Kaoruko's instructions, the American had turned his car around and parked by the side of the road. He got out and walked round the car as if looking for something.

"It really won't do," continued Kaoruko. "The man who bought the car paid him ten days ago, but Ryosuké still hasn't handed over the money although I've been on to him about it time and again. Have you no idea where he is? Surely he can't have left Tokyo."

Taeko's face clouded over, and she was unable to reply.

"Such irresponsibility!" continued Kaoruko. "He really might have considered my position a little. I'm caught between two fires."

"I'll tell him," said Taeko.

"There's no chance of canceling the transaction. This sort of thing is especially difficult when one's dealing with a foreigner. It could all have a very bad effect on our future business. I tried straightening the matter out myself by speaking directly to the man who bought the car, but he showed me a receipt in which Ryosuké acknowledged full payment."

Taeko still felt unable to make any comment.

"The trouble is," continued Kaoruko, "that Ryosuké is perfectly capable of going and spending that money in the most stupid way. It's terribly worrying. Try to have a serious talk with him and explain that the thing has to be settled by tomorrow at the latest. I don't suppose he really can have gone and spent the money, but if by any chance that is what he's done I don't know what will happen."

Taeko felt as if everything was going dark before her. What she found particularly hard to bear was the memory of the hundred thousand yen that he had given to her sister.

Meanwhile the American had taken out a cigarette and put it in his mouth. Evidently bored with standing, he squeezed his large body into the driver's seat and sat there looking straight ahead. He left the door open so that he could quickly jump out and help Mrs. Iwamuro into the car when she had finished her conversation.

"I can hardly believe it," said Taeko, and she felt that the blood had drained from her face. "Is it a large sum of money?"

"He's handed over the deposit. That leaves eight hundred thousand yen to be paid."

"I know he'll bring you the money," declared Taeko. In her excitement she forgot herself and raised her voice. The very fact that such a large sum was involved made her feel that the situation was less dangerous than she had originally feared.

"Well, Taeko," said Mrs. Iwamuro in a slightly sarcastic tone, "so long as you give your guarantee I'm sure it's safe. But when you meet him don't forget to say that the matter is urgent. I have to go somewhere now, but I'll be back at the hotel this evening, and I'll be waiting for him. It really is too irresponsible of Ryobei-san that I should have to get people to search for him. It's a large sum of money, so I know he won't let me down, but he shouldn't worry me needlessly like this. He really is too easygoing!"

. . .

It was getting dark when Ryosuké appeared at the hotel. He had been there so often that he knew most of the employees by sight, and he greeted the elevator-boy jovially: "Well, well, how's everything going these days? Working hard?"

Ryosuké's briefcase was bulging with bundles of thousand-yen notes. It made him feel cheerful to be carrying large sums of money, even when they belonged to someone else.

A glance in the hall told him that Kaoruko was not there, and he went directly to her room.

Kaoruko was in no position to afford the luxury of a permanent room at the Nikkatsu Hotel. She had, however, arranged to leave a suitcase full of clothes with the porter and quite frequently she would decide not to go home and would take a room for the night, its essential function being that of a dressing-room. Besides, Kaoruko had a number of possessions that she did not wish her husband to see; these she kept locked in a solid trunk which she left at the hotel, intending to move it to the Mitsubishi Repository as soon as she had succeeded in hiring a locker there. For some time now she had no longer been frightened of having secrets from her husband.

Kaoruko seemed to be constitutionally devoid of a real sense of sin. That is, sin in her mind was merely a social fact. So long as something was not proscribed by law it was not sinful. If she could commit an act without people knowing about it and without risking criticism, she felt that she could go ahead with a perfectly clear conscience. One of the reasons that she had made such a point of cultivating foreigners was that in their company (unlike that of her compatriots) one could go to certain extremes without any danger of publicity or scandal. The fact that their morality and their manners were so entirely different gave her a sense of emancipation. The Western way of living, in which one could shut oneself off from the outside by simply turning a key in a lock, had opened up an entire world to Kaoruko that she had never known in the past.

Takabumi seemed to have a very similar attitude, and he was remarkably broadminded as a husband. Recently he had shut his eyes to his wife's behavior and accepted all her infidelities so long as they did not become a subject of gossip. In a class which only valued appearances there had for some time been a tendency to forget the possibility that people may be tormented by sins they have committed even though no one else happens to know about them. When it came to outside criticism, Kaoruko was remarkably pusillanimous; but so far as her own judgment about herself was concerned the idea of sin did not exist, and if she did something wrong she was in the habit of forgetting about it promptly. Even in the rare cases when she was clearly aware that an action of hers was wrong, a couple of nights of good sleep were enough to erase any unpleasant feelings from her mind. To suffer the pangs of conscience in solitude was entirely alien to Kaoruko Iwamuro.

Ryosuké found out from a waiter in the corridor that Kaoruko was in her room, and he tapped lightly on her door. Before she had time to answer, he turned the handle.

"Good evening to you, Madam," he said jovially and walked into the room.

Kaoruko was standing by the looking-glass arranging her hair. She turned round instantly.

"What's happened?" she said accusingly.

"Happened?" said Ryosuké. "Nothing in particular."

"Oh really, Ryosuké, you're too irresponsible for words! I've been so worried."

The young man took off his hat and coat and threw them nonchalantly on a chair. There was something heavy and replete about the expression on his youthful face. He smiled fixedly and said in a lighthearted tone: "It looked pretty risky for a while. But anyhow I've brought the money—or rather, most of it."

He placed his bulky briefcase on the table and extracted a number of bundles which were tied with string. Without a word Kaoruko started unwrapping them. She had evidently been lying on her bed, for she was still wearing a nightdress secured by a narrow *obi*. Sitting down on the sofa, she put the money on her lap and started to count.

"I'll bring you the rest very soon," said Ryosuké with a slightly embarrassed, apologetic air. He got up and went to the looking-glass. The sum of two hundred thousand yen was missing.

"Ryobei-san," said Kaoruko, finally breaking the silence, "what's the meaning of this?"

"I'm sorry but you'll have to make do with that for tonight. I've had a bit of bad luck." He turned round from the looking-glass and glanced at Kaoruko. "Tell me," he said casually, "how do you like this tie?"

"This is no laughing matter," said Kaoruko. "You owe me an explanation."

"Come, come," said Ryosuké, "there's no need to get so angry."

"What did you spend it on? Or haven't you spent it? In that case, kindly hand it over."

Ryosuké stood by the looking-glass and carefully adjusted his tie. "I do wish you'd stop," he said with a smile. "When you get cross it makes you look much older than you really are. And since you're a very beautiful woman one gets the impression of one of those splendid female demons one sees in paintings. Anyhow, there's no need to be angry. I've told you I'd bring the rest of the money. So why ask how I spent it? It's my loss, not yours. But what a damned fool I've been!" he added in a self-mocking tone.

"Well, Ryobei-san, what have you done?" said Kaoruko softly as though all the energy had gone from her.

"I bought some stocks. I had planned to double the money by the end of this week." Ryosuké smiled wryly and sat down on the arm of the sofa. There was a solid, immobile look about his broad shoulders. "I'm afraid I came a cropper—or at least a partial cropper. I managed to cut my losses and get out before things had time to get worse. I was in a tight squeeze for a while, but I saved most of the money from the wreckage. The market's fallen even further today. It's a good thing I sold out when I did."

"You seem to take it all very calmly," said Kaoruko.

"It's best to be calm when you lose," said Ryosuké with a grin. "If you lose and then brood over it in the bargain, you're taking a double loss."

"Look here, Ryobei-san, I'd like to remind you that the money doesn't belong to you in the first place."

"Yes, yes, I realize that. But tell me one thing—if it had worked out all right and I'd made a packet, would you be quite as angry as you are now?"

"Yes, I should," replied Kaoruko, putting her head to the

side. "I couldn't forgive such irresponsibility."

"Well, I'm not so sure myself," said Ryosuké. "If the stocks had gone up, I was going to give you half my winnings. It would have been a nice bit of extra pocket money for you. But I was out of luck. You may be annoyed with me, but you can't say that I didn't bring you the money, at least the greater part of it, all neatly tied up in bundles. I knew you'd be getting worried, so I decided to sell out. If I'd waited another ten days or so, the market was bound to go up again and things would have started getting interesting. It was rather a nuisance having to sell out, but I didn't want you to be too worried."

"Very well, Ryobei-san, when are you going to let me have the rest of the money."

"There's no desperate hurry, is there?"

"Really, my young fellow," said Kaoruko icily, "I wonder if you don't have something missing." Her manner was cold, almost to the point of being brutal, and there was a glare of anger in her narrow slanting eyes. "I used to imagine that you were just happy-go-lucky, but that seems to be too generous an explanation."

"What's the matter?" said Ryosuké calmly, and chuckled as if to laugh the whole thing off. "I'm taking a practical view of the matter."

"Practical, you say?"

"That's right. I've brought the remaining six hundred thousand yen that I owe for the car. You can't question that, can you? That leaves two hundred thousand which represents our commission. All I'm doing is to ask you to wait a little longer for your part of the commission. I haven't said I won't pay you. It's just a matter of raising the money. With a sum of that kind I shouldn't have much trouble."

"Well, if you are going to pay me, I wish you'd settle it at once. It costs much more than you would imagine to stay in a hotel like this."

"Surely you can get someone to foot your bill for you," said Ryosuké impassively. He knew that the suggestion would annoy Kaoruko, but he felt that he was in a position to put things strongly: a look of self-confidence appeared on his face.

"No," said Kaoruko. "It's up to you to settle your debt. But I don't suppose you know how to go about it."

"Oh yes, I do," declared Ryosuké. "Someone in Kobe owes me one hundred thousand yen, and that's not the only credit I've got. If I ask my friends, they'll help me out too."

"Well, please do something—and quickly."

"It's silly, isn't it," said Ryosuké, "all this talk about money?"

"Not in the slightest," retorted Kaoruko, and her tone was more glacial than ever. "So far as I'm concerned, money is strength. There's certainly nothing else I can depend on in this world. And you don't have any reason to consider it silly either. If there's one thing I can't stand, it's irresponsibility in money matters."

"Oh really," said Ryosuké with a smile, "this is getting to be a bore!"

"So you think you can laugh about it, do you?" said Kaoruko, her coldness now turning into hatred. "You won't get anywhere in the world with a lot of irresponsible prattling and giggling. You're too old to treat money matters lightly. You're making a great mistake, my dear fellow. And if you don't wake up to realities, you're going to get it in the neck one of these fine days!"

"It's only because I lost that money that you're talking to me like this," said Ryosuké, a smile still fixed on his face. "I'm a little sounder than you seem to think."

"You still don't know what fear means, do you? One often finds your type among ill people. They refuse to believe that they aren't perfectly well, and they go on doing one reckless thing after another until in the end it's too late for a cure."

"If I get ill," said Ryosuké in an infuriatingly cheerful tone, "I go to bed. It's as simple as that. At my age you can get over anything by going to bed."

"All right then, have it your own way," said Kaoruko. "But please see that I get my money promptly. This involves other people, not just yourself."

"Are you still going on about that wretched money?" Ryosuké's manner overflowed with self-confidence, and there was a look on his face that seemed to say: "I know one thing that will make you stop talking." The young man was entirely unaware that the trump card of physical seduction which he thought he held in his hand would only infuriate Kaoruko fur-

ther. He walked up to her and tried to take her hand; she
quickly withdrew it, and the look in her eyes became still
colder.

"Foreigners don't behave like that," she said quietly. "At
least they realize that business is business."

She glanced at Ryosuké with an expression that was not
only cold but disdainful and hostile. The young man was unpleasantly conscious of a sense of oppression that came from
the difference in their ages, and he could find no satisfactory
reply. He gazed at the voluptuous body of the woman who
sat near him on the sofa and decided that the only way to improve the atmosphere was to channel her pent-up feelings of
antagonism into some concentrated physical action. Looking
into her angry eyes, he put his arms round her and lightly
lifted her onto the bed. It required only the slightest effort to
carry the pliant body of a woman across a room. Now that she
lay there, still startled by his sudden action, Ryosuké felt that
he only had to use a little force to put things on a completely
new footing; then he would have won the game. He felt completely confident in the ardor of his youth, and already he could
visualize the woman's total submission. He was about to put his
hand to her sash when Kaoruko sprang away from him. She
fixed him with a look that was more hostile than ever. "Go
back to Taeko-san," she said. There was a finality about her
tone that made Ryosuké's entire scheme of forceful seduction
collapse like a pricked balloon.

"I'm not going to have you dictate to me about such things,"
he said.

"All right. But you'd better leave, in any case, not only for
your own sake but for mine."

Ryosuké looked at her fiercely; he was lost for an answer.

"You needn't think I'm all that easy to deal with just because I'm a woman. Anyhow, please go back to Taeko-san."

"Yes, I'm going," said Ryosuké. "But there really was no
need to get upset about such a trifle."

"I know," said Kaoruko. "I took you much too seriously."

"Took me seriously, did you?" said Ryosuké and a defiant
look came on his face. "I'm afraid, my dear lady, that you have
absolutely no understanding of us young people. For us this is
something that happens on the spur of the moment. It's just a

matter of a man's skin touching a woman's. We don't think anything of it."

Ryosuké had no particular intention of slighting Kaoruko; he was surprised to see her turn white with anger after he had spoken, and he wondered what had annoyed her.

"Please go," she said.

"I see. You want me to leave. But, of course, you still want the money."

"Certainly. You needn't bring it yourself, though. You can have Taeko-san deliver it."

Without a word Ryosuké put on his coat and picked up his hat.

"Bye-bye," he said, using the English word. With a cheerful wave of his hand he left the room.

THE HOLIDAYS had started, and Sutekichi Ata was staying at Soroku's house in Kamakura. Professor Segi had helped him to find some extra work. This time it was not proofreading but translation, and it was to devote himself to this task that the young man had come to the country. The work was done under a subcontract, and Sutekichi himself received no credit for it; but since he was paid by the page it not only helped him to defray his living expenses but allowed him to buy certain books that he had wanted for a long time. For the very first time since the war he had gone to the Maruzen bookshop in Nihonbashi, and as he had stood in front of one of the shelves laden with newly imported books from Europe and America a sense of joy had sprung up in him—the joy he had known years before when his mind had been full of hopes and plans for future studies.

Now in Kamakura he was beginning to feel grateful to Soroku for his generosity. The pride of youth, however, made it impossible for him to show this feeling openly. The notion still lingered somewhere in the back of his mind that it was only natural for rich people to shower favors on poor students like himself. This feeling carried over from the anger that he had once felt for the rich people about him who seemed to live useless lives while all his plans for study and research were being balked for lack of money. The indignation of his early youth had given way to a greater serenity, but he still could not bring himself to express his gratitude to Soroku in words.

Since arriving at Kamakura, Sutekichi had made a point of getting up early in the morning, and he had taken on the morning and evening housework. Whenever he was able to give a hand, he would put down his pen and hurry along with a cheerful look on his face. Now that the sear winter season had come Soroku was trying to put his garden in order and it was Sutekichi who did the lion's share of the work.

"Don't bother about it," said Soroku, looking sympathetically at the young man. "Go and get on with your own work."

"No no, it's fun. And it occurs to me, Mr. Okamoto, that I've never had any experience of messing about in a garden. I enjoy it."

The young man really looked as if he was enjoying himself while he helped Soroku make a bonfire of the dead branches and the rubbish.

"Do the *yatsude* plants actually have flowers?" he asked as he carefully examined the thick shrubbery of the hopelessly overgrown garden. With their small, jewel-like clusters and their delicate blue-tinted white color the *yatsude* gave a sober, slightly sorrowful air that fitted in perfectly with the wintry aspect of the scene. The smoke from the bonfire floated over the garden and crawled up between the dark green leaves that served to enliven the melancholy *yatsude*.

On the afternoon that Taeko abruptly appeared at Kamakura Soroku had gone to Tokyo to attend a performance of traditional *rakugo* story-telling at the Mitsukoshi department store.

"Do you suppose he'll be back very late?" the girl asked Sutekichi with a crestfallen look.

"Yes, I'm afraid he may be a bit late. Is it something urgent?"

"Yes, rather."

The sight of Taeko had instantly filled Sutekichi with a

sense of buoyancy; with a happy look in his eyes, he scurried about, putting the sitting-room in order. In Soroku's absence the young man had been entrusted with the task of watchman, and for this purpose he had brought all his books downstairs.

"Your uncle may be late," he said, "but I'm sure he'll be back before the last train. Do make yourself comfortable and arrange to spend a quiet night here. This evening I'm going to invite you to dinner. I've earned a bit of extra money that I didn't expect, so I'll get some meat and cook it for you in my special way."

Taeko gave a tired sort of smile; she had lost her usual cheerfulness and made no effort to enter into Sutekichi's happy mood.

"What's wrong, Taeko-san?" he said. "Aren't you feeling well?"

"Oh no, I'm perfectly all right, thank you."

It was getting dark outside; looking out at the dusky garden, Taeko suddenly asked: "Those white plants over there—are they *yatsude?*"

As the butcher was fairly far away, Sutekichi decided that he would go himself rather than send the old woman who worked for Soroku. He set off hurriedly, and the dog followed with a great jingling of his collar. There was still a touch of blue in the sky, but the road was sunk in shadows. By the time that he left the shop, night had completely closed in.

When Sutekichi returned to the house, the old woman informed him that Taeko had left.

"She's gone back to Tokyo, you say?"

"Yes, she said she had an appointment that she'd forgotten about."

There was no sign of Taeko in the sitting-room. The thought of cooking the meat that he had bought and of eating it by himself filled Sutekichi with gloom.

"I wonder why she should have done that," he said.

"I happened to go to the front door," called the old woman from the kitchen, "and there was Miss Taeko putting on her shoes and getting ready to leave."

"It's funny," said Sutekichi. "She said she'd wait till Mr. Okamoto came back."

"Perhaps she decided it would be too late. Well, sir, I was just getting ready to light the stove in here. What would you like me to do? Shall I bring you the little portable stove?"

"It really doesn't matter now," sighed Sutekichi in spite of himself. "Since it's just for me," he added, "I'll have my dinner later. I'll go on working till I reach a good place to break off."

He sat down in front of the little table that he was using as a desk and gazed absently at his books and papers. He did not feel like getting to work at once, and he took out a cigarette. He was thoroughly despondent, as though he had lost all his bearings.

Then suddenly he remembered something and quickly looked under the large, flat cushion on which he was sitting. A moment later he was in a panic. He jumped to his feet, rolled up the cushion, and searched all round. It was a Saturday, and early in the afternoon someone had come to deliver a sum of money to Soroku; since he was going out, he had entrusted the money to Sutekichi, who had carefully placed it under the cushion where he sat working. The young man turned pale at the memory of how much money was involved. He made an effort to collect himself and called out to the old woman, "Have you tidied up in here while I was out?"

"No," she replied calmly.

"Has anyone been in here apart from Miss Taeko?"

"Why? Has something happened?"

"No, it's all right," said Sutekichi. "I was just wondering." He realized the need to keep cool and lit his cigarette. But he couldn't sit there smoking; once again he jumped to his feet and began a meticulous search under the table and all round the room. His heart was pounding fiercely.

Already the thought was taking shape in his mind that there must be some connection between Taeko's sudden departure and the disappearance of the money. For a moment he found himself on the verge of rushing out of the house and following her to the station. Then he felt ashamed of the suspicion and forced himself to lean against the little table and not to move until he had finished his cigarette.

Meanwhile the old woman brought a few lighted pieces of

charcoal in a shovel and placed them on the brazier. Sutekichi examined her in as calm and nonchalant a manner as he could assume. Some time before, he had been given the unpleasant task of observing the pupils in his class to find out which of them was responsible for a theft that had occurred in the school. What had happened this evening, however, was far worse; for the ineluctable fact was that the theft was his responsibility. He felt the blood coming to his face, and he broke out in a cold sweat.

"They say it's going to get much colder tonight," remarked the old woman as she put the charcoal on the fire: there was a look of complete innocence on her wrinkled face.

Late that night Soroku alighted from the electric train at Kamakura station. As he made his way through the crowds, he noticed Sutekichi standing by the wicket.

"Good gracious!" he exclaimed. Soroku had not expected to find the young man waiting for him; no doubt he had come to fetch him because it was so late. "What brings you here?"

Sutekichi smiled ambiguously. "There are no more buses," he said. "Would you like me to call a taxi?"

"No, we'll walk. Since I went to Tokyo purely for my own pleasure, it would be wrong to take a taxi."

The two men set off on foot along the busy neon-lit side streets. Near the station the rows of small eating-houses were still open and the streets were crowded, but when they reached the wide dark road by the Hachiman Shrine there were few people to be seen, and they could feel that it was the dead of night.

"Well, I really enjoyed myself," said Soroku, and with an air of satisfaction he started describing the performance that he had attended. As they walked along the tree-lined avenue that led to the great shrine, they heard the drunken voice of an American soldier shouting something incomprehensible. His companion, who appeared to be a rather pleasant young soldier, was evidently reproving him for his rowdy manners and at the same time was skillfully steering him in the direction of the station.

"I've done something inexcusable," said Sutekichi as they

passed a dark side street by the hospital. "I've lost the money you entrusted to me."

Soroku turned round and looked at the young man. "What happened?" he asked. He spoke quietly, but Sutekichi could tell that he was far from calm. And indeed, he thought, who could be calm after losing three hundred thousand yen? "Did the money disappear while you were in the house?"

"No, it happened outside."

"Outside?"

Noticing the shade of suspicion in Soroku's voice, Sutekichi started to rattle off his story. "Yes, I decided to go out for a walk. It wouldn't have been fair of me to entrust all that money to the old woman, so I stuck it in my pocket. The next thing I knew it had disappeared. Evidently it had fallen out somewhere. I went back and searched every inch of the road, but there was no sign of it."

Soroku walked along with his head bowed; he did not say a word.

"It was terribly careless of me. I really don't know what to do. All I can say is that there's absolutely no excuse."

Soroku still did not say anything for some time. Then he suddenly seemed to recover his spirits, and in a gentle tone he remarked: "On the contrary, it's my fault for having put you to such worry. It was wrong of me to entrust such a large sum to someone who's not used to taking care of money. Of course, it will be a calamity if it doesn't turn up, but . . ." He paused for a moment. "Have you reported the loss to the police?"

"No, not yet," replied Sutekichi. "But even if we do report it, there's not much chance of getting the money back, is there? After all, it was in cash."

"I'm not so sure," said Soroku. "Anyhow, we'd better go to the police station directly."

Soroku's words pulled the young man up with a start. He realized now that it was perfectly natural that his host should want to report the loss to the police, but for some reason the possibility had not occurred to him before.

"The police?" he said falteringly. At that moment his suspicions about Taeko, which until then had been vague and fluid, assumed a solid, immobile quality. He knew that he must do what he could to prevent a visit to the police. The trouble was that he had no reasonable pretext to dissuade his host from reporting the loss. They had stopped walking now, and Sutekichi realized that Soroku was about to turn back in the direction of the police station.

"I'm afraid that all sorts of unpleasant suspicions may fall on me," he blurted out. He knew that there was something rather pusillanimous about his argument, but he could think of nothing else to say.

Soroku did not seem to consider the young man's attitude particularly odd, but he disposed straightforwardly of his objection. "No, no," he said, "why should anyone suspect you? It's just a matter of making a clear report to the police that there's been a loss."

A tardy moon hung in the sky and lit up the deserted streets. It had the look of a moon that one sees on a fiercely cold winter night. As they started walking, the moon moved with them.

"There's really no excuse for what I've done," repeated Sutekichi. If he was going to cover up for Taeko, that was all he could say. Once this became a police case, he realized, he would have to be more careful about what he said. For he had already resolved to carry out what he conceived to be his duty until the bitter end and not to bring Taeko's name into the matter even if it meant making himself look like a thief. As to why he should do this, he himself had no idea.

It still astounded him that a gentle young girl like Taeko should help herself to someone else's money and then rush back to Tokyo without a word to anyone; at the same time he was beginning to feel that there was something inexplicably sad about the whole incident. It was clearly not for himself that he felt sad, but for Taeko. How wretched and pathetic, he thought, that a human being should take such a drastic action and then run away into the night! In the background was the idea, which seemed to have become an inherent part of Sutekichi's nature, that he himself was a poor student, to whom the wealth and possessions of this world were always denied.

"Yes," said Soroku, abruptly bringing the conversation back to the performance he had attended, "it was a very fine performance." Their two shadows moved next to each other along the surface of the road. Was Soroku deliberately trying to avoid talking about his carelessness? wondered Sutekichi. Or was it that he did not really believe his story about having lost the money? The thought of this last possibility prevented the young man from saying anything that might sound like an excuse.

The moon brushed against an icy cloud, then entered it, and the earth became dark. They could hear the sound of a dog running from somewhere. It turned out to be Soroku's dog.

"Friday!" exclaimed Soroku, patting the dog. "Did he come with you to the station?"

"No, I had no idea he was out of the house."

"He must have decided that it was late and that he ought to come and fetch us home."

Sutekichi felt that Soroku was purposely trying to act as normally as he would have had if the money incident had never occurred. He remembered hearing that the impulse which had finally restored this man's memory was his concern at seeing the money that Professor Segi had carelessly left on his table. At the thought of what the sum of three hundred thousand yen must represent psychologically to Soroku and of what effect this might have on Taeko's fate, Sutekichi was cast into gloom.

It was close to midnight when they reached the police station. The officer in charge of lost property had already gone home, and a young policeman heard the report in his place.

"Three hundred thousand yen?" he said, evidently amazed at the amount of the loss. He took out a report book and examined it. "No, I'm afraid it hasn't been turned in. Was it in cash?"

"Yes," replied Soroku, "it was all in thousand-yen notes."

Sutekichi had a presentiment that things were going to go wrong. Now that he was actually in the police station his story struck him as hopelessly puerile and implausible.

"Really?" said the policeman. "Three hundred thousand yen in ready cash!" A smile came onto his slender face, and he looked at the two men with an expression of curiosity and surprise. "Quite a sum, isn't it?"

In the quiet of the night the sound of footsteps could be heard in a passage at the far end of the building. The policeman tilted his head to one side; apparently he was considering what to do next.

"What time was it when you lost the money?" he asked after a while.

"It was a little after five o'clock," replied Sutekichi. "It had already gotten dark."

The policeman listened with a cold businesslike air, then produced a pencil and some paper and asked Soroku to write down his name and address. "Let's hope that the person who found it is honest," he said. "But I'm afraid it doesn't look too good. It's past midnight now, and we still haven't heard anything. Whereabouts did you lose the money?"

As he replied, Sutekichi felt his face go hot and the figure of Taeko flashed uncomfortably before his eyes. He explained that he had lost the money somewhere along the path where he usually went for his walks. He was aware that the young policeman was eying him intently as he spoke.

"Why should you have taken such a large sum of money out of the house? Rather unusual, isn't it?"

"Oh no," said Soroku, replying for Sutekichi. "I was going to Tokyo, and since it was a Saturday I couldn't deposit the money in my bank. So I entrusted it to Mr. Ata."

The policeman barely heard him out before fixing his eyes on Sutekichi and saying: "A sum of money like that must have made quite a bulky packet. About this size, wasn't it?"

"Yes, I should say so."

"And where were you carrying it? In the sleeve of a kimono? Or in the pocket of a suit?"

"In my pocket."

"I see." There arose an increasingly intense look on the policeman's face. Then abruptly he broke into a smile—a smile that for some reason made Sutekichi's blood run cold.

"Would you mind telling me in which particular pocket?"

Sutekichi felt for the right-hand pocket of his jacket and patted it.

"In that one, eh?" said the policeman. "Are you quite sure it wasn't the inside pocket?"

Aware of his interrogator's sharp gaze, Sutekichi was momentarily at a loss for an answer. "I didn't pay any particular attention," he said after a while. "But that's the pocket where

I always put any book I happen to be carrying, and I expect I stuck the money in there without thinking."

Again the policeman was silent for a while. Then abruptly he said: "I don't think you could have dropped it."

Sutekichi felt himself change color. He tried to speak, but it took him some time before the words would come out. "If I didn't drop it," he said, "do you suggest that I've hidden the money somewhere?"

The policeman looked younger than Sutekichi, but he kept his eyes fastened on him imperturbably and smiled. "I could understand it if your pocket had been picked, but I really can't believe that you dropped the money on the ground without noticing it. Were you carrying a book at the same time?"

"Oh yes," replied Sutekichi. "I remember that the book was exactly the same shape as the parcel of money."

"Well," said the policeman, "several people have had their pockets picked on the trains from Tokyo, but I don't think it's ever happened to anyone on the streets of Kamakura."

Having thus canceled his earlier suggestion, the policeman looked down on the floor and seemed to be thinking intently. Sutekichi felt that each inadvertent remark he made was somehow being used against him. There was not an atom of good will in the policeman's attitude.

"I'm sorry to have caused you so much trouble by my carelessness," said Soroku hurriedly. "It's getting late now, and I think we'd better be getting home. We'll call here again tomorrow morning."

"Would you mind waiting for just a moment?" said the policeman, and went to a desk at the back of the room where a much older colleague was still on duty. He spoke to him in a low voice, then the two men talked to each other for some minutes. The elder policeman craned his neck and looked carefully at Soroku and his companion.

"What's happening now?" muttered Soroku impatiently. "I do wish they wouldn't keep us waiting like this."

Sutekichi was now quite certain that the suspicion had fallen on him; he also knew that, so long as he was determined to keep Taeko's name out of the matter, there was no way to avoid this. Strangely enough, now that things had reached this point he felt much calmer, as though he had finally succeeded in mustering his courage. He certainly intended to deny any accusations that might be made against him, but if in the end the only way to vindicate himself was to mention Taeko he was prepared to take the guilt upon himself. It was unclear to him why he was willing to do this, but he felt that it had something to do with his own perennial poverty. "This is how things always turn out for people like us who have no money," he thought defiantly. Until then he had never imagined that his feelings for Taeko could go so far.

The two policemen were still talking to each other at the other end of the room. "They're really carrying it too far!" exclaimed Soroku in an exasperated tone.

"It's all right," said Sutekichi with a smile. He knew that there was something weak about his expression and that this came from his feeling of guilt at having told a lie. "They're wondering what I really did with the money. It's unpleasant for me, but since it's my fault it can't be helped."

"It's all too absurd," said Soroku.

The young policeman returned with a smile and looked at Sutekichi. "Would you mind going over there," he said, "and having a few words with my colleague? He's going to ask you what happened all over again. Please answer him in as clear and detailed a way as you can." Seeing that Soroku was about to object, the policeman added: "And you, sir, won't you come and sit by the stove for a while? It's getting rather cold. There are a couple of things I'd like to ask you about. I'm sorry but this is our job. As long as there are any doubtful points left we can't get anywhere."

Soroku remembered that Friday was still outside. Since he had thought that he could briefly report the loss to the police and then go straight home, he had kept his dog waiting.

"Excuse me for a moment," he said and started for the door.

"If you want the toilet, it's over there," said the policeman.

"No, it's my dog. I've left him waiting outside."

Friday was sitting patiently by the entrance. When he saw his master, he jumped up and started wagging his tail; he was obviously eager to rush out into the street and go home. Having made sure that Friday was still waiting (a rather unnecessary precaution), Soroku closed the door and sat down by the stove.

Meanwhile the middle-aged policeman took Sutekichi into

a separate room. Looking at the young man from behind, Soroku had an unpleasant feeling. The Sutekichi whom he had
come to know during the past months had a simple, straightforward quality that appeared to be very rare in present-day
youth.

"What's the matter?" Soroku asked the young policeman.
"I'm completely at sea."

There was a touch of reproach in his voice. Instead of replying, the policeman countered with a question of his own.
"Tell me, sir," he said in a business-like tone, "does that young
fellow work for you as a student-houseboy?"

"No," replied Soroku sharply, "he's not a houseboy.
Though he's a great deal younger than I am, I consider him a
friend. He's the student of a certain university professor in
Tokyo for whom I have the greatest respect. At the moment
he's come to stay with me to do some studying."

"In other words, he's not a member of your family or a
relation?"

"That's correct."

"You must have the greatest confidence in him to be able
to entrust him with an enormous sum of money like three
hundred thousand yen."

"Of course, I have."

"But don't you think, sir, that there's something a bit odd
about stuffing such a bulky amount of money into one's coat
pocket and then dropping it without even being aware of the
fact?"

Soroku was conscious of the young man's powerful gaze
as he replied: "No doubt he was thinking about his studies.
Anyone can be absentminded at times. I for one would never
suspect anything that Mr. Ata told me. If he says he dropped
the money, drop it he did!"

Seeing that Soroku was becoming heated, the policeman
smiled with embarrassment and turned aside. "Surely, sir, there
are limits to absentmindedness," he said. "How can one go and
lose such an enormous amount of money when one has been
specifically asked to look after it? And besides, isn't there something rather strange about carrying such a sum on one's person when one goes out for a short stroll? Of course, there's
nothing to stop you from trusting him implicitly if you want to,

but our position is rather different. Once we think there's something odd about a case we can't just let things go as if nothing had happened. Anyhow, all I wanted to ask you about were your relations with this young man. If you tell us to drop the matter, we shan't be bothering you about it any further."

Soroku bowed politely to the policeman. There was nothing now to stop him from leaving and withdrawing the case from the hands of the police. Yet he felt depressed. The shadow of suspicion that had flashed through his mind when he had first heard Sutekichi's report of the loss had suddenly taken on form and weight. He realized that the young policeman's judgment was a simple matter of common sense.

Soroku was still at some distance from Segi's house when he noticed the professor walking along the pavement. At once he asked the taxi-driver to stop. The professor had obviously not seen him, and he continued walking briskly down the street. It was a rather squalid street, typical of the city's outskirts.

Soroku ran after the professor, who had still not noticed him. Segi was wearing an overcoat, and there was something very familiar about his back which was bent slightly forward. As he walked he caught sight of a handbill stuck to a lamppost. The professor paused for a moment to read it, then chuckled to himself so that his mustache moved up and down, and continued down the street.

"Professor!" Soroku called out.

"Good heavens!" said Segi. "What are you doing here?"

"I was on my way to your house, and I happened to see you from the taxi."

"Well, well," said the professor with an astringent smile. "That was lucky. You might easily have missed me. I'm just on my way out."

"Where are you going, Professor? Are you in a hurry?"

"I'm not going anywhere in particular," replied Segi. "I suppose most people would find it rather shameful of me that I shouldn't be going anywhere in particular, but there it is!"

"In that case, do you mind if I walk along with you?"

"Come along by all means! As a matter of fact I've been

wondering where to go ever since I set out on my walk. It's remarkably warm for a winter's day, don't you think?"

Soroku was perspiring lightly and he realized that the sun was showering its heat on the wintry streets. He was about to broach the subject of Sutekichi and the money when the professor started off with his usual verve: "Ever since I was a young man I've always enjoyed going out for a walk without any particular destination. I suppose that's the real meaning of 'a walk,' isn't it? Some day I'd like to undertake a real journey in the same spirit, but that would be rather an expensive enterprise, and I don't suppose I'll ever be able to afford it. Of course, it can be fun to travel with a fixed destination in mind, but even if it is fun it's a fixed kind of fun. To travel, not in order to arrive, but for the sake of the journey itself—what a delight that must be! For that is the sort of journey in which the real humanity of a human being can come into its own."

Professor Segi always spoke in a light tone, but one could sense the depth behind his words. Soroku was not sure when he had first become aware of it. The professor certainly did not try to impart any special significance to his remarks; it was just a matter of chatting away in a desultory fashion about anything that came into his head. Sometimes the listener would wonder whether the professor was not simply pulling his leg, only to find that he had switched to an entirely different topic.

"I wonder whether Bashō wasn't a man who succeeded in making precisely such a journey. In *The Narrow Road of Oku* and *Journey to Yoshino* (those *are* the names of his books, aren't they?) his travels have been neatly committed to writing, and one might get the impression that he knew exactly where he was going. But I'm quite sure that in his heart Bashō had no fixed destination. He walked in order to walk. Arrival was never his objective. And this doesn't only apply to Bashō's travels. It applies to his entire life, don't you think? It was all a journey without any fixed destination. For us poor worldlings, on the other hand, the destination has become everything. It's always hovering there in front of our eyes. And the more hectic things become, the more insistently do our shabby little programs control our lives."

As usual the professor did not give his listener a chance to put in a word. To hear him was like being confronted by a typhoon, and one had to wait until it had blown over before one could hope to have one's say.

"If only it were possible," continued the professor, "to live, like Bashō, with free, unshackled spirits. Why must we all be in such a hurry to fix our destinations for good and all? Why can't we enjoy the journey itself instead of always thinking about where we are going? The world is a large, open place, and our lives too should be large and open. I know that earning our daily rice is a matter of grave concern, but to go through our whole lives absorbed in that one aim—well, it's as if we'd been born into this world just in order to scurry about and fill our rice bowls. Where does such a life really get one? All that one's left with in the end is utter exhaustion. Let's see now. How did Bashō's farewell poem go? Ah yes.

> *'Fallen ill on a journey,*
> *In my dreams I run about*
> *Over the barren fields.'*

"Wasn't that it? Yes, I'm sure that's how it went."

"I'm afraid I really don't know," said Soroku.

"Yes yes, that's how it is. He was a man who kept journeying until the moment of his death. He never thought about the point of arrival. When Bashō died I believe he was fifty years old. He had lived only fifty years in this world of ours—less than you and I have lived already. It gives me a strange feeling, you know. What on earth have we been doing all these years? —that's what it makes me think. Of course, in those days people grew up much sooner than now, so their adult lives started earlier. All the same it's rather amazing that Bashō should have died in his fiftieth year and that even in his lifetime he should have been referred to as an old sage. He was a fully developed human being and that's why he was thought of as being old from the time of his early forties. If he was regarded as old when he was only in his forties, we who are in our sixties must be utterly decrepit. Yet, old though Bashō was, that last poem of his about running over the barren fields is the work of a sprightly young man. There was nothing old about his spirit, was there? People are always referring to the 'quiet taste' and 'elegant simplicity' of Bashō, but I don't believe a word of it. If he was really old, what does that make you and me?"

The professor paused for a while, then continued: "I've heard people say 'When I come to the end of this particular work of mine, I'll be quite happy to die. I ask no more of life.' What a stingy way of looking at things! The path is wide, very wide. And who has decided that we must fit ourselves into some limited framework? Each of us is given a journey to travel, and if we attach due value to our lives the journey is quite a long one. What could be more foolish than to deliberately set up barriers around ourselves and to make the path narrow? Everyone has a separate personality outside the one that he so fondly believes to be 'himself,' but very few people ever seem to think about it. Most people are content to limit their journey by assigning a fixed distance and a fixed destination, and once they reach that destination they're ready to call it a day. What a waste! For each of us has the possibility of something strange and unknown. Of course, there is always the danger of being crushed by the practical difficulties of life. But if we have the sort of nature that enables us to get clear of these difficulties, to stick out our tongues at them, so to speak—well, then we have the possibility of developing. Planning and calculation will get us nowhere. It is only the spirit that can enable us to run freely over the fields."

There were signs that the professor's typhoon had finally abated. "Well, after all that," he said, "which way shall we go?"

The time had come, thought Soroku. "To tell the truth," he said, "I came to ask you where Mr. Ata lives."

"Good gracious!" said the professor. "I thought he was staying with you in Kamakura. Didn't I hear that he had imposed himself on your hospitality once again?"

"Yes, that's quite right. But the fact is that there was a silly misunderstanding, and I caused him a lot of needless worry. He was at my house until yesterday."

Without noticing it, the two men emerged on a new road that led past rows of little houses interspersed occasionally with small sunlit cornfields. Now it was Professor Segi's turn to listen, and he walked along silently as Soroku told him about the suspected theft.

"Hm," he muttered dubiously, "young Sutekichi made an inexcusable mistake."

Soroku looked thoroughly embarrassed. "To tell you the honest truth," he said, "until I received my niece's letter, I couldn't help finding something a bit odd about Mr. Ata's story. I never for a moment believed that he had hidden the money for some ulterior purpose, yet when I discussed the matter with him face to face, I felt a definite change in the atmosphere. It was as though something insoluble had come between us. No doubt Mr. Ata was aware of the same uncomfortable atmosphere. Otherwise he wouldn't abruptly have announced on the following morning that he was going back to Tokyo. My niece's letter was delivered just after he left. When I asked my old cook about it, she told me that my niece had come to see me on the previous afternoon. She had evidently been planning to stay, but then for some reason she had suddenly left. It all came out in the letter. After Ata had gone to do some shopping, she had noticed something sticking out from under a cushion. The moment she saw that it was a packet of money she forgot herself completely. She put the money in her bag and left the house. Once she was outside she realized that she had done something wrong, but she still had no desire to return the money. She would apologize to me later on and take whatever blame was coming her way. In the teashop by the station she borrowed a pen and paper and wrote me her letter. You can imagine my surprise. Mr. Ata hadn't even mentioned my niece's visit. When we got back from the police station that night I went to bed. But I couldn't get to sleep. The policeman's suspicions had started working on me. I had a very bad night. It was wrong of me, of course, but however hard I tried I couldn't put my mind at rest. It had given me such pleasure to feel that I could trust this young man and become friendly with him. This of course made my disappointment all the keener. It's a terrible thing, I know, but it has taken me half a lifetime to develop my particular foibles about money, and, though the amount itself wasn't as enormous as all that, I couldn't stand the idea that Mr. Ata was trying to hoodwink me with ambiguous statements."

"But that's all perfectly natural," said the professor. "I understand exactly what you felt."

"I'm old enough to know better, though. It's shameful that I should have let myself get so upset."

"It's nothing to do with age. If anything, people become more avaricious as they get older. I expect it's connected in some way with the death wish. An old person's love of money, you see—No, I mustn't go off on a side-track. Let's get back to our Sutekichi. What on earth made him tell you that cock-and-bull story about having dropped the money? He's full of little quirks, but there's nothing dishonest about him."

"That's why I feel so guilty about having—" began Soroku, but the professor interrupted him.

"No, no, he deliberately turned the suspicion on himself. There was nothing wrong in your suspecting him. I should have done the same myself. The fact remains, why did Sutekichi—"

The professor broke off, and a new expression came onto his face as if it had suddenly been lit up. "Ah yes, of course!" he exclaimed. "I see now. Well done, Sutekichi my lad!"

Soroku did not understand what the professor meant, but he was struck by the happy look on the man's face. Professor Segi was rejoicing by himself.

"As his teacher I never told him how to lie, and he obviously isn't very good at it. Really, I'll have to give him a good talking-to one of these days."

"Oh no, Professor, you mustn't do that. I'm the one who should apologize."

"Don't worry, my friend. What matters is that you got the money back. You did get it back, didn't you? I'm afraid it sounds rather inquisitive of me, but naturally I'm interested. I'm interested in young people, you see. Youth is very liable to stumble. And their manner of stumbling is quite different from ours. There's a sort of foolhardiness about the way in which they go astray, or, if one wants to put it in a kinder way, a type of wholehearted sincerity, which doesn't allow them to calculate the consequence of their behavior. You can compare them to the sturdy little sprouts that grow off a tomato. Some blind force makes them grow and expand. They have no idea how to stop themselves, and often they end up by doing things that we adults regard as excessive."

It looked as if a new typhoon was blowing up, and once

again Soroku felt himself pushed into the passive role of listener.

"Perhaps it's a matter of taking a lenient attitude to my own former student, but I feel sure that this very uncharacteristic dishonesty of Sutekichi's comes from the type of wholehearted sincerity that I was mentioning. Look, Mr. Soroku, it may sound rather inconsiderate to you, but I can't help feeling that in this case even dishonesty has something endearing about it. 'How very young you are!' I feel like telling him. And now may I ask you a favor? I've never met your niece, but I should like to offer my services as counsel on her behalf."

"I beg your pardon, Professor," said Soroku with a bewildered smile.

"No, I'm dead serious. I don't know why your niece should have borrowed all that money from you without saying a word. But I'm quite convinced she did it on the spur of the moment without really considering what it meant. She too belongs to the 'wholehearted sincerity' school, and when she took the money I'm sure it didn't even occur to her that she'd be putting her uncle to any inconvenience. This may sound strange to you, but try looking at it in a new way. After all, don't forget that on one occasion you actually disappeared from this world of ours. Try imagining for a moment that you aren't living on this globe at all but on some entirely different planet." The professor paused for a while. He was smiling, yet there was something almost frighteningly serious about his tone. "I should like you to turn this one bad deed upside down, so to speak, and regard it in a good light. The ardor that caused your niece to make off with the three hundred thousand yen may be evil, yet in this mediocre day and age such wholehearted behavior is something on which we should set a very high value."

Soroku could not help bursting out into laughter at his friend's argument. " 'Let real evil be done!'—is that what you're saying, Professor?"

Professor Segi looked surprised. "Where on earth did you hear that? Those are the words of Prince Fumi Matudaira." Evidently the professor had forgotten that this was one of his pet quotations. "Well, be that as it may, the important thing to remember is that young people grow like tomato sprouts. So long as you've retrieved your money, let your niece forget about the incident. Help her to make a fresh start, won't you? I hope you don't mind my asking you this."

Soroku gazed silently at the professor. For a moment he looked as if he was going to reply with a chilly refusal. Instead he said: "That's what I've already done. And I didn't ask her to return what she took from me. I told her that if she needed the money she could keep it."

●

THE PINE GROVE of Enju Beach lies outside the town of Gobo in Kii Province. It dates from the beginnings of the clan adminstration of the province when a solid row of trees was planted for two and a half miles along the beach to serve as a windbreak. From the distance it stands out conspicuously, giving the impression of a castle wall.

Taeko's bus passed the pine grove on its way to the village of Mio. On the other side was the rich plain of Hidaka. From the windows of the bus one could see plum trees with their white blossoms, trees colorfully loaded with tangerines, and sunlit houses dotted across the fields. The grove was brightly lit from the south, but the trees blocked the sun off from the highway so that it was sunk in shadows. The sea lay directly on the other side; the trees, however, formed a barrier five hundred yards deep and effectively hid it from view.

Here and there inside the grove one could see neat piles of pine needles; the sandy ground was as pretty as a garden. Everything was planted in orderly rows, not only the pines, but the low-growing *yamamono* evergreens which grew in dark lines, like garden plants. Pine groves near the seashore usually have little depth, but this one was as dense as a forest. The pine resin, warmed by the sun, mingled its aroma with the smell of the seashore and drifted through the afternoon air into the bus.

The hills on the right hand side of the road came closer and closer; then suddenly there was a break in the pine grove, and the sea came into sight, sparkling brightly. Taeko gazed at the gentle undulations of the reefy, windswept shore, and it occurred to her that this was really one of the southern parts of the country. On her way through the region near Kyoto the light snow had still lain glittering on the ground, but here little spring flowers were already dotted about the fields which cut their way into the foothills. It was not only the vegetation that suggested the end of winter; there was a warm brightness about the sea that augured the beginning of a new season. For a moment Taeko felt that she was back on the coast of the southern Izu peninsula and that by scanning the horizon she could make out the silhouette of Oshima. Then she remembered where she was and realized that what she saw far in the distance was either the hills of Shikoku or the coast of Awaji Island. The sea stretched out in all directions. There was a bend in the road, and now from the edge of the beach Taeko could take in at a glance the long pine grove along which they had traveled; then it disappeared.

"There's the Hinomisaki lighthouse," said the young bus conductress, pointing along the coast. No doubt she remembered that on boarding the bus Taeko had inquired whether it went past the lighthouse. In the distance behind the hazy promontory Taeko could make out a low, chimney-shaped building standing high on a hill; that must be the lighthouse. As the bus ran along the sinuous coast road, the building was soon blocked from sight by one of the cliffs. Presently a group of women appeared on the road. They had evidently been up to the hills to collect bamboo, and they were carrying heavy bundles on their back. The women formed a single file to let the bus pass.

"The trees you see over there," announced the conductress, "are called *hamayu*. They have beautiful flowers in the summer." What a kind girl she was, thought Taeko, smiling at her.

The light played lambently on the vast surface of the sea. Apparently the Black Current came all the way up here, for one could make out a surprisingly dark shadow under the water. Presently the Hinomisaki lighthouse came into sight once again, but this time it looked quite different. Its white walls stood out in bold relief against the blue sky.

On reaching Gobo earlier that day Taeko had been informed that Ryosuké had gone to look at the lighthouse. It was some ten days now since Ryosuké had come down to Wakayama to visit his uncle. Shortly after arriving he had written to Taeko suggesting that she should join him there, and she had decided to accept the proposal.

Ryosuké's aunt and uncle were a simple, middle-aged couple who lived near Hinomisaki in a little hamlet which had recently been written up in the papers as the "American Village." Even now about 60 per cent of the population went to the United States or Canada to work. People from the village of Mio had in fact been crossing the high seas ever since the Meiji Period. After years of hard work in America they would return to the village to spend their old age. As a result Mio showed signs of Western influence that one would be unlikely to find in any other Japanese village. "It's an odd place and well worth seeing," Ryosuké had written to his fiancée.

Taeko's first view of the American village had been a small brick house by the main road; it lay next to a little ricefield, but was built entirely in the Western style with a concrete wall and stone steps leading up to the front door; the owner had even planted some red hollyhock at the foot of the steps. The house had obviously been designed by someone who had returned from overseas, and for a fisherman's dwelling it was a very fine structure indeed. Through the glass window Taeko could make out a pair of lace curtains.

The road ran between the mountains and gradually started to dip downward. Presently the bus reached a point where the hills came down to a small inlet, and from here one could see the cluster of roofs in the village. The bus stopped at a crossroads, and Taeko noticed a signboard on which were written the dates of departure for various ships going overseas. It was something that one would find in no other village in Japan and bespoke the fact that young men in Mio were constantly on the lookout for shipping services to go abroad.

The bus passed a large tropical banyan tree and emerged on a road that ran along the inlet. A high stone windbreak had been built along the sea front to protect the village in case of typhoons. There were crowds of people walking along the wall, and from the bus it was impossible to see either the beach or the bay itself.

The houses stretched in a solid mass from the highway to the hills in the back, but they were blocked from the road by still another high concrete windbreak, which had been erected on top of the stone wall, and, although one could see the slate roofs of the houses, it was impossible to look inside. In fact, what with the stone wall and the concrete barriers, there was very little that one could see from the road as it ran round the inlet.

The bus reached the far side of the bay and came to the end of its line at a point where the road ran into a steep hill.

"They're working on the road now," announced the conductress. "By the time the flowers are in bloom it'll be possible to drive all the way to Hinomisaki." She got off the bus especially to tell Taeko how to reach the lighthouse. "You take this road out of the village," she explained. "It goes along the coast for a while and then up that hill over there. It's a straight road, Miss, so you can't go wrong. You've only got just over a mile to go."

Standing on the beach, Taeko watched the bus as it turned around and ran along the parapet until it was back on the main road. When it had disappeared, a fantastic quiet came over the village and the windless sunny bay. A few women trudged along the beach; they were carrying stones in their straw baskets and were evidently working on the new road to the lighthouse. Apart from them, there was not a soul to be seen. A fishing-boat had dropped anchor in the bay, but there did not seem to be anyone aboard. Taeko remembered hearing that the actual population of Mio was far smaller than the number of its inhabitants who had gone abroad. Since it was the younger people particularly who left for America, there was hardly ever any noise to be heard in the streets. The houses were all stoutly constructed to withstand typhoons, and not a sound came through the thick walls.

Taeko walked part of the way along the beach, but then it occurred to her that by now Ryosuké would already be on his way down the hill from the lighthouse, and there was no point in her going all the way up. She decided instead to go back along the narrow street through Mio. Reaching the village, she was surprised to see that even the smallest lanes were carefully paved; the houses were all solid structures of a type that one would never see in a Japanese fishing-village and, though it was broad daylight, the doors were all securely shut.

After a time Taeko caught sight of a village girl dressed in bright Western clothes, but almost instantly she vanished into one of the houses; once more the place looked deserted. There was not a sound on the clean stone streets, and the village gave Taeko a strangely forlorn feeling. She imagined the old people lying on their Western-style beds, with all the doors and windows shut, dreaming about their youth in America and all the exciting things that had happened to them until they had returned to their village in this remote corner of Japan.

Finally Taeko went back to the beach and walked along the cove. She noticed a strange black bird perched on a rock off the shore and realized that it was a wild cormorant. There was still not a soul in sight.

The sun beat down on the beach and it was hard to imagine that it was still winter in Tokyo. The cove was as narrow as a pond, and the water sparkled beautifully. "So I've really come all this way!" thought Taeko, looking out to sea. "And there before my eyes lies the Sea of Mio in Kii Province."

As she stood there, confronted on all sides by the clarity of the sky and the water, she recalled how she had made off with her uncle's money and how she had used it to repay Ryosuké's debt to Mrs. Iwamuro. Now that she stood by the sea, all that she had thought and felt during that period seemed like a dream. Perhaps it was because she had left Tokyo so far behind her; or again, perhaps it was because her uncle's unexpected forbearance and generosity had released her from all the feelings that had weighed on her during the past weeks.

Strangely enough, it was precisely her uncle's treatment of her that had brought home to Taeko the real meaning of sorrow. At first she had been convinced that this money would bring her happiness; but, after handing it over to Mrs. Iwamuro, Taeko had perceived that she herself no longer believed in the happiness which she thought she had purchased. If, instead of forgiving her, Soroku had severely berated her as Taeko had expected, perhaps it would all have turned out differently.

The fact was that her uncle's attitude had completely thrown her off balance. Yet, if Taeko had really been confident of preserving her own happiness, she could have settled everything by taking advantage of Soroku's kindness and simply writing him a letter of thanks. It was not until after her uncle had forgiven her that Taeko had become ineluctably convinced of being in the wrong. Much as he might be prepared to forgive, she could not be happy within herself. Soroku had not imposed the slightest obligation on her, and if Taeko now began to feel burdened with a sense of obligation it was one that she had sought herself. Her suffering was entirely self-imposed and for that reason all the harder to eradicate.

Standing by the water's edge and looking out at the magnificent sea, Taeko was inevitably reminded of how she had immersed herself with Ryosuké in the water below the golf links at the Kawana Hotel. Even now the memory of that moment seemed to awaken her entire body and to set her senses tingling. Her body had been utterly naked then—as naked as when she was born. Indeed she had been reborn at that moment, and it was the intoxicating joy of rebirth that had given her the strength to act fearlessly as she did.

Was it really possible, she wondered, for people to feel that they are being born anew? Taeko was at the fresh and vital age when one can answer positively and without hesitation: yes, it can happen again and again in one's life. She was full of the youthful self-confidence that demands such an answer. It was, she felt, precisely by rejecting the type of happiness that depends on worldly considerations that one could find both strength and confidence. Taeko was on no account unhappy, although for the moment she was estranged from happiness. So long as she was fulfilling herself, there was nowhere for real unhappiness to enter.

Painful as things might be at the moment, the first consideration was life itself and the process of living. She must not stand still on the road, but must keep on walking. This idea had somehow become embedded in her mind and she felt the power of it. She would not let her life become like standing water, which is bound to stagnate; no, she would make it start flowing, like a fresh river. At present her destination might be a blank, but she would move ahead depending on the very strength that motion gave her. For everything outside her—the world and all the people in it—was moving and changing, and she too was part of this constant flux. No doubt it was possible simply to let oneself be carried along; but Taeko was conscious of her own resources, and she was determined to watch herself move and act.

It had been purely by chance that she had seen her uncle's money. At first she had thought that it belonged to Sutekichi, and it had not occurred to her to take it. When she realized that it was Soroku's she had completely forgotten herself. It was as though someone outside herself, Ryosuké perhaps, had entered her body and removed all power of discrimination. The act had been performed in a moment of passion, and on this occasion the Taeko—the special Taeko who usually watched from the outside to see what she was doing—had not been there. Ever since her childhood this other self had guarded Taeko in her loneliness; but now it had become confused and had lost sight of her. As a result she had not been conscious of the ugliness of what she was doing. Even the letter she had written to her uncle from the station had been a mere explanation, a sort of memorandum or receipt, in which Taeko's real nature and conscience had not been involved in the slightest. During all this time she had been completely oblivious of her uncle's peculiarly sensitive attitude to money and of the concern that she must be causing him.

In view of all this how was she to explain Soroku's amazing magnanimity? "Don't worry," he had told her. "Do whatever suits you best."

Taeko was not worried. But the act that she had committed in order to procure her own happiness had paradoxically led to disbelief in this happiness. She no longer really understood why she should have taken her uncle's money.

Taeko noticed a shadow moving across the sand. She looked around and saw Ryosuké advancing toward her. He was wearing a sweater, and there was a happy smile on his face. Taeko had not seen him as he came along the cliff road. Not having seen him for some time, she looked at him with new eyes and her first reaction was to be impressed by the youth and health and size of the man.

"Ah, Taeko," he exclaimed with an unconcealed expression of delight, "so you came after all!" Taeko looked at his mouth and memories of their intimate moments together flooded up in her. "I somehow thought you'd come. When did you get here?"

"I arrived on the noon train." Taeko answered calmly, but she was dazzled at seeing Ryosuké's body before her, the same as it had always been. "What a peaceful place it is—this village!"

"Yes, it's a funny little place," said Ryosuké. "I've just been up the hill to the lighthouse. There's a terrific view all the way to Shikoku."

"I thought you'd be on your way down, so I waited for you here."

"Did you meet my uncle and aunt?"

"Yes, I met your aunt."

Ryosuké looked as if a new thought had come into his head. "The sooner I can get back to Tokyo," he said, "the better."

"Have you spoken to them about the money?"

Ryosuké smiled bitterly. "You can't get anywhere with these country people," he said. "They're too tightfisted for words! It takes them ages to make up their minds about the simplest thing. To get them to cough up a little money you've got to keep after them day after day."

Just then a bus appeared by the parapet. Taeko was surprised to see a large crowd standing by the bus stop. It was hard to imagine how so many people could suddenly have emerged from the peaceful little village. The bright dresses of the girls stood out conspicuously. Someone was carrying a small Rising Sun flag. One of the men looked like the village priest.

"It looks as if another of their young fellows is off to America," said Ryosuké.

Ryosuké and Taeko climbed up from the beach onto the main road. As they stepped into the bus they felt everyone looking at them. Presently a young man wearing a Western-style suit emerged in the bustle and confusion of the crowd. The villagers surrounded him, and a boy, evidently his younger brother, lifted a cheap-looking suitcase into the bus. Shouts of greeting came from the crowd. Looking out of the window, Taeko noticed that even the old people in their sixties and seventies were wearing Western dress. They were different from the Western clothes one saw in Tokyo; there was a decidedly more foreign air about them.

Several people crowded onto the bus. The young man who was leaving for overseas stood on the steps, and presently amidst a medley of cheers and farewells the bus started to move. All the way through the village people were standing at the crossroads and at the corners of the alleys; as the bus passed, they waved and shouted. "Good-by, good-by! Good luck to you!" A group of girls was standing in front of the house with the red hollyhock, and they too waved enthusiastically.

When they had finally left the village behind them, the young men settled down in their seats and embarked on a lively conversation. From what they were saying Taeko gathered that the young man had already been overseas once and that this was his second venture. Despite his Western suit, he looked like a typical sunburned country lad and had a simple, healthy air. He spoke in a strong dialect and Taeko had trouble in making out what he was saying. Several more country people boarded the bus at the next stop, and now it was hard to distinguish the young man who was about to leave for America from the others who were simply going as far as Gobo to see a movie.

Soon the bus was running along the pine grove of Enju Beach. Beyond the ricefields one could see the low afternoon sun lighting up the hills and mountains.

"The famous Dojo Temple is over there," said Ryosuké, pointing to one of the hills. "You know, the temple one's always seeing on the stage in Tokyo and Osaka."*

Taeko smiled by way of reply. She was wondering how she should let Ryosuké know of her decision.

"Will you see me off at the station in Gobo?" she asked after a while.

"The station?" said Ryosuké, looking at her quizzically.

"Yes, I've got my return ticket."

"Why?" He seemed thoroughly surprised. "You aren't going all the way back to Tokyo already, are you?"

"Yes. I just wanted to see you for a moment."

Taeko felt her breast heaving, and she forced herself to look out of the window.

* The Nō play *Dōjōji* was adapted as a Kabuki in 1753 under the title *Musume Dōjōji* ("The Maiden of the Dojo Temple"), and is one of the most popular in the Kabuki repertoire. It tells of a girl whose love for a priest is spurned and who turns into a monstrous snake.

"Do you have to get back for your work?" asked Ryosuké with a touch of annoyance.

Taeko shook her head silently. She was on the verge of telling Ryosuké that she had repaid the money to Mrs. Iwamuro; then she decided that this matter at least should be left unmentioned.

"I still don't understand," said Ryosuké. "If you don't like being at my uncle's, we can go and stay at an inn."

"No, I'm sorry," said Taeko. "I have something to tell you, but we can't talk here."

"No, we can't. All the more reason for you to spend a night or two so that we can talk things over quietly."

There was a slight smile on his face as he looked at Taeko, but she was determined to reject its implication.

"We can talk at the station," she said.

"Are you still worrying about that woman?"

"No, not in the slightest. Other people have nothing to do with it any longer."

There was no dishonesty or bluff in Taeko's reply. She had already broken away from Ryosuké, and she was ready to nurse her wounds in private without help from anyone.

"Well then, what's it all about?"

"I think we should leave each other now."

"Now?"

"I mean for good."

The bus crossed the bridge over a swollen river, passed the white façade of the new post office, and entered the town.

"Well, here we are at Gobo," said Ryosuké. "This is where I'm getting off. Come on, Taeko." He started to get to his feet, but the girl did not move. She was still resolved to get on the train and separate herself from Ryosuké; if she obeyed him now, she would be defeating herself and everything would once more become hopeless.

"Won't you see me off at the station?" she said.

There was a new weakness in Ryosuké's expression; the young man seemed cruelly deprived of his normal self-confidence. The bus came to a stop, and most of the passengers alighted. Ryosuké made a final effort to persuade Taeko. "Come on, do let's get off here."

Taeko remained steadfast.

Apart from the young man who was going to America and

the friends who had come to see him off, the bus was now almost empty. Taeko glanced at her watch: the train for Tennoji would be leaving in half an hour.

"You're still laboring under a misunderstanding, you know," said Ryosuké. Taeko could not stop herself from smiling. The idea of a final parting had filled her with sentimental emotions; yet she had felt certain that these would clear away once she started speaking. Now that the time had come she felt strangely lighthearted. If they were to part, she hoped that their leavetaking would be something light and cheerful. She knew that this was a great moment in her life; but surely she ought to consider it as being simply one stage on a journey—a journey that would in all likelihood continue for a long time.

"It's you, Ryosuké, who must avoid misunderstanding," she said. "I myself have no regrets about what has happened, nor do I feel sad about it. We should both make a fresh start—each in our own way."

"You've taken me by surprise, I don't mind telling you."

"I can't go back to where we were before, Ryosuké. If I tried to, it would mean gradually wrecking myself, without even being aware that I was doing so. I should be terrified of growing up like that. I want to be born again and to try living afresh."

"Is that what you came to tell me?"

"Yes . . . but that's not the only reason. I wanted to see you once more." Taeko's voice reflected her deep affection. "I was weak, you see. And since I was weak, I wanted to meet you again and to see whether I was capable of carrying out my resolution."

"That's all very well, but don't you think you're being rather heartless?"

"A man shouldn't speak like that. Even after we part I shall go on praying for your happiness. But if we went on as we have been, I'd be too worried to do anything." She gazed directly at Ryosuké and continued: "Please try to understand me, my dear. If we went on, it would only make us both miserable."

Ryosuké felt oppressed. It was not only Taeko's words that concerned him, but the feeling that mere masculine pride was no longer sufficient to oppose her will. Taeko seemed to have entered a new emotional world, and, even though they were still sitting close to each other, she had drawn away from him.

"And what's to become of me?" he said.

"I never thought I'd hear such weakness from you." For the first time Taeko sounded thoroughly discouraged.

"It's just that you've thrown me off balance," said Ryosuké, and turned aside.

The conversation broke off. The bus ran between the last wintry rice fields and pulled up in front of the station.

"Last stop, ladies and gentlemen," announced the conductress. "All off, please!"

The young men from Mio alighted from the bus, followed by Ryosuké and Taeko. Inside the little station the benches were crowded with passengers waiting for the train.

"We still have twenty minutes," said Ryosuké with a forced smile. Taeko began to feel sorry for him. She was no longer frightened that she herself might weaken, but she wished that she could now see in Ryosuké the young man she had known during the time when she had been so intoxicated with happiness.

"I've thought about all sorts of things," she said. "I wish you had a really good friend, Ryochan."

"I do have friends," he said.

"Really?"

"My best friend was that fellow called Mé. But he's dead." The young man's eyes suddenly clouded over, and he was silent.

Then abruptly his face lit up, and Taeko saw the same bright, lively expression that she had so often remembered when they were apart. For a while he seemed stuck for words, but with an impulsive gesture he took Taeko's hand and shook it powerfully.

"I'm sorry," he blurted out, looking her straight in the eyes. "It's you who have been my best friend. And that won't change even if we part. Every time I remember you it'll stop me from doing anything shabby. From now on I'll manage to get by without doing anything I'm ashamed of. I can promise you that."

Taeko felt overwhelmed by this sudden access of passion, and she could say nothing.

"I understand perfectly what you've been telling me, Taeko-san. We don't need to say any more. You've always been honest and gentle with me, ever since we've known each other. And it may very well be that what you've done today was the kindest thing of all. If I were to tell you now that I could make you happy, it simply wouldn't be true. I might want to, but I couldn't. Ever since I was in the war I've been unable to feel any real respect for people. I've taken my fellow beings for what they are, and on the whole I consider them a pretty worthless lot. That being the case, I've never felt any particular need to deal straightly with them. You're the only exception. But even in your case I haven't been able to feel the proper respect. That was wrong of me. Yes, there I was really wrong."

Taeko looked at him but did not speak.

"I suppose that in a way I'm ill. Perhaps I'll recover one of these days. But even then I'm not going to request your sympathy. I don't consider I have the right ever to ask you to come back to me. One thing I can promise you, however—I shall never forget that you are a good person and that I behaved badly to you."

"Don't think unpleasantly of me," said Taeko, and she felt the tears coming to her eyes.

"Me? Why on earth should I think unpleasantly of you?" Ryosuké sounded almost angry. "Oh well, let's say no more about that. I shan't pretend that I shall be praying for your happiness. The gods may listen to your prayers, but I'm sure they wouldn't pay any attention to mine. Well, Taeko, they've started collecting the tickets. I shall say good-by to you here. Don't worry about me. Look after yourself—that's the important thing. *Bon voyage!*" He said the final words in French, and once again shook her hand firmly.

The train drew into the station. As she stepped onto the platform, Taeko turned round and waved. Ryosuké was standing by the entrance. There was something unmistakably military about his bearing. He lifted his hand and waved back at Taeko. In the failing light of the winter afternoon his face became smaller and smaller in the distance until he looked like a little dark statue.